About the Author

Devon was born in South Africa and now lives in Scotland with his spectacular wife and crazy thoughts. He works as a veterinarian but lives life with one foot in the world of fantasy, ensuring a tenuous grasp on reality at the best of times. When he is not working to ensure the medical wellbeing of his four-legged friends, he can be found diving into anything even remotely related to the world of fantasy. From table-top games to practicing sword play in the park, he is always looking for ways to add a little magic to life.

Arcanum

Devon Seaton

Arcanum

Olympia Publishers
London

www.olympiapublishers.com
OLYMPIA PAPERBACK EDITION

A CIP catalogue record for this title is
available from the British Library.

ISBN: 978-1-80074-953-5

First Published in 2023

Olympia Publishers
Tallis House
2 Tallis Street
London
EC4Y 0AB

Printed in Great Britain

Dedication

I dedicate this work to The Fish Team.

Acknowledgements

In the world of procrastination, there are many that can consider themselves proficient. I can easily say that I count myself amongst their number which is why I would like to thank my wonderful wife, Lindsey, for her passion shown towards this project, the countless hours she spent editing drafts and her endless patience with me and my ramblings. Your creative input and control over the literary arts astounds me and I enjoyed every second of working on this book, thanks to you. To Olympia publishers, you all worked tirelessly to get this book to where it needed to be. You provided not only the road but the lanterns that lit the way too and you have my sincerest thanks. For the readers of this book/series (hopefully), I would like to extend my love and thanks to you all! You can now count yourself as members of Etroah, having walked these lands alongside myself and all those who worked on this project. Where would any of us be without our family and friends? We are all the product of those around us with a few rolls of the dice thrown in. Not only have they put up with me, but they have provided an endless source of encouragement and kindness through all trials faced in this wild ride. My father, Des, inspired me from a dangerously young age to pursue a love of literary works and to question the world around me. He took my hand and showed me how to love a world of creativity, knowledge and humour. Not only that but there was not a day that went by where, if I wanted to read a book, then he would be there at my side to help me find a copy and then compare notes the moment I finished. The world can be tough sometimes but there are those in my life who have displayed particular strength beyond what I could have ever thought possible. My wife, Lindsey, my mother, Mandy and my nanna, Yvonne (Nan, Nanna, the one and only). The trials faced and overcome by you all have given me the confidence to take on the world with my head held high and a smile on my face. To all the table-top crews and gaming guilds out there: You are all fantastic people, and you add your magic to the world every day. Thank you for creating worlds of fantastical wonder to enjoy amongst friends and loved ones and giving a place for people like me to call home. Please forgive me lest this last one feel a bit strange. There have been many low points in my life and during those times, I have found myself turning to the unconditional love of my pets. Few bonds are stronger and more unconditional, and I dare not imagine a world where we do not have our furry little friends there to brighten up our lives and to accompany us on our many adventures.

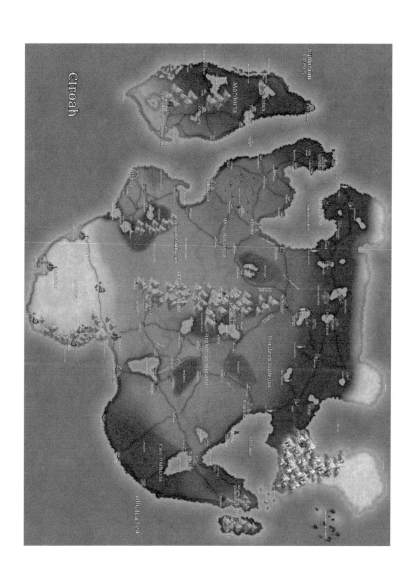

Prologue

Crashing Thunder

Crashing thunder, streaking lighting, the sky tainted red. Rangers stood upon the crumbled walls of Dilen'Nahen, their armour struggling to cling to their beleaguered forms. Captain Yvlynne stood above the main gate, commanding her sinking ship, the storm of the Ilvithiirians having proven too strong for her to navigate, now sending wave upon wave to crash against the prow.

The haggard form stood resolute, grime-slickened strawberry hair clung to her brow as the captain raised her fist and shouted, "Nock arrows! Raise shields! To the depths with these vermin!"

The elves began bashing their shields with their swords while stamping their feet.

The archers began the chant, *"Arensela lu alunala[1]! Arensela lu alunala! Arensela lu alunala!"*

The Ilvithiirian army lay before the ghost of Dilen'Nahen, its sentinel tower now reduced to a heap of rubble, its walls shattered and crumbling like the hearts of the elves that guarded them. The Ilvithiirian force began their advance, the rhythmic beat of their marching spurring the fire in the hearts of their warriors. The drums of war pounded as the footmen began their battle cries. Yurinduur charged ahead of the Ilvithiirian troops, their superior size and strength sending them forward with the swiftness of a galloping steed, tearing at the ground on all fours, throwing the earth behind them.

Alikain and Goronil burst forth from the clouds, arrows peppering their wake. The gryphons, that they had stolen upon their escape, straining with each beat of their colossal wings. The elves drove them on desperately, every corner of their minds urging them forth. They heeded the urgency demanded by their new masters, their chests heaving as they struggled to

[1] For the light we fight

stay ahead.

In the wake of the two elves sprang their pursuers on demonic wyverns draped in war banners, spitting fire into the crimson sky. Their riders brandished shortbows, firing arrows in rapid succession, sailing through the air toward the fleeing elves.

Goronil and Alikain drew their stolen recurve bows, returning fire as their mounts stabilised their altitudes and propelled themselves forward into the storm clouds ahead. Goronil downed one of the riders, his arrow striking the thalenar in the neck, his mount roaring its retreat from the storm, no longer bound to her master's will. The lead rider flew up next to Alikain, dodging the elves' arrows with ease. Alikain gained altitude then jumped down onto the rider's wyvern, lodging his dagger in the thalenar's spine, then pulled the wyvern up, allowing him to jump back onto his own mount.

The pursuers continued their onslaught, firing arrow after arrow, dodging any return fire they received. Mighty plumes of flame shot through and bathed the air between them.

Goronil shouted, "To the storm! Lose them, drop altitude then fly into the keep with weapons at the ready."

Alikain nodded, his hands shaking, trying not to let his fear overtake him as his many wounds poured blood down his legs.

The elves urged their gryphons into a dive, burying themselves in the upcoming storm. The air grew thick with their hair standing on end. The lightning sent veins of energy to split the sky and strike the ground, plumes of fire flying off the bolts as they did so. Alikain struggled to urge the gryphon further into what lay ahead, using every ounce of willpower he had left to push on, to fly faster.

They entered the cloud, the rain now bombarding their blood-stained cloaks, the wind threatening to tear them from their saddles at any point. Their pursuers were not perturbed at the new course of assault and flew on into the clouds after the elves, fearless and bloodthirsty.

They battled the storm for what seemed like an eternity, trying to share what energy they could with their mounts but, out of arrows, they could now only watch as the thalenarian attackers drew in closer and closer with the colossal wings of their wyverns beating at the storm. Two of the riders had boxed Goronil in, drawing their swords and swinging at the mighty elf. He repelled them as best he could, but his shattered body could do little to defend him now.

He looked up at Alikain, their eyes met as he gave a defeated smile. A single tear ran down his cheek, the rain hitting him like thousands of tiny arrows. He thrust his blade into the air as if to stab the very stars, and a bolt of lightning struck the elf, tendrils arcing through him and into the flanking riders. Sending all three and their mounts plummeting to the ground in a ball of fire and smoke.

Alikain banked right toward the falling corpse of his mentor, racing the thalenarian riders, racing time, racing the storm, trying to outrun his horror. He spun his gryphon, reaching for Goronil's satchel, snatching it with the tips of his fingers.

He stabilised his flight path, flung the satchel around his neck and drew his own sword. The remaining thalenarians dove down upon him with swords and spears, like owls to a wounded rabbit. What Alikain couldn't dodge, he deflected with a snap of his blade, his eyes feral in the onslaught. An arrow flew from one of the riders and clipped Alikain in the leg as he pulled at his reins, sending them into a straight dive.

The elf shuddered but urged his mount onward, crying out in agony, with their silhouette akin to a spear sailing toward the armoured ground. The thunder deafened him, but then, as if rising from beneath a lake, he exited the clouds to the light of the world. The rain had not died down, but the wind had subsided, becoming more laminar. He opened his eyes to see the fires below, the elven keep was under siege by a force numbering in the thousands.

The defenders were kicking down climbers, shooting arrows and letting loose mighty torrents of magic – to little effect. Alikain plummeted toward the ground, his speed increasing until he could barely keep his eyes open against the wind. He waited until the last possible second before he kicked the sides of his gryphon, signalling her to spread her wings and break the dive.

He careened towards the keep below, hoping beyond all hope that his timing was perfect. The thalenar in pursuit, too heavy, shot past him and crashed into the ground. Alikain stabilised and sailed over the attackers, mere metres above the tips of their weapons.

He flew over the wall and into the keep, diving off his mount and tumbling across the ground before coming to a sudden stop as he collided with the cold marble of the central tower. Rangers dove in his direction, spears aiming for his throat, stopping inches away at the sight of his elven features.

Captain Yvlynne ran toward Alikain. "By the light, Alikain! Did you get it? Where is Goronil? *Oronnsela estrala*[2] Alikain, where is he?" She asked, her voice beginning to tremble.

Alikain clutched at the shaft of the arrow in his leg, looked up and shook his head, unable to meet her gaze. He held out the satchel for her, his arms shaking with his head bowed.

"Keep it, you need to get it to the council. The mages have started the ritual. We have a plan to stabilise the portal and need to ensure that the evacuation is ready to begin. Go now, it is time to show these treasonous dogs what we think of them," she said, a dark conviction taking over her demeanour.

The yurinduur's second wave were fast approaching now, their pace quickening as they got closer and closer to the taste of fresh blood. The elves raised their bows and all at once, released their arrows in wave after wave. The yurinduur began crashing into the ground, their thick hides no match for the arrows and a ranger's precision. Where one fell, three took its place and the shock waves were soon upon the breaches in the walls of Dilen'Nahen.

The elves braced their shields for the impact, the footmen shouting in unison, "*Arensela luestrala selunua foretdinela*[3]!"

As the yurinduur charged into their ranks, some of them pierced by the outstretched spears, others met the elves with such force that it sent them flying backward. The gaps in the ranks were quickly filled and the line held, their pitiful numbers not leaving room to spare the wounded from the fray.

The mages upon the walls hurtled balls of fire and sent arcs of lightning through the attackers, all the while, maintaining their wards against the assault of the magical projectiles fired from the cataclysmic siege works. Arrows struck any elf that dropped their guard whilst others were torn apart by the yurinduur.

The thalenarians distanced themselves from the frontlines directly, shedding the blood of the lesser races this day. Their captains grinning at the fall of the elven stronghold. They kept the trebuchets and archers firing blindly at the walls and over them. Every fifty yurinduur that fell to the fire would be worth the cost of every one elf who died.

---

[2] By the stars
[3] For the light of the stars and the life of the forest

Wave upon wave drove into the wall of steel and blood and wave after wave was repelled. Mages hurled their apocalyptic magic into the fray without concern for the fatigue caused. The very air around the keep was turned into a maelstrom of cinder and screams whilst the elves within tended to the wounded, dodged trebuchet stones and answered calls to breaches in the defence.

Coronation

The fireworks shattered the air itself, exploding into a dizzying array of colours through a rain of drifting leaves and flower petals. Their metallic smoke clouds mixed with the sweet honey nectar set in the air by the merchants working the crowds offering treats; from toffee apples to steaming fruit tarts. The parade moved through the street with opulent carriages decorated to represent each of the noble families of the *forehaltha*[4], the wood elves.

A carriage of clear ice drawn by steeds of flowing water followed by not a cart but a cloud moving through the air as it would to form the first rains of spring. Another had a mighty water buffalo spun together from vines pulling a terrarium which, at its centre, showcased a cherry tree in full bloom whilst butterflies and bees danced between its flowers. Two lumbering spruce trees drew a carriage of flowers that would continuously bloom and fall, leaving behind a floral carpet of stunning pinks, yellows and whites.

The elegant and simple display of a clear iceberg floating millimetres above the ground, carried Rylia, the daughter of Quilin and Diala, the previous Master of the *Tamore Narana*[5], and the elf who would become the new Queen of the *forehaltha*. Drawing the carriage were two snow-white mares without reins or aids, attached to the cart by ethereal strands of focused moonlight hanging slack in the breeze. The air surrounding the display seemed to be that of twilight, as small flakes of snow fell in its radius, gently kissing those within.

Rylia stood, the picture of elegance, waving to the gathered masses with the relaxed grace and surety of one seemingly destined for the role. Her emerald eyes scanned the cheering faces, gleaming in the morning light. Coruscating gems, forming small stars, adorned her chestnut hair which cascaded down her back, baring intricate braids woven in. Her ivory

---

[4] Wood Elves
[5] Council of Healers

skin blended into the dress that flowed off the back of her icy podium in a waterfall of the purest white silk, fitting to her graceful form.

Rylia's smile set passion and loyalty into those who looked upon her. The celebrants cheered and sang as she rode past, accepting her eye contact with deep gratitude and pride. Flowers, motes of earth and pitchers of water were laid out before her as an offering of both land and nature.

The noble houses that formed the parade, displayed their culture to the people gathered. Members of such houses in the crowd bowed or sang house anthems as they passed by, pride welling up in their chests with tears in their eyes.

Acrobats of the *tarviahaltha*[6], the sky elves, tumbled in the air and spun around lengths of ribbon made from pure light. They wore porcelain masks disguising their faces and had a sourceless drum beat synchronising their movements in rhythmic waves. Richly coloured tunics augmented with fine jewellery and intricate designs bolstering the spectrum of the floral parade.

Next, the mages of the sea elves, the *merhaltha*[7], had cast dolphins shaped out of water that danced around the procession and swam through the crowds. Birds of mist and cloud soared overhead, sparking with bursts of lightning in their bodies, crackling amidst the fireworks. The mages themselves sailing forward in their royal blue robes with silver masks homogenising their features.

All the noise of the parade was enough to wake Ara from her deep slumber. She snapped up out of bed like a chameleon's tongue to an unsuspecting fly, her limbs flailing in panic as they threw off her blanket.

"Parade!" she repeated to herself, over and over, as she whirled around her room picking up clothes and brushes to get herself ready, knocking over tables and chairs in the chaos. Bags littered the furniture with her room in disarray from a night spent packing. Trinkets and clothes left out serving now as shrapnel in her flurry.

She dove to her door and snatched her staff from beside her writing desk before careening down the stairs and out of her dwelling. She halted at her threshold, trapped by a thought. Spinning around, she deposited her staff back beside the entryway and resigned herself to the race.

Ara barrelled in the direction of the citadel tree, weaving her way through the celebrants, snatching the odd fruit tart or two as she did so.

---

[6] Sky Elves
[7] Sea Elves

"Good day! Yes, she looks gorgeous. Already late. Wonderful day for it…" she remarked to the many elves attempting to engage her in conversation. She answered, not breaking her stride, and not minding that her replies had to make their way through mouthfuls of sweet elderberry tart.

She arrived at the *Foretarla*[8]. Here, the crowds were gathered by the tree roots, staring into the centre where the coronation was to take place. Each were dressed immaculately in the natural colours that nature brought to bear, with the effortless grace of the elves merely seeking to be a part of the display. Ara, herself, wore an emerald, green dress that hung down to conceal her sandaled feet in cascading linen. A silver pendant of the *Foretarla* hung around her neck as her only jewellery for the occasion and at the centre of her ensemble was her glowing smile between rosy cheeks.

Ara made her way through, making the final adjustments to her ceremonial garb, pinning back the stray strands of her chestnut hair as she reached the main entrance to the *Foretarla*.

The wardens, of the royal guard, surrounded the citadel at attention, holding back the enthusiastic crowd. Their mahogany-tinted armour and green cloaks blended them seamlessly into the foliage of the tree to form the roots of the citadel's defence.

"My dear, you have… something on your hands," said Diala, grabbing a cloth from a hidden pocket and wiping the sugary substance off of Ara's hands and from the corner of her mouth.

Ara, still attempting to catch her breath, grabbed the cloth and finished wiping herself down before adorning her formal demeanour. Together, they hurried through the guards' wall, taking up their position in the ceremony. Ara reached out to hold her mother's hand, tightly in adoration.

"Thank you, Mother, how is everything proceeding?" she inquired, her breathing now beginning to settle.

"Well enough, I would say. Your sister should be in any minute now. I believe we have everything ready for her arrival," Diala replied, gesturing toward a nearby guard who gave a subtle confirmatory nod, his expression unreadable behind his decorated helm and unwavering posture.

At that, Ara settled and took her place at her parents' side, clasping her hands neatly in her lap, blowing at a loose strand of hair that had already

---

[8] Heart of the Forest – The great oak tree at the centre of Foretilatava

escaped its bindings.

Looking over the celebrants, she smiled, noting elf, human and dwarf having gathered in Foretilatava for her sister. The foreign and local dignitaries stood, eagerly awaiting the commencement of the ceremony, each seeming more confused than the next.

The dwarven clan leaders had sent representatives of the crafter's guilds, the merchant leagues and the ambassadors from all their halls except for the southern halls of Rotamur. The human kings had resisted sending representatives of any real political weight, most of them being superstitious spies that had to be kept under constant guard lest they pocket anything on sight.

Ara had a run in with one of their spies, Jackson, two days prior. He was wandering the city making diagrams of butterflies in a crude cryptographic depiction that must have been a map of the city and its defences. It was a valiant effort but according to a brief scan, he had clearly misidentified one of the phytomining groves as a syrup farm. Goodness knows why he thought the *forehaltha* needed that much syrup.

Twilight mist and snowflakes seeped into the room, as the sound of the parade grew steadily louder. Rylia's carriage could be seen approaching *Foretarla*. The crowds gathered at the base of the stairs as she ascended into the tree to meet her destiny. Wardens saluted her as she passed them by then returned to their position at attention, stoic and resolute.

The musicians within *Foretarla* rose to play their melody, a tune so soft, so pure and sweet that it sounded like fresh drizzle falling on a field of heather. The strings sang in a breeze that danced with the willows beside a stream whilst the percussion set a beat of clouds rolling over the trees for a summer storm. The pipes were the last to join in to raise the emotions and build atmosphere in the crowd to match the crescendo of the ceremony.

Rylia walked up to meet her parents and her sister at the head of the congregation, nervously summiting the stairs with her dress meandering down behind her as a great river. The corners of her mouth twitched upward revealing the slightest hint of elation in her royal visage. Her nerves were tightly under control, but Ara noticed the tremor in her hands and the flush in her cheeks that betrayed her. The way she tucked her arms at her sides and her deep breathing were the only indications of anxiety in her; otherwise, flawless show that commanded the attention of her congregation.

She spun in one fluid motion to face those gathered within *Foretarla*, losing all previous tells of her anxiety. Her dress responded to the intangible breeze that held it in constant flowing motion around her feet. Vexhimarith, the head druid of Foretilatava, stood from his seat at the front of the audience. He wore a form-fitting green tunic with woven ivy epaulets that held a forest green cloak extending to his boots. His ash blond hair nested a crown in the form of miniaturised antlers made from carved birch. He climbed the stairs to the throne's podium to stand before Rylia.

In Vexhimarith's arms was a cushion of flowers woven in to hold aloft a crown of platinum that now caught the twilight glow surrounding Rylia. Simply woven as vines around a tree, the settings held three emeralds inlaid into its brow. The crown of *Foretarla* that had been a symbol of the nobility since the elves first set foot onto Etroah with the great northern forests welcoming them and protecting them from the wilds of the world.

"Welcome one, welcome all," he began in his unnaturally booming voice. "Thank you for journeying here today so that we may all stand as witness to the crowning of the new monarch of the *forehaltha*. Rylia, Arch Druid of the *forehaltha*, daughter of the full moon and former Master of the *Tamore Narana*."

The congregation broke into applause, enthusiastic at first before being reined into a formal acknowledgement with a wave of Vexhimarith's hand. Rylia stepped forward and held her arms open toward the congregation.

Vexhimarith gave a deep bow, his green eyes aglow with pride.

"Rylia," he said, turning to Ara's sister, "you stand here before us, a humble servant to the people, a healer of the sick and protector of the lands and culture. For many years now, you have upheld our values and opened your heart to all. Now, chosen by the forest itself, we ask that you might accept the responsibilities and duties set before you, as Queen. That you welcome all the *forehaltha* into your arms to be treated as your blood kin. That you dedicate your life to the prosperity of the people and their lands, ensuring the protection of our home and the endurance of our people. The forest has chosen you. Will you answer our plea? Do you accept our plight?" asked the druid, dropping to one knee and bowing his head, presenting the crown forth.

The humans and dwarves shifted from side to side, unsettled at the customs set before them. Their gazes wandered around the tree's interior, scanning the faces of the elves in the room, inspecting their fellow emissaries and remembering to politely clap every so often.

The dwarven merchants, clad in fine red velvet robes with heavy gold chains around their necks and a dazzling multitude of rings on their fingers, scowled at the conserved propriety of the affair, clearly eager to get back to their business. Jackson, the ambassador from Westhold, had barely noticed the ceremony with his gaze instead falling upon the backless dresses of the elven nobility, unable to keep his cheeks from flushing.

"I accept the rights and responsibilities, the duties and privileges and all tasks of the crown that lay ahead of me, as this honour is bestowed," Rylia replied, lifting the crown into the air.

Branches of the tree slowly erupted from the floor, entangling her bare feet and wrapping around her legs. Rylia paused, smiling at her expectant audience. "I, Rylia, accept the lifeblood of the forest, to become its voice, to hear its plight and to connect our people with our homeland. In the gaze of our ancestors, under the light of our stars and with the guidance of our gods."

One more deep breath. She placed the crown on her head.

A pulse of green light shot down through her, to her chest and into her torso. The light flashed through her legs and into the roots that now engulfed them. As blood flows through one's veins, so the light dispersed through *Foretarla*, causing the tree to erupt into an explosion of blooming flowers.

The old tree that had looked too mature for such displays regained the theatrics of youth in this sudden show of vigour to the cheering crowds. Lilac petals rained down within and around as those caught in the flower fall sang, cheered and danced.

Imara, a member of the *forehaltha* nobility, grabbed Balduur, a trade merchant of Myngora Wiatalawald, by his shoulders and gave him an enthusiastic kiss on the lips. The proud dwarf shone a luminescent crimson through the thinner patches in his coal-black beard. At this, he decided it best to engage with the festivities and his cheering rose to a mighty roar to meet the audience.

"*Eleia iaraiña Rylia, foretarla unua arlarla'a orela[9]*!" proclaimed Vexhimarith throwing his hands into the air.

Rylia composed herself, grinning at her subjects and taking in the flood of emotions that welled within her chest. The branches around her legs

---

[9] All hail our Queen Rylia, heart of the forest and heart of our hearts

released their firm grasp but she was now a part of the forest. Every leaf, each blade of grass and each new shoot was now a part of her and though Vexhimarith had trained her to withstand the sensory throughput of the entire forest, she couldn't help but feel faint and overwhelmed. She shut her eyes, breathing deeply, focusing her thoughts.

The ordeal was proving far more than anticipated and the colour seeped from Rylia's face. Ara, still cheering, walked towards her sister and embraced her in the natural rhythm of the moment.

"You are doing great, just breathe. Take your time," she whispered to her sister, magically extending her mind to share what energy she could with her.

Rylia, having been steadied, opened her eyes, her cheeks adopting their previous pinkish glow. A smile of gratitude and a single tear that ran down her cheek. The sisters embraced tightly, stealing a moment amidst the roar of the crowds. Rylia walked to the front of the throne's podium. She was more elegant than ever, losing her twilight effect to an ethereal glow that radiated from her skin in royal iridescence.

The highest ranking of the dignitaries lined up and down the row in order of arrival. The dwarves had anticipated this rush and made short work of the intervening distances. Gifts of jewels, fine metals forged into ornate statues and jewellery so intricate in design that it would turn the heads of even the elves. The merchants presented spices vibrant in both colour and scent, bolts of fine silks and other exotic oddities, each beaming with pride at their gifts and how it compared to the others being presented.

Gholon, the dwarven emissary from Myngora Staernbaum, had his assistants hand over bottles of fine whiskeys and meads brewed underground in the mountains of Mardacia. The other dwarves looked on derisively until a stone chest was brought forth. Within it was a set of sapphire tuning forks that had been expertly shaped to their respective notes.

Rylia received each gift with equal gratitude. From the sapphire tuning forks to the family quilts of Balmkalmeine, still dusty from the journey. The dwarves were elated at their gift giving and to have been in the presence of one as flawless as the new Queen of the *forehaltha*. Replete with pride, they returned to their seats to brag about the subtle differences in the manner in which their gifts were received and the perceived implications therein.

The humans adopted a reserved approach to the podium, surveying the situation with their keen political minds. Eyes darting to and fro, calculating their posture, timing and tone according to the situation around them. Each deciding their place in the line, they presented their gifts after the rush of dwarves.

Lord Threspin of Silverfort was first, kissing his toes with his bow. He presented a collection of coins from across the realm set in order, starting with Eastern Anthuria and ending Athraz. Clearly relations are being strained, Rylia thought as she smiled, impassively receiving the gift.

The melsoans had sent a single ambassador for the transcontinental journey. Lahkar Kamiir, a gentleman of exceeding charm and social grace, snatched Rylia's hand to give it an ingratiating kiss.

"Your eyes glow like the summer pools of the oasis springs and my heart dances at the sight of you," he said, his voice smooth and masculine with the poetic accent of the melsoans – Rubahari, as best Rylia could guess. "My gift is one befitting of your wild nature and I hope you find it as beautiful as your mirror in the kiss of dawn's fresh light," he concluded, handing over a curved dagger with a gold handle and jewelled ivory scabbard.

Ara stifled a chuckle at his attempts but stared in awe at his presentation. Lahkar was a handsome gentleman indeed and he struck quite the intriguing figure with his crimson and ivory satin robes. The dagger he had presented was a work of art as much as he. The pommel was blown glass housing the red sands of the Melsoan desert gently cascading within as the dagger was handed over.

One by one, the human ambassadors presented their gifts, each more transparent and obsequious than the next. Weaving their words and tying their tongues into promises they would never keep. Sabille had not sent anyone out of sheer defiance. The High Ambassador of Athraz, Trent Emberlind, was the last to present a gift.

He grew nervous as the elven delegations lined up behind him, but he kept his air of pre-eminence around him, nonetheless. He handed over an embroidered silk dress of the deepest black Rylia had ever seen. It inhaled the light from its surroundings, forming an abyssal void within. The colour had an impact but just as it unsettled her, she found it incomprehensibly beautiful.

"Never fear the darkest night. Embrace it and its power shall be yours. Wear it so that you may control it. It is the will of those lesser to fear the dark," he said, snaking his words around his meaning.

"My gratitude to you for this unique gift. I shall look forward to such an occasion where I may wear it," replied Rylia, folding the material between her hands, marvelling at the colour's effect for a brief moment before smiling impassively once more.

Finally, the faces of her fellow elves approached to present their gifts. They were not here to impress or gain favour but merely to congratulate the *forehaltha* on their new Queen. They held no gold nor gem for this, much to the shock of the dwarves and confusion of the humans.

Admiral Kespin of the *merhaltha* knelt to one knee with a friendly smile. He presented a scroll with silent approval. Rylia unravelled the paper to reveal a complex list of additions, upgrades and repairs to be requisitioned for the *forehaltha* ships by the expert shipwrights of Sinien Tarvia. The magnitude of this gift was too immense for words. To secure ocean trade for the elves in Foretilatava was no small gesture. Rylia nodded silently in thanks, the understanding between the elves as clear as the sun in a desert.

The final presentation of the assembly was from Chancellor Nildinar. He was a new face to the Council of Isfrisairis but one that Rylia was happy to acquaint herself with. His silver-blond hair fell to his shoulders as he spoke with the quiet grace that she had come to expect from the officious *tarviahaltha*. His words were simple but drove the point across with brutal efficiency.

"I request a private audience," he said, his tone friendly but his gaze intent.

He handed over a broken sword, wrapped in crushed velvet. The crossguard was open as the wings of an eagle with a tear cut aquamarine in its pommel. It was the blade of a sentinel which meant grave news for all elves, especially when delivered with such urgency that it could not be done after the ceremony.

Understanding the message, Rylia nodded, not immediately turning to hand off the gift to Vexhimarith but instead, taking a moment to ponder the implications of the presentation.

"Of course, I also have this," Nildinar said with a polite smile, handing over a book filled with schematics, formulae and diagrams that took a few moments for Rylia to decipher.

Once she had, though, she chuckled with excitement and thanked

Nildinar. He smiled and walked toward Admiral Kespin, handing him a bent dagger in a pine box. It was less impressive looking than the sword, likely belong to a soldier or even a ranger but the manner of its presentation sent a shiver down Ara's spine. The admiral was less able to retain his composure and immediately sank into concern, looking to Rylia for confirmation.

With the ceremony at a close, there was little sense to waste time on social platitudes when such pressing matters had just arisen. Rylia gave Nildinar's gift, of updated magical ward glyphs for the city, to Vexhimarith. Her mood was modulated at the news and now, the celebration had turned into a meeting to decide the future of the elves.

Their parents, seeing the events unfolding, melded into the procession to distract any confused guests. They assisted the wardens in directing the assembly back in the direction of the city proper where the coronation festivities were to continue.

The orchestra recognised their cue and leapt into action once more, leading the masses out with the flowing high tempo of a song Ara recognised as *The Springs Bloom*.

Foretilatava

Foretilatava, a city of life. Trees formed the buildings, sung magically into the required shapes with staircases that spiralled, around their trunks, toward the sky. The forest's canopy bore the residential homes of the *forehaltha*, the dense leaf cover providing seclusion within the cities heart. The understory had the larger meeting places of family groups and small businesses in the branches of the living landscape. On the floor, the public buildings lined the walkways, their frameworks being spun from buttress roots and roofed with a dense network of vines and leaves.

Festivities ruled the city and involved every corner of the city's floor. Magic permeated the air in showers of sparks, illusory birds and mystical scents. Food stands were set up in all the buildings and drink was flowing freely. Musicians, acrobats and performers of all imaginable arts led the festivities and gave substance to the atmosphere around them.

Quilin arrived with his arms full of fruit cocktails in ornately carved mahogany mugs with little umbrellas in the crushed ice, handing one to Diala and another to Ara. The trio set about their beverages and surveyed the crowds. Jackson was amidst a battle with the dwarves, attempting to keep his feet as they handed him drinks and jostled him during their stories of combat ability and amorous prowess.

The other dwarven group were trying their hand at the *forehaltha* delicacies. There was no cost for the food or drink which was bordering on insult towards the dwarves so, instead, they would hand over small trinkets from their homelands in equable exchange.

Balduur had cornered Vexhimarith and the two were in deep conversation about the goblin hordes rising up from the depths to assault the dwarven holds, Vexhimarith trying to avoid such topics during this joyous occasion. Balduur was shorter than Vexhimarith, standing in around one and a half metres which had him at Vexhimarith's shoulders but stood twice as broad with muscles that could shape steel.

Lahkar Kamiir had taken the podium at a poet's stand and was currently in possession of a small crowd's attention as he recited *Mesnat Areia* – The

Midnight Sands – in its original Melsoan dialect. The elves made a point to understand the world's languages, but without having exposure to many native speakers, the subtle nuances of the language were a rare treat to their ears. Lahkar was all too pleased to provide his performance, his tongue rolling around the syllables as he theatrically gesticulated.

Quilin broke through Ara's reverie, saying with a playful chuckle, "You did well in the ceremony, Ara. We were however worried that you would not make it in time."

"I slept in." She grinned through her sip of apple and kiwi cocktail. "I got a little carried away with the packing last night."

"Has Rylia got any idea where you might be off to? I must say, Melsoa does not seem like a bad choice," Diala asked, eyeing out Lahkar's performance.

"Or the heroic lands of Mardacia with peoples on their quests for greatness and renown? I hear their gods have been growing more active in recent years." Interjected Quilin, clearing his throat to break Diala's facetious gaze toward Lahkar.

"I have no idea and she has been annoyingly logical on the matter. She was awaiting the talks after the coronation's primary festivities. She may want to send me on a round trip of the elven cities first. Get a feel for travelling and dealing with the political doublespeak before taking on the human and dwarven groups. Chancellor Nildinar may have changed things though," she said, now eyeing out a sorbet stand.

Before she could get distracted however, Diala halted her with a subtle gesture. Striding towards them were three finely clad nobles with vaguely elven features. One wore a red dress cascading down into tails of orange and yellow, with burgundy hair that matched the colour of her piercing eyes.

She led the procession to stop respectfully before them, and began her greeting, "*Yralui*[10] and good tidings to you all. Our blessings upon Queen Rylia. May her reign be prosperous and long."

The male with near black hair, a blue tint breaking through when it caught the light, stood to her flank. His clothing was similar in style with flowing robes from the black shoulders to the royal blue tails. His eyes glowed cerulean in the shadow of his brow. At her other flank, a female in a green dress, matching some of the *forehaltha* celebrants. Her eye colour

---

[10] Good rain

was the emerald of the forest lakes, her skin was vibrant and sun kissed. She had a wildness to her form that resonated with the *forehaltha*, her mahogany hair shimmering ever so slightly to reveal its dark green tint of a philodendron leaf.

Dragons. Ara had only ever seen them from a distance and now, up close, three of them together. They had not participated in the ceremony and had likely only arrived to privately wish Rylia well, now extending such platitudes to her family.

"A pleasure to have you in Foretilatava, and a true honour to have your blessing in this. Rylia, the *forehaltha* and indeed, all the *haltha*[11] would like to see her reign usher in a new era of peace for us all and we will be glad to have you counted amongst our friends," Quilin responded, bowing his head.

"Perhaps. The unity of Etroah may yet be required," the lead delegate responded, cryptically ending the interaction before leading the group to the periphery of the festivities and into the forest beyond.

"Is it me or was that more of a warning than an exchange of good will?" inquired Ara.

"The dragons have been pushing to make peace with the other races, however… The dwarves hold grudges tighter than they hold onto their clan histories, the two often becoming one and the same. The humans, bless their souls—" she continued, shaking her head at the Anthurian, Jackson, who was now on the table, dancing and swinging his coat around his head to the raucous encouragement of a group of cheering dwarves "—will not seek peace unless they it bolsters their personal power. Finally, us *haltha* have peace, but certainly no alliance or friendship with them. Isfrisairis struck the final blow in the Dragon Wars, and as you well know, have kept the nature of this to themselves. It is still a point of great contention between the *tarviahaltha* and the dragons, one which overflows to the rest of us."

"Perhaps I need to start there with my political tour?" Ara offered.

"We shall see. In the meantime, Ara, Vexhimarith needs to be saved. Perhaps you can be of assistance?" she offered, wincing at Balduur as the dwarf had just stabbed his dagger into a nearby fruit stand to drive a point home.

Ara nodded and jogged over. The clans of Wiatalawald were chief among all dwarves. They were in charge of the clan meetings between the

---

[11] Elves

dwarven kingdoms and thus, their personalities were generally the most intransigent.

Ara seamlessly integrated herself into their conversation, having been able to hear Balduur's side of the engagement from twenty metres away where she had stood with her parents.

"Lord Balduur, *forsonrander*[12]. My name is Ara, I am bloodkin and sister to the Queen," she opened.

The dwarf's eyes lit up at his new political intermediary. He puffed out his chest and lowered his voice to its more booming and honorary register.

"M'lady Ara. Light fall upon your steps and leaves, uh, grow in yer hair. As I was saying tae this fellow here. Myngora Wiatalawald is being tested by the goblin hordes. Though the might of the dwarves is more than ready to fend off any tide that crashes against our shores, we could still use some support from your esteemed workshops. Our magic runs low, and our shamans are spread thin as it is. Etroah is stirring and we need to be ready. If we are to maintain trade then we may need spell casters or more charged gems to be sent through, else you'll be dealing with these vermin too."

"Of course. Well, the might of the dwarves is to be supported by the *haltha*, not limited by it. Dwarf blood is too precious to waste on such a foe. I am sure my sister will see it this way as well. I shall bring this matter to her attention personally and shall ensure that I have Vexhimarith's support in this as well. From there, we can come to an arrangement that will benefit both our nations and secure us from the threat of the deep. In the meantime, however, Vexhimarith is due to escort me through the city and to my sister so that we may discuss such issues. If you would excuse us," she finished, bowing deeply, her head passing her knees.

The dwarf looked appeased for the time being and gave a grunt of acceptance. He snatched his mug and his dagger from the fruit stand and made his way to Lahkar who was now finished with his performance and sampling the elven wines, unprepared for the tornado heading in his direction.

Ara ducked into the building behind the fruit stand, through a curtain of flowering vines. The city had lost its wildlife residents with all the commotion but at least the flora remained its stunning self. She sat at a table and let loose an exhausted sigh. Vexhimarith leant forward and filled his

---

[12] Greetings

mug with water from the xylemic tap in the middle of the table.

"Thank you for that. I did want to talk to you though," he said, revealing his anxiety.

"Well, if it is to teach me about tone and posture when addressing the dwarf clans then be prepared for a derisive laugh," she responded sarcastically. Her mind wondered, reminiscing on their long diplomacy lessons in the evenings after her normal hours spent at the University Druidica.

"No. It seems that the dwarves did not study the same textbooks we did and thus some of our information may be off in that regard. Or perhaps, we were following the teachings of Wolfrith, a ranger posted in Myngora Haezelahol and thus, his take was based off of the central clans, so perhaps—"

"Vexhimarith, not the time," Ara interrupted.

"Of course. Yes. Fascinating though. Anyway, the *tarviahaltha*. They have a custom of handing weapons over as gifts to one another. If they hand you an intact weapon, then they are offering to fight at your side and aid you where possible. If they hand you a broken weapon—"

"Chancellor Nildinar gave a sword to Rylia and a dagger to Kespin."

"Yes, broken ones. A broken weapon represents a call to battle. They are asking Kespin and Rylia to assist the *tarviahaltha*. The sword was wrapped, suggesting that the owner is still alive. Admiral Kespin received a broken dagger in a box, likely belonging to an elf who is deceased."

"What wars are they fighting? I thought the towers were keeping the humans at bay. The dragons certainly are not attacking otherwise we would see the smoke from here. The dwarves? Goblins?"

"Athraz has been stirring but I have not heard of any conflicts that have arisen involving the *haltha*. Nildinar did ask for Rylia's attention in a private meeting with Admiral Kespin, myself and you. In fact, he asked for you by name. I suspect that our *tarviahaltha* brethren have a plan and seek to amalgamate our nations into it."

"I am to be the Queen's envoy. Perhaps he sees a diplomatic resolution to the conflict and would like my assistance in that?"

"We can only hope. He travelled here with a small army of rangers and sentinels. He is scared and it is showing. This is very uncharacteristic of him and yet, here we are."

The festivities had faded into a gentle hum in the background with

Ara's senses being overrun by her growing nerves. She was looking forward to a political holiday abroad but had never expected to be involved in a conflict over anything more than trade disputes or border grumblings.

"Be prepared and have your wits about you, Ara. I have a feeling that this will be no small task they will ask of you," he finished, pondering the reflection in his mug.

Daltorus Comes

The *tarviahaltha* followed Ara and Rylia to the council chambers. Their numbers had grown to include multiple sentinels all carrying locked mahogany crates with steel reinforcing brackets; a shimmer of magical wards around them with symbols that pulsed with energy.

When Ara was younger, she had heard stories of the heroic, dragon slaying sentinels. In her mind, they had been stars that had fallen from the sky to protect the elves in their time of need. Their armour gleaming through the darkest of nights. Seeing them up close though was even more impressive. The grey cloaks of the Isfrisairis *tarviahaltha* with the golden eagles embroidered between their shoulders, wings outstretched, lending their majesty to the elves.

Where the sentinels wore suits of full plate armour, crafted of polished moonsteel and engraved with a rich tapestry of their homeland in the Isfrisairis Mountains, the rangers presented a more modest appearance. Their green cloaks and brushed steel breastplates helped to meld them into their environment, being the silent and unseen protectors of that which they safeguarded.

She caught a few of the elves' expressions as she scanned them for their motives. There are refined differences between a serious expression and an officious one in *tarviahaltha* culture. A slight furrowing of the brow, the focused stare, but mostly the eyes that adopt a dangerous glint. The latter of the expressions was also so rare that one couldn't help but feel anxious in its presence, which is why Ara held her stomach in her throat as they made their way up the final flight of stairs, through the royal halls, and into the council chamber.

The sentinels spread out around the room, placing the crates down with heavy impacts on the oaken sung floor. The most decorated of these sentinels then set about unlocking all of the crates, placing the contents onto the table in the centre of the chamber.

There were shredded and bloody banners that still smelt of smoke and battle, weapons of an alien design forged from an unfamiliar alloy, and various scrolls, books and maps spread out to be viewed. Nildinar's shoulders sank as his eyes grew dark. It was as if he hadn't slept for the past month, and it had only now managed to catch up with him.

A tremble climbed into his voice. "A year and a half ago, the mages, of the University Arcanum, began noticing spatial fluctuation signatures inconsistent with normal variations. There were radiation spikes at ground level with no apparent source and, whilst harmless, they were troubling. We sent out scouting groups to investigate the sources for these disturbances but for the first year, we were met with little to show for our efforts. It was not until one of these anomalies was detected in the elven lands, on the very doorstep of Tour Mardesi, that we were able to investigate fully."

He paused, bracing his hands on the rosewood table and leaning forward to inspect the artefacts before him.

"They found that it was a portal leak. The energy signatures picked up were similar to those found at the other sites which, considering the frequency and patterns of emergence, we were able to conclude that said portals were artificial in nature."

Admiral Kespin's jaw almost fell to the floor as he pieced the puzzle together. "Why were we not informed?" he inquired, raising his voice. Where *tarviahaltha* were reserved and officious, the culture of the *merhaltha* was one of action. Kespin wasted no time in reminding Ara of this.

Nildinar raised a hand to delay his answer before continuing, "We are centuries away from such feats of magic, but our research teams were able to stabilise the portal and secure the surrounding areas. Nothing had come through, so we expected that our continent… or plane… was merely being probed out of curiosity and data collection. There was little reason to report this as we had no idea what it was that we were dealing with," he said, now gesturing for the congregation to take a seat around the table.

He fished for a booklet containing multiple graphs and tables. "We collected some of our own data. There were atypical isotope ratios, a slight increase in alpha and beta ultraviolet wavelengths but not to a vast extent. The atmosphere had higher nitrogen concentrations but, in the end, was remarkably similar to that of our own. The council decided to send in a research team accompanied by a non-occupational scouting force, totalling two hundred. This was three months ago." He ran his hands through his hair and rubbed his eyes. A sentinel brought him a goblet of water and he drank for a few moments, pausing to compose himself and let the current information sink in.

Rylia had called in a scribe to assist her in gathering the information. She scanned over the transcript to confirm the tales she had heard. Ara could not believe the implications set before her. A separate atmosphere. Did that mean it was another planet, or indeed another plane? And why had they kept this secret until now? These questions raced through Ara's mind as she reached over to get a closer look at the strange symbols on the banners.

"Who are they?" asked Kespin flatly, flicking through the volumes set before him.

"Multiple races actually. The race that concerns us most however, are the thalenarians. Worryingly, they have a culture similar to our own. They focus heavily on research into the arcane in which, despite their aptitude for portal conjuration, they are not much more advanced than ourselves. They have a heavy focus on the arts, and research into the physical world as well as a language that we were able to translate and adapt to our needs with relative accuracy. Interestingly, they are monotheistic with their God as their leader. Emperor Xalmilanthris. A mercurial character from our reports and one that is in possession of unimaginable power. It is our current theory that the thalenarians actually have a very basic understanding of portal magic and, instead, utilise the sympathetic magic of their emperor to summon them but without much accuracy or understanding."

Rylia spoke up in a tone so calm that it slid like a thorn through skin, "How did relations turn sour?"

Nildinar almost chuckled at this. "Well, we lost the ability to contact the team just as soon as they entered the portal, relying on information they were able to send through. Our attempts to manipulate the portal from this side made it unstable, so we thought against taking any chances untoward. The group was greeted by an unholy and hostile land which, if their accounts are to be believed, consists almost entirely of creatures bred to kill. As it turns out, this was not the first time the thalenarians had opened portals. In fact, they had collected all manner of creatures from their travels and enslaved them to suit their purposes. Now, initially, we had not known this and were able to develop diplomatic relations with the thalenarians, even going as far as to send envoys into their cities so that we may learn more of each other's cultures. While this was under development, the group had taken residence in an old fort…" He began paging furiously through the notes set out on the table before grabbing a banner instead. "Dilen'Nahen," he said, displaying a purple banner with a silver wyvern wreathed in flame.

"This God Emperor of theirs, what else is he capable of? Do they have paladins to their faith?" Ara probed.

Startled, Nildinar responded, "Well, we do not know. Contact with him was limited and we are still translating some of the stolen texts. He does have paladins, but they are essentially holy mages. Acolytes, they call themselves. To continue: everything was going rather well until we discovered their role in ordering hostility in the creatures that had been relentlessly attacking the expedition base. Their questions then became more… severe. We realised, before we revealed too much, that they were merely probing us, only offering us information as they never expected any of our elves to return home," he said, gesturing towards the head sentinel who unlocked a lead chest. Wards on the container faded as he reached in and brought a satchel from its depths. "Knowing where they stood, they made a plan to return with the inquisitors being sent in under the guise of being researchers familiar with our world's pantheons."

Ara nearly scoffed at this. The thought of a religious inquisitor was the most incredulous thing yet, and that was despite all the talk of extra-planar travels and God Emperors.

"Inquisitors Goronil and Alikain were sent in exchange for the political envoys."

At the mention of these names, the entire room held their breath. Inquisitors were the executioners of elven society. In a world of mages, they had to be the most cunning. On a field of sentinels, they had to be the better fighters. In a forest of *forehaltha* wardens, they had to have the sharpest eyes. Worst of all, they were brutally efficient and would never enter a room unless they knew they could kill everyone inside and escape unharmed.

"They were able to retrieve this," Nildinar said, pulling a crimson leather-bound book with gold-leafed pages. The head sentinel gave copies to Kespin and Rylia. "It is the definitive holy text regarding the thalenarian emperor. From our research, this race has no chink in their armour but, if one existed, this book may have it. The information is convoluted to say the least and we have merely transcribed it as written. However, we have thus far been unable to decode it. The research team did find a reference in another text that alluded to a manual of portal magic that, if deciphered, could give us a method of predicting the portal locations or even closing them once opened. From the little information received from beyond the portal, it seems that the inquisitors are currently on a mission to retrieve this book."

"Decode?" Ara asked.

"The acolytes have their own sublanguage that they write their texts in. It is secret to them and upon fear of the annihilation of their immortal soul, their emperor has sworn them to secrecy," Nildinar answered.

"So, we need this on the off chance you decide to send in another scouting party and need to tug on this god's strings? Is that it?" Kespin remarked, sliding a book across the table, back to its centre.

Nildinar ignored his tone and answered, "The inquisitors were able to gather a fair bit of information regarding the workings of their culture. The thalenarians find a world, investigate it and take what they want from it. Valuable resources, useful creatures, powerful artefacts and so forth. It seems, however, that we are the exception that proves the rule. The inquisitors stumbled onto some information regarding a prophecy given to Xalmilanthris not soon after his initial ascension. Basically, it stated that they would one day find a world which housed beings called the *'Suineassa Litani'*, which we believe to be the *haltha*. This world, our world it would seem, would hold the key to the undisputed supremacy of the entire thalenarian race as Xalmilanthris achieves his final ascension to godhood."

Filling the room was a silence so heavy that the elves slouched their shoulders forward in contemplation. Ara's mind was reeling until she could stand the reticence no more.

"Nature finds a way. What is our plan to stop this? Aside from deciphering and translating the book," she asked, her confidence sending a spark of inspiration to Nildinar and piquing interest in the others.

"To start, we need to get our people back. The portals have remained unstable. We are unable to stabilise them from this side and they do not have the magical power necessary to do so from over there."

The weight of the silence had alleviated but was rapidly replaced with that of guilt. So many lives were on the line and yet what could the elves in this room do? Nildinar was, however, a politician. He was building up the pressure before providing a solution that would be costly for all involved. A cost that they would all happily pay after hearing what was at stake.

Ara wondered what could possibly be done to save these elves from this God Emperor, and his apparent army of monsters from the diagrams set out before her. Isfrisairis and the Arcanum were known for their magical prowess. Even the inquisitors had not fared well, so why were they kneeling before the Queen of the *forehaltha* with hands outstretched?

"Estimates are that over half of the two hundred have died. We have little to no information… But what we have before us is a glimmer of hope. You see, the portals are an enigma but we feel we are beginning to unlock their secrets. Items appear to pass back through with relative ease although this expends a vast amount of energy with the actual location seeming to vary wildly through our methods. The items before you have been collected from within a three-kilometre radius of the portal. What is worse though is that they attune to the magical frequencies of those around them. The closer you are to them and the longer you stay there, so the more disruption caused when interacting with them. This is why we are here," said Nildinar, building on the momentum of the room.

"The Arcanum will be able to send down enough *lenlialarla*[13] to fuel the building of a small city. With this, we can send a representative from Foretilatava to go through the portal and deliver them. There sh… they will also be able to witness what we are up against for themselves so as to corroborate our reports. From our calculations, there will be minimal damage and no permanent injuries sustained from the portal should a member of this city go through. This, and Sinien Tarvia being far enough away to make time a worthwhile consideration. Well, you can see why we are asking for your assistance in this matter," said Nildinar, his posture submissive and his hands visibly trembling as he wiped the sweat from his brow with a ragged cloth from his pocket.

"—And why you offered Ara a seat at this meeting," stated Rylia, finishing Nildinar's request.

"Yes. Ara is royalty and she has your trust. She graduated from the University Druidica and has demonstrated significant ability in the arcane arts. She is not just the political choice in this matter, she is also the safe one," he said, pausing for a moment to allow for possible objection. "We have secured the portal, and the inquisitors managed to burn vast portions of their libraries along with much of their research relating to our world. We have bought ourselves some time with which we can now plan. We will

---

[13] Spell gems – Able to store magic or spells. Often inscribed with runes which must be read to activate the spell contained within

find out about this latent power that they seek to harvest from our world, determine how to counteract their portals, and we shall develop a method of disposing of this god emperor. What we need to do now is stabilise these portals to get our people back. Messages and artefacts have passed through the portals with minimal damage, but we need their first-hand accounts. We have questions that need to be answered and none of that will be possible unless they make it back. That... and we owe it to our kin after sending them through to study this potential threat on our behalf," proclaimed Nildinar, a hint of defiance building in his tone.

"I have copies of all the texts and information for you to peruse, and I shall be sending survivors of the expedition to each of your cities once they have been debriefed. If we are to go ahead with this, then we must leave tomorrow as we have no idea how long our forces can hold out. No matter your decision, we will be going ahead with this plan. We have rangers returning from the south if neither you nor Sinien Tarvia decide to send an emissary," Nildinar concluded, rising to his full stature.

Rylia stood to meet his gaze. "Ara will accompany you to the portal as my personal correspondence on the front line of this issue. I will get my scholars to look over these documents and ensure the guard is ready. We will prepare the reserves and begin bolstering relations with the other nations," Rylia said, her hand on Ara's shoulder, addressing the congregation as only a queen could.

The chancellor and the admiral nodded their agreement before leaving the room.

Ara swallowed away the sour taste in her mouth. Her heart pounded, sending waves of pressure through her body. Looking around, she was not alone in this. No one else had made a motion to leave and were all soaking in the new data presented. This was no longer just the historic day of Rylia's coronation but a day beginning the prelude to war.

Duty Abroad

Ara padded through the city's groves. The ground litter and loamy soil suppressed her footfalls as she went hopping between branches and ricocheting off tree trunks. Her shoes long abandoned, she landed with the sure footing of a jungle cat on the hunt; twisting in the air, leaping over rocks and skidding on moss-covered branches to make short work of the forested city's outer districts. Official matters tended to, her stomach filled with cake and her family members permission to leave? There really was only one thing she could justify doing now.

Rounding the final bend, swinging on an aberrant tree root jutting out from the embankment as she did so, she saw her solution. There, on the city limits, were the equid stables and grazing encampments. Standing at the ready were Galviir, Anmas's groom and Anmas himself with his bitless bridle adorned and saddle at the ready. The stallion was idly chewing to placate his frustrations at being tethered whilst nosing the covered quiver attached to the saddle.

Anmas had a black coat and white mane, having been born under the light of a full moon, resulting in his unique colouring. Standing at 14.2 hands tall with muscles designed for dextrous manoeuvres and athletic jumps. Being Ara's friend and adventure companion for many years, the two worked together like a ship and the winds.

Galviir held, under his arm, a parcel wrapped in green linen with silver twine bindings where, upon closer inspection, the royal seal could be seen. Ara greeted Anmas with her hands and touched her nose to his before turning to Galviir so that he might put an end to her curiosity.

"Good morning! I trust all the ceremonies went well?" Galviir greeted.

"Well indeed. Your contribution was noted. All the horses looked majestic. Dare I say that they may have even outshone my sister's dress!" said Ara with a snigger, not minding Anmas who curiously sniffed at her tunic pockets.

"Do not go around telling people that or I will have her tailors on my doorstep, sewing needles and lit torches in hand!" he replied, matching her level of enthusiasm. He had been the caretaker of the stable yard since its inception, which extended past the history books, yet still; greeted each day with a hearty smile and an untamed passion for his work.

"It is a pity you could not attend though. She really did look quite stunning, and I mean it about the horses. The whole crowd stood in awe at every moment," said Ara, sobering her tone with sincerity.

"I had to look after Filistrad. The poor dear had colic last night, but she seems to have turned a corner and is on the mend now. She may even let me get some sleep tonight. However, I digress. I foresee a period of great prosperity ahead with Queen Rylia at the reins, and I am sure you will agree with me, as for starters…" he said, bringing attention to the parcel "…she managed to arrange this for you," he concluded, handing it over, unable to conceal his excitement.

Ara accepted the parcel and her fingers immediately recognised what lay within. A grin exploded across her face as she carefully unwrapped the bindings.

"No, she did not!" she exclaimed, placing the cloth on her shoulder and revealing the recurve bow that it had concealed.

The dragon tooth seers curved forward and were carved to show the design of tree leaves, cured in a manner that had dyed them a rich natural green. Etchings in the rosewood limbs displayed a masterwork of detailing; carved leaved vines wrapping around with dew-drop flowers dispersed between. The central leather -wrapped handle was stitched on with the finest of silver threads and left no space for an arrow rest allowing for ambidextrous use, just the way she liked it. The fine counter-twist string bore two green wool silencers and was, itself, intertwined with delicate silvery strands. The nock was made from a seamless silver ring with a finger rest of wrapped green twine, all forming a testament to the quality of the design.

Ara sat down next to Anmas so that she might achieve the appropriate levels of concentration required to fully appreciate the work of art that now lay in her hands. This was beyond the work of legends and of that which even her dreams could have mustered. She stood back up and strung the bow with delicate precision, treating it as though it was an ancient relic of fractured glass.

She held the bow out at her arm's full extension, admiring the curves that it conformed to, now that it was strung and in its natural shape. It resembled the smooth winding of a river through the forest, natural but with intent. Next, the draw. She pulled the string back, allowing it to gently kiss her cheek, holding it at her perfect draw length. Perched as a falcon, waiting for its prey.

Ara blinked away her glittering tears, clearing her vision.

Galviir smiled. "Quite the sister you have there. A bow that beautiful deserves a name." His voice carried with the breeze, barely more than a whisper. Then, shaking himself out of the bow's trance. "Yes, of course, there is more to this gift too," he said in his usual tone as he turned Anmas to reveal a quiver set on the preferred side.

The quiver itself was of flowing silver vines matching the bow's etchings. The modular design allowed for storage of the arrows whilst having the ability to be broken down to a quick draw quiver for either horseback or for if Ara was on foot. The arrows seemed to be hewn from the same vision as the bow they were intended for. The shaft of rosewood, matching the draw length, and green spiralled feathers.

Their nocks were the same pine green of the seers, although probably not made from dragon's tooth; perhaps goat horn? The tips, when examined, were shining steel of various shapes for their intended purpose, but all resembling a leaf that could be found in the forest. From the long thin lanceolate bodkins of the white willow to the thick broad heads of the poplars.

A pouch attached to the storage section of the quiver held a bag with spare arrow heads, nocks and feathers. Something Ara chuckled at, remembering how many arrows she used to have break on her when she missed her mark, hitting a sidelong rock instead of the target.

She gave Galviir a tight hug, thanking him for his role played and for his unwavering and excellent care of Anmas. He reciprocated but appeared as eager as she was for her to get a move on and hit the trails to test out her gift and give Anmas the exercise he was becoming desperate for. She vaulted into the saddle, setting off on one of her preferred archery trails.

First, they walked until the path had officially begun and she had settled in her saddle, sliding her clothing into position so that neither her movements nor her comfort would be impaired. She broke out into a trot at the start of the trail, feeling her muscles loosen and relax into the motion. Then came the canter. She didn't have reins, nor did she need them. Instead, she used her legs and her body position to communicate in her secret language with Anmas. Subtle changes told him that now was the time that he could let loose, as he had been begging to do from the moment they left the courtyard. Ara held him back no more and together, they burst forth into a full gallop, bracing against the wind and centring their focus on the path ahead. Their hearts quickened with excitement and their movements synchronised perfectly. Turns were shaved off with the blade of a carpenter's knife and they flew over the small rises of the trail, matching Anmas's gait to the obstructions faced. She was now galloping as much as he, acting as an extension of his weight, urging him forth in a dance they had practiced a thousand times prior.

Ara fixed her gaze on the trail ahead, but her focus shifted to the bow. She flicked her wrist from side to side, testing the weight and feeling the balance. She nocked an arrow blindly, her muscle memory finding no difficulty with the task. Seeing the target in the distance, she raised her bow and drew back the string. It was an old log, showing multiple impact craters already. It had been hung from the tree by a vine, swinging freely in the breeze.

Ara leant forward into her shot as time stopped. The bow was speaking to her, guiding her, and she felt her body begin to listen. Right then, between Anmas's strides, at the trough of her exhalation, she let loose the arrow. She knew the trajectory was perfect, but she could not bring herself to break her gaze from the arrow's inaugural flight. The arrow sang as it cut through the air, spinning forth. It bent from side to side, dancing with the laws of nature and then, with a solid thud, returned time back to its regular pace. The arrow struck true. It sank deep into the log, protruding through the other side of the deadwood, sending it spinning and swinging wildly through the reaches of its vine's tether.

Anmas sensed Ara's elation and relaxed at the completion of her test. He slowly broke down his pace until he was walking back in the direction of the target. Ara patted him on the neck and gave him his due praise. She ran her fingers over the bow again, appreciating every grain in the wood and every carving set therein. This was no simple hunting implement or weapon meant to wage war; it was a work of art. The true artistry though, lay not in the aesthetic or the quality material, but in the precision and accuracy of its functionality. Where Ara wanted the arrow to land, so there it landed. It was an action without conscious thought as the bow acted as if it were a part of her.

"This deserves a great name indeed," she smiled.

Ara retrieved her arrow with no small amount of forceful persuasion. Anmas didn't laugh physically but she could sense his friendly judgement of her actions. Once the arrow had relinquished its target, she placed it carefully back into the quiver. She set off at a walk for the rest of the trail, dusting her tunic and securing the bow over her shoulder. Her heart was still racing, it needed time for a cooldown. The to and fro of her hips matched Anmas's stride, pulling her into a meditative state where she was able to contemplate nature's beauty as it unfolded in the forest around her.

The great oaks towering above created a world, in the canopy, all of its own. That land was filled with birds, insects and reptiles that may never feel the ground beneath their feet, yet still, they led their fulfilled lives not knowing the happenings of that beneath them. Their stories and their adventures to be had were completely unknown to Ara, yet there they were, unfolding in the world around her.

She then took notice of the many birds hopping between the branches in the sub-canopy. Chirping happily as they rooted around in the vines that clung to the trunks of the mighty trees. With Ara's honed gaze, she was also able to spot a stag eyeing out the activity in the forest with casual suspicion as he grazed amongst the ferns. She thought about all the critters that she couldn't see. Hiding amidst the brush or darting around within the ivy, maintaining their safety from the daytime predators whilst hunting for food in their own unique ways.

Anmas made his way along the pathway, concealed mostly by the ground cover. They skirted along streams, up embankments, and down steep hills. Down the straights, they cantered to better facilitate the jumps that Ara had set up with those moments spent in flight adding to the wildness of their trip. Even at a slow walk, this was no leisure route for horse or rider, but that was part of the excitement. As Ara ducked under a low branch, images of the crowd's adoring faces crossed her mind as she fondly recalled the day's events thus far. She remembered the fruity sweetness of the baked goods that she had liberated, their tantalising aroma flooding her senses, bite after bite.

Galviir was awaiting her return from their regularly scheduled adventure, knowing that despite all the change in the world, there would always be a few things that would stay constant.

Sounds of the bustling city ahead roused her from her pensive state and, with that, she regained her focus to tackle the social tasks that lay ahead. She felt her stomach on the precipice of a mighty roar of borborygmi to summon forth another elderberry pastry or cream tart. Who was she to deny such a request? She entered the stable yard and hopped out of the saddle. She took the tack off of Anmas and gave him a good brush before setting him out to graze for the evening. Galviir had already cleaned and packed her tack away and had himself turned in for the day when she finished.

She dusted her hands and cleaned the grime from her fingernails. A smile clung to her expression, persevering through the final hill leading to her room. The city limits were relatively barren of activity with the festivities luring folk toward *Foretarla*.

Jogging the final stretch to evade capture by the gaze of Lahkar Kamiir, Ara slipped into her home, shutting the door behind her with a contented sigh. Grabbing her staff, she climbed up the stairs to her room, falling face first onto her bed, spreading her arms out.

An unexplained giggle escaped her chest as she sat up, surveying her efforts from the night prior. Her staff would stay, it was from when she was planning to apprentice to Vexhimarith as a druid and would not be needed now. Clothes littered every surface, leaving little of the floor exposed. Her floral pallet of vibrant colours intermingled with the modest greens, browns and blacks of her work attire made for the appearance of a grassland in the spring.

Paintings she had made with Rylia were on the wall, the two finding comfort in sending incomplete artwork to each other, as well as letters of correspondence during Ara's time at the University Druidica. Each piece received would be added to and returned until they had a completed painting. Her favourite was that of a woodland fox, caught in a ray of sunshine amidst the great oaks of the forest.

She sighed at her bags, seeing her future pulling her away from home. New journeys awaited and her trepidation would need to be placed on hold. After all, this is how all the story books began.

Falling back, her bed welcoming her and consuming her doubts. Her eyes slid shut and a wave of relaxation crested over her. With a smile, she let sleep take her, eager to have her energy restored as the sun waited to present her with a new day.

***

Ara woke with barely an hour left until daylight. She didn't have far to go, but she could not stop herself from rushing to get ready and out the door. Vera was the blacksmith and arms-master for Foretilatava and Ara's last official stop before leaving. Well rested and not feeling nearly as burdened by the previous day's drink as most others, she flew out her door with a fresh step and a bounding heart.

She sprinted through the pathways of the city that was already awake by those seeking an early start to their chores. Vera was deep in the city's outskirts, at a shop known for its smokeless forge and musical ringing of metal.

An elf maiden, carrying a ceramic pot of water, nearly knocked Ara to the ground as she slid around a bend to meet her head on. The two were equally surprised but Ara was in a more appropriate position to make the evasive manoeuvres. She ran along the bark of an adjacent tree, swung on an overhanging branch and landed in a controlled tumble. Her bare feet shared an intimate relationship with the forest and her sure footing allowed her to treat the city as her playground with the trees as her running track.

The next obstacle to be met was the river crossing in the middle of the town. This bridge, although large, was currently in use by the many early risers heading to the market to set up stalls or to purchase the items they required to get their day started. Ara decided not to risk the slow-moving elves on the bridge, opting to hop from boat to boat, from turtle to fisherman's back and then to the other side. Onlookers chuckled at her display of dexterity. Even the fisherman smiled, happy to have been made a part of the show. She accepted their applause with a quick bow and a flick of her hair, smiling at their rose-coloured cheeks and enthusiastic chuckles.

Ara skidded to a halt within the soft glow of the forge. The lava rocks were being heated up by Vera's drake, with Vera behind her desk, organising her project sketches. She looked up at the disturbance and laughed at Ara's struggle to suck in more oxygen than the forge during a steel smelting session.

"Well dear, you made it eventually. Your sister warned me about your excitement. Sorry, the Queen."

"Sorry, I… fell asleep yester… yesterday while packing…" said Ara between desperate breaths. She straightened up and pushed back the pesky

47

strands of escaped hair from her clammy forehead as she struggled to form some degree of composure.

"I am glad you remembered to come here before you left. Your sister got you quite the gift. I took a few liberties with some of the finer details, but it was nothing that she would not have wanted," Vera said, fishing out a trunk from the storage area within her shop.

Now Vera, despite being a blacksmith, managed to keep everything, including her clothes and hands, spotless. Her hair was a vibrant array of reds and yellows to match the forge's glow with her elegant yet powerful frame providing a strong anchor point. She was beautiful and capable, yet what stood out most was her passion for her craft on a platter of dizzying intellect.

Lining the walls of Vera's shop were gem-inlaid cuirasses and helms with weapons of all types scattered between them. Display cases flaunted her ability, sporting everything from prosthetic limbs to masks, tiaras to artisans' tools and ornate daggers to medical equipment.

Forehaltha had sought out her expertise for their armour and weapons for over a century now. Seeing them march by was akin to walking through an art gallery displaying the greatest works of Vera's forge. Her mastery of moonsteel and keen eye for perfection, incorporating the silvicolous nature of the *forehaltha* into her work.

"Here you go, this should fit you just great. If you could check the balance on the sword then maybe I can swap it out if it does not suit you," said Vera as she drew a set of plate armour, and a longsword from the trunk.

Ara stood dumbstruck by the beauty of the pieces being handed to her. The armour covered her body in interlocking segments. She put it on with the aid of Vera who made adjustments as they went, not that many needed to be made in the first place. In fact, once Ara stopped fiddling and getting in the way, all the changes being made appeared to be purely aesthetic. Cutting straps short, folding in the buckles and polishing areas here and there.

Once in the armour, Ara was amazed to find how light it was. She was a walking metal ingot, yet she could move as well as if she was merely wearing clothes with a little extra starch. She tested out her unhampered range of motion and let loose a few explosive movements to test if the armour made any noise, but there was nothing. The folded fabric edges dampening the metal.

It was like a second skin for her, looking as if it belonged in the Queen's treasure room with its knot symbols and leafed tree branches wrapping and twisting around, giving the armour texture and life. A forest green, emerald lay set in the centre of the chest piece and in the helm with the embossed design of *Foretarla* on her breastplate. The helmet was something magical in its own right. It was constructed with silvered leaves placed upon a framework of filigree, allowing for air flow and protection around her face whilst keeping her attuned with her surroundings.

Ara, now suited in her armour, stood back for the final inspection. Vera clapped her hands together with a proud grin. "Perfect! No dragon tooth nor hail of arrows can touch you now!" she exclaimed, the elation in her voice exploding forth. "You may be safe but, say you want to give something a good seeing to—try this," she said, handing over the sword as gingerly as one would present a bottle of fine wine to a dignitary.

Ara knew the basics of swordplay, but this piece of art made all other swords she had used in the past seem more like poorly weighted clubs. She gave it a test swing and even engaged in a flurry of practice blows with Vera. Ara left her top guard open and took a strike to the top of the head which nearly made her spring from her skin. She realised that she had been wearing the armour the whole time, and Vera's blade glanced harmlessly away.

Next came the fitting of a cloak that matched the colour of her gems, bearing the royal symbol of Foretilatava— the Silver Great Oak, *Foretarla,* of the city centre. It hung from her shoulders, cascading down her back, being wide enough to wrap around her shoulders if needed but resting now, keeping the attention on the moonsteel armour.

"You are now ready to represent us all in the big bad world," said Vera, standing back to admire her workmanship, her soft eyes glistening. Even her drake, Mithilgilaz had lifted her head to stare in awe at the shining steel, puffs of smoke rings shooting out in appreciation.

Ara sprang forward like a cat to a ball of string and embraced her in a grip tight enough to make Vera gasp, "Thank you! Vera, once again; your work has not failed to astonish and amaze me. This is such a beautiful gift. I would not have believed that it was for me if it did not all fit so well."

Vera glowed at the humour, bid Ara farewell, and wished her good luck on her journey. She was eager to return to her work with the glowing forge beckoning her with its rising heat.

Ara returned the gesture and set off to meet the convoy. She walked with regal strides, showing the world just how great she felt in her new suit of armour. When she came across two elves carrying a large crate set upon waist-high carry poles, she decided that she could no longer help herself. She sped up to a jog, then a sprint, dove over the box, then tucked into a silent roll.

She didn't stop to look back. She felt amazing and so she rode the wave of excitement, in an energetic jog, all the way home to where she met her companions. They had just finished loading the carriages with the last of the luggage, turning to greet her with mouths agape at the site of her new accoutrements.

"My lady, you look about ready to slay a hydra and address the thirty seat council. You will be heading out now but first, the queen will have her audience with you. You can catch up with the convoy at the gate. Harley will be your mount for when you are ready to join us." Vexhimarith said at her arrival, gesturing toward a bay destrier gelding who was stalking a nearby fruit stand.

"Thank you, I will see you there," replied Ara, her ivy green eyes already searching for her sister.

She saw the queen standing in the shadow of a nearby redwood, wearing a green dress with silver thread, embossed in a design similar to Ara's armour.

"I see that you are enjoying your gifts. Do not worry, there is a case amongst your luggage that I added a few extra items to. Nothing really to your immediate desire but it should do you well should you come across a royal ball or masquerade," said Rylia, her lip quivering slightly.

"Goodbye, my wonderful sister. Thank you for the many gifts and thank you for this opportunity. Despite what my tears suggest, I am actually excited," replied Ara, failing to maintain her own composure.

"I was hoping the armour would be ceremonial, but I guess its functionality will prove useful with the recent change in plans. Have a wonderful trip and know that I will be thinking of you always. Keep me updated when you can and let me know if I need to send the full force of the elven coalition army and its allies to come and kick some rude prince out the window for you, okay? Oh, and for the sake of the stars; have some fun and make some stories of your own. Those books you read are going to seem awfully dull after the world sees what you can do!" Rylia said, tears now streaming down her face.

Ara could only manage a nod and a quiet, *"Im sinarle[14]."* Before turning away and forcing herself into the embrace of Harley's saddle.

"Im sinarle ilor[15], dear sister," came the near inaudible response.

Ara gathered the reins allowing herself one last look back to where her smile met with that of her sister's, the queen. The queen and her best friend. She urged Harley forward with a small squeeze and rode forth along the paths toward the main gate.

The Isfrisairis convoy saw her coming and sprang into life, all their horses stepping onto the forest road. She caught up in no time, riding next to one of the shining sentinels, at the front of the convoy, tears still filling her vision and obscuring the vortex of excitement that she had blossoming within her.

The city guards bid them their final farewells as they left the city, *"Sa sela estrala sinmarilma unua lual sinuruasa[16]."*

---

[14] I love you
[15] I love you too
[16] May the stars light your path and bless your travels

A Storybook Start

The journey was tense, arduous and most of all, boring. As it turns out, nobody talks freely and jokes around with the sister of the new queen of a powerful nation. Ara took to the nomadic lifestyle like a bird to the air with the only real exception being the hygiene rituals—she had already decided on day three that she would never get used to cold showers.

The sentinels were always on guard with Nildinar being too busy writing letters and consulting advisors to be of much help in the duty of entertainment.

The first evening was spent at a well-worn camping spot beside the road. Piles of firewood from the more conscientious of travellers before them making for a quick start to the campfire, around which the tents and carriages were arranged. Ara was not a part of the finely tuned ecosystem of the convoy and could simply look on as they set up the campsite in record time with the grey Isfrisairis tents sprouting up amidst the camouflaged shelters of the rangers.

She untacked the bay destrier, giving him a thorough brush before turning him loose with the other horses to graze for the night. All horses received a quick inspection, Ara eager to shake off her role of delicate noble in lieu of one with more action and responsibility.

The wagon carrying their supplies, and her luggage, was parked next to a towering sequoia with its thick umber bark. The sentinels had finished setting up the campsite and the rangers had faded into the surrounding wood to fetch supplies and to take up strategic posts.

Around them, the ground had been levelled by the previous campers with the undergrowth encroaching ever closer. Limbs of the ferns stretched over as rhizomatous roots tested the limits. Nearby berry trees held back their blooms, desperate for the warmth of spring to call them back to life.

Ara meandered over to her carriage, idly playing with the stiff leather straps holding her new quiver at her waist and hoping for a task to present itself on her journey. Her keen eyes darted about, looking for an opportunity to step in and lend a hand. This convoy had been travelling together for years, it seemed, and they moved like a shoal of fish in the shallows in both coordination and group purpose.

She sighed, her fingers running through the fletching of her new arrows, brushing the steel of her gauntlets. With nothing to do, and no one to talk to, she sat down in a huff to ponder her predicament. The Foretilatava carriage, which had served as a resting station for the convoy during the march, was now her podium of thought.

Nildinar was scurrying about the campsite, pulling scrolls and books from various chests, handing them to assistants who carried them to his tent. Deep in contemplation, Ara's entertainment would be the last thing on his mind for the evening. His hoard gathered, he turned in for the night, the silver glow of the *lenlialarla* within keeping him company. Resigned, Ara realised that he was a dead end as far as the night's activities were concerned.

A ranger stepped around the edges of a thicket, his arms full of dry wood, adding his stash to the rapidly growing pile near the centrally placed fire pit. Of course, there could never be enough firewood and a ranger was ill at ease when they were not preparing for the worst.

She pushed off from the wagon and turned towards the forest, her eyes already flicking between the trees. There was more than enough firewood but perhaps a few herbs or roots would serve to bolster everyone's spirits come dinnertime. This was Ara's home after all, and she knew the local flora better than most.

Not more than three steps from the campsite's boundary and she was halted by a ranger. "My lady, it would be best that you stay within the camp. The rangers shall gather the necessary supplies. Let me know if there is anything you require and we shall attempt to have it arranged," he said in an officious monotone, his hood pulled so far forward that Ara could barely see the colour of his eyes.

"But... I want to help..." she attempted feebly, stepping away from his herding of her, back toward the campsite.

The ranger shook his head. "Everything is taken care of. Please, rest within the bounds of the camp."

He turned away and faded back into the shadows of the foliage, waiting to ambush Ara the next time she strayed too near the dangers of the great beyond. With a huff, she returned to the wagon, her fingers once more straying to fiddle with the fletching on her arrows.

The other elves had now begun milling around the camp, attending to their personal chores or gathering in small groups to pass idle chatter amongst themselves. A few off-duty rangers had even set about cooking dinner by the fire.

She stepped away from the wagon and made her way to the neatly stacked pile of firewood. Attracting the occasional curious glance, she inspected the pile until she found those that met her criteria. She liberated two oak logs that held too much moisture to be placed on the fire, without spitting and crackling, but enough moisture to keep the wood soft. She tucked one under each arm and made her way back to the wagon.

Both were placed in front of the wagon, its warded sides likely able to catch any ricochets with minimal scuffing to the treated oak.

Ara knelt and spread a clean cloth on the loamy earth before her. She removed the pouch of spare arrow heads, selecting the sturdy practice tips from the collection and attached them to a set of five of her arrows. Satisfied that they were not going to splinter the wagon, or impale a hidden ranger, she rose to her feet and carefully unwrapped her bow, stringing it with the utmost care.

Marvelling at its beauty once more, Ara stroked the smooth grain and steadied her breathing, falling into a trance where she was at one with the forest around her. Her fingers stroked the fletching of her chosen arrow, liberating it from the quiver and planting it on the string.

She closed her eyes. A rogue breeze surged through the limbs of the trees, rustling leaves and cloaks alike. She breathed in. Twigs strained at the footfalls of an elven walker to her east, likely a sentinel with heavy plate greaves. She held her breath. An owl ducked to the floor after a shrew that saw to get a head start on the twilight of dusk. She exhaled.

She released a volley of all five arrows in rapid succession, letting her subconscious control each shot. Arrows slid from the quiver, springing onto the string, eager to set sail. The bow's silencers turned the twang of the string into a swish of a raptor's wings, flicking her hair across her cheek in a dance. She smiled and opened her eyes to reveal the tight cluster of arrows in the first log that had now collided with the ground, the force of the arrows tipping it over.

To her right, a clearing throat brought time to its regular speed, leaves from the trees falling to the ground and smoke from the campfire rising again. Ara blinked as crackling flames and mumbling voices became a part of her world once more. The ranger, previously assisting Nildinar with his bibliotheca, was standing there, inspecting Ara's handiwork.

He had his hood down but had just come off duty as he was still wearing the characteristic brown leather armour and dark green tunic. The steel of his breastplate and vambraces had been brushed so as not to reflect the slightest of glimmers in the forest's dappled light. His hair was pulled back in a half pony tail, hiding its true length, but some of the bronze strands had escaped and tickled his chin as the breeze continued to frolic in the clearing.

Ara looked at him, ready to challenge any objection he may have to her filling her time. He broke her expectations with a hearty chuckle and a gesture for other rangers to join them. Ara smiled and stood to the side, welcoming all challengers to her makeshift practice range, eager to see the rangers of Isfrisairis in action.

"Are you truly so bored, by our journey, that you wish to sabotage our transport?" he said, his posture easing as he uncrossed his arms and walked over to her target, removing the arrows on her behalf.

Ara blushed, shaking her head. "No, the logs will... I am sorry," she ended feebly, tucking her hair behind an ear and looking to the grass around her feet for assistance.

"I am joking. It is quite an elegant solution, but with aim as good as yours, far too easy of a setup. If an enemy is this close to you then it is time you contemplate putting away the bow and opting to put some speed to your stride."

Ara smiled in earnest. "Well, ah, thank you. I did not want to stray out of the boundaries of the camp. It is a new bow and I wanted to get in some practice before... Well, you know." The ranger chuckled again, this time with a hint of an edge.

"My name is Ara, by the way," she added.

"Lethrik," said the ranger. "Would you allow us to join you, Ara? See what your fancy new bow can do against my tried and tested one?"

Ara beamed and nodded enthusiastically. "How about a game?" she asked.

"That sounds like a good way to spend the evening. How about it all? Fancy a game of pendulums?" he asked the group of rangers.

There was a general consensus of approval and they set about hanging the targets from a low branch at a tree, casting magical wards on its trunk to prevent any dangerous misfires from harming the bark.

The group set up on the opposite end of the camp and began taking turns at the range. Lethrik would call out a number and the participant would have to hit the corresponding log. All logs would be swinging out of time with each other and have the occasional wandering elf get in the way.

Their aim did not falter, despite additional rules being added. Ara suggested blindfolds but even the jaunty Lethrik had his second thoughts. The rangers were masters with the bow, showing themselves to be worthy advisories for Ara, but they still thought too much when they fired. A bow is meant to be an extension of oneself. Just as you would not think to aim when tossing an apple to a friend, so you should be releasing the arrow.

Lethrik chuckled when Ara pointed this out and merely nudged her to the side, releasing arrows that cut through the ropes of their targets, releasing them from their bindings. With a sly wink, he signalled the games conclusion with dinner now underway in the camp.

"You did well Ara. Do not rely on 'feel' for every shot. There are times where your judgement may be clouded and that is when logic should take over. Emotions are powerful but are vulnerable to influence. Logic is infallible and you will need to know how to draw on that should the time come when emotions are clouded. That said, you deserve this," Lethrik said, his eye snapping to the branches where he reached up, retrieving two malachite feathers. "A small token for your victory at pendulums. May you have many more."

Ara beamed, feeling her cheeks flush at his praise. "Thank you, Lethrik. I have a lot to learn from the *tarviahaltha* and I am certainly fortunate to be able to receive some of those lessons from a ranger. Which bird does this belong too?"

Lethrik chuckled, attempting mock outrage with little success. "That is the feather of an Isfrisairis macaw. A rare find this far west, but one does not question omens of good fortune. Whilst not the famous eagle of Isfrisairis, they still serve as a welcome reminder of home," he smiled, tucking one of the feathers into the tail of her hair.

***

The previous night had helped her integrate with the group. The rangers were now more relaxed and even exchanged pleasantries with her around the breakfast theatre.

On the road again, Ara found that she missed Anmas. She often thought of all those times she had been wandering around the forest, pretending she was off with him doing exactly this – travelling to some far-off location on an exciting adventure for the good of all *haltha*. Harley was a pleasant enough replacement. His stride was long and comfortable, often lulling her into a meditative slumber during the quieter parts of the day.

Time spent not riding was focused on ensuring the happiness and well-being of the horses and her fellow travellers' stomachs. They ate rations mostly but not for lack of other food being available. This was the forest, after all. It became evident that her companions were simply content with their lot. Devoid of imagination when it came to flavour and seemingly too busy doing other things to sprinkle a dash of spice on their meals.

Waking early for breakfast wasn't really Ara's style, but she took it upon herself to ensure that the dinners served were bountiful delights compared to the grey porridge or the pressed fruit and grain bars they had been subsisting on until now.

Ara could not be sure, but she thought she even saw one of the sentinels smile at his cheese-covered flat bread with its tomato and basil smiling-face toppings. It might take the whole trip, but she was sure she could get under their skin. At least one of them had to be capable of humour.

Lethrik often joined her in the evenings when he was not on duty. His acceptance of her tentative friendship gave her the courage to approach the other rangers in turn. She livened up the evenings' activities by casually challenging the rangers to competitions of marksmanship. All too eager to wield her new bow, she was able to hold her own against the best that Isfrisairis had to offer in the art of archery, filling her with pride and camaraderie.

Two days of driving the horses at a solid pace brought them to the bustling town of Foret Dela. Trade caravans bound for Tour Aine were making their way through from all over the elven territories. Carts, bringing raw materials from the south, passed through taking the dwarven ingots to smiths, specimens of preserved Mardacian monster to the alchemists and casks of dark red wines of East Anthuria to the tables of the Isfrisairis elite.

Ara's excitement bubbled to the surface as they entered the bustling market town. Shops lined the main roads and the square at the centre of the town where everything from herbal remedies to hand-crafted scarves, dwarven style crockery and *lenlialarla* could be found.

It was not often that Ara and her sister ventured from the isolated depths of the forest, but there was something intoxicating about the sheer volume and variety of wares on display. Each shop sported a dizzying spectrum of colour with exotic scents, intriguing textures and flashes of magical lights sparking through display windows, bringing attention to the wares within. Goods and trinkets from the farthest reaches of the world might be found in such a place, if you knew where to look of course.

Alas, the rangers of the convoy did all the shopping on behalf of the procession whilst the sentinels formed an impenetrable wall that guided the horses through the crowds and kept them moving. Ara, smelling a bakery not five minutes out of the way, gave a pleading look to Lethrik. He nodded with a wry smile, snatching her coin pouch from the air.

Ara chuckled and leant back in her saddle with the gentle rocking to and fro.

The city guard was not a feature in most cities – except for the capitals and border towns of Isalsolla and Northern Tour Aine. Today, however, there were guard patrols moving through the crowds, methodically scanning faces as they did so. Guard towers long converted into residences were now being repurposed back to their original design. Sentinels and accompanying mages were flying overhead on their alithaers, the giant eagles of Isfrisairis, scanning the lands below like hungry predators in the winter.

Seeing this peaceful elven town apparently preparing for invasion brought Ara back into the present and into the shadow of her future. She pulled her hood up and hid from the world as she pulled out one of the bestiaries Nildinar had lent her, opening it up and resting it on the pommel of her saddle.

Smiler:

Carnivorous ambush hunter

Characteristics:

- Varying, odd number of eyes on the frontal plate
- Rictus grin with jaw capable of unhinging
- Nictitating membrane suggestive of aquatic or subterranean adaptation
- Can turn invisible for brief periods, seemingly at will

- Only hunts those in groups fewer than four
- Multiple rows of long, smooth teeth similar to canines with few, seemingly rudimentary, molars
- Highly venomous – poison resulting in rapid onset delirium and paralysis
- Generally nocturnal but has been seen hunting at dawn and dusk hours or in periods of mist and increased cloud/ash cover
- Creature will ambush and lash out with elongated, serrated claws then bite and drag prey away into a tunnel system where it will become impractical to rescue the victim. If a smiler is cornered, engagement may become unavoidable
- If seen, do not engage where possible. Group up, light all torches and wait out the low visibility period or make your way to larger groups
- Note: Smilers have been known to bury themselves under paths and ambush those that walk over them, dragging them to their burrow as fast as possible. Features to look out for are wilted plants in the area as they react poorly to the smilers' tissue oils. Their burrows, if near flora, can be located by looking for vegetation with similar withering

Ara looked up and shuddered as her mind pieced together an image of this creature, saliva dripping from a mouth of horrors as its many eyes stared through her. It was the smell of cheesecake that reached a hand down and pulled her to safety. Lethrik was handing out the baked goods to everyone before getting to Ara.

"You should have seen the baker's face when I placed the order! He said that cheesecake is his speciality and that, to quote him, 'If the gods had taste buds, then the crumbs of these cheesecakes would forever be found resting upon their chins.'"

She thanked him with a quiet chuckle, not quite able to rid herself of the mental image of what a smiler might look like but glad for the distraction. The ranger glanced at the book in her lap before handing her a box containing a whole cake. She slid the manual into her pocket a little too roughly as she focused all her attention on the source of the heavenly smell before her.

The convoy rode forth into the embrace of the great oak trees and the gigantic sycamores, leaving the clamour of the market behind. There was an additional sense of ease that Ara had in the forest, knowing her sister was the one watching over them as the new queen. She would still be attuning to the power of the forest but even now, she would be able to sense them walking through the trees, drinking from the streams and picking through the bounty that the flora had on offer.

Nildinar had planned to leave the convoy at the city outskirts. A contingent of gryphon riders awaited his arrival just outside the city limits. The first Ara heard of this was when he bid farewell to the lead sentinel. Having choked on a barrage of inhaled cake crumbs, she approached him for an explanation.

"Ara, I need to fetch the *lenlialarla* for you to take through the portal. Unfortunately, it is a significant requisition from the university, so they are insisting that I be there to join the mages escorting them to Tour Mardesi. I will meet you there. Likely not long after your arrival, lest those academics swamp me in paperwork again. If you arrive before me then you may have guided access to my library. It should have all the volumes required for you to prepare for your upcoming journey through the portal. Some private tips though: Keep your head down and keep yourself safe even above those of the other elves there. You are the voice of your people in this matter. We need you to survive so that they know what is coming," he said, not waiting on ceremony before mounting his gryphon. His mind was already in the clouds and his non-committal stare let Ara know that her time with him was fast running out.

"My sister knows something is going on, she would not have reacted so severely, based on your reports, otherwise. I will go through, and I will get your people back. We have a beautiful home here in Etroah and I would hate for them not to be able to see it again," she replied, a polite smile on her lips, bringing his attention back.

He offered her a soft smile, his *tarviahaltha* propriety reeling him in. He fought with himself before settling on a sigh, returning his focus to the clouds. "Keep her safe. I will endeavour to reach Tour Mardesi as soon as possible. *Sa sela estrala sinmarilma[17],*" he finished, nodding to Lethrik.

Immediately, the rangers began to relax. Lethrik chuckled through a freshly stuffed mouthful of cake, mounting Nildinar's horse and getting the convoy moving.

"And just why are you so happy?" Ara inquired, gathering Harley's

---

[17] May the stars light your path

reins.

"I mean no disrespect, my lady, but I am glad that we only have the one noble that we are protecting now. What is that saying about eggs in a basket?" he answered, dusting crumbs off his jerkin.

"You are the rangers and sentinels of Isfrisairis! This job should have been a breeze for you no matter the challenges," she said, a little shocked at his remark.

"Of course, but from what I hear, that entire family of Nildinar's has always had something of a knack with getting into trouble. Now that Nildinar is a chancellor, well, let us just say that we are all holding our breath until he comes up with some world changing idea that has us in the middle of all the danger. And, from what we have been told, this was beginning to sound just like that," he said, giving a polite nod.

"You underestimate me, good sir. Plus, we are four and a half days out from the centre of it all, so you are by no means out of danger yet," she said with a huff, trying to think of something irresponsible to do that didn't involve her relinquishing her remaining cake.

"Oh, two and a half days, I think you mean," he said, moving to a trot and cutting off the road along an obscured forest path that, if not for the lead horse, she never would have found.

Looking back, the sentinels were already well into removing their belongings from the carriage and packing them onto the extra horses from Foret Dela.

The following days of travel were gruelling to say the least. Lethrik's shortcut had them riding through thick forest that involved countless banks and jarring dashes. Multiple acrobatic manoeuvres had to be employed to have them avoid being scraped off their mounts by rogue trees or thorny shrubs. The many stream crossings then left them oiling their tack in the remaining ache-filled time each evening.

Time blurred together as blisters turned to sores and aching muscles began refusing to operate under command, resulting in some rather embarrassing jolts and awkward strides following dismounts from the saddle each evening. Harley was beginning to show signs of fatigue as well with his stiff muscles no longer recovering overnight which only made the morning ride more difficult for Ara. Still, she kept everyone's spirits up by dishing out a plethora of treats from the bakery that Lethrik had pillaged, being sure to keep a few of the fruitier options for the horses.

Free hours not spent massaging leg cramps or cleaning equipment had Ara reading by the light of a *lenlialarla*. She figured the bestiary would be a good place to start, studying the pages in depth to prepare herself for what may likely be hunting her soon. The entries were far from complete and painting a picture that Ara hoped was more horrifying than the real thing.

Yurinduur:

Characteristics:

- Two metres tall with horns included. Horns not being used for martial engagements but appearing to be of social significance
- Canine teeth present, replacing molar teeth morphology
- Widened oral aperture, extending to the mandibular ramus
- Slit eyes that focus on movement detection. Moderate vision in darkness
- Thick hide in hues of black, grey and brown
- Humanoid with bestial features
- Rudimentary linguistic structure, communication not having been possible to establish due to outwardly hostile nature
- Can wield basic weapons relying on strength-based strikes
- Social hierarchy present but not determined
- Bipedal but quadrupedal when charging with claws on all four limbs
- Weaknesses: Magical attacks but no contraindication against martial attacks. Bones are strong, avoid the skull where possible, especially the frontal plate. Blunt weapons are not advised
- If seen, prepare for engagement as highly aggressive and territorial. Capable of causing significant damage with or without weapons and can run at great speeds
- Note: Highly muscular; meat can be used for sustenance in emergency scenarios

A slight drizzle brought a sombre mood to the trip, now two days out from Foret Dela. Everyone huddled in their respective tents having abandoned all hope of keeping a fire going in the frigid rain.

Ara would glance up, startled at the occasional falling branch in the rain, thinking it an Ilvithiirian wyvern assaulting the camp. She eyed out the undergrowth with suspicion, half expecting the eyes of a smiler or the glint of a reaver's chitin to shine through and alert her to her impending demise. She stroked her malachite feather of the Isfrisairis macaw, but it did little to settle her racing mind.

Ara nearly jumped out of her skin at the hulking form that had snuck up on her flank whilst she was inspecting the roots of a nearby sequoia for signs of a smiler burrow. He had no reaction to her gasp and sat down next to her in her tent cover.

"You scared me..." She chuckled; nervously clutching her heart, tucking the bestiary under the blanket over her legs.

The sentinel lifted the visor of his helm, revealing the sapphire blue eyes of a *tarviahaltha*. He had delicate and angular features, a narrow nose and soft lips that curved into an apologetic smile. "Please excuse my intrusion. I have brought your dinner and wanted to ask if you would mind my company while we eat? Also, some tea."

Ara nodded mutely, and awkwardly scooted over. The sentinel presented her a plate laden with fruit and seeded bread covered with cheese along with a flask of steaming tea for Ara's cup. The cheese, she noted with a start, was cut into the shape of a smiling face.

She looked up, delighted, as the sentinel removed his helmet completely, and brushed back his shoulder length silver hair with a chuckle, the flash of a malachite feather having been tucked behind his ear.

"Th-thank you!" exclaimed Ara. "This is wonderful."

She placed the plate on the floor before her and picked up the bread, inhaling deeply before taking a bite. It was stale, and the cheese a little too alive, but she smiled as she chewed and pinched her fingers together in the air before her, silently gesturing her appreciation. The sentinel shrugged, not quite able to hide his smirk after seeing through her facade, taking a bite of his own sandwich.

Ara hurried to swallow, "You are my new hero! My name is Ara."

"Yildrin. Pleased to meet you."

"It is a pleasure to meet you too, Yildrin," Ara said, before taking another huge bite of her sandwich.

She chewed slowly, trying to buy time so that she may think of what to do next. The sentinel's sudden offer of friendship was more than she could have hoped and had thus caught her unprepared.

Yildrin ate quietly beside her for a moment before speaking again, "If our enemies are anything like those logs swinging from trees then I foresee a swift victory in our future with you and the rangers at the helm."

Ara laughed and fought off a rogue piece of sandwich that was now trying to choke her. She nodded, sipping her tea to settle her coughing fit, still waiting to get in trouble for her unorthodox entertainment methods.

"You have some skill with that bow of yours, does it have a name?"

Ara frowned. "Not yet. I guess I was hoping that it would be presented to me in the thunder of a storm or in the song of the trees like in the storybooks. Any ideas?" asked Ara, now cutting her apple into smaller wedges.

"Zephyr? Albatross? Kestrel? You will find one soon enough, likely once you have fought together, properly."

Ara bit into her apple and nodded absently, adding the names to those dancing around in her head. The sentinel leant back and crooked his legs to rest his gauntlets against his knees as he peered out at what was now a full deluge. Water ran the length of the tents edge, falling down into the stream running out of the campsite.

They spent the time enjoying the world together, Ara feeling much safer having a sentinel in sight. They finished their dinner and made short work of the tea. Content to go about the meal simply enjoying each other's company and the crisp scent of the forest rain.

Night had settled and fatigue got the better of them. Before Yildrin left the tent, he turned to Ara. "Let me know if you need some training in a melee. Those rangers can twirl a sword, but they should definitely stick to the bow," he finished, giving her a wink.

The next day had fresh air and soft ground with the sky having relented from the downpour. Water had found its way into Ara's tent, making her less than ready to deal with the day in her current mood. Still, she adorned her armour and strapped her sword to her hip, lamenting at the moisture content of her socks.

The rangers, now backed up by the sentinels, were having none of it though and they were soon all laughing and chatting together with high spirits. The peak of the day's events involving a berry-tossing competition between Yildrin and Ara with Lethrik's hood as the target and his bronze hair serving as the bystander.

That night. Lethrik sat next to Ara, the groans he made waking the eastern half of the forest as he did so. He looked at her and dumped a pile of berries over her head with a flat expression.

After Ara finished her reaction, complete with squeals and flailing arms, he smirked; "I will be honest. I appreciate the speed, but I much prefer my own two feet," he said, sitting back and stretching out his legs, dusting the horse hair from his breeches.

"Sorry, your feet are far too funny looking for me. I think I prefer horses," Ara chided.

He chuckled, tossing apples out to the sentinels, who sharpened their weapons and tended to their armour. They had been through all that the others had, and yet, if they were feeling any similar effects then they certainly did not show it.

Ara had heard the tales of what the sentinels were capable of. They were the original dragon fighters after all. Since then, they had kept up their training so that, no matter the threat, they would be prepared. She had never actually seen them in action, but she could begin to imagine the power they would hold on the battlefield.

The travel grime on her brow distracted her. She felt gross and her skin had grown sticky from her travels. Asking Lethrik to mind her bow, Ara escaped to find a secluded recess at the nearby stream where she could bathe. She refused an escort from the sentinels at the price of taking her sword with her, not minding the stipulation as it was strapped to her hip already.

She took off the half plate that she had been wearing and rested the sword on the ground beside the stream. Wearing the entire suit of armour made her feel foolish when she was walking around in a forest that she had known all her life. Sure, there were dangers to be aware of, but that was the thing. They were dangers that you left alone. You never went poking at them, so why would armour be needed?

She rubbed her wrists, now liberated from the gauntlets whilst her toes greeted the icy waters of the stream.

She disrobed and sat on a rock, where she then went about the unceremonious duty of washing the travel grime off herself. Not quite ready to go back to her ever-vigilant escort, she lay back in the shallows, completely submerged but for her face, watching the canopy rain leaves down from above.

Having been away long enough to make the sentinels concerned, she dried herself off and got dressed into loose-fitting slacks and a linen shirt, picking up her armour to walk back to the camp. She refused to put her shoes on unless the world was ending around her, or it was dawn and time to ride again.

Nodding to the rangers who acknowledged her return with a brief glance, she packed her armour away, carefully, for the next day. Lethrik had a lute out and was playing a simple tune; one that raised all their spirits more than any steaming pastry could. Ara sat nearby, leaning against the trunk of a giant oak tree while she brushed out the tangles in her long, damp hair and idly nibbled on an apple.

Yildrin sat next to her, still in his armour, his tabard barely showing a crease despite the long day. "We should get there tomorrow afternoon."

"I will be rather glad to have *him* behind me," she said with a nod in the all-too cheery ranger's direction. "This is such a lovely trip when you take your time. It all just seems like a massive rush. I mean, I understand the reasoning, but we also need to be in one piece when we arrive. This is just the beginning after all." She sighed.

"Of course. Well, there will be some time to rest tomorrow as I am sure that every politician, captain, mage or otherwise, will want to brief you before you head into the portal," he said, then taking note of her concerned expression. "Do not worry, listen to what they have to say of course, but remember, they are working on similar information to you. It will be very different when you get there. Keep your wits about you and you will be fine. Or just find the nearest sentinel and stick to them," he finished with a wink.

Ara laughed. "Thanks, Yildrin. I just hope we can get them back, that I can do my part to help. There seems to be a lot that we do not know… It terrifies me."

"It terrifies us all, my dear, but that fear can be a good thing. Being fearless in the face of danger is called stupidity. Controlling your fear in the face of danger, now that is bravery. Take charge of your mind, take time to think through your actions then act without hesitation. Trust in your plan. Trust in your fellow elves." Ara allowed herself a smile, and Yildrin nudged her. "Now, let us see how good you are with that blade of yours shall we?" he said, rising to his feet and unsheathing a practice blade from his pack.

Ara hopped to her feet, keen for a break in the evening's routine and happy to let the others sort out dinner.

***

The dawn's light kissed the sky as the party was stirred into motion, like birds to their migration call. Ara's body hurt, but her many bruises were not without a heroic story attached. Sparring with a sentinel, cutting paths through the forest with a ranger and perusing journals written by battle-worn mages. It all made her feel like a character out of the story books. This was her final training, and soon, when she was shoved through the portal, she would be able to put it all to use and fulfil her duty to save the elves.

What Little We Can

Today was different in that Ara would need all of her defences up. With assistance from Yildrin, she suited up to become one of Foretilatava's finest. With a flare, she placed her cloak over her shoulders and deftly hopped into Harley's saddle, the silent moonsteel plates obeying her every movement. She faced the day with renewed intent. Today, she was going to show the world what she could do.

Lethrik led the way to Tour Mardesi. The road was nestled within the forest floor, shielded on both sides by a steep embankment and a blanket of season worn leaves. As they drew closer, they saw troops from Isfrisairis travelling to and from the tower in their patrols, greeting them as they entered sight. The tower itself came into view not soon after, previously having been obscured by the trees ahead.

Set to its eastern front was a war camp unlike anything Ara had ever seen. There were wooden towers erected all around a central point, the ballistae atop them all facing centrally. Trenches were dug into the ground, forming a maze of death before reaching lines of rangers with bows at their sides and arrows close at hand. Sentinels were standing on the front lines, their armour showing signs of recent repair.

Hospital tents to the outskirts of the campsite were bustling with activity as the injured were being tended to within. Healers, smiths and engineers worked in the camp, rushing between the duties as if afraid they would get rained on. Their convoy rode straight to the command tent before the tower. They passed a conflagrant pile of corpses. The devilish creatures contorted in a myriad of twisted forms.

Mages were incinerating the pile as one of the bodies began twitching and rising up. At that instant, three rangers turned around and sent a volley of arrows into the creature. Those arrows not finding a joint, simply bounced off. Enough found their mark that the creature fell back down in a booming howl. The mages doubled their efforts and made short work of infusing the pile with magical fire, pouring pitch-black smoke into the air.

"Do not worry, Ara, let us find out what is happening before we let our emotions take the reins, shall we?" came the calm voice of Yildrin through the smoky haze from behind her. He was in his armour but left his faceplate lifted for Ara's sake, his warm features doing their best to reassure her.

Ara merely nodded, not able to pull her eyes from the pile of burning creatures and spitting flame. Some she could loosely guess the names of, from the bestiary, but others were created from nightmares themselves.

The creature at the base of the pile, and likely the reason for the pile's odd location, appeared tall enough to tackle Tour Mardesi alone. A thick black haze seemed to surround it, smothering each tongue of flame that got near.

The convoy halted when Captain Polvin exited the tent to greet Ara. Elf captains had a reputation for being fierce and battle hardened and Polvin refused to be the exception. The only thing sharper than his features was the gaze with which he regarded them. His hair was braided back forming a continuous cascade of silver with his Isfrisairis cloak. The tip of his left ear had been cut short and was now on full display to all he faced. His armour was well kept with his sword showing signs of recent battle.

He nodded to the creature. "A 'blight-shambler' they call it. Nasty piece of work. The mist around it tends to melt armour and skin alike if you stray close enough. Thankfully, a sentinel's spear and a few ballistae to the chest were enough to bring it down. Fear not, they are rather rare from what we have gathered. If you run into one of them, over there, then you were never meant to make it." He smiled, regretting his poor choice of humour as the words left his mouth.

Ara dismounted. "*Yra irasestrala*[18] , Captain. My apologies. There has been a lot to take in. I hope a full written report is being kept for Foretilatava as well as Sinien Tarvia and Isfrisairis?" she asked, looking to buy time to gain her composure. Her own tone drenched in fear when placed in tandem with his icy words.

"Of course. A full written account. Creatures have also been sent off to the University Druidica for dissection and study. Please, this way. The portal has been unpredictable the last few days so it would be safer to conduct your briefing inside," he responded.

The casual business-like manner was beginning to annoy Ara. It was passing the point of bravery and edging into the realm of audaciousness.

---

[18] Bright stars to you

Yildrin, Lethrik and the others offered Ara nods of assurity that did little to assuage her concern. Their relaxed familiarity faded; giving way to their duty as they slotted into various roles around the camp. Ara followed the captain, pushing down at the knot in her stomach as she walked into the tent in his wake, minding the blood stains on the tent flap.

On the heavy oak table were maps of Etroah, the elven kingdoms and Tour Mardesi, as well as a basic reconstruction of the battlefield by the portal. Sections of the forest were circled, revealing locations where patrols had run into trouble with the numbers and species indicated in a logbook off to the side. Above the table was a chandelier, supporting cerulean *lenlialarla* that bathed the tent in a cool glow. Message amulets were hung by the captain's post with labels beneath them. Spears already shattered and shields too dented to use now littered his armoury with his participation in the battles being clear.

He offered her a seat and poured her a drink of water. Flakes of ash danced in the tin mug set before her. She eyed them suspiciously, politely accepting the offer but choosing not to drink from it. There were pages of the bestiary with notes added to the entries. Creatures that haunted her dreams were on the table before her and burning in the pile of bodies just outside the tent.

Her chest tightened as she thought of the task set out before her. It was her going through this portal. Just her. She grabbed out at more knowledge, her breath quickening and her mouth feeling dry. "That creature outside, the one with the smoke—"

Captain Polvin raised his hand, cutting Ara off. "Nildinar is on his way with the *lenlialarla* and will be here any moment. In the meantime, he has given me permission to brief you on your task.

"The elves were sent through three months ago, when we first detected the portal. Usually, they pop in and out of existence without much notice but this one was right next to the tower. It set our wards off and the mages here were able to stabilise it until the Arcanum arrived. The predesignated research team were then able to get in without issue, but it seems too many went in at once and the portal nearly collapsed on itself in the process. It appears that our resonant magical frequencies cause it to break down and we are unable to stabilise it from this end. Think of it like lifting up a basket. It is easy if you lift it when it is by your feet. Put it at the end of a stick, thirty metres away, and you may find it rather difficult. They do not have enough mages there and we are running out of time to fix it from this side… Which is why you are here. You are not linked to the portal, thanks to your distance from its creation. The longer you stay here, the more effect you will have on it so we will need to get you in there as soon as possible. Gods only know what they are facing over there with all the trouble this trickle of monsters has caused us. You are a good candidate according to your qualifications. That, and you have some impressive political connections," he said with a respectful nod.

"With the portal instability; how have those creatures outside been able to make it through without collapsing it?" Ara asked.

"The portal is a gateway into our world from which, there appear to be many entrances. The thalanarians who created the portals have attuned them to their creatures, as such, they have minimal effect on their stability. They choose a doorway on their side and get spat out over here. Mostly, they arrive through the portal tear at the centre of the camp but there have been exceptions. We have sent objects through before, but it seems there is some variation in where they arrive on the other side. Should these *lenlialarla* land in the incorrect hands then that is a lot of power we are just handing over to the thalenarians. If you go through with them, however, then you can ensure that they reach the group on the other side. They can then use that extra power to stabilise the portal enough for them to all come home."

"Seems simple enough. Hold onto the stones, find the elves on the other side and take plenty of notes along the way. Oh, and do not die?" she said, her sarcastic confidence shaking a little, revealing the anxiety beneath.

"Precisely." His polite smile interrupted as his concentration seemed to falter for a moment. He abruptly rose to his feet. "Apologies. My mages have informed me of Chancellor Nildinar's arrival. He has the *lenlialarla* and is inspecting the site, but it would be best to get you through as soon as possible. One more thing, we have not received much information from the other side for the past three days. They know to expect you and should be waiting for you, where you land, but if they are not there when you arrive then cast this spell – do you know how to use one of these?" he asked, handing over a carved *lenlialarla*.

Ara's brief affirmative nod was all she was able to add to the conversation before Captain Polvin had his hand on her pack, leading her out the tent.

"Good, then you will have their direction revealed. They are in the ruined fortress of Dilen'Nahen, although I would not go asking the locals for directions once there," he continued.

Ara studied the *lenlialarla* for a moment, the runes inscribed pertaining to a locator spell of sorts. She tucked it into an easily accessible nook in her belt, fastening the flap in a quick release knot, tucking the rest into the pouch so that the tails would not hang loose. Only then did she look up and meet Captain Polvin's patient, searching gaze. She nodded quietly, offering up what she could only hope was a reassuring smile.

Awkwardly stumbling through the mud at Polvin's guidance, she felt for her sword and counted out her arrows. She had her travel pack, but her food was in her saddle bags along with her cutlery. Polvin pulled her back into line as she attempted a final escape toward Harley to check her bags. Looking up, her fate was sealed. Yildrin was giving his report to Nildinar, the two looking expectantly at Ara.

"Glad you made it, Ara. Here are the *lenlialarla*. This is Master Paylorn of the Arcanum," he said, gesturing to a regal looking elf with smooth, pitch-black hair that was tied back behind his ears. "He is the Master of Abjuration there and is going to cast a few wards on you if you would let him?"

"Chancellor Nildinar, good to see-oh, yes, he may." Ara panicked. Master Paylorn was already working spells into her armour and didn't seem as though he expected a formal greeting from her. Nildinar and Polvin were talking now, the chancellor seeming to have dismissed any further input from Ara. Yildrin passed her the *lenlialarla*, securing the pouch over both shoulders, adjusting the straps so that its weight would not be a hindrance. He tugged on the straps, shaking her about as she looked around, attempting to focus on one of the many potentially life-saving conversations happening around her.

Nildinar and Polvin spoke of the number of injured soldiers at the tower and the hideous assaults endured. Paylorn hissed as magic poured from his fingers into the wards surrounding Ara, his tongue moving too fast for his words to take root in her mind.

"Here, take this, they will need it over there," ordered a ranger, handing Ara a bushel of arrows.

"And this. Remember, aim for the joints on those ones, stay away from the blight-shamblers and look out for smilers. If you see Rolnidiir, he will help you." said another ranger, handing Ara a bag of clinking bottles, weaving his words into the flap of a hummingbird's wings. Ara looked down in terror, her arms filled, as everyone began forcing her in the direction of the portal with straps being pulled, advice thrown, and equipment shoved over.

"Is she prepared to go?" Nildinar asked.

"As much as we can prepare her, yes," responded Captain Polvin, "and we have informed Ruunidil on the other side – they will have a party waiting for her."

Ara opened her mouth, only to have Nildinar's voice fill the air, "Yildrin, get her to the portal, send her in. I put some basic provisions in the bag as well as a few emergency trinkets. As a last resort, this spell will destroy all the *lenlialarla* in the bag as well as anything and everything nearby," Nildinar finished, handing her a red gem in a velvet bag.

She nodded, her mouth opening and closing, desperate for more information. With not a second to think, she stowed the latest of the *lenlialarla* in a pouch on her belt. She reached out for Nildinar's attention, but he was already in retreat, amidst his personal guard.

The group dispersed, leaving Ara and Yildrin to make their final preparations. Yildrin relieved Ara of the extra arrows, tossing them to Lethrik, who strolled past. He smiled and gave Ara a reassuring wink, the worry in his face noted only by the sullen nature of his eyes. He tossed an apple to her. She attempted to catch it but didn't bother chasing after it as it bounced off her hand and rolled harmlessly away in the muck.

"*Raéna ilpa[19]*, if anyone can get them back, it is you. Trust me," he said, giving her a reassuring smile before walking off to the front line at Captain Polvin's summons.

Ara looked up at Yildrin in desperation, her lip aquiver. He chuckled at the sight of her and offered a warm smile. He fixed the pauldron on her left shoulder, allowing her a moment to breathe by shielding her from the expectant gaze of Nildinar, and then placed her helmet on her head, ready for her to secure.

In the shadow of his colossal form, she hid away, checking her straps and counting her bags. He caught her hand, stopping her from pulling the visor down. "You look far too pale to be doing that. We do not want you losing your lunch only to have it then stuck inside your lovely helmet for

---

[19] Baby fox or little fox

73

the rest of the week."

"*Raéna ilpa*?" she asked, not caring about the choke in her voice as she tread water.

"You will find out for yourself. Lethrik pointed it out. Now, those arrows will weigh you down, but this bag of potions may serve those folk on the other side well enough to risk strapping it to your bags. Are you ready?" he asked, kneeling down and locking her eyes with his, searching her heart for doubt.

Strengthened by his support, she gave a weak chuckle. He squeezed her gauntlet lightly and led her, through the battle-soaked mud, toward the portal with the bag on her back and her sword drawn. Rylia's gift was strung and at the ready, but she had no idea where she was going to end up, and if it was in the middle of a battle then a sword in her hand might prove faster to swing. The elven war horns sounded as they drew near and the front line parted to let her through, their shields locking to form a passage to the centre.

Paylorn was still muttering spells under his breath, but for the life of her, she had no idea what they were, only that the poor fellow looked like he had just summited a mountain by the end of it. He stumbled a few steps from the portal, managing a languid nod to Yildrin before making his way back behind the line to safety. Magical wards were wondrous but hardly instilled the required confidence. When an arrow is flying towards your chest, it is not some invisible barrier that you will be wanting to rely upon. Moonsteel armour inspired far more confidence but still, what Ara needed at her side in this was a friend: Rylia, Lethrik, Yildrin, Anmas… anyone.

Ara walked through the maze of battlements and defences, trying to ignore the claw marks in the shields and the tunnels dug through the ground from the direction of the portal. She wondered if any smilers had snuck through and were waiting to grab her ankle. Trampled ground is not the best biome to go looking for wilted plants in, however.

At the centre of the defences was a shimmer to the air, like heat waves coming off the red Melsoan sands, shifting the fabric of space before her. Seeing it up close made it difficult to understand why all these defences were warranted. It seemed so small, so insignificant, and yet the effects of the portal could be seen all around her, felt beneath her in the blood-stained ground.

Ara pulled at the bag straps to ensure it was still there and gave Yildrin a final smile. His eyes were fixed intently on the portal, shield and sword at the ready.

"*Raéna ilpa, arensela lue strala selunua foretdinela alunala*[20]," he whispered, his posture relinquishing her defence back to her, releasing her toward the control of her own two feet.

She took a deep, solitary breath and stepped through the veil.

---

[20] Baby/Little fox, for the light of the stars and the life of the forest, we fight

An Unwelcome Visitor

Ara felt her body being stretched and pulled over impossible distances as the sound of a million crashing trees assaulted her ears. Her chest caved in as her breath left her with a silent scream into the torrent. She could not open her eyes as she was no longer present to control her muscles. She was only there to feel the pain of her body being reformed, time and time again, with bones cracking and muscles tearing.

Silence. She fell no more than a metre onto her knees, crumpling to the ground, gasping for air. Her lungs clawed at the foreign atmosphere desperate to fill again as she hunched over trying to orientate herself in her own body. Waves crashed in her head with throbs of agony sending flashes through her vision.

She vomited onto the floor, a mixture of blood, bile and breakfast. Tears streamed down her face from the torture endured as she looked up, trying to ready herself for any potential threats. She lifted her sword and opened her eyes, releasing a flood of light that burnt her mind. The crimson sky loomed overhead. Storm clouds rolling over each other, sending arcs of lightning across the expanse. The ground was covered in ash and the trees around her were long dead, their gnarled and desiccated trunks recalling a story of agony and woe.

She was alone. She was alone but safe, for now. She rose slowly to her feet and sheathed her sword in favour of her bow. Nocking an arrow, keeping three spare in her left hand. She knelt to her knee, waiting for her ears to stop ringing. Her eyes darted wildly across the hellscape before her, ready to give way to instinct should anything catch her eye.

The world was in chaos. There were the sounds of battle on all horizons and the thunderous sky set a beat of destruction to the ambience. She pulled out the locator *lenlialarla*, her fingers wasting no time with the straps. In a shaking hand, she released the spell, reading the runes out loud "*Marilma. Opas. Yvlynne. Faire.*[21]"

---

[21] Path. Guide. Yvlynne. Reveal

A spine of blue light was erected from the milky crystal. It led to the… well it could have been any direction. She wasn't even sure if this place had a north or south. Even up and down seemed up for debate with her stomach still turning from the portal.

Ara crept forward, keeping alert for the slightest sound or flicker of movement. Branches from the trees reaching out from the pages of horror stories, ready to grab her and pull her in. The ground cracked around her feet, ash floating up with the lifeless bistre sand giving way.

Step after step, she crept forward stopping only to rid herself of the last of her breakfast in one final salute to portal travel. She came across a denser thicket of dead trees which gave her more cover. There were neither birds to flick between branches nor rodents to scurry in the undergrowth. This sterile wasteland rejecting Ara's very presence by pulling the moisture from her skin and covering her with ash in acrid gusts of wind.

Over the tops of the trees to her right, she saw the colossal figure of a blight-shambler striding in the opposite direction. It was vaguely humanoid, at least ten metres tall with long, razor tipped fingers at the end of arms that reached its knees. A creature made seemingly of smoke and shadows, whose gaunt yet towering form sapped the light from the air around it. Ara couldn't tell if it was lingering portal sickness, undiluted fear or an effect of the creature itself, but light seemed to bend around it. The light was afraid to stray too near lest it become trapped in its form, unwilling, or unable to bounce off it in any natural way. She turned away, definitely not alone anymore but at least she wasn't found.

Her pulse throbbed in the vessels of her head, her mouth bitter and lungs coated with ash. The blight-shambler strode from view and had been gone long enough that Ara felt safe to start creeping forward once more. She moved from tree to sand ledge and from wind carved boulder to petrified log.

Clouds of ash rose with each step, and then slight trembles. At first, Ara thought the trembles to be caused by the land itself but then the trembles grew to vibrations. Ara stopped midway between trees, remembering the tunnels at the portal site. She stood still, hoping that the creature making those tunnels would not be able to find her if she were motionless. The vibrations eased as she stood still, biting her lip and holding her heart in her throat. She was shivering in her armour despite the intense heat with sweat clinging onto the ash that blew into her face.

One step was all it took to reawaken the vibrations, this time, not easing as she froze in her panic. There was no time for a new plan as the ground beneath her exploded and a creature erupted from the earth beneath it. Its six spider-like legs stabbing at the ground as it rose to a height almost double Ara's. She dove back and sent all four readied arrows in its direction as it searched the surface for its prey.

Her bow sang with each arrow fired, the glistening leaf shaped tips finding their mark between the onyx plates that glinted with violet. There were more eruptions around her and soon dirt was raining down on her from all directions. Shrieks pierced as the reavers discovered their prey, cowering in the sand and ready to be shredded by their ravenous mandibles.

She panicked and scrambled to her feet, determined to fight as she fired a second volley of arrows into the tide of insectoid monsters now charging her down. Arrows were not enough. She readied her magic with flames growing in her hands as streaks of silver entered the fray from her rear. At the centre of the ambush, a sentinel of Isfrisairis now stood, slashing creatures in half and cleaving limbs off in singular strokes of a mighty greatsword. Arrows blew through the trees like a coastal storm, collapsing the shrieking figures as they struck. Ara was pulled back before she could summon an iota of relief and before she knew what was happening, she was at full sprint with a ranger of Isfrisairis on either side of her.

"The sentinel!" she cried out in her retreat.

"He is fine, get down!" came the response. Nothing about the tone implied that Ara had a choice in the matter.

Instinct took over as she dove into the recess of a sand ledge. The sound of a thundering herd of yurinduur ran past mere metres from their location.

The male ranger to her left had an empty quiver, no bow, and a tarnished dagger at the ready. To her right, the female ranger hunkered down, four arrows remaining, her armour made more from bandages than from steel at this point. Ara, in this free moment, split her arrows between the rangers and gave her bow up without a second of regret, drawing her sword as quietly as she could. No pleasantries were exchanged but she saw the relief in their faces. They now stood a chance, turning from hunted to hunters.

The herd moved on and the sentinel joined them, covered in the hissing yellow ichor from the reavers. "Our apologies, Ara. Dilen'Nahen is currently under attack so we were all that could be spared. We must hurry, everything is ready for the arrival of the *lenlialarla*."

She made her response clear by silently vaulting over the ledge toward the distant castle-like structure that was surrounded by a hoard of these nightmares. Ara, shocked at the sight, let herself be led forward by the others, toward the heart of the battle. The sentinel pulled a horn off his belt as they neared the edges. He signalled his defiance in a sonorous blast that caught the attention of the battle.

The mages on the keep's wall turned and walls of flame flowed over the assailants with carpets of lightning that carved out a path of safety. Sentinels jumped down from the wall and ran to meet them with shields raised, receiving arrows and spears from the remaining attackers nearby.

The group dashed forth, arrows flying from the ranger's quivers without thought or hesitation. The sentinel cleaved any creature not already dealt with by the mages. Sprinting through, a twitching hand of a dying yurinduur grabbed at Ara's foot, tripping her and spilling the contents of the bag out before her as she hit the ground. The group turned and immediately surrounded her with their shields, but the forces were filling in the gaps already. She scrambled to replace the contents, spitting out mouthfuls of acrid sand as she did so. Finding her feet, she began running as the tide of yurinduur arrived to clash against the shields of the sentinels.

She sprinted as fast as her trembling muscles could manage, up a ramp of bodies and to the wall where she was lifted up. The male ranger had joined those sending volleys forth to rescue the sentinels of the rear guard, who were surrounded. They were pushing their way through with shields raised, protecting each other in a wall of steel, allowing those on the wall to open up a route for their retreat.

Ara panicked and began casting spells of her own. She brought back all that knowledge she had gained from the University Druidica, bringing forth the primal power of the magical weave to bear and unleashed her own destruction on the army before her.

Her first few attempts were balls of flame colliding with individual reavers, bursting into the flesh beneath their chitin. Then, as she secured her magical channels, so the size of the flames increased and with a final push, she threw up a wall of fire that curled around the sentinels and incinerated the relentless forces of the yurinduur.

They charged up to the keep and formed a wall of shields, taking advantage of the time afforded by the spells being hurled into the fray from all around. From a shoulder, one of them placed the body of the female ranger at the feet of the mages. Ara fell back and burst into tears at the sight of her mangled chest and lifeless stare, contorted into agony with blood trickling from her mouth. A mage briefly touched the ranger's neck and shook her head before moving along the line. The male ranger took Ara by the arm and dragged her to the keep interior. She hobbled behind him; her mind reeling in shock, comprehension far from her grasp.

"Ruunidil, we have the *lenlialarla*," he announced, presenting Ara to the lead mage in the keep as if she were a child caught stealing toffee apples.

The brass-haired mage stepped away from the healer he was assisting and hurried over to them.

"Ara, *oronnsela lu*[22]! Do you have the *lenlialarla*?" he pleaded, his arms stretching out.

She could not get the words past the lump in her throat, so she just pushed the bag in his direction. The elf's robes were in ruin. It was impossible to make out any features past the ash and blood that clung to his face save for his soft features, tormented by the vicissitudes of battle. His eyes darted around as he shuffled through the contents of the bag and brought the gems out, relief washing over his whole body.

"Inform the captain that the ritual will take around ten minutes. Once the barriers are up, we shall begin work on stabilising the portal. We are leaving this lightless desert!" he shouted victoriously, an insult directed all around him.

Ruunidil ran to a side room, summoning his fellow mages and leaving Ara to release her tears.

It was the tentative contact of the ranger on her shoulder that came to her rescue. "We need you back on the western wall. There are cracks forming and if we get overwhelmed then that barrier will not mean very much," he said, summoning her to his aid.

Her eyes widened with shock then began to focus on him as his request took root.

Ara looked down at his hands. Through the blur in her vision, she could see him trying to hand her something: her bow. She grabbed the curved shape, her fingers finding strength in the smooth feel of the polished Foretilatava rosewood. It was the faint smell of the wood and the feel of her

---

[22] By the light

bow that settled her trembling hands. The carved vines running the length of the limbs with the leaves showing the abundance of life from their home. Foretilatava had arrived in Dilen'Nahen and was now ready to fight back.

She nodded, walked over to a pile of loosely stacked arrows, loading them into the empty quiver at her waist.

"Lead the way." She managed, nocking an arrow and falling into stride beside him as he started jogging away from the central room in the tower.

The ranger did not look back as he began carefully picking his way over and around debris, each foot falling to its mark as he led her across the castle interior. The grey stone of the castle was scorched and chipped with battle scars both young and old. The four story keep struggled to stand on its crumbling foundations with the desperation of the *haltha* being the only thing keeping it standing. It lacked all artistry with its squared angles and brutalist architecture, the building's scars providing the only decoration.

They made their way through a maze of corridors that might have once been an armoury, the roof of which was still smouldering after having been burned away by some colossal force. Elves rushed the halls, carrying with them the weapons destined for the front or wounded in need of healing. Ara passed the bag of potions to a healer, insisting he take the bag when she was met with confusion.

The ranger led them to the periphery of the tower where the devastation was too severe to provide any protection for those hiding amidst the masonry's skeleton. Holding up a hand, he motioned for her to stop at a crumbling doorway in the ruined eastern wall. Cautiously, he peered round into the courtyard beyond, motioning for her to follow before ducking out in a crouched dash.

The cacophonous sound of battle was all around, smothering them in the threat of impending death. Clouds of smoke blew past, carrying burning embers and torrents of ash. She kept her eyes trained on the back of the ranger's heavily stained hood, only allowing herself the occasional glance around at the broken terrain and fiery skies.

There was a scattering of intact buildings near the periphery of the courtyard. They appeared to be making a break towards the northernmost building, plotting a course between the projectile fire that sailed over the walls, landing in earth-shattering explosions.

Weaving between the spears and arrows, imbedded in the cratered earth, Ara held her breath. Soldiers on the walls around them were holding the line despite the onslaught with the full might of the *tarviahaltha* magic being brought to bear. Sentinels threw the attackers from the walls with crashes of their shields and rangers poured arrows down from their posts. Mages, too tired to throw spells, had lifted swords and fought amidst the rangers with snapped bows and empty quivers.

After the eternity that mere seconds can feel like in the heart of a battle, they darted across the expanse and into the building. A group of elves had huddled in the darkness. Their bloodied bedrolls were the only evidence that this might be a place of rest as their weapons were close at hand and most still wore what passed for armour. Four sentinels leapt to their feet and two rangers aimed arrows at their throats as they dove through the threshold.

A petite, iron-haired elf squeezed through, from between the sentinels, lowering her companion's weapons. "What is it, Aeradil?" Her eyes widened at the sight of Ara. "Oh, is this…" Her lips twitching towards a smile as the ranger nodded.

"The mages at the tower are tapped," he said quietly, "we need you to get word to Captain Yvlynne across the keep. Ruunidil is preparing the ritual, he needs ten minutes. When the barriers are up, they will see to the portal."

She closed her eyes and a slight frown appeared above her brow. A moment later, she nodded. "Done. Is the perimeter holding?"

"Poorly," he said solemnly, knowing the implications of his response.

The spent elves patched their defences with dented steel and ran out with Aeradil at the lead, their loose armour plates clanging with each stride.

"We should head to the northern breach, where we climbed in. We summoned something of a feeding frenzy there," he said, leading her to the northern line by skirting the wall at a jog that lit a fire in Ara's thighs.

Elves were running through the chaos, carrying arrows, water and the wounded. The perimeter defence looked meagre with frequent gaps forming faster than they could be filled.

They climbed the stairs to observe the sea of reavers and yurinduur making a push. Ara wasted no time and had three arrows sailing through the air before looking at the defenders beside her, their resolve shattered for all to see.

The body of the female ranger had been removed, a point that both Aeradil and Ara noted at the same time, sharing an austere glance.

A yurinduur war horn blasted and a wedge charge formed to the rear of the reavers. Those creatures that did not get out of the way were trampled under the stampede. Arrows sank into their chests and, one by one, the yurinduur collapsed, being devoured by the charge behind.

One by one was not enough. The rangers fired as fast as they could. Ara felt arrows being pulled from her quiver by those around her and within seconds, all the arrows were down range. With no time to think, she slung her bow around her shoulder and summoned ravenous walls of fire to clash into the yurinduur front. Roars of flame and rage erupted before her as she pushed her energy into her magic, pulling on her need to protect her kin, encouraging her hatred and giving in to her fear.

She felt her legs becoming weak but the yurinduur charge was not halting. She gritted her teeth, trying to retain consciousness, her ears ringing and her vision fading. Still, she pushed herself further, dug deeper into her well of magic, ignoring the blood that started trickling from her nose as old warnings from long forgotten Druidica lectures rang through her head. Shadows tore out at her vision with her mind screaming out at her.

A hand grabbed her collar and yanked her back, taking her place on the lines. Through the haze, she could see a fresh pile of arrows at her replacement's feet. Flashes of spells arced before the silhouette in focused pulses. Ara stumbled back, wiping furiously at her face, smearing blood, and sweat as she wobbled unsteadily, taking deep breaths to fight for her consciousness.

She was stronger than this… What was a few minutes of fire compared to the months these elves had spent facing this horror? She tripped over her feet, and fell to her hands and knees, the air escaping her lungs. Panic swelled in her mind as she could no longer feel the ground beneath her fingers. She could not hold on any longer. Ara made one final push to her feet, but her body gave way. She blacked out, her eyes falling upon the elf who took her place. The fading image of his inquisitors badge welcoming the void.

Glowing Eyes

A pitcher, of what could once have been water, hit Ara in the face and she spluttered her way back into the hellscape. Aeradil knelt beside her, barely able to stay on his feet. A bandage covered his left eye and there were burns on his neck and jaw.

His silver eyes gave him an almost ethereal presence, so different from the natural hazels and greens of the *forehaltha* that Ara was used to. His blond hair was a mat of grime that clung to the sweat on his face with free strands reaching down past his chin.

The barrier's dome of magic was now up, a few hundred metres past the perimeter wall. Reavers clawed in vain at the magical structure, crying out and jumping back as each of their strikes bit at them with the spell's fury. The assault on Dilen'Nahen had alleviated for the time being. Few creatures clung to life as the last of the arrows brought them down to clear the field between the outer walls and the dome. Ara gave a sigh of relief. Her hands clawed at the slick stone atop the wall, lifting her up. Aeradil assisted her to her feet, his face contorting in pain as Ara noticed the fresh blood on his torn jerkin.

Around her, soldiers took advantage of the reprieve provided, leaving some of their rank to keep watch with the rest repairing breaches, refilling arrow baskets and tending to their wounds. The healer, with the Ara's bag of potions, was dutifully going around, applying tinctures to the larger of the wounds, and rushing to the aid of the grievously wounded.

Silhouettes scouted the keep from within the clouds above, flashes of lightning revealing the magnitude of their wingspans. Bodies carpeted the ground around the keep with heaps leading up to the tops of the walls. Mangled corpses of yurinduur, reavers, blight-shamblers, elves and many more; discarded unceremoniously by the machine of war.

Aeradil was now being held upright by Ara whilst he caught his breath. He shut his eyes and fought for his balance. With shaking hands, he turned to Ara and handed her a war horn. It looked as if it had been carved from a yurinduur's horn. Its hastily attached mouthpiece showing signs of rust, with the spiralled groves up the horn having gathered enough grime to make Ara's stomach heave.

She looked into his silver eyes; his expression was not unreadable—it was simply not present. He was a puppet working through his instinct for survival with fatigue weighing him down at each action. He placed a callused hand on her shoulder.

"We need to go and fetch the arrows. The sentinels are going to start pulling the bodies from the wall, but they can handle themselves. I need you to watch my back. If you see anything sneaking up on any of the rangers in the field; blow this horn and we will come running back," he said, his voice falling like grains of sand through an hourglass in-between his laboured breaths.

"But… the barrier, it is up?" pleaded Ara.

"Creatures have methods of getting through these fields. Some of them are also adept at hiding in plain sight," he said, drawing a shortsword and stepping from the wall, making his way through the corpse-strewn battlefield.

Ara furiously wiped at her eyes trying to clear the water, tears and ash from her vision. Aeradil wasted no time in darting from body to body, stabbing them before retrieving the arrows, not taking any risks that he didn't have to. Occasionally, a yurinduur would attempt to stand but he made short work of those with a scavenged spear or with a flick of his sword. Ara would lift the horn to her lips at each engagement, begging to have Aeradil back in the keep, safe, at her side.

Five rangers were now in the northern battlefield, picking arrows from the bodies, all under Ara's watch. Her eyes darted from torn banners to twitching arms, from the rangers dashing between the bodies to clouds of ash swirling in rogue wind currents. In her mind, Ara was staring through the trees, tracking signs of movement, attuning herself to the natural motion of the branches so that she could filter out the normal flickers from the deadly ambushes.

Aeradil moved further and further away, opening up separate bags for his arrows, leaving the full ones in a line to collect upon his return. He would tuck to his haunches, reacting to sounds and fine movements that only he could perceive, creeping ever further forward.

A reaver slid out from a pile of bodies, thirty feet from the closest ranger, its spider-like legs kicking at the dirt to liberate its extensive form from its tunnel. This one was different though. At nearly four times the size of any Ara had seen thus far. Its body was supported by legs and arms, scuttling in a more horizontal position like a centipede, serpentining across the ground toward its prey. Its elongated tail curved up and over in anticipation, baring a hideous-looking stinger at its tip, large enough to kill an elf with the impact alone.

Ara brought the horn to her lips and unleashed the contents of her lungs in a pathetic puff of air. Panicking, she tried again and again, the rangers not turning around to see the impending threat. She tried to scream but all her chest could give her was a rasped whimper. Tears welled in her desperate eyes, Ara reaching her mind to Aeradil's begging him to let her message through but all she found were his wards.

A flash of shadow leapt over the wall from beside Ara. An elf sprinted to the creature's flank, his speed startling Ara as he seemed to sail over the uneven terrain of the battlefield. He dove at the creature's tail, severing it with a swipe of his sword as he leapt over it in a twisting dive. It doubled back, emitting a gut-wrenching screech that warned the rangers of its presence.

The elf dodged a feral pounce then rolled between its legs in an eruption of mud, punching its underside and unleashing a neat explosion of lightning. It collapsed, steam spouting forth from its chitinous joints with lightning arcing between its limbs.

The rangers doubled their speed as the elf ran back to Ara. Defeated, she shoved the horn in his direction. He looked beaten to within an inch of his life, bruises and slashes covering his body. Black hair reached to his collar in tattered lengths, framing his angular features, and accentuating the eyes that were currently scanning Ara's very soul.

A singular glance from those storm grey depths let Ara know who was in charge of the coming exchange. Suddenly, she was a child having scraped her knee, in the presence of a warrior who commanded the battlefield.

He accepted the horn from her and wordlessly took over her charge. She refused to give up however, and watched over the rangers, trying to keep them safe as best she could. The elf next to her tensed up like a cat, bringing the horn midway to his lips. She doubled her efforts but could see no threat. He sounded the horn in a short blast.

"Shadows!" he shouted, running to a brazier in the wall and grabbing the torches leaning up against them. "Place them along the wall!" he ordered, as he began lining them up himself.

Ara grabbed an armful and ran the length of the wall, sticking the torches into the makeshift holders, echoing his cries from the unseen threat, "Shadows! Shadows!"

The rangers left their arrow packs, diving onto the wall in their haste, sourceless shadows on the floor appearing to be chasing them down. At the level of the torches, they formed corporeal spectres that screamed out at the world, their elongated jaws unhinging in gaping maws. The rangers turned and made short work of the creatures with quick slices in their direction, their scythe-like arms doing little against the attacks.

Eerie silence descended, interrupted only with heavy breathing of the exhausted rangers and the crackle of the fire from the torches. Wasting no time in answering their duty, they returned to the battlefield. This time, simply retrieving the arrow packs they had set up, pushing their bodies to the limit so they may return as soon as possible. The wavering safety of the keep welcoming them back after a few tortuous minutes.

"Th…" Ara spluttered, evacuating ash from her lungs. "Thank you," she finally managed.

The elf did not break his gaze with the perimeter, his brow was furrowed, expression unchanging.

"Ara, correct? The 'thanks' goes out to you. This barrier came at the perfect time. Let us hope that it will be enough," he replied, hopping off the wall and gesturing for her to help him clear the embankment of bodies alongside the sentinels. His collected tone slid over his words like water across ice.

She would grab one half and he the other; together, they would throw the bodies down the slope of death that had formed before the walls.

"My name is Alikain. You did well. Much better than us on our first day over here," he offered with a glimmer of emotion, seeing her melting away into herself.

"What were those things?" she asked, trying to break his focus on her defeat.

"The first was a reaver. A female. Much bigger, much nastier. Their exoskeleton render weapons useless so you have to hit the joints or attack them from beneath. We call the other creatures: shadow stalkers. They can travel as shadow projections on the ground making them impossible to kill. Get them in direct light and they are forced to take form. From there, it is pretty straight forward," he finished, casually brushing away a dying yurinduur's grasping hand with a flick of his foot.

"Straight forward…" she whispered, exasperated.

"Follow me," he offered, apparently satisfied at the ingress they had made.

Confused, Ara dared not decline. She climbed gracelessly onto the wall after him, too tired to manage anything more.

"You saved a lot of lives today. It was wonderful seeing a fresh mage enter the fray, albeit a little chaotic. You need to look after yourself. If you run yourself into the ground then you will not be able to help anyone out, down the line," he said, potentially attempting to comfort her. "If you go sacrificing yourself then you better have a damned good reason for doing so."

She nodded. Alikain was an inquisitor. The stories she had heard about them were enough to shake her resolve even in a place like this. Every word out his mouth would be a calculated move on a board that he would never not be in control of.

She understood what he was saying but could not allow herself to find comfort in his praise nor could she see the logic in being reprimanded for pushing herself and killing those creatures. They would have overwhelmed them if she had not. How many would have died then?

The keep's interior was littered with sheltering elves attempting sleep or making their way through their meagre rations. Healers worked furiously to stabilise those on the brink whilst rangers and mages alike saw to the other wounded, changing bandages and suturing up basic wounds.

Ara felt a sickness enter her mind. Her regal kin, the valiant *tarviahaltha*, were scattered about the floor, fighting for survival and yet, were expecting to fight the moment the next assault came. Alikain rested a hand on her shoulder for a moment, partially breaking through the dark cloud that was creeping through her mind. Ara looked to him, desperate for the inquisitor to reassure her; to let her know that everything was under control, that the job was done and that these elves would be safe, but he was interrupted before he could speak.

A panicked-looking mage shouted, "Alikain, Ruunidil needs you. There are negative energy floods forming at the portal."

"Ara, you did well today, but you will not be of much use when the next battle comes if you are still exhausted. Get some rest, we may find ourselves in need of more *forehaltha* chaos," he managed with a smile, his teeth not filed to points as some would have had her believe.

She was left alone amidst the dead and the dying. She couldn't take it, and there was no way she would be able to get any rest in here. Aeradil had still not returned so she looked around the keep for a hole to hide in, seeing a staircase heading up. It was no grand sequoia tree for her, with floral scents and choiring birds, but she needed her feet to be detached from this tainted ground.

She took the stairs one by one, leaning on the wall for support, dragging her shoulder along the hot stone. The air made her feel nauseous, the amaroidal heat consuming each breath she took. There were no elves up here, so she braced the climb for the reward of solitude, for a moment free of battle and expectation.

The stairs spiralled higher and higher. Not being satisfied with the middle floors, she kept climbing until the summit. She pushed her doubts about the foundations damage to the back of her mind. The roof of the castle was in terrible shape. Rocks had punched through in many places, with support beams actively smouldering. She looked out of one of the impact holes and saw the expanse of Ilvithiir spread out before her.

Pulling herself through the rafters, she reached the apex of the roof, scanning the skies as she did so. Here, she was alone. Here, she could rest.

She leant against the broken precipice, propping one foot up on a piece of crumbled wall, using it as a makeshift table. She rifled around in her backpack, retrieving one of the books that Nildinar had included for her. In it, was a crude map that revealed the landmarks that now stretched between her and the horizon.

To the west, on the horizon, was a colossal city, a crown rising from the ruined landscape. The thalenarian capital of Xilmiranth. Its ominous silhouette watched her as she sat there. In the north, the gnarled forest lay dormant as a snap lily, waiting for those to stray too near the portal site before springing its trap.

Blight-shamblers strode across the expanse, patrolling, waiting for creatures to cross them so that they may release whatever horrors they were capable of. The skies played host to terrors all of their own. Creatures flying in the clouds and screeching in the distance, swooping down to prey on those below.

She added sketches and notes to her maps and bestiaries. The briefing provided to her was but a fraction of what they actually faced. She wondered how she was going to report all this to Rylia when she couldn't rationalise what she was seeing herself. The plague that was the reavers, in its own rite, was enough to cause widespread terror in Etroah yet in Ilvithiir, they were the bottom of the hierarchy, the grunts of the army sent to draw enemies out of their nest.

With that, though, she began wondering what it took to make an apex predator in this land. What were the thalenarians like? Then, what was their god emperor, Xalmilanthris, like? Who was he to control such horrors.

The roof was hardly comfortable, but it was quiet. She took a deep breath and folded her book, taking in the emotions of the land. If she were to report on this, then they would need to feel the fear as she did. See the land through her eyes. Feel the pain of all the wounded below, not simply the cuts and stabs but the mental torture they had all endured from being hunted for so long. They would have the facts of the *tarviahaltha* and the heart of Ara.

No sun could be seen but the clouds mosaicked with rays of light cracking through. There were no insects or animals to call the world home, merely creatures that were stored here as a barrier of protection for the thalenarians, an army to be kept on hand.

She shut her eyes, fatigue drawing her to sleep. Heavy breathing came from her left, rousing her from her reprieve. She glanced over expecting an exhausted elf to poke their head from beneath the roof. Instead, a wolfish creature balanced on the top of the crenel opposite her, staring her down.

Glowing red eyes froze her breathing as the realisation of her mistake became apparent. Alone, she faced this beast with limbs as long as she was tall and talons that could cleave her in two with a single stroke.

A grin crept across its features. Not a grin… a snarl. Saliva began pouring from its maw and the bristled grey hair on its body stood on end. This wolf with an oddly humanoid body was focused on every potential movement Ara could make but all she did was sit there, frozen in fear.

A hand yanked her by the collar of her breastplate, as Aeradil appeared, and pulled her back into the keep. The roof strained as the beast dove at Ara, chasing her down and swiping through the hole she had been sitting next to.

The two elves fell down the stairs, gliding on their feet to try and control their descent. The roof was shredded by their pursuer, the stairway too narrow for the creature's full range of movement. There was no time to consider their actions. There was one way up and now they scrambled to follow the only way down.

The sound of their terror was evident to those below and when they hit the ground floor landing. Aeradil threw her to the floor as arrows sailed over them, flicking at their clothes and hissing past their ears. The beast's hide reflected the projectiles with ease, arrows ricocheting into the walls and falling to the floor.

Alikain was prepared. He dove forward and levered the creature against a spear, the other end being lodged in the ground. The creature vaulted on the spear point; the tip unable to so much as scratch its flesh. It turned to face Ara again when Alikain dove forth, not allowing a chance for it to recover.

Lightning erupted from his hands and the wolf yelped, running from the keep. The elves chased it out with scavenged weapons, only to see it burst through a shield barricade that the sentinels had formed in response to the chaos. Rushing toward the perimeter barrier, it bashed against it over and over until a crack appeared for a fraction of a second, allowing it to fall through and disappear from sight. The barrier reformed behind it.

Ara watched it disappear with her heart in her throat. The sentinels returned to their posts on the wall, or trailed back into the keep to rest, unphased by this latest development. She got the sense that Aeradil was right: even with the barrier up, there was never a chance to fully relax. There was always something waiting to drag them into the shadows.

The new threat was Alikain who stormed towards Aeradil and Ara. "Did you not see the wounded down here? Pull that crap again and I will watch as it tears you to pieces. If you survive it then I will be the one scattering you across the cobblestones," he seethed, his tone dangerously flat, his eyes a raging storm.

He walked back to Ruunidil, who was calling for help with the portal again, panic slowly rising in the mage's voice.

Aeradil patted Ara on the shoulder and returned back to the keep with a wordless sigh. Ara simply fell back, curling up against a pile of rubble by the entrance, her rage holding back the tears. She buried herself in her cloak, searching for the faint smells, of the forest, saved within.

A Heated Escape

Sleep was not something one managed in Ilvithiir, but Ara had achieved a few moments where her eyes were shut, and she was not causing impending doom to those around her.

Menora, the creature that chased her. The only note present in the bestiary was; 'Hunter. Carnivore. Killed six already. Weapons are useless.' A grim entry, even by the bestiarie's standards.

She slammed the book shut, unable to summon the courage to add a sketch of the creature. Those red eyes gnawed away at her, even from the depths of her repressed memories. Her ears twitched to the sounds around her, tensing her muscles whenever anyone walked too close. Magic was slowly returning to her. She could stand her quiescence no more, deciding that she needed to make herself useful before Ilvithiir drowned her in fear.

The healers declined her help with the injured appearing stable for the time being. Ara did not have enough magic to compete with the refined techniques of the *tarviahaltha*, so she reserved her own power for the defensive line.

Aeradil was looking over her from a nearby perch, cleaning and repairing the arrows retrieved from the field. They used any resources they had left to lend lethality to the projectiles with some of the arrow tips looking like cold-shaped steel, wrapped around the shaft. Many of the arrows even incorporated fletching or shafts scavenged from the Ilvithiirian forces.

She sat next to him, grabbing a pile of arrows and sifting through them herself, smiling at the occasional arrow she came across that had come from Vera's forge, the leaf shapes setting off her memories of home. She picked up an arrow with the poplar-leafed tip, showing it to Aeradil for his opinion. He nodded, not appearing to manage much more.

Ara remembered the Isfrisairis macaw, reaching beneath her helm and pulling out the malachite feather. She flipped it through her fingers. "Lethrik, a ranger gave this to me. He said it was from an Isfrisairis macaw," she said.

Aeradil raised an eyebrow, managing a brief nod but his gaze lingered for a moment longer than what a simple acknowledgement required. Ara slipped the feather into his hand, squeezing his shoulder. He lifted the feather, marvelling at it, tears welling in his eyes. With a deep sigh, he picked up a heavy grain arrow of Isfrisairis design, placing it on his lap. He trimmed the feather, using it to replace the missing fin on its fletching.

Ara's gaze dropped. There were no such luxuries in Dilen'Nahen. An arrow can remove a creature that may otherwise have killed you or your kin. A pretty feather had little place in this world.

A line of four sentinels had marched to the wall above the keep's gate to the north, flanked by two hastily erected wooden towers, each hosting a nest of rangers. Captain Yvlynne, a recognisable figure at their centre. There was a thrum of activity being stirred up to the west and the nature of the reaction had Ara concerned. She offered Aeradil a smile, but he too had realised what was happening, tears welling in the corners of his eyes. He nodded to Ara as she ran to the western wall.

Looking to the horizon, Captain Yvlynne wore a mixture of concern and hatred. She was adorned in the armour of a sentinel with a golden Isfrisairis eagle on her chest and a clear ruby at its centre. She was much taller than Ara and stood with an air of unquestionable authority around her. She had a pendant on her neck, a life-link amulet if Ara had to guess, although it was not glowing as it should. She had a sword at her side with an inquisitor's badge and a matching pendant wrapped around it. Goronil…

Concerned, Ara made her way onto the wall, slipping through the hurried mages that darted along the walls, casting their defensive wards. A creeping shadow extended from the direction of Xilmiranth, great plumes of dust being kicked up in its wake.

"It seems like we have something they want," Captain Yvlynne said through the veil of her copper hair, noting Ara's presence on the walls.

Ara's mouth fell agape. "Will the barrier hold?"

"We will find out soon enough," she said, turning to the keep and blowing an elven war horn.

"How can I help?" Ara pleaded, desperately looking at the state of the walls, seeing nothing but potential breaches, weak points and injured soldiers.

"You can make sure that you get back alive. Alikain chose you for a reason, Ara. As I understand it; your sister is the new queen. You will be the one making certain that the *forehaltha* join the *tarviahaltha* in championing against this cause. Etroah needs to be ready."

Ranger, mage, sentinel; all were called into action at the horn's sounding, running to their posts. Torches were lit and arrows piled up in regular stations near the clusters of rangers across the walls. Shields were raised on the front line with the elves casting their wards and readying the last of their resolve for the final push.

The army marched, ever onward, toward the keep. The distance was closed in unrelenting speed. Strident cries of reavers amidst the yurinduur that roared in rhythm with their war drums, smashing their shields and kicking at the dirt. The magical dome was the only thing stopping the sea of destruction from crashing against the keep.

The roaring grew into mania as a thalenarian mage sauntered forward, the forces giving her a wide berth as she made her way to the barrier. An intricately detailed golden mask with two crescent horns extending back. Scaled engravings guarded the frontal plate, covering the top half of her face. Her purple-shadowed alabaster skin in stark contrast to the void-black gossamer dress that hung delicately from her shoulders, dancing around her bare feet where around her, no ash nor dirt dared to enter.

She raised a hand to the barrier and a cruel grimace took over her expression, her eyes glinting as abyssal pearls beneath the ocean. The magical dome shattered around the remains of Dilen'Nahen along with the hopes of the elves. Ara's heart sank as the army roared in victorious blood lust, reavers shrieking to where Ara needed to cover her ears. The cadence of their drums rose up as the tsunami broke forth.

Calin, Captain Yvlynne's private mage, looked up to the defiant leader. "The portal is almost stable. We just need more time. The main gate has been sealed, and the western breach reinforced. The walls are still not high enough though. They will be able to climb up above the main gate before long. The southern line is the thinnest as reinforcements needed to be pulled to sure up the west. Maybe we should consider pulling back now?"

"Dilen'Nahen will be buried in corpses before long. Move the more wounded to the keep but have them ready to cover our retreat. The western flank last. Get Alikain to light the ritual fires and tell him there is an acolyte on the field. Get yourself inside now. I need you to assist Ruunidil with the portal."

Calin nodded, too tired to argue. She closed her eyes briefly to send her message then ran towards the keep. Captain Yvlynne watched her go and then turned back to the fight. She drew Goronil's sword and bashed her shield in a sentinel's salute, summoning the courage of her fellow defenders that joined her in her resistance.

***

Alikain, we are starting the retreat. Light the fires, the western ones last. Hurry, there is an acolyte on the frontlines of the western approach! Calin's voice sounded in his head.

He dropped back, his position at the front line already having been taken from him by a ranger. He ran as fast as his body would let him toward the southern barrel stock, his leg sending arcs of pain with each step. He flicked his hand and a tongue of flame spat out to light the fuse of the first fire, the accelerant hungry for the spark. He barely paused before proceeding to the rest, dodging retreating soldiers and projectile fire as he did so.

The army swarmed around the keep and pushed against the torrent of arrows and spears. Clawing at the walls and throwing spears of their own. The speed of the advance began to overwhelm the sparse remaining forces. The valiant defenders giving their last in these final moments, too desperate to hope.

Captain Yvlynne motioned for the rest of the soldiers to begin their retreat, and they moved back as one, maintaining their shield wall. Arrows flew over their heads from the keep's second floor, felling the incoming yurinduur. Before anyone could react, however, a ball of flame struck the shields, shattering the ranks and incinerating those with weakened wards in an instant.

"Dragon!" A desperate call came from the wall above.

Captain Yvlynne shouted, "Retreat! To the keep! Get inside! Now!"

All the soldiers spun around and ran towards the keep, too disciplined to panic. Some paused only to hoist the remaining wounded onto their shoulders before continuing their retreat, desperation pulling forth the last of their energy reserves.

Alikain had only just managed to douse the flame on a spearman near the final brazier when he looked up to see a dark shape shimmer through the clouds above him. He pulled up the wounded soldier and ran inside, his body screaming at him to give up and simply accept his fate.

Other wounded were being dragged or pushed through to the keep by anyone who could still stand. Alikain ran around to the western front line to cast what wards he had left to shield the remaining forces against the dragon fire. From the ash clouds ahead, a spear pierced through and hit him in the calf, knocking his feet from under him and sending him, crashing to the ground.

The gossamer-clad thalenar emerged from the haze, already in the walls, chuckling at Alikain's crumpled body. Haughtily, she stepped over the slumped bodies of the fallen, her hips slipping out the lateral cuts of her dress.

Ara saw Alikain fall, the mighty inquisitor clutching at a golden spear that stuck through his greave. Nocking an arrow, she prepared to shield him, waiting for her moment to strike. Seeing the thalenar's focus now locked on Alikain, she took a deep breath and let loose a mighty flurry, casting her magic through her arrows to do as much damage as possible. The arrows were vaporised in her wards, the splinters dropping harmlessly to the ground.

The acolyte turned, intrigued at this development, and sent a shadowy bolt of magic directly into Ara's chest. Her wards glowed, then shattered, returning the spell to the caster as they did so. The bolt struck the thalenar and shattered her defences, causing her to stumble at the attack. Rage contorted her face and she paced towards Ara, violet energy swirling in her hands.

Alikain seized the opportunity, removing the spear from his calf in one smooth motion. His greaves had absorbed most of the energy, only a surface wound adding to his exhausting list of injuries.

The spear was perfectly balanced, if a touch heavy for his liking. He crept forward, the thalenar now distracted, her wards appearing to be down. Launching the spear, he watched it sail through the air, before charging soon after it. The acolyte sensed the projectile and sent forth a burst of magic to splinter it in its flight, Alikain piercing through the shards.

Her eyes widened as she realised her mistake. Her other hand threw a wave of purple tendrils, arcing toward Alikain, who was now dangerously close. He gave her a sickening smile and caught the energy in his hand, the arcs forming a protective net around him as he harnessed her magic. The acolyte began to falter.

A yurinduur charged Alikain down but, with a flick of his fingers, the energy turned the creature into a cloud of dust. The inquisitor siphoned the energy of the acolyte's next spell, a portal – her final attempt at survival, and deflected the feral charge she made with her dagger. Wasting no time in piercing her heart with a snap of his arm, the runes on his sword glowing bright as he did so.

The acolyte let loose a torrent of magic onto the field, directing her dying fury at Alikain. His smile faded as he concentrated, his sword now absorbing any magic she was attempting to call upon. The web of energy surrounding him grew in intensity until he could hold onto it no more. He screamed, ripping his sword from her chest and sending a bolt of lightning into the dragon flying above, just as it was about to bathe the keep in flame. The thalenar slumped at his feet, dead.

The energy struck the dragon's chest, and it sent a mighty roar into the storm. Alikain used the lightning as a tether, and dragged the dragon downward, forcing it to collide with the upper terraces of the keep. A husk of smouldering flesh that shook the masonry with the impact.

A fireball from the siege engines sailed over and hit Alikain's wards, shattering the last of his innate defences. Shrapnel scattered over the ground around him, residual fire licking at his exposed skin.

Captain Yvlynne was now in the centre courtyard, wings of fire erupting from her back, the flames of the braziers forming a tornado around the keep. Glancing back at the portal, the last of the elves escaping, she caught Alikain's eye.

This place took Goronil from me. I will take everything from them. Slaughter them all, Alikain. Every last one. Was the last message he received from her, and with a solemn nod, he was relieved of his duty to her. She was now surrounded by pure destructive energy and was not going to allow Alikain any time to argue. He hobbled over to the entrance of the keep and toward the portal.

Ara had run along the wall and began making her way safely down as soon as Alikain had begun his attack, unleashing too many spells for her to keep track of. She looked back at the field. Her eyes caught sight of the acolyte's golden mask on the ground, its false eyes empty and soulless. Captain Yvlynne was wreathed in a fire that was threatening to overwhelm Dilen'Nahen and she was exposed to both her fire and the charging army of Ilvithiir. She ran toward the keep, her senses threatening to overwhelm her at any moment.

The air left her lungs as Alikain grabbed her shoulders, picking her up and throwing her against the wall. A wave of black energy shattered the rock of the wall behind where she had stood, the keep now collapsing in vast partitions from the damage sustained. She panicked and looked around, seeing the fading light of the portal through the falling debris. As she attempted to make a break for it, she was swung round once more, almost in a dance with the inquisitor. Focused on scrambling to the portal, it took her a moment to realise that he was bullying her to protect her from the flight of evocation spells being flung at them from the figure descending the stairs to their right.

The dragon walked down the stairs, its draconic form having been shattered by Alikain when he pulled it from the sky, forcing it to drop its form in favour of a thalenar's, masked and hungry. He growled and threw spell after spell at Alikain, his partner in the fierce duel. The inquisitor sent bolts of lightning in return, shielding the dragon's spells or absorbing them to use against him.

A ball of fire struck Alikain head on, with his wards too weak to shield them both. Ara cowered, her arms thrown up to cover her face as the last of Paylorn's wards flared to life, absorbing most of the peripheral fire before shattering and falling to the ground like fireflies.

Waves of heat from the burns on her wrists made Ara hiss and her fingers trembled within her still glowing gauntlets. She collapsed against the wall, and cried out, trying to release the steaming buckles and free her hands.

Alikain helped her, casting her gauntlets from her hands to swing from her wrist strap, but allowed her no additional time to recover as he pulled her in the direction of the portal. At the base of the stairs, laid the dragon with a hole in his chest; Alikain having concluded the duel.

They darted forth, into the portal room, their salvation at hand. He whirled her around, pulling her down, onto the floor with him before rolling them beneath a table. He stifled her anguished cries with a panicked hand clamped down over her mouth. Ara frowned and whimpered in pain, but the inquisitor's expression turned deadly, silencing her as his body froze and his grey eyes flicked up. Ara's gaze followed his, and she felt her heart freeze over.

The menora had broken through Yvlynne's fiery torrent and was feasting on a corpse that had not made it through the portal. It looked up, red eyes glowing in the darkness as it sniffed at the room, apparently unfazed by the keep collapsing around it, looking around for the source of the intrusive sound within its feasting ground.

It turned and got onto all fours, its hackles raising with a low resonating growl. Ara's eyes widened in terror as it tasted the air, all its senses engaged in searching for them, shattering furnishings with wide swipes of its claws. Dozens of reavers now skittered through the doors and flooded the room. They were officially overrun with their path to the portal becoming a death trap.

Ara shivered as a sickly wave of fear washed over her, she wanted so badly to shut her eyes and pretend she was back at home. That Alikain's hand clamped over her mouth was Rylia's instead. That they were hiding from a deer's sight to get close to it before it scampered off. That the tears behind her eyes were from looking at the sun through the forest canopy and not from fear of being torn apart by ravenous teeth and razor sharp, chitinous limbs.

In this moment, Yildrin's words rang through her mind; *Controlling your fear in the face of danger, now that is bravery. Take charge of your mind... Trust in your fellow elves...* Ara turned her tear-filled eyes to Alikain's. She carefully pulled the small velvet pouch from her pocket, offering it to him as a last resort. He released his grip on Ara, and a smile of relief relaxed his features, only serving to worry Ara further. He grabbed the crystal with it now glowing in his hand.

He stood, pulling Ara up with him to resume their dance. This time Ara was ready, moving with him, her magic bubbling to the surface, awaiting the perfect moment. He threw the *lenlialarla* into the room's centre, where it hovered for a moment, spinning slowly at first but then, at Alikain's incantation, it sped up until it was a ruby blur of flashing lights, emitting a high-pitched scream. The menora pounced at the elves but Alikain predicted the creature's movements and spun Ara out of the way, where she was able to unleash the last of her own magical reserves, clearing the route of the chittering reavers.

The final dash was made in the light of Captain Yvlynne's cataclysmic fire and the shattering of the *lenlialarla*, through the tunnel of fire that Ara created and into the portal.

Ara flew through the realm between realms. Her body bending and twisting. In the moment before, she had forgotten the horror of her previous portal experience, but she was all too glad to go through it again knowing that it was sending her home. She landed in the marble halls of Tour Mardesi, breathless and vomiting blood. Ruunidil ran to her and got her to her feet.

"Here she is! Alikain too!" he shouted to white-robed figures that faded into shadow as Ara lost consciousness.

A Foreign Mind

Ara woke in the halls of the Druidica, her skin covered in soaked bandages and the smell of herbal remedies suffusing her sinuses. She was alone, in a stone hall, but definitely in the Druidica. She had visited Rylia many times in this very ward when she was still a healer.

"Isol… Isolation! Really?" she exclaimed, tearing the bandages that had adhered to her healing skin.

Wincing with each step, she strode to the main doors and began hammering relentlessly at their steadfast latches. Her skin was covered in burns, already showing the first signs of healing, though that didn't stop her eyes from watering as each rap on the door brought forth a fresh image to her mind. Her own bloody handprints reached out to her each time, grabbing at her fists.

Rap: Flames, engulfing monster and elf alike. Rap: The lifeless eyes of the ranger. Rap: Sentinels surrounded. Rap: The golden mask. Rap: The tears that ran down Captain Yvlynne's cheeks. Rap. Rap. Rap.

She fell to the floor and burst into tears. Sobbing and huddled on the cold marble. She was alone, save for a pair of red eyes staring out at her from the darkness.

The doors opened. The healers ran in and got her back to her bed. They brought her food and drink and spoke to her gently, trying to calm her down. She sat, hugging her knees close, refusing the bandages, unable to get words in through the sobs. Their hands grasping at her… tripping her… ripping at her. Their voices… their cries… their screams.

"Stop, stop!" she managed.

That was not the healer's job, however. Ara needed help. Her wounds were opening, and blood was starting to drip onto her sheets. She was becoming hysterical and needed to be calmed.

Ara snapped. These were not healers. The reavers needed to be stopped. The bed moved and she felt the ground erupting from beneath her. She screamed and her hands turned to flame as she leapt across the beds, out of their grasping limbs, turning to face her assailants. They fled out of the doorway. Around the corner came a figure in a long green dress wearing the crown of the *forehaltha*. This crown, this false mask, these were the thalenarians again. She unleashed her fury at the figure as the world faded into the abyss.

Dawn's cool kiss welcomed her into the embrace of a grove of great oak trees. She was still in the Druidica but... how? She had just been... somewhere. Crimson skies of rolling thunder replaced by overhanging branches that rained down green leaves as opposed to suffocating ash. Song of insect and bird alike had chased away the clashes of battle with their sonorous melodies.

"Drink this," the figure sitting next to her said, her tone gentle and soothing.

She grabbed the cup. It was tea. Cold... but that wasn't the worst thing, perhaps.

"Who are you? Where am I?" Ara begged, tears welling up inside.

"Rylia. You are in the Druidica," the soft reply came.

Ara's blinks were taking too long, but her eyelids were too heavy to rectify this.

"My sister is named Rylia. She is a Queen," she replied softly. Her words seeming foreign in her mouth.

The figure chuckled. "A Queen you say? Well, she must not be a very good Queen. If she was, there would be more cupcakes in the world and perhaps she would not have sent her sister away. Do you not think so?"

"I guess. Cupcakes are nice. She is a good Queen though. She will be the best Queen. Except for the cupcakes," Ara said. Curling back up and giving in to the weight of her eyelids, melting into the undergrowth.

***

Her eyes opened, this time it was in the dead of night. She was back in her own room. Her pillow had that tea stain on it from the beginning of the year when she was reading in bed and got a fright at the thunder outside. She thought of that thunder and images came flooding to her mind again. She shut her eyes tight and sobbed until her body ran out of tears.

She lay in her bed until her sweat had soaked the sheets and her tears, the pillows. Her head was pounding and the muscles in her jaw ached. She needed to feel the forest. She needed to be away from the darkness. She was at home among the trees and there, nothing could chase her, nothing could beat her. She would be safe.

Late at night or early morning, either way, Foretilatava was sleeping. She had no jersey nor shoes, but she couldn't turn back. She needed the trees and was already feeling better with the grass between her toes and the fresh air in her lungs. She slid silently between the buildings, ignoring the faint glow of the *lenlialarla* and ducking toward the equid stables where she might find Anmas.

The trip was lengthened by her stealth, a thief in her own city. Avoiding the bridge, she knew of some trees to climb whose branches crossed the waters, eliminating the risk of running into anyone. She kept wind blowing through her mind, chasing away any thoughts, allowing her to simply focus on her goal, one step at a time. These steps just happened to be very large steps. She needed to climb one in order to see the next, to see what lay ahead. So that is what she would do.

Ara tucked in the back of the open stables, the horses not reacting to her stealthy intrusion. She found her way to Anmas's stable to find it empty, devoid of hope. This was the next step. She took a deep breath, focusing on the sharp smell of the barn. There was warmth and comfort in this scent, familiarity, but not the kind she was craving. To the fields. Anmas must have been turned out for the night and was merely sleeping with the herd in one of the groves. She turned to leave. Ahead, a pair of eyes staring hungrily into her soul. Those piercing red eyes. The beast snorted and steam, no, fire! Fire erupted from its maw.

Ara ran deeper into the barn, towards the back exit, the doorway forming a portal into the moonlight. She was panicking, tripping on her own bandaging and ripping at her wounds. She ricocheted off of the building's pillars and walls, spinning into each step blindly, her legs no longer able to support her. She hit the ground and screamed as the world faded from view, the humanoid figure next to the menora ran and leant over her.

"Ara! It is just me; Galviir!" the thalenar said, reaching a hand down to finish her off. His golden mask replaced by one of shadow.

***

Thunder cracked and Ara snapped up in her bed. Her linens were clean and smelled like citrus and lily. The air was heavy with the incoming. She clenched her fists on her blanket, her mind was clearer, and she was able to focus on controlling her breathing.

The door opened and Rylia entered with a tea tray. She handed Ara a mug and a fresh cupcake with strawberry frosting. Rylia was in pyjamas, pausing at the foot of Ara's bed.

Rylia smiled and walked around the room, collecting chairs and spare bedding... Ara watched her curiously for a time and then chuckled. A blanket fort. She climbed inside the rickety structure, her body screaming at her as her skin bent and stretched with the movement.

She sipped at her tea and ate the frosting off her cupcake in silence. Hiding from the thunder in her mind. Rylia fiddled with a music box and set up a gentle tune as it began to drizzle softly in the forest outside. Ara smiled at the safety of their little bubble, looking up to see Rylia wipe a tear from her cheek.

"I will be fine. Sorry about all this. Galviir? Did I... the healers..." Ara started.

"He is fine, the healers are too. They should have known better, plus, they all needed to be brought down a peg or two. Their medical abilities are excellent, but their bedside manner has always been lacking." She managed a chuckle and met Ara's gaze.

Ara smiled, "Glad to help... Rylia, it is real. It is so much worse than we can imagine. There were just too many, and they were just playing with them." Her tone was sinking.

"I received the report from the head of the expedition, Ruunidil. He was impressed with your abilities by the way," Rylia said, lightening her tone.

"I got a ranger killed and nearly sacrificed six sentinels because—"

"I have the report of everything that transpired. What you did was nothing short of miraculous. The fact that any elf made it back alive is beyond what we all could have dreamed. We had no idea what it was you were facing over there," Rylia interrupted, decisively.

"How many... How many made it back? Where is everyone else?" Ara asked, not sure if she was brave enough to hear the answer.

"Fifty-five, including yourself." Rylia touched the back of Ara's hand, gently breaking through the panic that had started to form behind her eyes. "Fifty-four who would have died an unimaginable death, in a land not their own, had it not been for you." She pulled her hand back and tapped the side of her teacup. "Ara… Daltorus has been called. The council will convene at the University Arcanum where we shall deliberate on the next course of action. Sinien Tarvia has agreed and will be sending representatives as well," Rylia said. Her royal demeanour shining through her pyjamas and cupcakes.

"Not that buffoon, Kespin, I hope," Ara jabbed.

Rylia laughed that musical chuckle of hers. In that moment, the world made a promise to repair itself, just for her.

"I am not sure exactly, but the report sent through was undeniable. They will be sending the best person for the job. Of that, I am certain," she said, finishing the last of her tea.

"I am going on your behalf," Ara proclaimed.

"Ara—" Rylia began.

"Nope. You got me into this. I started something terrible here and if you do not let me fix it then I will tell all the fellow nobles that you have a foot fetish and enjoy the smell of boiling cabbage," Ara said, lifting her nose defiantly, her shaking tone and sniffling nose betraying her.

Resigned to the fate of the argument, Rylia replied, "You use that threat far too often. It makes me worry about the books you have been reading. So be it. You shall be one of my representatives. The congregation leaves three days from now. Be warned though, you are passing your medical before you will be allowed anywhere and that much I am not budging on."

Ara chuckled, taking a deep sip of her tea.

Walking Dead

The sun stood high in the fresh mountain air, the breeze carrying the mist from the waterfall onto Alikain's back. He was smeared against the cliff face as he launched himself to the ledge above, locking in his fingers and securing his hold. He lifted his feet, and with a sigh of relief, he planted them on a less precarious groove in the rock. He was thirty metres up at this stage and a fall would have him tumbling into the frigid mountain pool, in a manner slightly less gentle than being caught in a stampede of wild horses.

He surveyed the landscape below, taking in the view of his little mountain vale, his secluded grove. The winter trees were blooming, and the fruit would start forming soon. His hut was little more than a roof to keep the rain off, but it was his and it was safe. The waterfall that he climbed beside came from a mountain spring another twenty metres further upward. The stream the pool then formed would snake its way through until eventually becoming a direct tributary to the River Isfrisairis.

The family of trees in the grove consisted of elders, oaks, willows, birches, yew and many more. Fruit trees were also present. Alikain was particularly fond of the pomegranate and the citrus trees although something about the harsh environments required by apple trees also intrigued him.

He rolled his shoulders, feeling the pull of the many scars he would rather forget. The climb was easier from here on up, and with only two metres left to go, he made short work of it. This high up on the face, with the constant moisture of the waterfall and the increased sunlight hours, grew a species of moss that was of particular interest to Alikain. He swung a leather satchel off his back and scraped the moss into it, using a knife. He left enough in patches along the face so that the regrowth would be swift. He packed the knife away and tossed the satchel into the trees below, slowing its uncontrolled descent.

The azure sky above, the mountain birds calling and the air free from smoke and torturous screams. Alikain closed his eyes and stood on the precipice taking in the peace of the world. His ears rang, slowly at first but then to a cacophonous clanging of scraping metal, roars of rage and tormented cries. He opened his eyes with a start, glad to see that the scenery before him was still his home. He steadied his heart and let himself fall forward, bracing into a dive.

He sailed through the air, not caring if he lived or died. The roar of the waterfall and the wind rushing past drowned out his thoughts and emptied his mind. He broke the surface into the icy pool, his chest constricting and his limbs burning. He surfaced and quickly dried himself off on a towel from a nearby tree. The satchel was caught in a branch close by and was liberated with a quick nudge. Alikain changed into dry breeches and put his linen shirt back on before making his way to the hut.

Inside, the kettle had begun to sing. Alikain made a pot of tea, leaving it on the table to steep. Next, he retrieved the moss from the satchel and set about bruising it with a mortar and pestle. He added boiling water and set it to steep. When the steam stopped rising, ending its trance it had on him, he strained the tea.

He took it with him to the side of the pool, close to the waterfall, and drank peacefully. Only when he had finished did he notice that he had his sword drawn and at his side. He grimaced and went back to the hut to oil the misted blade before returning it to its sheath.

There were a few items of food that had been delivered and he was slowly making his way through the supplies until he had time to set up his own production again. He retrieved some sugar, flour, salt and eggs to mix together. He added some starter dough and set his creation out on a cloth-covered wooden plate to rise. Orange marmalade today, he thought, sifting through the jars set out on a shelf by the hearth. Finally, he set about juicing some oranges until he had a pitcher filled to the brim. The bread had been placed in the oven above the hearth and was already smelling heavenly. Patience is key when making bread, but Alikain's patience abandoned the sinking vessel when his stomach grew louder than the waterfall.

With the late lunch completed in his usual spot, Alikain ambled back to the hut to return his dirty dishes and his sword. He cleaned up and packed everything away in its respective cabinets, sighing at the completion of his duties for the day. He strained the second cup of moss tea and drank it soon after, feeling his newly healing wounds relax and cool down. Night was creeping across the sky and so he set about lighting the lamps in the grove. One hundred and forty-six in total, afternoon turned to dusk and dusk turned to evening, as he filled and lit all the lamps one by one.

Once the moon was the dominant force in the sky, he found himself unconsciously fiddling with the loose leather strapping on his sword's handle. With a grunt, he went to sit in the centre of the grove, amongst the highest concentration of light. Here, he had dug out a small burrow at the foot of an oak tree in which to sleep. Filling it with cushions and linen to lend the arrangement some sense of comfort and civility. Alikain crawled inside having his sword drawn and at his side as he let the sleepless night take him.

Morning eventually came to bathe the mountain peaks in its warm glow. Alikain crawled out from his little burrow and dusted himself off. He rubbed his weary eyes and returned to his hut, tossing his sheathed sword onto his bed. He set about chopping up some fruit for his breakfast while the water boiled for his tea. Eating by the waterfall, he relaxed and even managed a small nap after his meal, waking with a start and almost crawling up the cliff face. He gathered his wits quickly and chastised himself for the reaction.

A few of the flowers had started to form fruit already. He watched as the bees visited one flower after the next, checking up on each of them in their turn. A mountain weaver was tirelessly building a nest, pulling leaves out, packing new ones in and soaring through the trees in the grove, hunting for the perfect building materials. He was not the only weaver to have picked the grove, so the competition for the best leaves was fierce indeed.

Alikain arrived at a clearing where he began the business end of his morning routine. He stretched out his tight muscles with ground stretches and various exaggerated poses. The squirrels chattered quizzically at the oddity before them, but Alikain paid them little mind. Next, he began pulling himself up on tree branches that he had dusted clear of any insects before finding a grip. Push-ups had him starting simple and ending so that only his hands were touching the ground as he pushed himself into the air. A series of jumps and lunges later and he was struggling to keep his breath. He then drew his sword from its sheath at his side and began striking poses, meticulously carrying out his practised movements. He would ensure his footing, engage all the necessary muscle groups and focus primarily on his smooth transitions.

During the workout routine, he had a wire loop maze with a bronze runner ring that he would concentrate on to keep aloft with his magic. It was simple enough for anyone to keep them floating so he would run the ring along the loop maze ensuring that at no point did the metals touch. Keeping his mind in shape was a perk at this stage as mostly, it kept him distracted.

Finally, came his archery training. He kept his focus on the maze whilst slowing his breathing and controlling his heart rate. He fired shot after shot, using an Isfrisairis ranger's recurve bow, with deadly efficiency. It was a half metre diameter target set fifty metres away with tree limbs blocking the path Alikain would shift his angle of approach and distance to the target, regularly, so as to not fall into a pattern.

With the day wasted away, he made more bread for his late lunch. This time, he allowed the dough to rise fully before baking. Still fond of the idea of the orange marmalade, he sat by the waterfall. He had some of the moss tea with him as his morning activities had only served to open some of the scars. He finished his meal and returned to his hut to smear honey on his open wounds.

His heart kicked at his chest, threatening to burst through. He was no longer alone in his vale. There was the sound of a snapping twig that seemed to echo through and send shivers down Alikain's spine. He had his blade out before his heart could finish its beat. He was on the hunt.

He crouched in the trees dancing between the patches of earth that allowed for his silent footfalls. Creeping closer to the source of the disturbance, a stag sprang through the blueberry bushes, giving him a start.

Not amused by the turn of events and his heart still pounding, he scanned the rest of the grove systematically and in a grid-like fashion. He searched the branches of trees and between the leaves of the bushes. Nobody had snuck in, and he was still safe.

Regretfully, he chased the stag out of the grove and sealed the entrance with some minor wards. Next time, he would have more warning should a sizeable intruder come barrelling through.

The start to the lamp lighting had been slightly delayed but he still made good time in illuminating the grove. All one hundred and forty-six filled and lit, he returned to his burrow for the night. He replaced some of the dirtier linens and cushions with fresh ones and settled down. Sleepless, in the shimmering glow of the grove's lamplight.

Morning came once more and Alikain made short work of his stretches and exercises. He spent some time reading by the waterfall, keeping his ring puzzle up as he did so, swirling it around his head for extra difficulty. It wasn't long before he found himself napping in a shallow slumber with a tight grip on his sword's handle.

His ward began tugging at his mind. Someone had arrived and was merely letting him know. His heart couldn't have handled another full-on intrusion like that of the day prior. Alikain made his way through the trees in the soft earth, sword at the ready and his own personal wards up. Waiting patiently at the entrance to the grove were two sentinels and Chancellor Nildinar of Isfrisairis.

He was one of those present at his debriefing and was less than keen on Alikain's need for recuperation during times of such urgency. He was very civil about the ordeal though and had even been the one to arrange the delivery of supplies to Alikain's grove on a regular basis. He had offered a guard detail too, but Alikain was still waking up in a start, finding himself screaming at his visions more often than he'd liked. Such seemed embarrassing to have witnessed by the hardened sentinels who had little idea of what they had all been through.

"Inquisitor. How are you doing?" greeted the chancellor.

"One day at a time." Alikain nodded.

"We need to get you to the Arcanum. You can continue your healing there, but they will have questions. The scribes finished transcribing the copies and they have been delivered. We need to leave right away. I am not fond the uncertainty of our future," said Nildinar, rubbing his eyes and dusting his robes.

"Let me pack, I will be out now," replied Alikain, barely able to keep the fear out of his voice.

The sentinels approached Alikain, but he dismissed them back to their posts at Nildinar's side. Letting them see the rabbit hole where he slept wouldn't be the greatest thing for his reputation.

He retrieved the linens and packed everything away, sealing the cabinets as he did so. He piled the supplies given outside his hut and packed all his intact clothes into a travel pack. His sword and a dagger were strapped onto his belt. He prepared a quiver with the remainder of his good arrows, storing the arrowheads of the others in a small pouch in his main bag. With a sigh, he turned to leave his little vale behind, bidding farewell to the trees and the waterfall, thanking them for their help.

Nildinar nodded at his readiness and agreed to send a cart to retrieve the supplies before they went off. The sentinels formed a loose column with Nildinar and Alikain each getting into their own horse-drawn carriage for the journey.

Coalescence

The market town of Ixilth was by no means small but, by elven standards, it was definitely rural. There were no towers reaching to the sky nor were there public theatres with packed schedules for the season at hand. Run mainly by merchants and innkeepers, the town served as the final stop before committing to the journey into the mountains, eastward and towards Isfrisairis.

Built at the same time, and hewn from the same stone, the white marble buildings stood out as a pearl in the forest clearing with the farmland extending around it. Nobody knew how the town received its name, but it was the one that stuck, now seeming to fit like a puzzle piece.

Ara had been in the town for a day already, awaiting Chancellor Nildinar's convoy, so that they might travel to the University Arcanum together. She kept to herself for the most part, the wardens sent to accompany her were friendly enough, but she craved solitude. Not quite trusting herself to be around company while she felt so raw inside. She managed to visit a few shops at a time, stopping each trip early with the sound of crashing pots or the smell of smoke from the cooking fires dragging her back to a place best left forgotten.

She was furious at herself, not being able to keep hold of her emotions at even the slightest of provocations. Still, she attempted the dizzying array of mental exercises the *Tamore Narana* had given her during the days leading up to her departure.

She had purchased a few pastries from the bakery on the way through Foret Dela, remembering the excellent selection that Lethrik had procured. She had even saved some cheesecake in case he was still travelling in Nildinar's convoy, although it was starting to look a little... aged.

A travelling bard walked past playing a gentle song on her fiddle, skipping through the streets with a flock of hummingbirds following in her wake. As fate would have it, Ara's gaze followed the bard's path and came across the bakery for Ixilth.

Not wanting to play favourites with Foret Dela, she entered the shop tentatively, smiling at the gentle ring of the bell above the door. A rosy cheeked baker popped up from behind the counter, standing on a box to be able to see over the display.

"Hello!" she chirped; her face covered in flour with a baker's hat balancing precariously on her head.

"Hi there! My name is Ara. How are you doing today?" she greeted.

The elf was extraordinarily young and seemed overjoyed at Ara's presence. "Well, Ara, it is a delight to meet you. My name is Peppa. What can I get you today? Tarts? Doughnuts? Jellies? Cakes? Scones?"

Getting the impression that Peppa was preparing to recite the entire menu, Ara interrupted with a chuckle, "I would like to try your cheesecake if you have any? Some scones would be great too. Perhaps if you have cream and jam as well?"

A small frown crossed Peppa's face as she disappeared behind the counter. There was a whirlwind of activity and small explosions of flour that puffed out before she rose again, her head spinning from the activity.

"Done!" she exclaimed victoriously. "I managed to fit twelve scones, two bottles of jam and a whole cheesecake in there! Oh, and a small jar of cream," she finished, heaving a small picnic basket with a wrapped central parcel onto the table.

"That is wondrous! What flavour jam? And how much does this cost?"

"One of the silver ones and two of the little bronze ones. Flavour of jam? Oh! Uhmmm… It could be any flavour! I guess you will just have to find out." She grinned. "Also, you have to wear this!" she finished, stretching over the counter and sticking a daisy into Ara's hair, tucking it behind her ear.

Ara burst out laughing and handed the coins over. "Peppa, you have made my week!" she said, waving goodbye and leaving the shop.

Peppa waved back manically before diving right back into the flour vortex she had going behind the counter.

***

The convoy came to a halt in the merchant's square. The horses were glad for the reprieve, being treated to fresh cut greens, clear mountain water and a grooming after their tack had been removed.

"We are meeting some folk here. We are to travel with them to the University Arcanum. Meet me back here in an hour, I just need to see if they have arrived," proclaimed Nildinar to all those that looked keen on stretching their legs in the town.

This was not the first time the town guard were seeing sentinels, but they found themselves staring in awe nonetheless. Despite having been on their feet for three days of hard walking, they looked as fresh as the day they had left. Royal banners waved from their spears with their mighty tower shields at their sides, baring the Isfrisairis eagle.

Alikain broke away from his group to visit the alchemist. It was a small shop that was no doubt attached to the greenhouses five hundred metres off on the northern edge of the town. Called '*Irin's House of Alchemy and Naturopathy*', the shop was small and spectacularly well fragranced. Flowers, dried leaves, and uprooted tubers lined the wall hangings whilst poultices, specimen jars, potions, and philtres filled the shelves. All this behind a storied mahogany door with a small silver bell that rang to greet each customer.

"It was just lying there, teeth gone, not even an attempt at skinning it!" a patron exclaimed to the shopkeeper.

Irin was old, even as elves were concerned, and probably knew her craft better than she did the back of her own hand.

Handing over a coin pouch and giving a sly smile to her patron, she replied, "It has been a while since I have had some basilisk scales in my shop. Thank you for thinking of Irin's as your first choice."

The patron, a woodsman, or potentially even a ranger, beamed at the sight of the coin pouch. He pocketed his haul, saying his goodbyes. Turning around, he almost scrambled over the counter to join Irin at the site of Alikain at the threshold. He stepped to the side giving free passage to the startled woodsman, who gladly accepted his escape, tipping his head in a bashful nod.

Alikain gathered his shopping items under Irin's calculating gaze: Manuka honey for any split wounds, turmeric to get blood flowing to his muscles and more of the mountain moss to reduce inflammation. Irin decanted and packaged the required amounts for Alikain and gave him an expectant grin. He returned the smile and handed over the coins.

"You need to see a medic," she said, breaking her shopkeeper's persona as Alikain's jerkin folded open, revealing a blood-soaked line on his shirt.

Alikain shrugged non-committedly, holding up his bag of recently acquired medicines. Irin frowned, blowing a strand of her steel-blue hair from her sculpted face.

"Even inquisitors need healers, Alikain," she said to his retreating form, his step faltering only slightly at her remark.

Leaving the shop with a deep breath and heading back to the convoy, Alikain saw that they had now been joined by a contingent of *forehaltha* soldiers. There were no doubt wardens on the rooftops, scanning the townsfolk, although Alikain couldn't spot any at this moment. The Tree Guard had added another carriage to the convoy and were looking just about ready to turn back to Foretilatava.

The final leg of the journey was about to begin, and for the last day they would likely be joined by gryphons and another few carriages bearing the nobility from Isfrisairis. For now, however it seemed they were only to pick up the *forehaltha* nobles. Nildinar finished off a conversation with their captain and made his way to the front of the train, where his carriage awaited.

Alikain attempted to sneak into the tranquil isolation of his own carriage, letting the sentinels know of his return with a clearing of his throat. As he opened the door, he shut his eyes and sighed in defeat.

"Hello, Ara," he said, catching a glimpse of the *forehaltha* royalty to his left.

She was smiling a little, which is far more than he expected. Her wounds had healed well, and she stood with a strength that suggested that she was doing better, physically. Still, like all who had escaped Ilvithiir, there was a shadow to her eyes, an echo to that smile.

"Hello, Alikain. It is good to see you."

"And it is good to see you. I believe we will be leaving soon. Would you care to join me in this carriage? Nildinar has threatened me with his company, and I could use some reinforcements. A journey with political commentary awaits," he said, rolling his eyes.

She ducked her head then replied, "No thank you. I wish you luck though. I am going to remain in the carriage that has cheesecake," she said, showing off her picnic basket.

At that, Lethrik's head popped around the corner. "Cheesecake?" he asked, grinning at Ara before jogging to her and giving her a hug. Ara reciprocated enthusiastically, all too happy to see the ranger. His hair was

114

just as bronze and his smile just as warm as when she had last seen him.

"I will hold on to this. Yildrin will be glad to see you in one piece," he said, liberating the picnic basket from her arms despite her incredulous protest.

Nildinar had finished speaking with the head druid, Vexhimarith, and was now intent on spurring the convoy into motion. Ara spared a moment to ensure her luggage had been collected before following Lethrik's rapidly retreating form. He shot her a wink and then disappeared behind the wagons, her picnic basket in tow.

Passively annoyed at the loss of her pastries, she climbed into her carriage and settled in for the day's journey. She pulled out her journal, as the carriage gently lurched forward. Staring at the blank page set before her, wondering how beneficial reliving her memories in written form would be for her mental recovery. The *Tamore Narana* had given her a full evaluation but at the end of the day, they did not see the horrors she did. The case studies they used to develop their treatments were not based off of Ilvithiir, nor did they include Ara.

Ara's stomach had been growling for some time now and she was becoming worried that they would soon think her a caged animal instead of elven royalty. It was mid-morning and lunch was more of an optional stop for these official types, meaning that little by means of a reprieve lay on the horizon.

Her carriage door swung ajar, and a sentinel reversed through, sitting down on the bench across from her, the vehicle straining at the added weight. She slammed her book shut and tried to look as important as possible to meet her surprise guest. The sentinel stared at her for a moment, painful silence filling the carriage. He broke the stare-down by reaching out of the window, opposite the carriage door and stealing a basket from outside.

"Hey!" came Lethrik's outraged cry.

He lifted the basket onto her lap. Her cheesecake! And only two scones missing! She beamed; her luncheon was saved.

Removing his helm, Yildrin smiled knowingly at Ara.

"Yildrin!" she exclaimed, relief clearing her worries and calming her fidgeting hands.

She leapt across the cramped space in the carriage and threw her arms around him. It was a little like hugging an anvil, but she didn't care. He chuckled and returned her embrace before releasing her back to her own seat. Ara sat and crossed her legs, pulling the picnic basket onto her lap.

"It is good to see you, my dear. That ranger is far too comfortable in the world. He did assure me that none of the baked goods were poisoned and that he was happy to test them on your behalf," he said, shifting awkwardly to better fit the cramped space.

"Well, that was mighty kind of him. I will be sure to thank hi—" She was interrupted as the wagon hit a loose cobblestone, jolting them harshly.

She let out a gasp, her arms shooting out to steady herself. She shut her eyes to settle her nerves, not wanting to break down in front of the sentinel.

"Take it one day at a time," he began, a tone expecting nothing from her. "Remember, nobody went through what you did. Only you were able to see through your eyes, feel through your hands and hear with your ears."

Ara opened her eyes, instinctively investigating the cabin for danger before turning to Yildrin. His eyes searched hers for a moment, their icy blue depths burning through Ara's fear as he held her gaze, calm and steady.

"You are going to be told how to deal with everything you have been through, but that will be the healers treating a disease they do not understand in a patient that they have never studied before. You have spent an awful long time in that head of yours and, thus, you know how to get through this better than them. Take their advice but ignore their pressure. Also, I would like a scone please. The elderberry jam I think," he finished, abolishing the expectation for her to respond and eagerly rubbing his gauntlets together in anticipation of lunch.

"…You saved my life, Yildrin. You saved so many of their lives too. You were the only one who was able to prepare me for what was out there. Thank you," she said, wiping her involuntary tears away with her sleeve as she tried to prepare the scone.

She wasn't crying exactly. She was happy but her body needed to do this. She chuckled as she sniffed loudly, handing him his lunch.

He smiled and patted her knee sincerely. "You did it all. I was just there to undo the damage all those academics and politicians did." He chuckled.

She had a lovely lunch with him, eating scones, with the gentle rolling of the wheels and chatter of the convoy preventing any awkward silences.

"Does it get easier?" she asked.

Yildrin looked up at her, confused.

"These experiences. I may have to go there again one day but… I need to know that I will be strong enough to handle it," she confessed.

"*Raéna ilpa*, you are already strong enough. You would have to be a fool, or an inquisitor, not to be affected by your time there. It changed you, but that may not be a bad thing. This is how we grow, Ara. It is how steel is forged and how roads are paved. Just be patient and allow yourself to go through your natural emotions. Holding yourself back may be more damaging. Use this and you will be stronger for it," he finished, grabbing another scone from the prepared pile, this time going for the apricot jam.

The University Arcanum

The cool crisp geosmin bathed the hills in the high-pressure air. The land now submerged in the shadow of the rapidly approaching storm clouds, rolling and crashing their way through the azure skies. It was a winter storm on its way to soak the ground and scare the terrestrial creatures back into their caves or into the forest shelter. Raethran, seeing the danger ahead, began his descent down the hill and into the rocky valley that lay below, his pack bouncing and clanging with its hastily packed contents.

The training yard was set out before him in Students littering the grounds went about their routines. Many were sparring with magic and weapons, some were running exercise drills with others dispersed between the action; reading and chatting whilst trying not to get hit by a misfired arrow or spell.

The marble lecture buildings were on the east side of the yard, each extending four stories up in modest elven architecture compared to the main hall of the Arcanum, with the ornate columns running along the walls, extending above and joining the upper tiers with flying buttress supports. The black tile gable roofs over the halls and the towers both spired and angled, testing the imaginations and exploring the abilities of the *tarviahaltha* architects.

The main hall, the first of the buildings to have been constructed, stood at the south of the yard and was the centrepiece of the University Arcanum. The greenhouses flanked the lake that was to the west of the fields, extending over the water with the many outdoor botanical experiments surrounding it. The mage towers of the Arcanum were no doubt crawling with activity but all that could be seen from Raethran's vantage point were the snow-white towers with cathedral windows spiralling upward to their opaline crystals, each the size of a horse cart, at their peaks. At the base of the towers stood tall stained-glass windows depicting sages and researchers in their chosen fields of magic, from the striking reds and blues of the evocation to the soft hues of cerulean and lavender of illusion.

Between the buildings, gravel paths lined with knee-high hedgerows guided students to their classes. Ivy, wisteria and foxglove reached across the marble walls, lying dormant for the season.

Raethran entered the grounds, approaching from the east and humming a sombre tune despite his jovial mood. He hopped along the footpath toward the dorms, keeping his face concealed with his hood. The students, he passed by, glared and sniggered, no doubt speculating on the punishment that awaited him.

With a dash of stealth, he flanked the dorm to the rear. He made the precarious traverse along the moss-covered rocks that set the foundation against the lakeside, flicking his arms through a disturbed wisp colony. Their faint ringing and gentle darting glows buzzed around his head before giving up on their pursuit as Raethran's gaze turned upward. After a subtle scan of his surroundings, he began the ascent using the masonry of the columns, ledges and windows to make short work of the climb towards the window of his room.

Move your feet, support, then move your hands. Check your footing and your hands will find their way. A simple climb but it wouldn't be the first time he ended up mangled in the rocks below, if he fell now. The icy water and the awaiting bruises were simply not worth the effort. With his hands on the ledge of his window and relief in sight, he fell.

Well, there was more than just gravity at play. He was being pulled. Pried from his hold and flung towards the softer ground, he landed before the four figures that stood, waiting to bestow their judgement.

He landed with an elegant crumple on a soggier section of earth, kicking mud into the air and sinking his right foot deep into the freezing quagmire. Raethran let out a deep sigh before lifting his head to face his assailants, still star-fished in the muck.

For what it was worth, he had attempted to make an effort with his appearance this morning. His robes, whilst not pristine, nor well laundered, were at least patched where it mattered. He had even taken extra time this morning to, well not to brush his hair, but to pull the brunette tresses back into some semblance of tidiness. His deep blue eyes were in stark contrast to the mud that now covered his face with him abandoning his soaking hood and facing his assailants.

"Stars above, boy! Get yourself up. Lest the land herself is rising, I see no reason for you to be this late?" inquired Master Selen.

Raethran winced. "Master's Selen, Graxith, Filthin, Ilkiir," he began, greeting them each in turn as he stood to attention, "I got a touch lost on the checkpoints, I assure you that all were completed. As for my route of entry… Well, I just thought that I could sneak by unnoticed and return to report my completion of the hike once I had cleaned myself up a bit."

Master Selen was the head mistress of the Arcanum and her reputation for having a stern disposition was not unfounded. "Master Graxith, I am sure you can handle this boy's punishment. I see no need to waste a formal inquiry here. The sooner you are gone, the sooner I can breathe a sigh of relief. You highborn will have me in the infirmary before long," she said, scrunching her nose and storming off with the sycophant and head of illusionary magic, Master Filthin, on her coat tails.

Raethran flicked his robes, removing the larger clumps of mud. A throat cleared and he met the gaze of his judge and executioner, Master Graxith, the head of martial skills, tactics and weaponry. His reputation was one not renowned for its excess of leniency or compassionate displays of forgiveness.

"Why are you late, boy? Though you lack many fundamental skills, I have never seen cartography or walking to be among them," asked Graxith, his monotone words slowly pushing a dagger toward the truth.

"I took a wrong turn, Master. Through the Ixilth valley," Raethran answered, straining to maintain eye contact and daring not to lie, instead, making liberal use of his ambiguity.

Ilkiir, the head of enchantment magic interceded, "Well, Graxith, the boy clearly has his head in the clouds again. Perhaps a group spar followed by laps of the lake and then cleaning out the greenhouse sap trays for that tailored flare you enjoy so much?"

Graxith growled his approval and strode off. Ilkiir held out his hand expectantly, the tall and imperious looking elf sighing impatiently. Raethran nodded, waited a few moments for Graxith to round the corner before pulling a wax-stoppered vial from his pack.

"What was it?" Ilkiir asked, inspecting the vial against the light with his piercing copper eyes.

"Basilisk, green… adolescent," Raethran said, dipping his head to the ground. Fear saturating his tone.

"You are lucky then. Is this it?" he asked, raising an eyebrow.

Raethran shifted uncomfortably before pulling a fang from his pocket within the travel coat. "And this, but I hope I may keep this one?"

Ilkiir pocketed the fang. "I will send more tomes to your room. You did well boy. Good luck for tomorrow though. Graxith has a lot of pressure on his shoulders to get you lot through graduation. Letting him down will not make your life any easier," he said, still in the middle of his organoleptic exam of the vial's contents. He was too distracted to notice the nose between his eyes yet alone any response Raethran could muster.

The two parted ways, this time Raethran using the main entrance, passing by Filthin on his way in. The elf's golden hair tied in a ponytail with his embroidered robes displaying multiple glyphs that seemed to fade in and out of focus at their own accord. He didn't take any note of Raethran as he came in, which sent a jolt of relief through his chest. He scuttled the rest of the way to his room, so keen to avoid people that he often spun through doorways, scraping his pack in the process. Once there, he closed the door and set about the various locks, shaking the cold from his fingers.

Raethran turned, lent against his door and let out an uncontrolled chuckle. Grindol, Raethran's roommate, sat up at the disturbance and put down his textbook that he had been making his way through. *'Toxicology of water plants in the Northern Freshwater systems'*, fourth edition by the looks of it.

"You came dead last! How, with all the celestials have graced you with, did you manage that?" Grindol said, concern and outrage wracking his expression.

Raethran smiled in response and swung his pack from his shoulder. He began unloading the contents onto his bed, for Grindol to inspect. The elf peered over with his ears pricked and mouth agape.

"Ilkiir had a runner chased off near Ixilth and wanted me to swing by and check it out. Turns out the runner is afraid of willow limbs on a windy night. I was however able to run into a merchant at the end of his rounds, looking to liberate the last of his stocks," he said, pulling out three more intact, wax-coated basilisk fangs and another vial and a half of venom. "Then there were these along the way and I thought you may find some use for them?" he offered, removing an array of healing herbs. Some were shoved in the pack, others pressed in a book and a few suspended in jars of water. "Plus, what worth would a pass to leave the grounds have if I could not get this?" he said, pulling out two bottles of mint-flavoured mead, baring the mark of the Ixilth merchants.

"This must have been your life savings plus your soul to a stranger at a crossroads. How did you afford all this?" asked a somewhat bewildered Grindol, fondling the basilisk fang and smelling some of the pressed rosemary.

"Look, what I spent is just a figure in the final formula. It is what I can sell it for that matters now. The merchant gave me an agreeable price for the lot, and he seemed less than willing to travel further than Ixilth with the meagre stocks he had remaining. Now the fellow has time to return, replenish and get back out there before the cold locks him in Isfrisairis."

Grindol laughed. "Fine, fine, but if the devil comes knocking at our door, then you better hope he chooses your bed to drag down. That is, if you do not get your head bashed in first. Whoever are you going to sell this overpriced liquor to? Even Tuliin would be hard pressed with these at your mark-ups," he said, inspecting one of the bottles, recoiling at the smell.

"Look, I do not need much more if all goes well. My classes are paid for now. All I need is my own kit and I will be set for the rest of the term," Raethran said, falling onto his bed and liberating himself from his travel clothes in exchange for his day robes. Tossing the mud caked mass, into a wicker basket in the corner, with a wince at seeing mud scatter across the room.

"Your pride will be the end of you. The sooner you realise this, the sooner your life will become infinitely simpler," said Grindol, his look of disapproval hampered by his wonder at the basilisk fang. "Why do they even coat these things? If you are worried about pricking your finger, then a sheath would do far better."

Raethran dismissed the advice. "They do it to keep the venom from oxidising. It loses its potency rather unpredictably once it yellows thus, making paralytics with it will become more unpredictable. The venom stoppers are waxed on too. Now, the storm is almost here. We better get to the mess hall before those apes in the mage tower start calling lightning on us again," he concluded, tying up his shoes and rolling out his shoulders.

"Those apes are my friends and that only happened one time. Plus, it missed you by two metres at least! If we had wanted to hit you then you would be well done, have crispy edges and ready to serve by now." Grindol chuckled.

Raethran shot him a glare worthy of Master Selen herself as he flicked his magic to sweep the floor clean of the mud. In a huff, he jogged out of the room, locking the door behind them.

The activity in the halls was rapidly increasing as students returned from their day's labours. Thriol, a behemoth of an elf, pushed Raethran to the side as he strode by with a war axe on his shoulder and blood droplets on his helm. His colossal foot falls strained the floorboards in time with the jostling of his loosened heavy plate armour.

The mage aspirants were darting here and there in a mad dash to gather what they needed for the experiments in the tower. Some carried beakers, others conducting rods, whilst the lower-ranked students were stuck lugging bottles of solvents and sacks of mischief in the wakes of the seniors.

Raethran danced as best he could between the hurried masses, but his dexterity couldn't save him from the twins: Lirith and Astril. They wash-lined him under each arm and dragged him into their room, not saying a word as they did so. Grindol knew better than to get involved. He waved over his shoulder without glancing back and grabbed a copper coil array from a first year, joining the exodus toward the towers.

Raethran was thrown against the bed in the twin's' room with little by way of ceremony. The room was covered in rare orchids and hanging flowers in a cacophonous assault to the senses. The flowers, though, were all rich shades of maroon, purple and black giving off a vibe as sinister as the twins themselves. Their desks were functional, yet each were set before large opulent mirrors with silver vines twisting around the borders and a single crystal sconce set at the top. A peculiar mixture of quills, makeup brushes and knives set upon the rich grained mahogany desks.

The beds, despite Raethran's position, were rather lovely. They had goose feather duvets and pillows. The heavenly mattresses, like everything else in the room, were brought in by the twins in conformance with their exceptional taste.

Amidst such a luscious décor, the grime covered, and travel worn Raethran was the only thing out of place, a mouse in the den of the twins. Acutely aware of this, he searched for exits but was soon confronted with the futility of his situation.

These two creatures were the visage of physical perfection to the point where they made their decadent décor look as if it belonged in a traveller's inn on a lesser road. Their angular yet supple features, their piercing eyes and aureate hair that danced in the windless room. Dressed in tailored, form fitting robes with embroidery to further accentuate their powerful forms. Cuts in their robes revealed more skin than was necessary, especially in the northern climates, but one could not help but be intimidated.

Lirith began the inquisition by setting her hands on her hips and biting her lip ever so slightly before, in a voice akin to a honey covered stiletto, asking, "Back from your trip? Lovely. I hope you had a good last meal in the wilderness. You see," she continued, slipping a petite vial onto Raethran's lap.

Both her and Astril leaned in close, placing their hands on Raethran's legs, above the knee and a little too high up for his comfort.

"We have been stuck here, using your little potions, elixirs and philtrum's…" They lent in even closer now, their hair draping against his chest with their weight now firmly rooting his legs to the bed.

Raethran had retreated to lying near horizontal at this point when Astril finished in little more than a whisper in her sultry tone, "But imagine our surprise when, after we made a fool of ourselves giving him all manner of compliments for the hour following, that nothing… seemed… to have worked?"

The final syllable sounded like a silver coin being dropped into a crystal decanter, their faces practically touching his at this point, their sweet breath warming his face. Escape options had become limited as now, their legs were crawling onto the bed, pressing in on Raethran from his sides.

It was at this point that Raethran noticed their free hands bringing long, silver daggers to his throat. He shook himself free of their siren charm and stood on the bed, crawling backward against the wall.

"My dears, this," he said, holding up the vial with his other hand ready to defend his throat, "is no mere poison, philtrum, elixir or otherwise. Let me guess, he did not drink whatever you spiked in its entirety? Pulled a face at each sip?" The twins answered the rhetorical question by exchanging a look. "This, my sweet harpies, is a perfume for you to wear and thus, it is not advised that one should ingest it. Though no harm shall come of it, save for a wasted glass of wine," he said, spinning the vial in his hand, revealing a small label explaining the application methods.

His reply seemed to only anger them further as illustrated by their hands tightening over the silver daggers, and their muscles clenching in their slender jawlines.

In response to this, Raethran offered, "Now, dab a little on the nape of your necks, and give him a hug. Get him in close. As stated before; it cannot bring him to love you, but it will cause the dopamine and endorphin rush from which you can capitalise. My personal tip, however? He is surrounded by sycophants, even on his off days. Play the tease, be what he cannot have and let him see you on the field with those blades of yours. Show him that you are a challenge worthy of his interest. He can find adoration in any corner of this place. What he seeks, is a touch of fear."

The advancing ladies paused to consider this, looking to each other for approval. This was all Raethran needed. Sure, it was good advice, but the twins enjoyed their torture and they had yet to have devoured their fill. He dove for the door and spun through it, shutting it behind him, praying to outpace their reactions.

His timing was perfect, for as he closed the door, there came two thuds and corresponding shudders mere nanoseconds apart of which he could only assume were daggers aimed at his back. With a sigh of relief, he ran off and dissolved into the mass of students, trying to shake of the smell of rose and oleander from the room.

Raethran ran to the east wing of the main hall and collected his meal along with the biggest mug of hot chocolate he could find. He sat close to a window at a yet unoccupied table. His joints were killing him, and he had gashed open his lateral right thigh.

Getting his wounds seen too was on his list but the infirmary would ask far too many questions. He thought of leaving it but the more he looked at it, the less he was able to convince himself that it didn't need closing.

The storm was upon them now and the rain was running down the windows, giving him a brief distraction. He loved the rain but having just finished his hike did give him some joy as this rain would have soaked him to the bone despite any amount of tree cover that he could have found. Being inside the hall allowed him to enjoy the cold misted breeze from the entryway whilst avoiding the hypothermia and drenched socks.

An elf walked over and sat at the table opposite him, bringing with her the sweet jasmine smell of the infirmary, "Three days late and nothing to show for it. Why did I ever think that throwing my lot in with you would be a good idea?"

She brushed a strand of mousy brown hair behind an ear, her warm blue eyes flashed to his and she quirked an eyebrow, waiting for his answer. Her soft features doing little to bolster her mock impatience as her smile began to shine through like the sun between the clouds.

Raethran awoke from his distraction; his face lighting up at Ahrayn's arrival. "Who would not want to be this close to a dashing rogue such as myself? Broke, broken and gift-less as I may be," he answered, standing up and giving her a theatrical bow.

"Hmmm, I guess you are in the clear but next time; a seed of an oak tree, a song sung in sunlight, a promise in the moonlight and for you to be on time," she said, picking at her own meal consisting of a fruit salad with a dollop of cream.

Her hair was tied back into a messy bun with rogue strands escaping, despite her efforts, rolling forward to tickle her chin and cover her face as she looked down to her dinner. Despite her happiness, reservation lingered in her activity.

Raethran's mood grew hesitant. "How are you feeling?"

"All right," she replied. "The new potion, Masters Oldiir and Hital have me taking, seems to be making the pain worse though. They wanted to see you when you got back. Apparently, you lot have been conspiring again and have a new approach under consideration?"

"I will head there after dinner, but you, *inunelunail*[23], need to eat something a touch healthier than this. You cannot expect your parents to do all the work!" he said, reaching for her bowl.

She withdrew her fruit salad horde and let loose a small growl at his hands until he retreated, "Excuse me, when you have your own body eating you alive from the inside then I will let you eat whatever it is you want."

"Fine, fine, fine then at least do it properly!" he exclaimed, lifting the hidden mug of hot chocolate onto the table, ignoring the few scolding drops that he spilt on his lap. She chuckled, happily accepting the offering.

They finished their meals together, exchanging stories. Ahrayn told him about one of the misbehaving horses in the barn that was on his third stable door of the month, and Raethran shared the tale of how he got pulled off the side of the dorms by Master Selen. He told her about the merchant he had met in Ixilth and a tree that he had passed which looked like it was leaning down to pick a patch of mushrooms from the forest floor. Of course, it was only the tree that she was interested in, but she entertained the rest of his ramblings, nonetheless, holding back her judgement at Raethran's knack for stepping into the sights of the masters.

"I need to scuttle off and you, my dearest swallow, need to go to bed.

---

[23] My moonwing (swallow)

We will greet the sun tomorrow, dark and early," he said with a wink, standing to give her a warm hug and a kiss goodnight.

They remained in their embrace, drawing out the time they had before parting ways. Ahrayn went back to her dorm room as Raethran headed to the alchemy labs in the lecture building. His heart kicking out at his chest for not staying in the meal hall a little longer with her.

The room was piping hot as the more dedicated of the students smelted precious metals into filigrees, pendants and connection arrays. Some were leaning over vast cauldrons hurriedly chopping roots, dicing leaves and juicing stems within the clouds of steam. Ringing hammers and smashing boards cutting through the gentle hum of chattering students and bubbling cauldrons.

Masters Oldiir and Hital were in Oldiir's office, in discussion over the pages of multiple opened textbooks. Raethran stopped to stir a cauldron for a student that had dropped his mandrake root on the floor where it was now running away.

The red-faced student dove to the floor and caught it in a burlap sack. He raced about cutting and juicing the root before pouring the contents into the cauldron with an exasperated, "Thanks," muttered to Raethran.

The masters' attention was drawn by the commotion and at its conclusion; they ushered Raethran in. His tears were thankfully masked by the steam of the lab, but he wiped his eyes nonetheless before entering the office and placing the vials of basilisk venom on the table.

Master Hital was the first to speak, her voice relieved, "Ilkiir's suspicions were correct, I take it?"

"Basilisk, adolescent, green." Raethran nodded.

"Collected fresh?" she asked.

"Within the hour, stoppered and sealed," he replied, looking at his feet.

She strode forward and embraced him for a blink of moment.

Master Oldiir patted him on the shoulder, inspecting the vials. "Well done, this will do nicely! We may finally be able to alleviate her pain. The colour is still pristine, and you have enough of it to last over eight months by the looks of it! What was Ilkiir's cut?"

"One vial, one fang," he replied.

"One of each? That… Does he know—" he began, his face flushed with rage, bashing his table as he did so. Master Hital shuddered at his visceral response, stabilising a teetering pile of books.

"I kept three fangs, all pristine and sealed. If you do not mind, I would like your permission to work them in your shop? They may sell for a bit more and cover the fare. It can be my masterwork project and I believe we can get a buyer come the winter market? At least then, we can afford to buy some more venom when the time comes."

"Should the time—" Oldiir began, this time being silenced by Master Hital.

"Thank you." She whimpered.

Raethran looked up pleadingly. "She cannot know, I mean, that is… I told her I bought this all from a merchant in Ixilth. If she knew… Well, it would be a lot more dangerous than a basilisk." At this, they both smiled, tears welling up in their eyes. "But I need to know. What sort of prognosis are we looking at here?" Raethran finished, maintaining eye contact as his voice crumbled.

"Six months," answered Oldiir.

"To a full year," added Hital.

Raethran nodded, retreating from the labs, allowing the masters to begin their work.

Quiescent Stirrings

Raethran awoke to the chirping of the birds that sang in the early dawn. He jumped out of bed, ignoring Grindol's protestations at the sudden activity in the room. He changed the cotton dressing on his leg and dressed himself in his faded black tunic and breaches with grey cotton wraps up his arms and shins. His belt was more a wrap to tuck things into and with that, his cloak was the last to be adorned. He ran out to the training fields where Ahrayn was waiting for him, looking fresh and cheery despite the hour.

They gave each other a wordless greeting and a kiss before walking around to the western shore, their hands firmly clasped. They climbed to the top of the hill overlooking the lake, not minding the frozen dew gathering on their legs. The Arcanum was lit up by the magical glow of *lenlialarla*, which were set in light sconces lining pathways and upon external wall mountings of the Arcanum's buildings. These providing the soft hue that set it glimmering in the dappled sea of green of the surrounding forest.

Ahrayn broke the silence, "So the new medication seems to be doing a treat. Not an ounce of pain. Something about a new muscle relaxant that they could add? Also, do not think I have not noticed your limp. If you were a horse, they would have locked you in a stable for the winter by now."

Raethran chuckled. "Well, that charade lasted long. All right, I had something of a detour through Ixilth and that merchant I told you about was selling an array of remedies. I picked some up, as per your mother's description, and delivered it to your parents last night. As for the leg, my wondrous dexterity was unable to save me from a fall I had, now four days back? Anyway, the infirmary has endless paperwork in the way so I thought you may be able to sort it out for me?"

She sighed. "Your lies have more holes than Vildloliad cheese. I am glad for the help though, thank you. Now, let me have a look at that leg of yours."

Raethran smiled and removed his breeches to show the wound. Removing the bandage, Ahrayn gasped when she saw it, releasing a flurry of punches on his healthy leg.

"You fool, why would you go and do this to yourself? It looks as if you slipped and fell on the talon of an alithaer! Look, it is already starting to fester," she said, poking the area next to the laceration, making him wince.

"Ow ow ow, okay, yes well, that is certainly not the treatment for a festering wound!" he exclaimed, laughing through a tear.

"And neither is leaving it for four days! At least it looks like you made some attempt to clean it…" she said, further inspecting the exposed tissues.

She hastily pulled her hair into a half-ponytail and rolled back her sleeves. Her petite nose and rounded cheeks were flushed from the cold, but she held onto her casual smile through her concentration. After a few minutes of planning, Ahrayn uttered a small incantation under her breath and the wound edges began to stretch. She cauterised some of the tissues further before pulling them off so that only the healthy tissue remained. Raethran was in sheer agony at this stage, collapsing at the completion of her debridement and spells, not being able to feel the cold water being poured over in the preliminary clean.

"Sorry about that," she said, genuinely concerned despite her outrage at his behaviour.

Scar tissue stretched together, forming a bridge across the gap in the skin that contracted like a drying river. She ran her fingers along the silver scar line, muttering comments on her work.

Raethran, catching his breath, dried his leg and pulled his breeches back on. "No, it is I who is sorry, for both your sake and mine," he said, massaging his new scar, "I will just have to be quicker next time! But look, the sun is about to peak over the horizon there," he exclaimed, leaning in and nudging Ahrayn's shoulder.

They sat together watching the sun rise with a flask of tea that Ahrayn produced from her bag, drinking and enjoying the moment as she hummed the sweetest of tunes to greet the day. The sun shone through the vales ahead, lighting up the treetops and reflecting off the frost on the grass. The rain had left the air clear and the day smelling fresh and ready for whatever lay ahead. The university was silent save for a few students, returning from their early morning exercises and meditation.

Master Filthin was running among them in the tiniest of shorts revealing his ghostly legs. Master Oldiir possessed his daughter's talent for waking early and had the fires in the lab smoking again with wisps of iridescent greys, blacks and even purples. The horses in the fields behind the main hall were slowly making their way to their troughs, waiting patiently for those with equine duties to give them their food, morning health checks and grooming.

To the south, students could be seen making their way through the trees carrying sacks of meat and fresh bedding for the gryphons. The fledglings were already hunting on their own but a little supplementary feeding during winter gave them some extra strength. Plus, it was a way for Master Graxith to punish those that dared cross him.

The breakfast bell rang, and students began emerging from the dorms in full force, the mages looking particularly bleary-eyed after their night of storm chasing. Ahrayn and Raethran smiled at each other, stood up, and set off down the hill humming in harmony and dancing along the grass. The Arcanum had awoken, and magic was in the air.

Ahrayn bid him farewell and ran off to her divination lectures without stopping for breakfast. They had delayed their departure, hoping that their tea would be enough to carry them to lunch time. Raethran followed suite but went to the office of Master Graxith instead, bracing himself for the sentencing that was to come.

Graxith was a firm believer that his lecture hall was the blood-soaked training grounds and that his textbooks were the bruises and gashes one collected therein. He was tough but he was brilliant.

Graxith's history was laid out in his expression of casual disdain for all that was around him. His short platinum hair combed back, not daring to get in the way of his concentration. Broad set for an elf, it was clear that he was ready for war, but, knowing Graxith, it was difficult for Raethran to think of a war that could be ready for him. He was also one of the few elves to grow a beard, it being the only manicured feature about him at a short trim with sharp edges.

His assigned lecture hall had been converted into an armoury, containing all manner of weaponry from across the continent. Some were ceremonial but rarely, did any of them have their edges dulled. After all, what use is having a tool that is never intended for use?

Training weapons were stored here too, leaving little space for indoor lectures. Mostly, they held lectures outside, where the fighting would take place and where the elements were as much a consideration as one's footwork. The first years received wooden swords for the first few weeks, but even these had iron cores that could cause significant damage if used incorrectly.

His office had windows that faced the fields, walls that were lined with various personal weapons and family crests representing the battles he had fought in. His crowning jewel was the oil painting of The Battle of Tour Hassette Harbour. It depicted Graxith on a boat that was set aflame, surrounded by no less than twelve Mardacian marines, with him wielding nothing more than a halberd and an expression he referred to as "The Warrior's Resolve", which is what he told the artist to name the piece. He did enjoy mentioning that he originally wished to call the piece "Slaughter of the Pitiful", but that the artist nearly fainted at the name. Considering that it was commissioned during the final peace talks, this was likely best to be avoided.

Raethran entered the room at attention, walking over with surprising ease now that his leg had been healed. Graxith was at his desk scribbling angrily on a piece of parchment, no doubt filling in injury reports from the day prior. He signed his name with a flourish that involved his entire arm, dotting the end by piercing the quill through the page and into the desk.

"Your timing is excellent, as always, young Raethran. Tell me, when will these saplings in politics ever realise what it takes to train you lot? You have a brother in the higher ups do you not?" Graxith said, moving onto the next page before scrunching it up and tossing it in the flame muttering, "He barely lost a finger, and it is attached now anyway!"

"Well, Master, they will fret that the training is too hard until the day of battle where they will then cry out that it was nowhere near hard enough. My only hope is that we come out of the other end, having lost only that which was necessary. My brother is a politician, Master. He has recently been appointed to the council of Isfrisairis."

"Humph. Well then, I suppose he is not all bad. I do not appreciate you using his politician's ambiguity, but there is wisdom in what you say. Time for your sentencing? What would you like?" he said, looking up. He preferred to play with his food before devouring it whole and, by now, Raethran was just a mouse at the end of his claws.

"Well, Master, I know of a two-hour trail route that has a couple of hills so maybe that followed by shovelling the gryphon roost and then to finish it off with some war hammer sparring," he offered sincerely.

Punishment was never unfair with Graxith, but he loved the idea of training his students past the point of university regulations, under the guise of punishment.

"No. The war hammer may hurt more but you are the weakest with the axe. I do not need any unnecessary injuries at this time. I will write that down for the next time you step out of line but for today, we have a meeting between the council and some or other *merhaltha* royalty. They are having a sit around the table to discuss how others need to fix their problems but would like a demonstration from the Arcanum to keep them busy whilst they wait for all to arrive. I was thinking we might get the final years to put on a little show for them," he said, a calculating grin pulling at his cheeks. "Do not think that you are off the hook, though, we will be needing to show these folk what we are made of here," he said, dismissing Raethran with his return to stabbing at the paperwork set out before him.

A day of what Graxith called 'showing off' sounded like a daunting prospect but Raethran was glad to be free of the other punishments. The gryphon roost had a nasty habit of leaving a smell on one's clothes that would have you sleeping outside for the following days. That and the thought of being pecked on the backside when kneeling to pick up a bucket was enough to make it a duty befitting of being used as punishment.

Being in the final years at the Arcanum was a mixture of complete chaos dispersed between periods of utter boredom. Sure, there were loads of tests, exams and research assignments but there were also fewer subjects and, better yet, they were subjects chosen by each student according to their aptitude and path. These classes covered every profession available to an adult *tarviahaltha* in modern society, from artists to Royal Sentinels in Isfrisairis; from travelling tradesmen to arcanists and artificers.

Ahrayn was studying to be a physician and was currently one of the best at the University Arcanum. She was so good, in fact, that she would often take shifts as head clinician at the infirmary and even consult on a few of the referral cases from the cities. Her workload was immense but mostly focused on the healing arts for which, she displayed a natural proclivity. She was also gifted in the art of divination, although she required some refinement in this regard. She had many visions and could put images of the future into tangible scenes rather easily, however her ability to do so would wax and wane. Besides she had never felt a calling to the art, unlike her choice to become a physician.

Raethran on the other hand went for the broad stroke. His goal was, initially, to become a ranger. He took alchemy, zoology and geology for his natural research classes. Martial works and riding would keep him alive as he travelled the continent and evocation, abjuration and illusion magics to satisfy his sponsor's basic requirements. Survivalism and artificing were included in the mix as rangers often spent time away from cosy hearth fires, opting for dungeons and ruins riddled with magical traps. A daunting course load in the best of times but Raethran was hardly the most studious of individuals. Sure, he passed his exams but only just. His primary focus was on the application of his skills over the numbers on his academic record.

His first task of the day was to finish his masterwork level alchemy task for his portfolio. He ran off to the labs, his mind dancing between ideas for the project, taking into mind his skill levels, what would sell for the most and what would be the most ethical to sell.

The thing about basilisk venom is that it kills you by paralysing every muscle in your body including your heart and those muscles involved in respiration. It does this efficiently. However, at smaller doses, you can induce paralysis and anaesthesia making it perfect for invasive surgery in the medical fields. Although it is usually too expensive for such with the alternatives also being safer. If you were to dilute it further then; it becomes a paralytic by relaxing all the skeletal muscles in the body and removing control of those muscles from the individual's grasp, making it perfect for bounty hunters, monster slayers and those that generally have the coin to pay for it. Diluted further still and you have a muscle relaxant and spasmolytic that can provide pain relief in even the most severe of cases.

Raethran set out plans for arrow tips. He could fashion six bodkin point caps, venom infused and armour piercing out of the enamel from each fang. This, he would set into a steel bracket for weight with a treated oak shaft and gryphon feather fletching. The range would be poor but mail or scale, this would penetrate it all whilst maintaining the accuracy needed for such an expensive arrow. You would only need to hit your target once after all.

First, safety. He retrieved goggles and thick leather gloves from the locker room when changing into his overalls. Then, he fetched a set of enamel files from the tool room along with a table clamp and a selection of hacksaws. Finally, he grabbed some polishes and polishing sheets of different gains. Once everything specific had been retrieved, he went about his work at one of the free workbenches under the meticulous and safety conscious watch of Master Oldiir.

He started by placing one of the fangs into a sealable jar with some tinder. He set it alight and capped the top with an airtight stopper that had a nozzle for an injection port. The tinder had a flame at first, then a smoulder, then nothing. After this, he injected oil through the port and agitated it until the tinder remnants floated upward. Next, he placed it in a holding apparatus and set a burner beneath it and watched as the wax melted off the fang and to the surface of the oil.

Soon, the fang was cleaned, and a small coating of the oil remained. Satisfied, Raethran removed the fang and set the saw blade to work, placing pieces cut out into a bowl of oil and splashing those exposed edges as he went. He had a catch tray in place to collect any dust or fragments that fell during the cutting process.

With the loose arrowheads cut out, he began shaping them one by one with the file, dipping them in the oil regularly. This work was particularly tedious as he had them spun into the table clamp which he had to undo and redo for each submersion. Finally, came the polish. An easy enough job after the filing and one that was mainly for aesthetic purposes. Once they were all complete, he set to work on the other fang, making sure the completed ones were in oil and sealed in a vial.

All the caps completed, he got a white-robed student, a first year, to fetch him the steel cap mountings, shafts and feathers from the fletcher's requisition room with Raethran's writ account. The student, Kaylith, then assisted Raethran in the setting and fletching process. He explained the helix angles of the feathers up the shaft, the advantages of using bone as a nock over woods or metals and the balancing of the final arrow and the effect it had on flight.

He went over the safety procedures when dealing with nonconventional arrowheads and how, when dealing with clay fragmentation tips to crystal incendiaries, you should always treat them the same and that is; with the utmost care. Kaylith drank up the information, elated to be able to assist on something so dangerous and story worthy for her fellow first years. Raethran was younger than her but had spent most of his years in the halls of academia whereas she was a new arrival.

"These are basilisk fang tips," he explained to the wide-eyed first year. "Now, the idea is that they still have enough residual venom in them to paralyse any target that the arrow penetrates and to do so with various efficiencies according to the surface area present. The venom oxidises relatively quickly so it is best to keep them sealed. They are single use, but the venom is slowly absorbed percutaneously so it is preferred that it penetrates the skin in order to work fast enough."

He then went over poison tables relating to the basilisk venom and its properties, discussing diffusion rates through the enamel at different temperatures, the effects of oxidation on the venom, and the toxicity of the venom according to the species. Together they calculated an array of surface areas for different sized targets and selected the required engraving tools to gouge out grooves at the depths required. They also debated the material properties of the enamel itself, seeing how strong it was but just how brittle that would make it and thus, deciding if the points were sharp enough to penetrate armour but thick enough to not chip.

The better half of the day had gone by but Raethran, with Kaylith's extensive assistance, had finally completed all the arrows and sealed their tips with a pull-away wax tab. They would not be suitable for anything elf sized, being far too deadly, but should a hydra come knocking then you would certainly feel safe in answering the door.

"This evening; I will be back to apply a resin to the tying threads and paint the detailing on the shafts. You are welcome to assist but it is just the boring stuff that is left," said Raethran, finally looking up from his work to see that Graxith had been waiting in the doorway. As he caught Raethran's attention he jerked his head towards the training fields, and then stormed off.

"I will be here. I need some help with my communication amulet assignment and was hoping you could lend a hand?" she asked, desperation clinging to her tone.

"Of course. Those links can be a nightmare to establish and identify. At least the atomic agitations are easy enough to magnify and then it is just a case of choosing your tonal transmitters in a pitch you enjoy," he said, clearing up the workstation as fast as he could. Kaylith saw the rush and, in her relief for his aid, motioned for him to leave as she remained to pack away the last of the files and beakers.

Raethran changed back into his day robes, the once black fabric now a faded grey with its many 'character' tears throughout the cotton outer layer. He placed the arrows and collected filings into his locker and shut it with the self-locking click.

Break a Leg

Raethran ran out of the labs, through the lecture building's corridors, fixing his dishevelled robes as he did so and placing his overcoat on just before exiting the building. With a start, he saw all the final years already gathered in their pristine black robes, serving as a welcoming party for the convoy of carts, horses and sentinels approaching. Raethran nodded to an annoyed looking Graxith who had joined a line in front with the other masters that were all adorned in their dress robes. He then found a gap next to Ahrayn who gave him a welcoming smile, picking off a fragment of desiccated lamia scale from his coat. The greeting party was silent to the point where all that could be heard was the rolling of cart wheels, the marching of elf and equine alike and the gentle breeze that now flicked at Ahrayn's hair in rhythmic gusts.

The musicians of the University had gathered next to the final years, a firing line waiting for their mark. One of the students, a harpist, was in her pale grey robes. A junior, in her second to fifth year, Raethran wasn't sure, that had to be the most junior member of the band to have played in an official ceremony in all his over twenty years of study. He smiled at this and pointed her out to Ahrayn who looked impressed, even going as far as to make a discreet clapping gesture.

The convoy grew closer with the tension being eased by the band starting up. They were playing '*Upon the Mountain Breeze*', a gentle tune but calm, beautiful and full of wonder. The weather was less autumn and more winter now with an icy chill, the sun just barely having crested over the surrounding hilltops into the university's valley. There would be snow soon and everyone knew it. The sentinels drew into the courtyard of the main hall first, forming a quick set perimeter and looking as fresh as if they had only just begun their journey despite their plate armour and colossal shields.

These were the Royal Sentinels of Isfrisairis, no doubt sent to escort the royal guests from Foretilatava and Sinien Tarvia as a show of good faith from the *tarviahaltha*. They had their grey capes embroidered with gold and silver thread on the edges, each in armour with the Isfrisairis royal motif of the sky eagle curving its wings upward with a clear-cut white sapphire in its chest. Their full-face armet helmets had the visors open in greeting. Each had steel shields bearing golden eagles on the polished steel background and bore flagged spears in their free hand. They all had weapons at their hips and on their backs, seeming ready for war at a moment's notice.

Thriol was beaming with pride, seeing his future in these gold and silver sentinels that awaited commands like an ornate chess set around the convoy. The elf may be a brute, but his aspirations certainly were honourable, even if his temperament suggested otherwise.

The royal cavalry dismounted and stood to attention beside their horses. Olethia, another of the final years, with copper hair and green eyes that could read your mind, had her sights set here. Their steeds were one of Isfrisairis' greatest secrets and said to be as smart as an elf and about as magically gifted too. Then, there were the gryphons, although they were only really ridden when they were needed or when there was a particularly auspicious occasion. Their rider's' armour was just as opulent but a lot lighter and better suited for mobility than that of the sentinels. They too had spears, shields and all manner of weaponry at their disposal, focusing on mounted combat and agility.

This was assumed to be it as far as the protection detail went but there were undoubtedly rangers covering every inch of the grounds, scouting for potential threats and planning for impossible circumstances, despite the University Arcanum being nestled in the elven heartland.

The sentinels that remained by the carriages moved to the side and out stepped the Isfrisairis mages in pristine grey, cotton fitted tunics, some with spell book satchels to match and others carrying staffs. They stepped off the carriage and to the side of the doorway, surveying what lay before them. Everyone here would have graduated from this very university and yet, here they stood, expecting assassins around every corner and dragons to descend from the skies and incinerate them all. The band went pianissimo, and the mages announced their charge one by one in clear, magically enhanced deliveries.

The first came, "Chancellor Nildinar of Isfrisairis, Head of Diplomatic Defence and Development." And out stepped Raethran's brother, shielding his eyes from the sun whilst straightening out his overcoat. He looked around and strode forward to begin greeting the masters in his official capacity.

The second mage began as Nildinar shook the hand of Master Selen, "Lady Ara, sister and envoy for Queen Rylia of the *forehaltha*, and daughter of the new moon."

Ara hopped out of her carriage, smiling and looking rather embarrassed at all the fuss before following Nildinar's lead. She walked uneasily as blood flow slowly returned to her legs, the sun blinding her and the cool air flooding her sinuses.

"Chancellor Kilorin, Head of Terrestrial Defence for Sinien Tarvia, Professor of Diplomatic Studies at the University Oceana and Captain of The Moon Chaser." Out stepped a figure clad in silver half-plate armour with a rich blue cloak guiding the wind around him. His skin was tanned, and his eyes filled with adventure. The masters treated his presence with the greatest curiosity, half expecting doves to flutter from within his sleeves or wings to sprout from his back.

The mage at the final carriage cleared his throat, "Inquisitor Alikain, Lord of the—"

Alikain refused to wait and escaped the carriage, giving his mage a casual tap on the shoulder. He strode over to the masters and greeted them with surprising informality. They had all tightened up and lost their colour at the mention of an inquisitor, especially one present in an official capacity. At this reveal, even the students were exchanging worried looks whilst suddenly shifting their weight as if they had all just discovered a stone in their shoe. Raethran and Ahrayn exchanged curious looks with Raethran shrugging it off, ignoring his growing concern.

The masters led the royal guests and the inquisitor into the great hall where a reception had been prepared. Thriol turned to the final years and put on his best sentinel persona, standing tall and pushing out his chest.

"All right, Graxith wants us duelling within the hour. Martial up first, starting with a weapons display. Partners on the board. This will be followed by a group battle, teams also on the board. Finally, there will be a good old fashioned free for all. Then, it is on to Grindol."

Grindol cleared his throat, looked to confirm that Thriol had finished before explaining; "Well… after all that mucking about with sticks, students of the Arcanum are expected to head over to the towers for demonstrations and project presentations. Apprentices will be doing flyovers and agility manoeuvres on the gryphons throughout the afternoon so do not mind them.

That should bring us well into the end of the day so… be impressive, for all our sakes," he concluded, looking worriedly in the direction of the masters. At this, the final years scattered to their rooms to change into their lesson attire.

Raethran instinctively looked to Ahrayn for the plan going forward. She offered a gentle smile and gestured toward the infirmary. The demonstrations had the potential to admit a few patients and there was much preparation required.

"Do not get yourself bashed up too badly. One day you are going to get an injury that not even I can heal," she said, kissing his cheek.

Raethran just smiled for his reply before running to his room. The students had made themselves scarce, only the black and grey cloaks of the final years now seen rushing around the hallways. Raethran threw on his lesson tunic before tapping Grindol on the back for a goodbye and good luck. He recoiled in fright, realising for the first time that Raethran had been in the room with him.

He was hunched over an intricate array of gears, coils and springs. It had been his pride and joy of the year thus far. A device that could record, store and translate any language programmed into it with potential use in the cryptography sector. That being said, you could have an easier time predicting the turbulent flow of water, through an irregularly shaped and angled tube, than predicting when the device would switch on let alone perform its function.

Gathering in the armoury that was Graxith's lecture hall, everyone was eyeing the board for their sparring partners and teams for the upcoming demonstrations. Raethran wormed his way through the crowd but found himself at an impasse when he got to Thriol. He looked up at him, barely being the height of his neck and about half as broad.

"You and me, Raethran. Try to put on a show, will you?" he laughed, bumping Raethran's shoulder on his way passed.

He retrieved a war hammer for his back, a sword for his hip, and a long spear and shield for his opening act, chuckling intermittently as he did so. He strode out of the armoury looking like a sentinel already, certainly carrying himself with the surety of one. The seniors not involved in the fight took note of his confidence, adjusting their betting tables accordingly.

Double checking the list; partners round – versus Thriol, teams round – on his team? He spun around, cursing his luck. Thriol was slower but he only ever needed to land one hit for the fight to be well and truly over. On the other hand, Raethran needed multiple well-placed hits through that armour of his to even make an impact. He chuckled at the irony of it all. Graxith had been the one to draft the table and here Raethran was, reaching for an axe. The only weapon he saw being of much use against Thriol's chosen combination with war picks being forbidden in sparring.

He added a shield and a dagger to his repertoire, but his defence relied heavily on his steel chest plate, vambraces and greaves. He had chainmail for his torso, covered in a leather jerkin, but that was mainly for show. One thrust of the spear or sword would peel through that, and the war hammer would make short work of a castle wall let alone a chest plate. He added a helm for good measure. It had a nose guard and cheek pieces but was otherwise open. Raethran enjoyed airflow above all when it came to head gear and there was no stopping Thriol's strikes to the head, merely the hope for a lucky deflection. He tightened all his straps for the fourth time now, adjusting the oversized shield before giving it up and tossing it to the side and grabbing another axe.

They all started clearing out of the room with Raethran taking up the rear, closing the door behind him. He was watching how his feet parted the grass, noting the plasticity of the blades. They wasted no time in returning to their shape after he lifted his feet with the moisture in the soil removing a vast proportion of the ground's friction.

"Raeth, where is your shield?"

Raethran looked up to see his brother with concern more than worry on his face.

Raethran nodded a greeting. "Hi, I did not realise you were visiting. Axes, faster," he said, gesturing rather pitifully to the weapons.

Nildinar shook his head and cleared the loose pearlescent hairs from his face, sighing and biting his lip. "Do not mess this up. I need you to get this right!" he whispered before touching his forehead to Raethran's. "*Erilsrahas alemen a huliasomene.*[24]"

Raethran nodded and strode forth, attempting to ignore the inspection that he was receiving from the inquisitor. He was scanning Raethran, making him adjust his stride unconsciously. Alikain stood up from his chair, whispered to Graxith before grabbing Raethran by the shoulder, leading

---

[24] Unwarranted haste leads to unwanted mistakes

him back through the door of the armoury.

"Bold choice! One that makes me think you have a plan," he said, entering the armoury and fishing around in the stores within.

Raethran, confused, looked over his shoulder to see all the other combatants already lined up, poignantly awaiting his arrival.

"Alikain, good to see you agai—" He was cut off as the inquisitor found what he had been looking for.

"Here you go, shake your limbs out. Get a feel for them before stepping out there. I want a show, not a dead student. Graxith would be most annoyed at my meddling should that end up being the case," he said, placing lead wrist and ankle weights on Raethran who was now too shocked to even begin to articulate his protestations.

"I would give you some tips, but I have seen who you are up against, and I am curious to see how you fair. Oh, remember to not die. I would hate to lose my first ever apprentice to a training exercise," he concluded, walking back to his seat.

His face bore the marks of a healing burn and its fair share of what could have only been a pitched battle yet maintained a controlled outward appearance which was more unsettling. Nildinar and Alikain had arranged for Raethran to apprentice under him, to become an inquisitor. It was a tough draw but a respectable one. Nildinar seemed intent on having a little brother that wasn't some reclusive ranger in the woods whilst he was off moulding the political landscape of the *tarviahaltha*. Raethran did not mind as he got on well with Alikain and this way, he could still travel the continent after his graduation.

Raethran took the field opposite Thriol who greeted him with a deep bow and a bash of his shield, his armour shining in the midday sunlight, embellishing the impenetrable fortress of equal parts artistry and savagery. Raethran bowed, crossing his axes over his chest before shaking out his arms and legs, getting a feel for the added weight.

The masters, with their royal visitors, had lined up by the great hall for the demonstration with only Master Graxith walking around, inspecting the students. Master Hital looked nervous but at the ready for the usual conclusion of such events. Her junior apprentices, with their white robes, were lined up along their starting line with the medical packs and stretchers.

The Royal Guard contingent had taken rest on the outskirts of the field, only two sentinels remaining at the flanks of Nildinar, Kilorin and Ara for propriety's sake. The gryphon riders had begun the first of their flyovers, scattering shadows across the grounds between those of the clouds. They began in the typical V-shape then performed a choreographed spiral dive out of sight.

Thriol, having chosen the slot front and centre before the spectators, had yet to break his iron gaze with Raethran despite Graxith's patrols and inspections. He was a mighty warrior and certainly looked the part. To have him working for the elves was a true gift but to have to face him in sparring sessions? Well, it was a lot more difficult to see that for the gift it was.

Raethran made to distract himself with his other senses. There were the gryphon screeches, idle chatter of students in the windows placing their bets and the sound of a tree swallow chirping on the rooftops behind Thriol. Raethran smiled, looking up at the sapphire glint of her feathers.

He gave an awkward nod in Nildinar and Alikain's direction, steadying the leather grips in his hands and giving gentle bounces with the balls of his feet on the soft earth. Calming his breathing, he faced his motionless opponent.

Graxith, satisfied with the layout before him, announced the rules of the duels. It was the typical run down they had all heard literally thousands of times during their studies at the university. They were to apply their defensive wards and then no other magic. Battle to submission with non-lethal wounds where possible. Sportsmanship was better left to the gryphon riders or the sinchal players. If they found themselves waking up in the hospital, in a month's' time, then at least they had fought to their limits.

The martial final years went about their pre-duel fidgeting rituals in silence, awaiting the signal. Tuliin adjusted his stance, switching his longsword between his hands with the flicking of his fingers. Olethia spun her sabre in clean arcs that dazzled her opponents and obscured her motives. The twins pacing the width of their arenas in their blackened, form fitting steel plates on tight black leather straps, only daggers and shortswords in their repertoires.

Graxith sounded his battle horn, the same one he had famously used in the Battle of Isalsolla Fields, in a thunderous roar that set the valley quaking. The world answered to his will and the duels began.

Thriol adopted the textbook pose of the sentinel's defensive line, bracing on his hind, shield raised and spear ready to lunge at the slightest of provocations. It was a formidable pose but one that the axes suited well.

Sentinels were unstoppable in a group but alone, Raethran stood a chance.

Raethran knew that time was not on his side. Thriol was smart and well defended. He could afford to wait until Raethran made the fatal mistake that got him stuck into a lunge on the end of a spear. This put Raethran in the position of move maker. He chose how the fight would proceed but that meant the mistakes were his to be made.

He lunged forward, dancing through and leaning back, under the spear thrust, hooked his left axe on the shield and pulled, twisting his body with all his might.

Shield walls are nigh impossible to break through but easy enough to pull a part where the hind leg brace just sets the forelimb as a pivot. Thriol's shield wasn't pulled away, he was too clever for that, but his flank opened up as a sacrifice.

Raethran stepped wide and swung the axe of his right hand into the side of his helm, setting a ringing throughout the field. With a flash of blue light one of Thriol's wards had been shattered.

He disengaged before the wild retaliation landed. This time, Thriol charged. Shield still raised and spear lunging for Raethran's throat.

Raethran ducked and spun on the grass, hooking Thriol's leading limb with his leg, sending him tumbling. His knee carved the earth with the steel armour as his chisel and his momentum as the hammer.

With a quick recovery, Thriol stood and launched his spear at Raethran. He ducked down but swung an axe to confirm its harmless trajectory. Students cheered as the spear shattered against the wards protecting the stands, Master Filthin not even flinching at the impact right in front of his face.

His weapon ready, Raethran left no time for planning to pass. He stepped forward, swinging his axes wildly but keeping a reserve strike in his timing, baiting a thrust by keeping his centre open.

Thriol recoiled at the smaller elf's ferocity. A bear doesn't expect a wolf to dive for the throat, especially when alone. He defended expertly, composing his form and seeing the opening in Raethran's high strikes. He shielded high and thrust low to his centre.

Raethran, hoping for the thrust, twisted to let the blade catch in his mail. The steel rings scattered across their footfalls, raining down on the grass.

Raethran placed his off-hand axe between Thriol's wrist wrap and carpal plate, relinquishing his sword from the fight as he tried to reset his posture. The sword fell to the ground and, with a flick of Raethran's foot, was swiftly dealt with. He shouldered Thriol's retaliatory bash and was pushed to the edge of the ring.

The shield bash hurt, as did the ripping of his chainmail but bruises healed quickly enough. Thriol was two weapons down and, aside from his dagger, only his war hammer remained. He tossed his shield to the side. It was weighing him down and would only serve to obstruct his vision at this stage.

Raethran was quick, devilishly so, but a war hammer when used correctly, can be just as quick and far more devastating. Thriol equipped his hammer and lifted the visor off his helm, greeting Raethran with a predatory grin and deep breaths, sucking in oxygen to fuel his furnace.

It's the healthy bear that's curious and the wounded one that's vicious. Raethran saw his predicament and submitted to his fate, now seeing himself as less the wolf and more the mouse. He gave Thriol a break to adjust his approach and removed his helm, tossing it to the side.

"Raethran! By the light you…" Nildinar shouted, bringing Raethran from the tunnel of the fight.

He looked around to see that most of the duels had met their conclusion. Olethia was being tended to by the physicians, and Astril was sipping from a potion vial. Graxith was on his feet and maroon with excitement, whilst the students threw insults and cheers.

Raethran risked a brief look at his brother but was quickly brought back into the duel as a war hammer swung past his face, Thriol dropping from full extension to spare him. Raethran dodged but it was Thriol's honour that kept his face from being shattered. Now that the duel was back on, no such quarter would be provided nor expected.

Duck. Dive. Roll. Deflect. Jab jab, low slash. This became the chorus of his song. Raethran was perpetually on the back foot, doing his best to stay out of the range of the hammer or stepping out of its trajectory as it shook the earth in mighty collisions. Thriol was on the offensive and Raethran was running out of time. He was planning his attacks and executing them with the precision of a musician finding the right chord with Raethran desperate to find the rhythm.

They were both growing tired, Thriol from his armour, Raethran from his costly manoeuvres and limb weights. By now, they were the only duel remaining and had gathered the invested focus from all left standing.

Left to right, lunge dodge, retreat, swing and deflect strike.

Rhythm. The rhythm. Find the rhythm. Raethran let himself become predictable, looking for Thriol's rhythm. Short. Short. Shoulder. Short. Long. No! – His hammer was thrust into Raethran's gut, wrenching his stomach and forcing his retreat.

Long, short, short upper, shaft – there! Raethran dodged the short to his head, tucked behind and leveraged his axe behind Thriol's ankle, throwing it forward to set him off balance. The gamble lost him his axe but Thriol, on the ground, was now scrambling to get up. Raethran threw his other axe at his head. Not having the time to bring his arms up, he shied away, his helm deflecting the strike with a satisfying dent.

In fights, it's hesitation that gets you run through. The dent had stunned Thriol, but it could do little more than that. Knife out, Raethran dove into the armoured form, rolling him out of the ring in the tumble.

"Hold! Concluded!" shouted Graxith through the stammering crowd. Raethran rose, calling the physicians who were already well on their way. He gestured to Thriol who was gasping on the ground, a dagger nestled in the shallows of his left axilla, through his mail, plunged downward to avoid his brachial plexus and thoracic cavity. It was still a gamble and Raethran could not be certain of the outcome.

Master Hital set about her incantations whilst her junior apprentices removed Thriol's armour and stopped the bleeding, checking for any major sources of haemorrhage that Hital's magic was missing.

"That was sloppy," Alikain's scrutinising register came from behind Raethran. "You baited that low thrust, yet you were surprised when it came. You were playing chess and he checkers – whilst you were working your way through his arsenal, you missed not one but seven opportunities to get the concluding hit. Finally, what will you do now? Axes on the floor and knife in your opponent?" he surmised, tossing him his helmet.

Raethran didn't know how to respond. Alikain had sent him for a spiral with everything he had done since his arrival. He was far too tired to deal with it the normal way, so he simply let the words spill out as he clumsily rose to his feet, "He is tall, my helm being off is what baited him high on his short strokes. He had a metre and a half to cover, to reach me, when I was ducking low. I will get faster. I need to," he finished, admitting defeat.

Alikain looked at him curiously, tapping him on the shoulder, giving way to Nildinar who took Raethran's hand.

"*Oronnsela lu*[25] little brother. That was quite the show! You martial folk know how to move. I thought that you were done for when he ran you through like that! You are still having trouble with your wards, I see?" Nildinar sang, inspecting the hole in the chainmail.

Raethran smiled, having reciprocated the embrace. "I am glad you came. Wait until you see what they are up to in the Arcanum. How are things going with you though?"

"The Arcanum? No dear fellow. You still have two fights left to win! After that, you can let your mind wander," he said, grinning like a true politician showing off his latest success story.

Exhausted and confused, Raethran nodded his thanks to Graxith who barely noticed over his preparations for the group event. He walked over to Thriol, helping him to his feet with the healers now packing up. The two elves shook hands, exchanging comments and tips over the fight. Thriol focused on the speed at which Raethran danced around him whilst Raethran admired Thriol's short grip work, showing off a couple of the bruises it had earned him.

The martial students replaced dented armour and retrieved more appropriate weaponry for the team's phase of the display. Thriol not changing anything but Raethran grabbing a longsword and dagger for his loadout whilst putting his helmet back on. The twins had their short swords and heater shields at the ready for their combinations that could take down even the most practised of warriors. However, their true talents lay in the bandoliers of throwing blades they had slung across their chests.

Olethia had her curved cavalry sword, a shield and a spear at the ready, her helm and armour mimicking that of the Royal Cavalry. The tassel on her helmet was an emerald green to match her eyes instead of the royal grey and gold of Isfrisairis. Tuliin, a black-haired elf of similar build to Raethran, grabbed a short bow and a short sword, opting for the support role with his medium armouring and keen aim.

Vexrith had long rose-gold hair and crystal-blue eyes which she had set on a sentinel position much the same as Thriol. She had something of a reputation for being the dainty rose with sharp thorns that could punch you out cold and empty a wine pitcher on your face in the time of an incredulous

---

[25] By the light

gasp. Something Raethran got to witness first hand when Grindol attempted a misplaced Jester's Day prank involving a mask and the element of surprise. The poor fellow had never snored since.

Yalthin was the final combatant although he was suited more to acts of subtlety and espionage than a pitched battle. He claimed the barbarity of such ordeals were best left to the lower classes and that one such as himself would be better suited at the right hand of a chancellor, gathering secrets, swinging around his rapier and most importantly, looking great.

He wore a velvet doublet with matching breeches under a breastplate bearing not his family crest but, one of his own design: an eagle carrying off the eyes of a lion. Such refinement wasted on anyone with a brain between their ears though. He generally stuck around the lower years, regaling stories of his many heroic exploits to anyone willing to swoon and drink wine with him.

The roster for this fight had Thriol and Vexrith with Raethran in tow facing Olethia, Tuliin, Yalthin and the twins; Astril and Lirith. It was weighted as such to show the proficiencies of Thriol and Vexrith in tandem versus the proven combination of the twins. The rest were merely there to fill the ranks and spice up the background engagements until the duos had decided how the battle was to end.

The twins led their team outside and to the field to talk strategy, Astril running her hand across Raethran's cheek as she did so. The sentinels-to-be made the finishing touches on their armour whilst Raethran attached his limb weights and tested his longsword's length.

"Raethran, let us handle this okay? See what chaos you can cause in the backline to buy us some time. I would hate for an arrow to make it through and cause a scuff," explained Thriol, fretting over the dent in his helmet.

"Oh, and be a dear – leave that worm to me," said Vexrith, gesturing towards Yalthin, before turning back to Thriol. "He snuck into my room two days ago and was just lying there on my bed, naked and covered in rose petals," she complained, making a gagging motion.

Thriol just laughed, putting on his helmet. "Go for distance," he said to Vexrith, holding out a fist.

She punched it. "Go for distance." She smiled, turning back to Raethran, placing on her own helm. "Coming?"

Having warmed up already, there was little left to cover before Graxith sounded his battle horn. The two sentinels formed their wall, their armour slotting into its natural, impenetrable shape. Raethran, wanting to waste no time, sprinted along the southern lateral, dodging arrows as he did so, making a mad dash for the rear.

He didn't turn to see the engagement, but it certainly sounded fierce with cries from both sides. Three… two… one… impact. Raethran found his mark before another arrow could be nocked. He jumped, knocking Tuliin's bow out his hand, landing with his knees on his chest. With a loud crack, his wards shattered into a green and black mosaic.

His face contorted and he tapped out. Raethran spun to meet the vanguard, Lirith, who greeted him with a precise flurry of sword slashes. Her strikes came faster than what Raethran could deflect but she was too used to fighting alongside Astril. Her left guard was down and Raethran twisted to exploit the gap. He found the stray slash and knocked one of her swords free, catching her other wrist in his hand. He put his sword to her throat. She submitted.

Looking to the back, Olethia was left alone at the mercy of Thriol. She was a force to be reckoned with, but she was not as comfortable on her own two feet as she was on a mount. Her poor footing had her at the business end of a shield bash and flying out of the arena, the flakes of her cyan ward falling away to the wind. Last was Yalthin, the performer. True to their word, Raethran and Thriol laid down their weapons, doing so just in time for the penultimate scene of this particular act.

With a deep bow and a flourish of his rapier, Yalthin greeted the duel.

"Vexrith, *luestrala inunore*[26], I regret that fate has set us upon this path bu—"

He was cut short as she threw her shield into his gut and sent him flying backward with an uppercut from the broadside of her one-handed mace. In an explosion of purple, as his ward disintegrated, the crowd erupted into cheers.

The masters clapped with the royals looking shocked, cheering politely, nonetheless. Even the physicians were happy as the wounds were minor if any. Just a few cracked bones here and there. Nothing Master Hital couldn't heal in her sleep.

Raethran looked up to see the blue swallow whistle a song whilst flying

---

[26] Light of my stars

to the infirmary. He walked off the field, helping Yalthin up on his way past, chuckling at the grass stains on his doublet.

"Tough draw, Yalthin. Maybe the next subject of your poems will have a weaker throwing arm?" offered Raethran.

Barely able to catch his breath, "It is the strongest of passions that hurt the most, dear Raethran. She has merely shown that she is up to the challenge, physically," he replied, being dropped to his knees by Raethran at this remark.

True to form, there stood Alikain, but this time he was bothering Vexrith and Thriol, introducing them to the head sentinel of the convoy's contingent. Quite the sight, they stood there receiving their praise whilst still riddled with arrows and throwing blades that were lodged firmly into their shields.

They seemed thrilled although saying it was destiny for them to become sentinels was putting it lightly. Raethran smiled at their good fortune and laughed at the heaving sounds of Yalthin from behind him. The physicians ran off to attend to him next, mainly to silence his now theatrical cries of pain.

The final round of this tawdry display involved the free-for-all pitched battle between all senior martial students. Those that needed to reapply their wards did so and picked up fresh armour from the barracks. Raethran got himself a double crescent cut oval shield, a spear and a short sword in exchange for his longsword. The others gathered unceremoniously for this final display of acrimony before the tour of the Arcanum, the real reason behind the university's success.

Graxith was walking around in the field, for safety or for wanting to be in the action. The horn blasted one final time for the day and immediately, there were arrows and blades sailing through the air. Unfortunately, many of them were directed at Raethran.

To his left; Thriol and Vexrith charging him down. His right; Lirith and Astril were sprinting towards him flinging blade after blade. Ahead, Olethia was making short work of Yalthin, and Tuliin was sending arrows at Raethran's chest. He ducked right, jumping and taking a high thrust at Astril. Lirith was quick to avenge her twin, but Tuliin's arrow struck her in the back.

Continuing his arc, Tuliin was easy work and didn't even cause him to break stride, the proximity of the fight doing little to favour the bow. Olethia stopped him in his tracks and had him retreating before long. He didn't have the time to be engaged with the sentinels fast approaching so he bashed with his shield. She was quicker and had a dagger between his ribs, sending him crumpling to the ground.

Thriol and Vexrith fell to infighting long enough for Olethia to mop up the scraps and take the victory, much to her elation.

Master Hital had the students up after an hour or so with her assistants stabilising everyone whilst she oversaw their efforts.

"No wards? What the hell were you thinking?" the Master said, packing away the chest drain after Raethran sat up. He shrugged, realising the futility in explaining his reasoning. She scoffed and walked over to see if Olethia was as unhurt as she looked.

On Display

The tour proceeded through the Arcanum. The master's showing off their fields and the students therein, with their projects and proficiencies. Ndolin had even gone as far as to arrange targets in the fields behind the buildings, forming their first stop.

He was an unassuming character, who would have been able to blend in with the students if not for his master's robes. His shaggy rusted brown hair disguising any formality, and his lack of jewellery leaving little but ability for him to display. Not being one to hide behind written reports and statements, he was glad for the chance to give a practical demonstration.

Students lined up in front of their targets. One was a crowd of humanoid figures made from oil-drenched tinder and others made from ice, representing the monsters of the world from the infamous cockatrice to the elusive bog-blights. These were Grindol's targets and so, when the command came, he bathed the range in prismatic flame, swirling it around to churn the heat within the vortex.

Whips of flame, crimson and gold, ran like raging rivers that spiralled throughout the hurricane that he had summoned. Heat bathed the faces of the crowd, Ara stepping back in shock at Grindol's theatrics; with even Alikain recoiling.

When the dazzling pyrotechnic display subsided, the ice sculptures had melted with the flammable allies remaining untouched amidst the charred range. Ndolin was not an easy man to impress, but this performance had earned Grindol a small nod, which was more than he could ever have hoped for. He beamed with pride, Tuliin pulling him from centre stage so that the crowd could continue onward.

Next were the twins. Their target was surrounded by shields and, for added theatrics, a patrolling squad of nervous looking junior martial students. The two tumbled around, juggling knives and carrying out acrobatic displays in vibrant suits of silver and sapphire. The dance of twisting forms and deadly blades was a display being worthy of praise in its own right. Ndolin walked between them and the twins and gave his command.

Their knives flew past his head, flicking at his shoulder length hair, and shaving the loose threads from his cloak. They bent their daggers in arcs around Ndolin, weaving through the defenders and into the targets with expert precision.

With a bow, the two commanded the crowd's attention, their beauty enamouring those not resistant to their charm. Even Raethran had to admit that they looked stunning, much like the flowers of the belladonna and wolfsbane.

Finally, Thriol and Vexrith. They were still dressed for battle, except this engagement allowed them the use of their more pernicious spells. Their blades lit up with white flame as steel rods were swung at them from the ends of ropes. With controlled strikes, one by one the rods were sliced in two. Their sword's' glow increased at the contact with the metal, making short work of the obstacles and incinerating any material in their path.

Blocks of granite were next; these too being cleaved with ease. Neither the swords nor the students showed any signs of being tarnished by the exercise. The lethality of the sentinels becoming clearer to the students watching from the windows as their mastery over both martial and magical combat was demonstrated.

A formal applause extended over the crowd, Ndolin not entirely dissatisfied at his students' performances. He was not the kind to punish his students, preferring an in-depth critique at every syllable in the spells cast and each nuance to their movements that pulled the magic to their command.

Ndolin led the way into the evocation tower, showcasing the diversity of *lenlialarla* and enchanted weapons they had been able to create. Raethran accompanied the procession, having ditched his armour in preference for his robes. He tucked in behind Alikain, pointing out a shield that had a dragon's open maw emblazoned on its surface. At the centre was a red gem that, holding a flame spell, flickered a maroon glow on the polished steel around. Alikain's eyes widened as he acknowledged Raethran's concern over it being housed indoors, skipping past the direction it was pointing. Raethran gave the shield a wide birth despite knowing it would do little to save him, having seen it spray fire thirty metres into the air on its original demonstration.

Ndolin was a savant at evocation magic. In fact, few in history had ever dreamt of pulling off what he could achieve when he was a student, let alone a master of the University Arcanum. Where his shortcomings lay were in public speaking; with the crowd soon finding themselves struggling through his lectures on the conduction tracings he had the final year evokers working on for their lightning spells. Raethran and Alikain hung back so they could quietly talk without interrupting.

"Your brother seemed rather impressed with your abilities, until, that is, you got steam rolled in that free-for-all," Alikain said, risking a chuckle.

"One of them I could handle. All at once like that? It just seemed mean. Next time I am just going to run laps of the field until they grow tired of chasing me," Raethran said, wincing with each step as his injuries tugged at his composure.

"I am sure your brother would love to see his future inquisitor brother fleeing from a horde of disgruntled classmates. Do you have any projects on display here?" he asked, a spark of interest in his voice.

"You took those magic disruption arrows I made so, I had to take a different direction. I made some boots that give a discharge of lightning on command, insulating the wearer of course. I thought it would make for a hilarious way to break out of being grappled or being surrounded by assailants. Plus, you could get a mean kick out of them. Ndolin said that it was an inelegant solution to a barbaric problem, so they got shelved for the tour," he concluded, fidgeting with some brass wire he found discarded at the cornice of the floor, twisting it around his index finger.

"I see their value. Not exactly what I would call masterful but valuable, nonetheless. Why are we not heading into the side halls with this tour? I can see a few items down there that would certainly be good for the chancellor to see," he inquired.

"They are hiding from the mage hunter, I believe. Having you learn all their secrets was enough to get even Ndolin to stuff his sock drawer with magical artefacts," Raethran scoffed derisively.

The tour moved on, Ndolin appearing glad to have the spotlight off his faculty. Next, Master Paylorn took the hot seat. A walkthrough of the abjuration tower was concise and to the point, befitting of the master's character.

There were cloaks enchanted with wards, blacksmith gloves designed to provide thermal insulation for one's entire body and gems capable of defending against any manner of attack simply by being placed onto a piece of armour. They had also found a way to enchant the glass in the building with a spell that used the energy from harmful wavelengths of sunlight to move heat across its surface to either heat or cool a room.

Paylorn's practical demonstration came at the end of his tour with Olethia being his student of choice. First, he invited rangers to fire arrows at her, only to have those arrows deflect off in a trajectory that impaled the straw targets of her choice. Next, he scanned the crowd, opting to call none other than Master Ndolin to the forefront to test his magic against Olethia's wards.

Ndolin simply chuckled. "She has been facing my students for long enough now and likely knows how to defend against some of my secrets already. How about a real challenge? We have with us *forehaltha* royalty and a top graduate of the University Druidica," he announced, beckoning Ara forth.

Ara froze, her legs trembling in front of the crowd of university masters and political elite that now stared at her expectantly. She managed a single step forward before looking too faint to continue. Alikain stepped in front of her, interrupting the crowd's gaze.

Raethran, at Alikain's signal, dropped a book to shake their concentration. The loud crash erased the past few seconds as Alikain proposed, "Ara is a gifted mage, but it would be unkind of us to expect such of our royal guests. Perhaps against an inquisitor?"

Paylorn gave a curious smile, nodded his consent, with Olethia turning pale. Alikain shot her a wink which she interpreted incorrectly, beginning to shake as he walked closer. His confident strides flicking at the knee length, void-black inquisitor's cloak that he wore. A firm grasp on his sword did little to comfort her either.

He let loose a stream of energy that crashed into her; fire, lightning and ice shattered against her wards in an explosion that tore at the world around them. Olethia held fast, bolstering her wards as best she could whilst Alikain turned to look over the crowd. Smoke, dirt and debris flew up from the force of the deflected magic, obscuring Olethia from view.

Boulders were tossed into the air like pebbles, flame struck out at Paylorn's wards over the crowd and lighting crashed against the marble walls of the tower and into the ground in sprays of dirt. A vague dome-shaped outline, in the centre of the maelstrom, was the only indication of Olethia's resistance. Her wards seemed to be holding.

A few of the student's gasped amidst the chattering of the masters. The crowd questioning Paylorn's sanity at pitching his student against the untamed might of an inquisitor's magic. Apparently satisfied that he had held their attention for long enough, Alikain cut his spell. Olethia was on one knee in a small crater that had formed around her, but her wards were still intact.

Alikain nodded, impressed. He lowered his hand and tucked the onyx strands of hair, framing his face, back behind his ears, returning to Raethran's side.

Paylorn, recognising the ploy, was the first to begin the applause, rushing in to break the stunned silence. After such a show, even the master's found themselves impressed and soon joined in.

Olethia beamed with pride as Yildrin, the head sentinel, walked forth and offered her a hand to stand up. He walked them back to join the procession giving a comforting smile in Ara's direction, one that blended in seamlessly with his acknowledgement to the rest of the crowd. Ara offered a weak smile in return, relaxing her clenched fists.

Raethran scoffed at Alikain's return. "Was that fun? Are you happy now? Everybody is scared of you, yes, very good, but now the students will have to go and fill that hole. And which student will they get to do so? Why not the one apprenticed to the elf responsible? Yes, great idea!" Raethran said, gesticulating wildly.

The tour group had already walked off toward the Tower of Illusion magic. Raethran took his sweet time to annoy Alikain who simply shrugged, casually dusting the few grains of dirt from his coat's sleeve.

Illusion magic had always been the hall of creativity. Its use was endless if you had the mind for it and it was responsible for more miraculous feats than any of the other fields. A visage of a dragon swooping down on a battlefield to sway your enemies' resolve. A poisonous scent created in a king's wine to inspire mistrust. A cloud of darkness to enable a rapid escape or a refraction of light in the air to render the caster invisible. Illusion magic certainly had its uses, but few could be displayed for tours such as these as it was one of the few fields of magic that required context.

Raethran saw Tuliin and Grindol sneak off toward the dorms and agreed that this was a good time to do the same. Grindol was standing a full head and a half above the height of Tuliin who himself was average size for an elf. The two were rarely seen together with Tuliin opting to spend his free time in the menagerie and Grindol burying himself in his latest projects. Tuliin was, however, an expert linguist and had been assisting Grindol with his current translator.

Not wanting to be roped in by one of the artificers and likely singed in the process, Raethran turned to Alikain. "I have some arrows to go and finish and a first year to assist. If you could avoid creating more work for me then that would be mighty kind of you. Would you like to meet up at the libraries later so that you can tell me what happened these past few months that got you incinerated? That it was big enough for the masters to risk enduring your presence at the university, for a council meeting, has me a touch concerned."

"We will talk about it later. I am hoping that this tour does not take too much longer. There is a lot that we have to cover, and I have the feeling that much will be changing soon," he replied ominously.

Raethran gave a sarcastic sigh and jogged off towards the labs. There had been talk of a winter market arriving soon along with patrons from as far away as Fanian Mair. Patrons that may likely be interested in his arrows or at least in buying them to resell to someone who would be interested.

Kaylith was slumped over a pile of books, slowly bashing her head into the precarious literary tower, building a cadence for the alchemy lab's activity. Two amulets were in braces before her, a scattering of tools in their proximity.

Master Oldiir was taking a junior class through the basics of matching solvents to solutes, using alcohol and healing herbs as his example. His focus was locked upon his students, and he did not seem to notice Raethran's arrival.

Raethran retrieved the items from his locker, throwing on his safety cloak, setting up shop next to Kaylith to begin the laborious task of detailing his creations. She lifted her head at his sudden interruption with a look of desperation taking over her expression.

"I have tried… everything. I have cleaned them. I have rebuilt them. I tried matching resonance frequencies," she said, frantically pointing out a diagram in one of the books. "Even overloading the crystals to catch a proximity burst and yet still, nothing! All I managed was to shatter the light sconce on the wall over there," she finished, shamefully pointing out a pile of crystal fragments near the wall as her head fell into her hands in a whimper.

Raethran chuckled and quickly set about sweeping up the crystal before Oldiir finished his lecture. He returned and inspected the amulets. They had a beautiful design with a central amethyst encased in a bronze setting serving as the source and conduit for the magic. The tracings were clear and the construction solid. Running a few trials himself, he concluded by fishing through Kaylith's book pile. Unsatisfied, and without explanation, he left to the textbook shelf and came back with a hefty volume entitled *Resonance of Materials and Energies – A Reference Compendium.*

Flipping through the chapters, and scribbling page numbers down, he pushed the book over to Kaylith with the page numbers written on a bookmark. "You made this mistake because you were trying to improve on the design. Your work is far beyond what most are capable of at your level of study. You should be proud of yourself for getting this far. A shielded communication channel that looks as if it will be able to join Isfrisairis with Sinien Tarvia? What you have here is a spectacular piece. Go through these pages and I believe you will find what you need. If you do not then we will tackle this together," he commented, sitting back and setting about the detailing on his arrows, leaning back on the alchemy benches until he got comfortable.

Exhausted, and a little embarrassed, she set herself to the task of the assigned reading. Occasional exclamations of "Of course!" and "Well that makes no sense! Wait… Yes, Okay."

Raethran sat back, setting the inlay into the oak of the arrow shafts. It was delicate work but rewarding as at the end, before him, were arrows worthy of the most decorated of rangers. He opted for a dark green for the fletching's' colour with a silver thread for the attachments. The resin, painted over, served to keep the ties from fraying, protecting against the decay of time.

Finally, he scavenged a length of hemp cord with which to wrap the arrow bundle in. A note on the side listed a space for a suggested price as well as the names of the crafters: 'Kaylith and Raethran under the supervision of Master Oldiir'.

Kaylith scraped off the glue she had used to secure the amethysts to their settings, being careful not to scratch their engravings. She had applied a solvent and polished the brass before applying a different adhesive per the book's suggestion. The amethysts were placed back into their settings and clamped in place once more. With a hopeful sigh, she looked at Raethran for his approval. He did not bother inspecting the piece, having watched her progress in his periphery.

He grabbed one of the necklaces and walked to the opposite end of the hall, waiting for Kaylith to catch on to what he was doing. She put on the other necklace.

"Not only do they look great, but they work perfectly too," he said, his words carrying across to Kaylith, on the other side of the room, through the magic of the necklaces. She let out a squeak of excitement at the revelation, one that pierced Raethran's mind causing him to chuckle and take off the necklace. He walked back, holding the piece out before him with care.

"I would suggest a final polish. They glow in their function, but they have a few tool marks around the edges. You are going to drop Oldiir's jaw with these. Are you working at the fair for the lab?" he inquired.

"Thank you!" she exclaimed. "Yes, I will do… and yes. Yes, I am," she replied, too excited to concentrate fully.

"If you could try to sell these arrows then we would all be a few coins heavier for it," he said, pointing out the label.

Her excitement turned to amazement. Not only was there a financial gain to be had but having one's name on a masterwork project like this was no small achievement, especially with items as rare as infused basilisk venom arrows.

She immediately began scribbling a similar label for her amulets but was quickly halted by Raethran. "Please, leave my name off of this one. I doubt anyone would like a secured communication amulet that was made with the assistance of an inquisitor's apprentice. I think it will be better that you take credit for the entire project. Anyway, all I did was fetch some books for you," he finished, sharing a grin with the first-year student as she admired her first project.

Birds of a Feather

Alikain had escaped the procession early to attend to the tutelage of his apprentice. That, or he could not stand another moment under formal scrutiny.

"The masters are going to think you are hiding in the shadows, waiting to catch them in the act, if you stay away for too long," laughed Raethran, remembering the nervous glance he received after dropping the book near Master Ndolin.

"Oh please. The most incriminating thing in this place is the size of the dorm rooms and that strange smell from Filthin that nobody seems to want to talk about," Alikain remarked.

"Say what you will, but it helps to be able to smell when he is nearby. You look like you are about to fall apart by the way. If the infirmary sees you like this then I will not be able to stop them," said Raethran, halting Alikain behind a corner to avoid the twins walking out of the dormitories.

"You are going to have to find a way. I am not having them stick fish skin on me and tell me not to move for the next two months," he scoffed.

"Are you going to tell me where you and Ruunidil went gallivanting off to? The elf disappeared for three months and then came back looking about as bad as you! I would ultimately prefer that you did not go knocking off our faculty members unless they really deserved it and even then, I would appreciate it if you waited until after my graduation," said Raethran, leading Alikain through the dorms.

"If you knew him half as well as I did... Wait, how did you find out about his wounds? He was looking rather pristine for the tour." inquired Alikain, a judgemental eyebrow rising for the occasion.

"I have an in with the infirmary team, remember. She was the one who tended to his magical burns. 'A small inferno' was her wording, I believe? Anyway, this does bring me to my next point," he said, stopping Alikain in the hall. He opened the door into his room where Ahrayn had prepared an impromptu medical bay. "Time for you to get patched up. You look far too... you," he concluded, shoving the elf inside.

Alikain rolled his eyes dramatically before greeting Ahrayn with a sheepish smile. She tapped her foot with impatience, gesturing to a chair next to her supplies. Alikain sat down and she began investigating his plethora of wounds. He made a point not to wince as much as he could, but ultimately lost the battle when she opened up a small wound and removed a fragment of reaver chitin.

"You two are the bloody same, you know that? Honestly. I do not think that there is a speck of self-preservation between you. And that is on a good day!" Ahrayn fumed, inspecting the fragment before throwing it into a treated steel dish. "And Raethran, I saw Thriol clip you with his spear. You do not need another scar added to your collection. So, shirt up and sit over there on Grindol's bed," she said, not allowing the illusion of choice to become an option.

"I was checked over after the bout. I got the all-clear. Some subcutaneous bruising. Nothing to sing a song about," he said, picking up a paper bag of dried berries to snack on, his face twisting at the sour ones. Ahrayn glared at him, letting him know of the repercussions that awaited if she had to ask a second time. He sighed, falling back onto Grindol's bed, with the crunch of a hidden stash of mechanical components startling him from under the duvet.

"Well, if you had had your wards up then you would be fine," she snapped, accepting her victory and returning her concentration to Alikain's surgery.

"He is not allowed wards," interrupted Alikain. "You can test a ward against a hammer in an office, but dodging attacks can only be done in a fight. With wards up, there is room for error. You become reliant on their safety. He needs to learn to avoid the strikes, to trust in his abilities and reserve his magic."

He instantly regretted his actions as Ahrayn locked eyes with him, swapping the small suture needle for one that was more suited for dragon hide. "Does he now? 'Avoid the strikes.' You say?" She gave a cruel smile and began closing the remainder of the wounds.

It did not take long for Alikain's composure to break with Raethran staring on in horror at what awaited him. Still, the wounds were cleaned and sealed perfectly, only the widest ones requiring sutures with the others being sealed by Ahrayn's spell craft.

The medical did not take much longer. Alikain and Raethran carried

Ahrayn's equipment back to the infirmary before taking a brisk trip to the dining hall to the sound of the dinner bell. Alikain led the way whilst Ahrayn and Raethran hung back, gossiping about the stories of the day's showcases. Raethran's favourite being Grindol's translator that got stuck on the curse word setting, letting out dwarvish profanities at a rate that would have startled even the most hearty of dwarven miners after a few ales.

"Paylorn had to dive in and cast a negative energy vortex on the thing to get it to keep quiet before Kilorin walked in. The room was smoke and bronze dust with a very bashful looking Paylorn amidst the carnage," Ahrayn finished, Raethran doubling over at the mental image.

The group wound their way into the dining hall. The marble columns and carved oak long tables stretched six metres at a time, setting the stage, for sudden silence to fall across at Alikain's entry. The room settled into a rustle of whispers, and chatter within the tables instead of between them. Dinner plates flew across the room bringing ordered meals to students, flying back to the meal stones after having delivered their payloads.

Ara sat amidst the class representatives of the Arcanum's academic faculties as they droned on about the importance of the angle of trajectories being pre-calculated by the meal stone and how stabilisation adjustments needed to be made according to the food's weight distribution and viscosities.

The debate had become heated to the point where parchment had been brought out for the equations to be confirmed. Apparently, the manner in which the illusion mages had achieved the results was over ten per cent less efficient than the method currently being tested in the divination tower.

Ara feigned interest as long as she could but saw Alikain walking between the tables. She owed the elf thanks, and not just because he presented the perfect opportunity for her to excuse herself from the trigonometric debate. None opposed her departure, with them seeming impressed at her affiliation with the inquisitor.

Alikain shook the pained look from his face as he saw her approach, burying it under a political smile of welcome. "Lady Ara. It is a grand honour we have to be entertaining you here, today!"

Ahrayn and Raethran bowed in greeting.

"Alikain!" Ara exclaimed. "Last I saw you; you were…" she began, trailing off as the slightest of shadows crossed his features.

"Well, I am much better now. It turns out that all I needed was a hearty

162

meal and to see the masters shiver under the responsibility of holding a council meeting," interrupted Alikain, his voice a slight tremor to an otherwise perfect performance.

Raethran, pained at the platitudes, interjected; "The royalty of Foretilatava! Well, as per diplomatic custom, allow me to show you what this little corner of the world has to offer by means of traditions," he said, picking a table for the group by swinging his leg over a bench; himself and Ahrayn on the one side with Ara and Alikain across from them.

"You see that stone over there," he said, pointing to an obsidian monolith with a purple crystal at its apex. "Point there, cast a mental message with your food order…" He closed his eyes. Moments later, a bread roll and bowl of butternut soup landed before him, its spiced aroma infusing the air, driven home by the scent of the freshly baked bread. "…and so, it shall be!" he explained with a simper.

"Yes, thank you." She smiled politely. "A message relay to a pre-set modular menu to create the limitless combinations available. Really, just illusion magic on protein and carbohydrate supplements I believe," she continued, adorning the formal acknowledgement with a respectful nod.

"Or an excuse for us to have a competition later! The magic theory is for Filthin and his lackeys to argue over. You see, there is a running competition over who can create the best dessert. I believe reigning champion is a raspberry reduction on a cheesecake lighter than the clouds themselves," he said, his mouth filling with bread at the conclusion.

"Is that so?" Alikain remarked. "In my day, we had what they called the chocolate volcano. A simple case of chocolate sauce inside a black forest cake that, when heated, would erupt from within to coat the masterpiece." He slumped, saddened at the fall of his hero.

"Well yes, but fifteen or so years back, Graxith was in a bad mood and saw a table of seniors tucking into it. He had them running laps through Gryphon's Pass after dinner. After that, people became too scared to order it," Ahrayn added, herself receiving an assortment of asparagus, mushrooms and bread sticks surrounding a bowl of melted cheese.

Ara chuckled at that and received a chocolate mousse with a whipped cream topping, as her starter, risking a grin at her dinner companions.

"There we go, she gets it! Foretilatava has the blessing and support of the Arcanum," declared Raethran, flailing his arms about.

Ahrayn laughed. "You have to pace yourself, dear. This one is prone to food-based competition," she said, shouldering Raethran, "and that one will not be outdone by his little apprentice," she said, tossing a mushroom at Alikain.

Ara smiled, shut her eyes and a chicken, coconut and pineapple salad arrived in front of her. Her dessert then taking off and flying to the exit hatch. "Wait!" cried Ara after the meal, a little piece of her heart withering at the site of her pudding's departure. "I was... not..."

They all chuckled at her misfortune. It only ever happened once, but it was still a lesson that all needed to learn here at the Arcanum: only one order at a time.

"So, what do you all do here?" she inquired, eager to hide her disappointment with conversation.

"Well, my name is Ahrayn. I am a senior student in the infirmary. I am in my finals to become a healer. I heard your sister was a member of the *Tamore Narana*?" asked Ahrayn.

"Yes. She has been a healer for over sixty years. It was something of a shock for her when she was chosen to become Queen," she responded, an unexpected jolt of homesickness hitting at the mention of her sister.

"Raethran, over here, is enrolled in all the subjects he should not be. Although, he never attends any lectures," Ahrayn said, sensing Ara's wish to shift the subject.

"I go to lectures, just never for any of my chosen classes. Besides, I wanted to become a ranger before this one conspired with my brother and chose me as his apprentice," he said, glaring at Alikain.

"Rangers have to have variety. It seems a bit of a running joke between them to see who can graduate with the most obscure major," said Ahrayn, delicately wiping up some spilled cheese with a stick of asparagus.

"That explains why you are only just passing everything..." mused Alikain. "Well, I am one of the mage inquisitors. I specialise in hunting mages who get a little carried away, or deactivating spells that have gone awry in a more lethal manner."

A shadow crept over Ara's expression.

Raethran, seeming practiced with the reactions Alikain's comments could prompt, dove to the rescue. "He also specialises in running away from basilisks."

Ahrayn inhaled her drink and began coughing on the side-line.

"Look, she is one of three remaining females in the area. I could not just kill her! Besides, she had my scent, what was I supposed to do?" he mumbled, slowly turning crimson.

"Wait, so an inquisitor, of Isfrisairis, is currently being hunted by a basilisk? And is now on the run?" Ara asked, incredulity saturating her tone.

"Not just that, but a group of elf-hunting propaganda pushers found out about it, and now, half the continent knows that the Basilisk Matriarch of Westwood is after Alikain the Mage Hunter," said Raethran, his smug attitude earning him a glare from Alikain.

Ara chuckled. It was oddly refreshing to see this side of him. She relaxed back into her seat with a shake of her head, and ate her salad, listening to the conversation spiral around mythical food choices people had made throughout the years. Ahrayn shot Raethran a knowing smirk and he winked back subtly as Alikain sought to redeem his reputation by blatantly ordering the illicit chocolate volcano pudding. He ate the forbidden gem in plain view of Graxith and the other masters to the envy of all those around him.

Raethran sat back and waited for his main course of spiced chicken, with a pepper sauce topping, to arrive. He smiled at seeing the twins stalking Thriol to his table, turning the group's conversation to their ongoing hunt with Ahrayn chastising his involvement with the perfume.

Yalthin broke the table's dynamic like a rock falling into still waters. He jumped onto the bench, sitting next to Ara, almost on her lap while strategically avoiding Alikain. Ara glanced up, midway through sipping her tea, startled at the proximity of the flamboyant elf.

"You know what they say, my dear; order from the stone and your heart's desire will be yours," he said, aiming a wink at Ahrayn who was eagerly awaiting Ara's reaction.

She panicked and forgot to swallow the last of her tea before managing an awkward, "Oh, ah… Hi there." Sending a stream down her chin.

"Do not worry, this kind of thing happens when dreams enter reality," he said, wiping her chin with a scented pocket serviette, lingering for a few seconds extra with his hand on her chin, staring into her eyes.

"Uh… all right. Um…" she stammered, confused at why her chin needed the support of his hand.

"Be gone carrion," chided Raethran, throwing a piece of melon from Ahrayn's dessert at him.

Yalthin scowled and rose to his feet, seeing that public opinion was turning against him.

"Look towards the light of the moon, my dear. Your destiny awaits," he whispered to her, striding off to the window ledge where he sat, practicing his silhouette performance, eating a bushel of grapes one at a time with the moonlight behind him.

Ara looked to the group for assistance in interpreting the events.

"It is not that we do not want you to have fun," Ahrayn said, pausing to chuckle at Ara's flustered protestations, "it is that, despite all his flirtations, his heart has and always will lie with Vexrith. Childhood sweethearts with a relationship more complex than the theorems of Almagarthis and Olnibiir."

"Vexrith is the one that ran him over in the team martial demonstration," Raethran added. "She has a mean streak and Yalthin is a sucker for punishment. When they do get together, I foresee an anthology of poetry coming at us from his direction."

Ara gave an awkward chuckle and ordered a fresh cup of tea to hide behind, eager for the attention to shift away from her once more.

"So, what are we all doing this evening?" asked Raethran. "I hear the theatre department is planning a sky dance over the quad. There is also a game of sinchal scheduled over the lake, the Evokers B-stream versus any and all challengers," he finished, giving Alikain a goading look.

"Well, there is a council meeting this evening, so I believe that Alikain and I will be attending that. Afterwards though?" replied Ara, not wanting to give up on this group of friendly faces.

Alikain nodded. "Yes, it does promise to snatch a significant portion of our evening from us… However, I heard the games are due to start late anyway. We can meet there, afterwards."

Ahrayn dusted the crumbs from her dress as she stood. Raethran rose to join her, sensing their dismissal as Ara glanced at the sky after mention of the council meeting.

"Well then, I wish the two of you the best of luck. Send Nildinar my regards and if he is in a good mood, then can you tell him that I would not mind a new set of boots?" he said to Alikain, lifting his foot to show off his current pair's dishevelled state.

Alikain chuckled and waved them off, his smile daring to linger after their departure.

Ara was left alone with Alikain. They finished their meals in silence.

166

When they were done, their plates flew off quietly. They rose to their feet and began walking off together.

"How are you doing?" Alikain asked politely.

"It took me a while. Well, I do not think that I am there yet. Soon perhaps," she replied, letting her chestnut hair fall to cover her face as she studied the gravel pathway before her.

"Just remember to go through it all at your own pace. Do not let anyone tell you what to feel or how to feel it. Let me know if you need to talk," he said, not making eye contact, instead, looking to the sky ahead, his angular features bathing in the light of the stars.

They walked through the marble hallways lined with portraits and hanging plants. The crystal light sconces gave the stone a cold and clinical feel. It was welcome when placed in contrast with the ashen wastes of Ilvithiir, but it was a new kind of feeling. A fresh, clean start, but one that could only get dirty from here on.

Necessary Formalities

Master Selen, the elf at the head of the granite table, stood up. Her figure imposed an air of authority over the room. Her slim fit tunic had no need for embellishments, only displaying a small broach of the Isfrisairis eagle and a sapphire set into the centre of her collar emitting a faint blue glow. Her silver hair was tied back, formally, giving her full control over her expressions power. Her eyes, the blue of an ancient glacier, stared at each member of the council in turn before calling the assembly to order with a subtle flick of her fingers.

Masters of the university were spread throughout those gathered. The chancellors of Isfrisairis and delegates from Foretilatava and Sinien Tarvia sat together, neat piles of research papers waiting untouched before them.

Ara sat beside Vexhimarith, her old mentor and the head druid of Foretilatava. Her eyes darted about the room, taking in the faces of those gathered, strange and familiar alike. It wasn't until Vexhimarith touched her gently on the back of the hand, and smiled reassuringly at her, that she realised many of those faces were avoiding her. A few of them shifting uncomfortably as she turned her attention in their direction.

She leant back in her seat, adjusting her sleeves to hide any scars that may still be visible, catching Alikain's impassive stare from across the room. He looked away, appearing perfectly serene. The smiling, lively elf from dinner was buried beneath the cold, calculating stillness of an inquisitor.

The room had a poorly lit periphery where stenographers and advisors lurked, absorbing everything they could. The elves shifted in their chairs and took gulps of water from their goblets, clinking their glasses back to the granite. Paper was shuffled here and there between officious whispers to advisors.

The headmistress of the Arcanum, Master Selen, cleared her throat. "The first Daltorus council of the Ilvithiir threat is called on this, the twelfth day under the first half moon of winter. We have all received the materials gathered and transcribed for us from the research party, run by the

Arcanum's own Master Ruunidil." She paused, casting a glance over those before her for a sign of interruption. "Tonight, we face the task of deciding the official approach the elven races will be taking in the defence of Etroah, against the threat from Ilvithiir.

"The threat is absolute and thus, as shall our actions. Before you all are experts in the many academic fields here at the Arcanum. As well as Vexhimarith, the head druid of Foretilatava. They are available to answer any specific questions you may have about the information gathered thus far. Ruunidil is here to assist with any queries we may have, pertaining to Ilvithiir, through his experience from Dilen'Nahen and the surrounding lands. Inquisitor Alikain is here to explain any points we may be unclear on regarding his reports on the thalenarian capital of Xilmiranth. Together, we are here to advise and facilitate talks between you, the delegates. Among us also are Ara, blood kin of Rylia, Queen of the *forehaltha* and the representative thereof, and Kilorin the Ambassador for elven affairs for Sinien Tarvia," she said, locking her gaze with each elf in turn. "Chancellor Nildinar has been at the centre of this issue. He has been involved in the administration of the difficulties surrounding the research mission, and in arranging the response of the *tarviahaltha* to the subsequent complications that have arisen," she concluded, allowing Nildinar his time.

Nodding to Master Selen, he cleared his throat, "Of the two hundred elves that entered the portal, only fifty-four returned. Of those, two more have so far succumbed to their wounds." Alikain shifted ever so slightly in his chair, Ara's eyes flicked to him but there was no break in his facade. Nildinar continued without pause, "The damage extends far deeper, however. We are outnumbered. Our control of the arcane is years behind theirs and above all, we have no way to counter the threat posed by their deployment through portals. We have received the portal codex from our mission which we hope, will enable us in overcoming this hurdle. If we are able to control these portals by locating them as they show up, then we can close them before they grow too large. If, and only then, we may hope to be able to counter this assault with manageable losses," he said, nodding toward Ruunidil.

The librarian shifted nervously under the scrutiny of the room. "We have a basic understanding on how to channel power into portals already present. Siphoning power from them has thus far proved too dangerous, resulting in multiple cases of energy floods through the individual attempting the procedure, inevitably resulting… in their demise," he said, glancing down at his notes. "The codex has thus far proven difficult to translate and decode, so we will need more time. It is our estimate that the time required for this will exceed that needed for a full portal tether to be created between Ilvithiir and Etroah. Approximately one year. Thus, we need a plan to stem the tide of their invasion long enough to complete our research, lest we are able to otherwise circumvent the portal threat."

Before the others could intercede, Nildinar added, "Which is why we need to seek a military union between the elven nations and form a combined front, mobilising our defences." Everyone appeared to agree with Nildinar, adding notes to their files.

"Based on these reports however," Nildinar continued, holding up his own binder. "This force will be a fraction of what is required. Upon our estimates, we will need a full coalition to be established, including; the races of the dwarves, dragons… and humans." At this, questions, objections and arguments began roaring from all directions.

Nildinar, expecting the onslaught, was still shocked back into his chair, trying to isolate a common theme in the words being thrown at him. Selen interceded on his behalf, calming down the groups, all that is, except for Graxith.

"Have you no regard for our history? Time after time…" he continued, ignoring Selen entirely at this point, "we have taken these races in and protected them, only for them to rebel against us! How many holy marches have we had to fend off from the Eastern Anthurians? Perhaps you were not there to see burning ships on every horizon during the war of Sallinenulan? What of the paintings of dwarves fishing their kin from the crimson waters on the gates of Myngora Haezelahol? Coalitions have been tried before and each time they end with tears on the graves of our kin," he finished, sitting back down in a settled rage.

An eruption began once more, duels between rival points forming across the table, opinions being declared to all who would listen.

Nildinar gestured towards the shadows behind him. Six sentinels brought forth a crate the size of a small cart, sliding it onto the table. The roaring debate slowly died down as curiosity struck the council. Nildinar reached forward and pulled a latch, releasing the sides of the crate to reveal a gargantuan clawed hand, oozing a shadowy mist onto the table. The mist flowed out in waves, sparking against a magical ward, flaring up like waves against a cliff..

"This is the hand of a blight-shambler. Based on our estimates, their number rivals that of the dragons of our world. It is unanimous amongst the survivors of the Ilvithiir expedition that one of these creatures is equivalent in power to a juvenile dragon. They were even seen as opportunistic hunters of the dragons in Ilvithiir. Let this add context to those bestiaries you have in front of you. These are real creatures. Real threats that are posed to us. We have no answer to this that does not include a union of Etroah and blood on our soil."

The room sank into silence.

Ara thought she should say something. She was the representative for her sister, for Foretilatava. Why wasn't she saying something? She opened and shut her mouth time and time again, her words retreating into her chest each time. She pushed herself and one final time, she went for it. Instead of her voice, however, it was Alikain's that echoed throughout the chamber.

"How are you planning to do this? Gifts? Lands? Treaties and contracts? You say this as if we have not been doing this for centuries. How long have we sent rangers into the south to improve the relations and assist the people there? How many meetings have you all had with these races where one day, peace and trade was promised to all and the next, they had a force building outside, calling for your ears on a necklace and your heads on a pike," Alikain said, his tone dangerously even despite his knuckles clicking and turning white.

"Alikain, please…" Selen attempted.

"How many holy marches have the humans launched? The Dwarven Trade Wars? I do not think there has been a breath of peace on the seas, whether it is the Melsoan trade princes or the Mardacian galleons chasing us down. So please, tell me, how are you going to do this?" he asked, his tone suggesting his request was rhetorical at best.

Nildinar stood back up. "We will go about it the only way we can. With respect and diplomacy. If we approach it any other way then peace, if achieved, will be on a foundation too weak to hold against the slightest breeze let alone the storm that is to come. We will organise peace talks with the nations of Etroah and, one by one, we shall reconcile. We will send through full reports of what we have discovered and with this, a common goal, we shall be able to find unity through hardship," Nildinar finished. His speech was not met with thunderous applause, but instead, with rapid whispers and worried looks.

"As Graxith stated, the foundation has been laid. You are now building off this very foundation and expecting it to hold? You use the same bricks from the shattered houses of the past in the hope that this time, the roof will stand. No, we need them to fight the enemy out of necessity. If they join us in our fight as a political ally then we will splinter. If they join the fight out of survival, seeing us as an ally, then perhaps they will see the value in this coalition as we do," reiterated Alikain.

"And just what do you mean by that? Hope that portals spring up and ravage their cities? Send their leaders through like you did with Ara? Forcing their hand to get your point across? I agree with Nildinar. We face this threat from a diplomatic stance. If we fail then we do so with the honour and conscience of our race intact," decided Chancellor Kilorin.

"Send your emissaries and watch as their silver tongues become tarnished in the courtly speak. Send me, give me the opportunity to do what needs to be done, to show these leaders what it is we face. This is no time for polite interjections or proposal request forms. We need to act. You know that I can get them to where we need them and deep down, you know that it is the only way." Alikain said, standing to meet Kiloran's ferocious gaze with one too calm to be friendly.

The council members recoiled from the inquisitor, siding with Nildinar, silently begging him to stand before them. His body language clear to all that he would not be entertaining further debate. He took a sip of water to calm his nerves, gesturing for Alikain to take a seat. An inquisitor loose on Etroah was just too much to risk. Alikain, seeing this, abandoned the chambers, ignoring Ruunidil's inquiries, the black tails of his coat flicking around the corners with his sword held steady at his side.

Ara sat, shivering in her chair. Her energy being sapped from her by the severed hand of the blight-shambler before her. They could all see the horrid claw, the hand of that... abomination. And yet, here they were, ignoring it. Burying the threat that it represented. They were happy to pretend they had come to some sort of decision, relying on the tired methods of the past, hoping that this time; more money, more gifts and more emissaries would be enough.

She could take it no longer and snapped, rising up, tears now streaming down her cheeks, "This is not a political exercise. This is not an army of farmers or misguided pilgrims on our border. This is an annihilation force.

We were there. We saw what they are capable of and yet, it was only their expendable troops that we faced. What happens when their true forces come marching out? The ones that keep this army in check? What then? When our magic is dead, our forests burnt and our gods bleeding, I hope you can find a political way to console whoever is left. *Arensela lu*, stand up and be the leaders your people need. Make the difficult choice. Right now, Alikain is the only one who can help. We can sing songs of their power, spin tails of their numbers but he was there. He looked into the minds of their acolytes, he faced their armies and heard the dying breaths of our kin. It is not letters nor speeches that will persuade the other races to join us, it is the fear in facing a yurinduur charge, the dread of seeing your own shadow reaching out to rip at your throat. The glowing red eyes in the forest you call home and the flash of magic as thalenarians annihilate your kin." She said, turning around and storming out, ignoring Vexhimarith as she did so.

She burst through the heavy oak doors and past the guarding sentinels; silent, and ever watchful. She wiped her face angrily and searched for Alikain through the mist of her tears, sprinting to catch up, her heart a raging storm.

"You better have a plan, inquisitor. It better be a damned good one too," she said, her stride falling in to match his.

St Albert's Flower

Ahrayn and Raethran explored the grounds. They had snatched frozen yogurts from the food hall before leaving and were now dancing between the displays, investigating all that the other students had to show. Patrons eagerly awaited the commencement of the festivities, set to start at the discharge of the council from the Arcanum.

The artificery had shelves of designs and prototypes on display, most of which were bolted to their podiums lest they fly away. The alchemy lab had its fire-resistant stands set before the labs with Kaylith, front and centre, strategically positioning the arrows for sale.

Vexrith and Yalthin were sitting together on the terrace of the abjuration tower, laughing and chatting above the festivities. Performer troupes had begun positioning themselves around the campus, the quad well and truly taken over by the Arcanum's own orchestra.

They hadn't begun the official performance yet, warming up with jovial renditions of famous ballads such as *'Ode to the dinner bell'* and *'Flight of the first-year gryphon rider'*. A student, loaded up with wine, usually taking centre stage for the lyrical portion of the songs. Grindol was even there, giving his all with the trombone, especially when it came to the chorus:

> If you see a gryphon rider who is flying into view,
> If they are wearing white, then you best know what to do.
> You run and you hide, and you duck and you flea,
> Before they get some height.
> For there are two things they are good for,
> With neither being flight

"So, what do you think this business with the council meeting is about?" asked Ahrayn, having just recovered from a case of mild brain freeze.

"Probably something relating to those anomalies detected down south.

Most likely the one near Tour Mardesi... Portals are my current guess. The reports, which I have been arranging from Ilkiir, have not exactly been clear on the matter." He trailed off, distracted by an off-duty sentinel having a drink, laughing at the orchestra. He shook his gaze free and chuckled, "It is like seeing a statue sneeze," he said, out of the blue.

"Focus, man! You are hopeless. How did you find out about those anomalies?" she replied, chuckling at his ridiculous attention span.

"Ilkiir has been filling me in on some of the local news. Something about temporal disturbances and radiation spikes. It all sounds like someone else's problem if you ask me. Naturally though, the university is going to poke them until they know exactly what they are and what temperature they prefer their tea. My guess is that they found something they did not like and now there is a general panic ensuing. We will probably get a lovely memo or university brief later this week explaining all the particulars regarding these new discoveries."

"I agree," she said. "It does sound like someone else's problem," she continued, her smile then fading to anxiety. "So, I spoke to my parents. They received the report from the *Tamore Narana*. They said that, even with the new medications, they are estimating a maximum of six months," she finished, watching their feet carve through the shallow snow.

He shortened his stride to match hers, placing his arm around her shoulders. "That council is always giving the worst prognosis. We are at the University Arcanum after all. If there is any way to fix this, then this is where we will find it! Not to mention, we have some of the best minds on your case and each one is more stubborn than the next."

"And if we do not find anything?" she asked softly, looking back toward him.

"Then, there is a lot that we can fit in six months," he said, layering optimism over his tone to hide the hole being bored in his chest. He stepped away now holding her hands outstretched, spinning her in a gentle dance. "Just think, we can snatch some gryphons and visit the red sands of Melsoa! I have always thought a god given quest in Mardacia would be fun? No? Well then, what of visiting the dragons in the Floating Isles of Sindal? What I have learnt in life is that anything is possible if you are crazy enough and, my sweet Ahrayn, you are with one of the best in That regard." he said, giving his best stage bow.

She laughed him off. "I have always wanted to see Melsoa. Crossing the Symmian Straight on gryphons? Well, we would certainly need to be crazy for that. As for the floating isles, I have been thinking of that. Apparently, the dragons have begun bestowing magical gifts on folk. A way to gain support for themselves or simply diversify their power," she said, baiting Raethran with a smile.

"Well then, the floating isles first! If we can still feel our legs after all that then we can decide between Melsoa and Mardacia. Perhaps even go via one of the legendary dwarven subterranean tunnels!" he responded, genuine wanderlust in his eyes.

She laughed him off, picturing the elf complaining after a trip of seven weeks underground, covered in dust, complete with a dwarven mining helmet and pickaxe.

They made a full circle around the campus before bumping into the rather annoyed looking pair of Alikain and Ara.

"Raethran, we need to talk. Now," said Alikain, his eyes carrying that intent look that the sinchal players got before declaring the need for a rematch.

Raethran glanced between them, "You two look like the meeting went a little too well. If you make a decision in this state, then I have a feeling we may start a war. How about we chat tomorrow, and tonight, we just clear our minds. Besides, I think my head is still ringing from the duels," he replied, stretching out his jaw and rubbing his ear.

Alikain's expression turned to ice, glaring at Raethran's casual defiance – which quickly hardened itself. Ara bit her lip as the two silently battled it out, their shoulders straightening and their necks tensing. Raethran made the slightest of gestures in Ahrayn's direction, softening Alikain's posture.

"Fine," he grunted, "I believe there was a game of sinchal we were to attend?"

Raethran chuckled and ran to a nearby exhibit. Ahrayn rolled her eyes. "Now you have done it… the game does not start anytime soon. We were just exploring the makeshift fair that your esteemed presence has rustled up." She sighed, watching Raethran dart about wildly, loading up his arms with food.

He returned, having picked them each a packet of assorted candy. "Come, I have a treat for you all," he said, jogging to a local unattended musician's stand. He grabbed the lute there and, after a quick tune check, began to sing:

Good old St Albert marched to war
    He was powerful but he wanted more
    To attack the elves was his task
    Using a righteous cause as his mask

He stood at the forest to give his speech
    Instead of talking, he began to preach
    To a task of murder, he sent his men
    Into the wood, the elven den

He ran in first, his sword was drawn
    Dodging the trees as he blew his horn
    He tripped and fell into a flower
    His end had come, in this hour

The plant ate him up in front of his men
    Poor old St Albert was never seen again
    A lesson learned to all that were there
    To trust an elven flower, you should not dare

Now in the bark of the trees
    Lay poor old St Albert's memories
    They warn the travellers of elven powers
    In sword and magic and their mighty flowers

The tune was a foot stomper that soon had a group of students chanting along. When Raethran completed his third iteration, he gave way to the lutist, whose stand it was, for them to continue the festivities.

Raethran nodded to the gentle smiles and platitudes but remained unsatisfied with the mood, Alikain still standing with his arms folded. The music, flaring up again, led him to do something yet more drastic. He grabbed Ahrayn's hand and spun her into a dance, swinging her around in a gentle to and fro as snow drifted delicately over the crowds.

Ara stood back, watching in glee, as dancing elves spun throughout the fresh fallen snow, becoming increasingly more raucous as the tempo increased. Their metallic hair and fine trimmed robes providing a glimpse into the *tarviahaltha* aesthetic.

After the second song, Ahrayn whispered into Raethran's ear. He turned to let her spin into Alikain's arms, the inquisitor knowing he could never deny such a request from Ahrayn. Raethran bowed gallantly before Ara and then took her hand, continuing the festivities that had them dancing well into the night.

Sinchal for Beginners

Under the light of the moon, the elves joyously went about their celebrations. Casks of spiced wine were brought out to accompany the teas and heated sweet drinks. It was close to midnight when the council finally let out, an event marked by the sudden eruption of formality from the orchestra. The students slowed their pace but for a moment, so that they could welcome the council into their jovial ranks, awaiting the time when they could return to their revelry.

Greetings made and officials welcomed, rangers around the university fired arrows into the air, each popping gently and scattering lights across the grounds in a prismatic shower that mimicked the snowfall. For a moment, Ara was transported to a land out of time with the music elevating her body in the swirling dance whilst the ethereal lights drifted down around them. The crescendo of the song had to come to an end but when it did, Ara's mood remained. She was grinning from ear to ear and felt her heart dancing to the rhythm yet still.

Raethran gave her a bow, his infectious attitude having performed its duty. He spun and proclaimed to the group; "To the sky dance and then a game of sinchal awaits. After which, the revelry will continue. For tonight, we race the dawn!"

They all chuckled and followed the eccentric elf to the quad where the sky dance had already begun. Floating over the orchestra as they played, a flight of acrobats tumbling down through the air in choreographed wonder. Below, crystal lights illuminated them each in turn, telling a story with their movements, the colour of the lights and the tempo of the music. The tale was to the orchestra's *'Four seasons'*. The performers mimicked the birth of spring's bloom, opening their postures with vibrant colours in pinks, yellows, purples and whites. Others darting through in rapid movements across the aerial stage. The activity of summer with wholesome greens had all dancers moving together, having found their rhythm. The windswept leaves in autumn blew over in amber and gold, gathering in swirling eddies that lay their heads down for the snow. Winter was celebrated for its quiescence and preparations. The slumber before the day's return, with quiet blues and pianissimo flutes riding upon the rolling mists of the strings.

The elves were enthralled by the performance. Half an hour had passed unnoticed by Ara who, at the conclusion of the piece, joined in with the enthusiastic applause.

Her ear tips were freezing in the cold that had settled with the night's snowfall. Her hands beginning to ache, she asked the group to accompany her in a hot chocolate. Olethia manned a nearby stand, showing off her selection of spiced drinks that included a delectable pot of hot chocolate, which bubbled away with hazelnut scented steam. Ahrayn chastised Raethran and Alikain for getting tea whilst being all too keen to join Ara in the steaming coco delight.

"So, what is sinchal?" asked Ara absently, staring at the twins as they juggled hoops of fire whilst performing acrobatic dances together, motes of flame spinning around them in lethal beauty.

Raethran let loose a gasp of mock outrage; "Sinchal is the game of the age! A game of magical brilliance and dextrous cunning. No, it is actually just an excuse to get the mages out of the library once in a while. You have it at the Druidica though?"

"We do. I guess, I just never really paid much attention to that sort of thing."

"Academics." Raethran scoffed, rolling his eyes. "Well, six plus two a side. The six field players fly around on floating disks that can be angled for a touch of vertical movement, but the main focus is on the x:y axis. There are the six elemental braziers a side, two of each for fire, ice and lightning. Two players on each team have gloves that can handle a specific element's type and can use those to catch and throw the elements at the other players."

"Oh yeah! I know that part. I saw them play a few times, but I never really understood the point of it all."

"Well, I do not believe there is one. Essentially, there is a ball in play. If you get frozen in place by the ice, stunned by the lightning or blasted off by flame then you are likely to drop the ball, allowing the other team to potentially steal it from you. They then try to get to your team's hoop, at your side of the field, where they toss it through to earn a point."

"Okay…" replied Ara, hesitantly.

"Let us go and watch a game. It makes sense when you see it."

Ara agreed; "That sounds like a good plan. I will meet you there. I need another coat as I believe that hypothermia is now becoming a real threat. On top of that, I need to find out where I am sleeping tonight."

Ahrayn smiled and decided to accompany Ara on her travels.

"This place is amazing! I cannot wait to see the rest of the Arcanum tomorrow," exclaimed Ara, once they were some distance from the crowds.

"You are going to love the forest around here, and the lake! Have you ever flown on a gryphon?" Ahrayn responded, giddy with the prospect of showing Ara around.

"I would love to see the lake in the daylight, and not just by walking past it in some official procession or in the background of some training exercise. We need to fly gryphons tomorrow. I mean, I will probably have other stuff that these people think I need to do, but I fail to see how learning to fly a gryphon will not help me in my future travels. I just hope that it goes better than in those songs they were singing earlier."

The two chuckled at the prospect, walking through the darkness towards the sentinel's' camp.

From the gloom, Vexhimarith stepped out and sobered the mood. "Ara, you walked out before the meeting was concluded. We need to discuss our plans going forward."

Ara looked up at him, her smile failing. It was not his fault, but for the first night that she was feeling a part of the world again, he was the one seeking to bring her back to the bog that Ilvithiir had trapped her in. Thankfully, Ahrayn came to her rescue with her musical voice breaking through Vexhimarith's stony expression.

"Apologies, Master Vexhimarith," she said, remembering him from her trips to the *Tamore Narana* at The University Druidica, "I have been showing Ara some of the student culture this evening and I do not believe that she is in the best mental state for such, at this current time. Perhaps in the morning?" she finished with a wry smile.

Vexhimarith looked to Ara for confirmation and conceded, "Of course. I shall look for you tomorrow and we shall decide our path going forward in this. I understand the importance of recovering but please, my lady, this is urgent."

"Thank you Vexhimarith. As my friends reminded me earlier, it is best that decisions are made with a clear head, lest one not see the chasm through the mist. We will meet tomorrow." She agreed, glad to have the support from Ahrayn at her side.

They bid each other a good evening before Ahrayn pulled Ara off, toward the camp. "Do not worry about all that. If there was something that needed doing, then it is likely that Alikain would be doing it already. Political meetings are not for this hour of the morning. Now come, let us find you a coat and watch the mages singe each other over the frigid waters of the lake," she said, hoisting the grin back onto Ara's face.

They skipped off to find the carriage that Ara had arrived in, greeting the sentinels and rangers in the camp as they passed through. She found a long, deep emerald cloak with a beige fur lining, better suited for the Isfrisairis climate that the Arcanum belonged to.

The crate that held her cloak also contained her armour segments that, whilst polished clean, were still a reminder of Ilvithiir. She clenched her fist and bit her lip, angry at the memories that came flooding through, not letting them control her this time. She shut the chest and adorned her cloak, Ahrayn admiring the fine silver embroidery in her flourish.

The walk back was swift as they could hear the excitement unfolding by the lake. Shoulder to shoulder, they took a quick jog through the cold, trying not to trip over the trenches forming in the snow.

Over the silver lake, a violent display of colours flashed through with the match now in full swing. The two water mages from each team, who did not wear the elemental gloves, were controlling waves on the "field" from the side-lines. Flaring up walls of water causing the riders to collide with them in heavy sprays. Some of the players being fast enough to flick their disks up in time to ramp over the waves as they formed, narrowly avoiding the icy plunge.

Looking over the crowd, Alikain was found quickly enough. Immediately assuming Raethran's participation in the game, Ahrayn and Ara joined the isolated inquisitor and began inspecting the players more closely.

Raethran had lightning gloves on and was after a player with the ice gloves. He picked a ball of lightning up from the appropriate brazier and sent it arcing through the air. The player was hit and convulsed in mid-air for a moment. His disc stopped but he continued forth with his inertia, being flung into the lake. Raethran spun his disk, dodging a ball of flame in the process, collecting the ball before the downed player had surfaced from the lake.

He sped towards the other side's hoop, dodging elemental fire and tucking behind his teammates so that they may either catch the hail of magic being sent his way or sacrifice themselves to allow him to pass unimpeded. He nearly made it too, but when he spun to catch a ball of lightning thrown at him, a wall of water rose up. He collided with it in a mighty slap that had the entire crowd cringing in their seats. The ball was picked up by Tuliin, who was on Raethran's team. The elf's acrobatic prowess stunned the evokers team as he danced his way through the final thirty metres of magical obstacles to score what was the third point in a row for the walk-on team.

The crowd cheered at the completion of the match. This turned out to be the warm-up for the A-team Evokers to play a game amongst themselves and their reserves, inviting a few of the B-team to fill in the ranks. Raethran climbed out of the lake and Ahrayn ran to him with a towel, trying to keep a straight face when confronted with his chattering teeth and bruised ego.

"You won at least!" she consoled, thanking Ara for her donation of hot chocolate to Raethran's cause.

He nodded, not yet able to form words with his paralysed face. He sat down at the fire with the other players currently battling frostbite, Ahrayn fondly pushing the waterlogged hair from his face. An abjurer was walking around, casting spells to dry them off, allowing the fire to begin warming their bones.

After a few minutes, and the addition of some extra blankets, they dragged Raethran away from the fire and re-joined Alikain at the periphery to watch what remained of the current sinchal game. He laughed at Raethran's scruffy appearance and comically large blanket stack that he had cocooned himself in. Soon though, they were all commenting on the techniques used and laughing hysterically as, time after time, the players found their way into the icy depths.

"Did you ever play?" Ara asked Alikain.

"I loved to play! It was the game that first sparked my interest in magic. Before that, it was just a method of making my life easier and for warming up my tea when I forgot about it. Sinchal showed me that there was finesse to magic. Everyone casts similar spells of comparable power, but it is how the spells are used that makes the game. Look over there," he said, gesturing towards an ice glove player. "If his water mage gets a tunnel then—" As predicted, a tunnel of water formed from the lake, and the ice mage sent his held ice ball into the water, freezing the tunnel in place and giving himself a safe passage through to the hoop. "You see, two spells both useless on their own but together, forming the perfect defence. They could not do anything about that if they tried. Magic's beauty lies in how you use it," he finished, his eyes glistening at the flashing lights of the magic being flung over the lake.

Ara turned to face the game again, seeing Alikain's appreciation for the sport and looking at it in a new light. The tactics of the spell use, the teamwork as each player used their element in a unique way, and the dexterity to ride the discs as well as they did.

"Would you play a game now?" she asked, not taking her eyes off the current tangle of players at centre field. The A-side water mage was shaping a whirlpool to hide the ball beneath the water's surface until all their players had climbed back onto their discs. The B-side's water mages created current interruptions, trying to raise it back to the surface to take advantage of having all their players up.

"It would be fun, but I have to play the part of 'Scary Inquisitor'. Keep all these mages in line lest they think about causing any mischief. A small sacrifice now to save myself a lot of work down the line," he said with a solemn smile.

Ara did not inquire further, sensing the topic was over. She smiled, seeing Raethran lying with his head in Ahrayn's lap. She gently stroked his hair, her gaze transfixed on the fire as opposed to the game. Raethran lay there, perfectly content with his lot in life, now only fighting off the occasional shiver with his eyes on his star.

Ara had a look at her new friends. Here they all were, happily going about their lives, finding joy where they could, yet all of them seemed to have a darkness behind their eyes. Alikain's and hers from their recent experiences in Ilvithiir and, whilst she didn't know what afflicted Raethran and Ahrayn, it was definitely there. The way they looked at each other in those quiet moments when they thought nobody was watching, stealing every second they could for themselves amidst the chaos of life.

A tear ran down Ara's cheek, this time one of neither happiness nor sadness but a leak of the excess emotion that had gathered in her chest. A moment of purity, hidden in the crowd and flashing lights.

Climbing the Hill

Ara, still fully clothed and humming tunes from the festival, felt as if she had just dropped her head onto her pillow when Vexhimarith was calling her attention from outside her frosty bedroom cart. She let out a whimper and rolled over to the door, keeping her blanket wrapped around her shoulders.

She cracked open the door to find Nildinar and Vexhimarith, impatiently glancing over their shoulders, awaiting her arrival. Before she could respond to the situation, Vexhimarith had his hand on the handle and had opened the door the rest of the way, offering an arm to help her out. She abandoned all hope of keeping her blanket and snatched her cloak off the floor, stepping out into the darkness with a crunch of the snow.

They walked to the centre of the campsite where the fire had been stoked into a warm aura. Cloaked figures patrolled the area, rangers covered in layers of frost and snow, keeping watch whilst Ara should have been sleeping. They sat at a table close by, Ara keeping her back to the flames, which warmed her but ominously lit the faces of Nildinar and Vexhimarith.

She was not surprised to see that Alikain was already waiting at the table, his back to the flame and his face in the shadow of his hood. His sword was not at his side but lying on his lap, to be ready at the slightest provocation. He had not said anything to her about a potential pre-dawn council meeting, but of course he knew about it, and looked as fresh as the falling snow. She scowled quietly, tucking her fingers into her coat sleeves, turning her attention to Nildinar.

"Good morning, all," croaked Nildinar, beginning his informal address, "apologies for the hour but there is much I need to get through today," he continued, rubbing circulation back into his hands. "Ruunidil has reminded us of the use you could provide, and of the elevated challenges we face, as you and Graxith had done during the meeting. Discussions on past attempts grew heated but he eventually made his point clear. We have decided to incorporate your plan into our own, thus, we are asking that you, Alikain, escort Ara, as the representative of Foretilatava to the kingdoms to begin talks. You will be available to answer any questions they may have on the topic of Ilvithiir with you will both serving as a gesture of good faith from the elven race." He paused, awaiting an argument.

Vexhimarith furthered the proposal, "In the past, we have opened communications on an even footing. We have recognised the need for both success and urgency in this matter and thus, would like you to travel ahead. If we are somehow able to get representatives of all the races, together in one room, to heed our call then we may stand a chance. There will be no deals, no renegotiations but a single, united Etroah that will be born from the ashes after centuries of conflict."

Ara saw the new side of Vexhimarith, the politician. He was now looking past propriety and toward results, no matter how they were achieved, all whilst disguising it as the best intentions. He was sending in an inquisitor to bully the races into meeting, knowing fully what that would entail.

She held her tongue, annoyed that her sleep had been interrupted for the sake of political correctness. She had already decided to go with Alikain for this, did it really matter that they now had permission to do so? Her duties abroad far outweighed her use as an intermediary between elven nations.

Alikain let the group sit in suspense before revealing the basics of his plan. The others wincing as he spoke up. "We will go to Erkotte first. We do not have time to negotiate formal alliances at each, but we may be able to get them to agree to talks in a more favourable light. I can answer their questions on Xilmiranth and do so at the capitals. The West Anthurians are likely to assist our cause, the dwarves and Mardacia can be persuaded, and I have a plan for the dragons. Melsoa is anyone's guess. East Anthuria, along with the midlands, will have to be last. They are the ones we need the most, but they are also as likely to side with Ilvithiir as they are with us. They will be dealt with one way or another. I am hoping that success with the other capitals will force them to realise the pressure placed on them to join too, even if they do so in their own capacity," he proposed, looking to Ara for confirmation.

"My sister has had me studying these royal families, trade dynasties, dwarven clans and clerical hierarchies for the past year. I will be able to assist Alikain in this, but I will then have to rely on you, Vexhimarith, to see to the interests of Foretilatava in my absence. It was always her plan for me

186

and now, I will simply be doing so alongside an inquisitor," Ara agreed.

"One final point," Alikain stated, shifting his attention from Ara back to Nildinar, "I will need Raethran's assistance in this. He has proven himself capable and it is time that he begins his apprenticeship at my side, in the field. His lessons can no longer come from the sheltered halls of the university, nor from his occasional outings upon my order. It is time he takes on his due responsibilities as a junior inquisitor, at my side."

Nildinar tapped the table in uneasy conclusion, nodding with his eyes locked on the fire. Vexhimarith looked to Nildinar for reassurance but only received a grunt as the golden-haired elf rose to his feet, straightening his robes before making to depart. "He has the final say in this. I will not hold you back. Master Selen informed me that he had enough credits for a graduation by mid last year so I doubt she will stand in your way on this, although I would not expect her to do so silently. It seems they are planning an academic career for him should he decline your offer."

Ara watched the silent forms of Vexhimarith and Nildinar retreating into the darkness. She groaned sleepily, swivelling on the frosty bench to face the campfire and free her fingers, wiggling them before the flames. As the heat reached out to touch her, she felt her tension begin to recede. She had always found herself favouring fire in her spells. There was something relaxing about watching the flames flicker before her now. Something primal in their movements, uncontrolled by trivial restrictions like politics or propriety. It may look chaotic but at least it was an honest chaos.

A frigid breeze drifted through the campsite, ruffling cloaks and battering tents, swirling the snow around her feet. The wind blew against her back, and then changed direction, pushing her hood back and ruffling her fringe about her face. She inhaled deeply, trying to catch the scents of the forest on her tongue, but the smoke from the fire overpowered her senses, and she opened her eyes with a start.

Before her, in the shadows beyond the flickering flames and hickory smoke, red eyes stared at her from the trees. She leapt to her feet with a gasp, a menora uncurled its talons, its dark form in stark contrast to the fresh blanket of snow coating the trees around it. Ara took a step back, bumping into the bench as the wind picked up, the claws reaching out for her...

She yelped as Alikain touched her arm. The menora faded into the illusion as the claws became branches once more, harmlessly swaying in the gentle breeze with glistening armfuls of snow clinging onto the last of the leaves. In a shaky breath, she turned to Alikain. His grey eyes were calm beneath the shadow of his hood. She freed her arm from his steadying grasp to smooth back her hair and straighten out her cloak.

Ara chuckled breathlessly and turned away, feeling foolish as she wiped her eyes, trying to calm her racing heart. She turned back to Alikain, pressing her lips together as she thought of an excuse, but the words turned to ash on her tongue. He was watching the treeline, the firelight illuminating the bottom half of his face as he stood with arms at his side, still holding his sheathed sword. Clouds of frost puffed from his nose as he peered silently into the darkness. Ara matched her breathing to his, clearing her mind and focusing on slowing her heart.

"The rangers will keep you safe here. Best that you get some rest," he said, his eyes flicking to her briefly.

She nodded, pulling her hood back up to protect her ears. There was an odd sense of comfort in knowing that she did not need to explain herself to him. She turned away, not entirely sure that she would be able to sleep in the few remaining hours before the sun rose, but wanting to be alone, and away from the smell of the fire.

"I will fetch you just before dawn," came Alikain's soft growl. "There is much we need to set in motion."

Ara paused, nodding without looking back. She curled into a ball inside her carriage, buried beneath the blankets without bothering to remove her shoes or coat, hoping that sleep would welcome her once more.

***

Morning's light came, but instead of the sweet song of birds, it was a harsh triple rap on the door that startled Raethran into consciousness. With the groan of an old oak door, he rolled out of bed and threw a coat on, desperate to escape the wine breath and overall creative atmosphere produced by Grindol. He poured the chap a fresh tankard of water and resisted the urge to wet all of his socks and freeze them in the frigid morning air. He was already splayed out on his bed with his neck at a jarring angle, allowing for his impending muscle spasms to be enough of a punishment.

Outside the room, Alikain was waiting with Ara and Ahrayn, all dressed in their winter coats. He sighed in resignation, nodded his salutations to them, and led the way to the dining hall. The grounds were quiet this morning and Raethran was trying to decide if it was due to the early hour or the festivities the night prior. He blinked at the somnolent haze in his eyes as he caught sight of Filthin doing his pre-run stretches, indicating that it was far too early for the living to be walking the earth.

He groaned, tucking around the various hallways and doors to make his way through to the dining hall. He removed his hands from his pockets and blew warmth into them, rubbing back the circulation, through his woollen fingerless gloves. They still smelt of the alchemy labs with a pinch of basilisk, twisting Raethran's nose.

Entering the marble meal hall, he looked up at the meal stone and ordered a round of tea for the group, eager to grasp the heat of the ceramic mug. His mind reached out on instinct, his routine pulling him to his corner table with his stomach calling for its due payment for being awake at this hour.

The hall was empty, save the odd student popping in to collect their food to go. They all sat with Alikain casting a barrier of silence around them. Raethran didn't have the energy to question the elf's paranoia and just let the ride of life take him where it needed him as he rolled his face in his hands.

The tea he had ordered was a strong blend of black tea, with separate flying saucers carrying the sugar bin and milk pitcher for those heathens that dared dilute their brew. Ahrayn was not averse to morning starts and loved seeing Raethran struggle with the vicissitudes of basic functions, so she sat, chuckling at his abounding mumbles and groans while stirring a dash of milk into her tea.

Alikain and Ara appeared in better spirits after the previous evening's activities, but were rather serious, nonetheless. Even subtle, harmless occurrences around them being treated with anxiety and speculation. Thankfully, this was partially broken by Alikain placing an order for a muffin for each member of the group.

"Ara, would you mind coming for a walk with me?" Ahrayn asked, sharing a nod with Alikain before reaching out to Ara with a casual smile.

Ara looked to Alikain, confused. She did not know how to decline Ahrayn's offer, nor was she given the chance.

"Perhaps you could show Ara the lake? Raethran and I are overdue for a chat anyway," he said, squaring his shoulders to Raethran in a move he loved pulling on those he wanted to intimidate. "I think the two of you might find a walk far more scintillating than our conversation over here," he finished, his tone icing over.

Ahrayn snatched a muffin from the plate flying past, destined for the table per Alikain's request. She smiled at Ara and gestured for them to head off. Ara gritted her teeth but followed Ahrayn, the two leaving with the scent of fresh blueberry muffins in their trail. Raethran looked at Alikain and lifted up the bran muffin, he had ordered him, with a frown.

"It woke you up did it not?" he replied to Raethran's grunt at the muffin.

He tossed the muffin to his plate with a solid thud that shook the table. "All right, so this is to do with the council meeting, correct? My guess is that the temporal disturbances with the radiation fluctuations were portals? Extra gravity, energy influxes, unless there is a magical bleed. But if all that is happening then there is definitely no point in this," he speculated, poking the illicit muffin with a spoon as if it were an unidentified gelatinous specimen in the labs.

"The land is called Ilvithiir. I have the notes for you over here," he said, lifting a satchel into view. "The synopsis: Ilvithiir has, an elf-like race called thalenarians. They have been using portals to reach other planes. They get there, subjugate the lands and then use it as a resource node for their empire thereafter. They have gathered magic, artefacts and, most importantly, a menagerie of horrifying creatures to add to their armies," he continued, punctuating the last sentence by tossing the bestiary over to Raethran.

He picked up the book and gave it a skim, focusing mainly on the pictures. "All right. A whole new world filled with scary creatures and now they have set their sights on us. You are getting ready to tell me the important bit though..." he probed, raising an eyebrow.

"It is their emperor, Xalmilanthris. He is on the path to ascension, and it appears, from what little we know of the process, that he is close. The thalenarians are guided by a prophecy that alludes to them coming into possession of the souls of an entire race, one much the same as their own. This will provide the final power boost required to complete the ascension and create a god. Per our predictions, we believe that race to be the *haltha*."

Raethran had now sat up and began scribbling notes in the margin of one of the more boring-looking books provided. Its gold leafed pages and illegible scribbles not being of much use to him at this stage, anyway. "Do they channel magic through him or pull from the weave like us?" he asked.

"They channel magic similar to ours, but do so through him, giving them a fine control over our magical countermeasures and the ability to snuff us out rather easily. Their mages have the edge over us in that regard, although I am unsure how our divine magic or that of the humans would interact with theirs. At this stage, I fear, only a pitched battle would be able to tell us," He answered, tapping the table idly with his fingers.

"If our magic is useless then we may need the human paladins regardless. How do they control these creatures? How are they summoning these portals, and do we have any control over them?" inquired Raethran.

"They have the bigger stick, and hold certain races hostage by controlling leaders, hive masters, etcetera. Some, they just cage, store and release as required. We know very little in this regard. What we do know is in your bestiary. As for the portals, myself and Goronil were captured by the thalenarians but were able to escape and cause a little havoc in their capital. We stole one of the acolyte's – that is what they call the emperor's mages – codex's pertaining to the portals. It holds what we believe will be the answer to closing them or predicting them at the least."

"All right. That would be a stall. If we shut their portals, then we enter a siege where we run around trying to shut portals as they crop up or until they change how their magic is channelled. We would need to knock this Emperor Xalmicrumpis out of the race, stop their arcane channel and fragment their empire, which could buy us a few thousand years at the least?" Raethran posed.

Alikain smiled. "Exactly my thoughts. The only issue is that we need to kill the leader of a hellish army, in the middle of his empire when he himself possesses powers akin to that of a god. All of this needs to happen whilst we defend ourselves from a threat that can literally show up in our back yard..." he said, posing the statement as one needing completion.

"Which is why we need to unite our front somehow, creating an army to delay or hopefully push them back so that we can find a way to knock him. Their divine magic; are there any major differences to that found in Etroah?" he asked, no longer bothering to look up from his note taking at this stage.

"No marked differences," Alikain replied, partially impressed at the elf's progress thus far.

"Then we need to shake his people's belief, break his own power and thus, decrease their ability to channel magic through him. I hope there is a theocratic brochure in this bag? We can think of all that if we are able to survive uniting our own nations against this threat," he finished, tossing his quill into the ink pot, leaning back and running his hands through his hair with an elongated morning sigh.

"Your brother is tackling the diplomatic route on our behalf, but I figured we could ride ahead and grease the wheels so to speak? I have some ideas but nothing solid enough to plan around. As time goes on, the frequency at which these portals show up will increase and the other nations will begin seeing them for the threat they are. The issue is that they need to start building their armies and planning their battles soon as the thalenarians are not going to wait for us to catch up," Alikain said, daring to take a sip of his tea.

"I know you are trying to make a point, but he may actually stand a chance. He has a liberal approach to politics that I believe we have needed for some time. As for getting the nations on our side, continental politics have never been my forte. I guess we head there, see what they need, see what we can do to help and if that fails then we move on before we damage any current relations?" asked Raethran, unsure at the validity of the plan.

Alikain chuckled. "As I said, I have a few ideas but essentially, yes."

Raethran absently leant in to take a bite of the muffin, hesitating before clamping his teeth. "If there are raisins in this... we are going to have a problem."

***

Ara walked out into the piercing air, staring in awe at the panoramic vistas before her. The snow-capped mountains, the coniferous forest mixtures to the south and, of course, the famous lake of the Arcanum.

"Why is it so cold today? I get that there are not as many trees, but this is just... new." Ara grumbled, pulling her coat back on and wrapping herself up again to brace against the icy needles in the wind that tore her hair from her braids.

"The wind is blowing from the east. The air chills over the Isfrisairis mountains. Just be glad it is not from the north." Ahrayn smiled, gesturing towards the path that circumnavigated the lake, ducking through the trees with cobblestone bridges stepping over the rivers and streams that fed into it. "This way. It is going to be cold but when the sun crests the eastern horizon and shines over the mist of the lake then all that will fade away."

Ara followed close by her side, breaking the silence by rolling her boots through the snow in musical crunches.

"Alikain has these little lessons with Raethran. It is usually just a series of mental exercises but in times like this, he will test Raethran's problem solving, thinking patterns and information gathering techniques. The last thing either of them need is you showing them up in their little game of 'Scary Inquisitor.'"

Ara smiled but an explanation for them needing to talk to each other did not solve the issue of her not being there. She sighed, stifling her protests, looking at her feet that carved through the snow.

"You have that look in your eyes. Alikain. Ruunidil. There was a sentinel too. They brought him to the Arcanum's infirmary; we could not tell his armour from his skin when he arrived. They all had that same look," she began, catching Ara's gaze.

"Ilvithiir… Those two are talking about it. It is not just their fight, but the fight of this world. I was there too, and yet I am not privy to their conversations," she jibed.

"I do not think you would want to be. At the most, he will simply be catching Raethran up to your level whilst allowing us to have our chat. Honestly though, it is just Alikain having his lessons with Raethran. He shows up every so often, steals him away from his usual routine and has him sparring with sentinels in the fields or being hunted by rangers in the forest. This does feel different though. It is difficult to explain but I know this time he will pull him away from the university. I know you will go with them as well. I think this is just the beginning of something far greater than we could ever imagine," Ahrayn said, her expression becoming pensive.

There was a moment of silent acceptance from Ara. It made sense, however odd it was, to be coming from someone supposedly separated from the situation. Alikain would need to leave to help solve this and, after the council meeting, there was no way that she was not going to be a part of it. She had to. She had a duty to.

"When I first met Raethran," Ahrayn continued, her voice sounding as if carried on a distant breeze, "he was in his second year at the university with myself, in my third. He had already been selected to be Alikain's apprentice by his brother, Nildinar. He was always buried in a book that had little or no relation to his current subjects and insisted on incorporating his efforts in every project he came across. I would catch glimpses of him flying across the night sky on a gryphon when he thought the world was asleep or sneaking through to the greenhouse when he was supposed to be sparring. We started talking and getting to know each other. His heart reached out to me, and I could do little but grab onto it. Then, he changed. I think he, well… We… fell in love. He lost who he was as we became a part of each other," she said, a weak chuckle stifling her sadness. "I am sick, Ara. The kind of sickness that only ends one way."

Ara grabbed at words from the air, taking a while before summoning a response. She struggled as the words squeezed past the lump in her throat, "My sister, she may be able to assist? She was the head of the *Tamore Narana*?" she asked. Seeing Ahrayn's patient, tortured expression, she continued softly instead, "What about a cure not from this world? These, well… the council has been gathered to talk about these portals to this new land, Ilvithiir. The land is poisonous, but they have different magic, different plants there. It is possible that one of them could be used to help you," she added with a hint of optimism, not really knowing how to handle the world anymore.

Ahrayn smiled. "We have done the research. The damage is done, everything else is simply catching up. It is not something that can be cured, only managed until it cannot be managed any more. The *Tamore Narana* gave me six more months. This is not why I needed to tell you the story though," she said, ashamed and a little confused at her own candour. "No, I wanted to tell you this because of Raethran. You have seen him in action to a certain extent, but he is so much more than that." She could not hold the tears back any longer, her emotional bark peeling away. "He is amazing. He is capable of greatness beyond imagination, but he cannot walk this world alone. It is his greatest weakness. He has and will likely always need someone at his side. Someone to be there for him. My worry is that, whilst Alikain loves him, he will be there beside him but not be there for him. Does that make sense?" she asked, looking pleadingly to Ara.

They stopped along the path, dawn's light now illuminating the silver streams down Ahrayn's cheeks. Ara felt the previous month's emotions channelling through her, being pulled to the surface by Ahrayn's torment. It was all too much. She began forging ahead to stop herself from showing her own pain, clenching her jaw and fighting her emotions for control.

"It makes sense. You need someone there who he can confide in.

Safely," she replied, focusing on the mists of the lake, watching them dance to the invisible currents in dazzling complexity.

"Yes… I was there for him, but I should not have been. I knew what was happening and now he is following me into my grave. I need him to… not be here. I do not know what he needs and cannot truly imagine the pain that lies ahead for him, but I just…" She closed her eyes and took a breath, trying to steady herself. "Something inside me just… Knows. I… I want you to keep an eye on him. You and Alikain are likely going to head off on some grand adventure regarding these portals. He is going to need help and when that time comes... My parents, Masters Hital and Oldiir. They see him as a part of the family already and will be going through a similar situation when it all happens, so yes, they will likely be able to help. It is just that they are not like him. I am their daughter, but they have each other. Raethran sees me as a part of him. When I am gone, I will not have to deal with missing him. But he will be left behind, missing a part of himself. I do not know what you could do to help. I just know that you are the only one who can." She finished, wiping her eyes clean taking deep, composing breaths in the echoes of her trembling words.

"Chancellor Nildinar, his brother? Will he help him?" Ara asked, defeated.

Ahrayn smiled, picking her tone back up. "His heart lies strongly with the people, and thus, less with his family. Placing that on him would not be good for either of them. Nildinar has also had a bit of a history with using Raethran to plan his own career, for the greater good of course, but he is much like Alikain in that way. They may work alongside each other, but not with each other."

"Ahrayn… I cannot. I am barely able to get out of bed each morning. I cry when I smell smoke, scream when someone drops a pot, and I can barely pull myself together whenever I am stricken with these attacks. I would do anything to be able to help, however I could, but I am not the one who can be trusted with this. Is there nobody else? His parents?" Ara asked, her words ringing hollow.

"…He has a sister. She would not help him. Her heart has been poisoned and she knows that it would spread to him if she grew too close. Generally, she keeps away from her brothers and most see that as a grace."

Ara hung her head. Her obligations were growing by the day with each passing hour chipping away at her heart. She would struggle to handle these tasks if she was at her best, but now? With the husk she had become?

Ahrayn cleared her throat and wiped her eyes with her sleeve. Her sorrowful smile acknowledging the weight she had added to Ara's shoulders. Her gaze trailed off to Ara's flank. She gestured toward a swirl of ripples in the lake, Ara snapping around, thinking it a threat. "Look over there."

Flicks of fins beneath the water's surface, cutting the icy stillness with large wakes giving away the size of the creatures beneath.

"Ara, do you trust me?" Ahrayn said, grabbing both of her shoulders.

Ara stifled her anxiety but seeing the tear-stained face of Ahrayn adorned with a mischievous smile was not helping her situation, "Uh... oh..." Was all she managed to get out before Ahrayn hit her with a flurry of spells that sent her plunging into the lake.

The waters enveloped her, consuming her in the past month's discord. She welcomed the darkness, but the shock of the cold never came. She rose to the surface, spluttering and confused as Ahrayn had finished her run up and was now airborne mere centimetres from the water. After the mighty explosion of waves that followed, they couldn't help but laugh.

"This way. We should have around fifteen minutes on these wards. Just do not get bitten by anything or it may cut that time down rather substantially." Ahrayn smiled and tucked beneath the waters.

Ara's clothes were pinned to her skin by the pressure of the water but stayed dry and warm thanks to the wards. Ahrayn's feet were barely visible ahead, so she began swimming after her to catch up in the murky blue water. They travelled close to the surface, making short work of the distance between them and the ripples seen before. Ara took the solitude that the water afforded to internalise the new distress that the day had decided to add to her mental vaults. Her gaze turned down, becoming lost in the depths beneath her.

She wondered what dangers and discoveries lay beyond that horizon of darkness. A vicious leviathan perhaps? A sunken ruin forming a sculpture garden with ancient statues? Or better yet, a kelp forest with merfolk markets and bioluminescent corals. A world entirely separated from the troubles of the surface. She strained for too long and returned to the surface for her next lungful of air.

Ahrayn gestured for them to halt, watching the fin swirls approach them like a creeping tide.

"What are they?" asked Ara, looking around and realising how far they were from the shore. Images of sharks circling beneath her feet and the tentacles of krakens reaching up to drag her to the abyss began flashing in her mind.

"Turtles. They migrate south down the river systems in the winter. The ice shelves tend to take over the Onien Mer. They have been known to go as far south as Twin Lakes. Mostly though, they stick to elven waters. The humans hunt them if they go too far south."

"I met a few at Foretilatava. They came through to trade their deep-sea pearls for a dizzying array of the most arbitrary of trinkets. The *Tamore Narana* would assist them in repairing any damage to their shells," Ara said, smiling now.

"I could never get that right. I can seal them up fine enough, but the patterns would always come out looking far too geometric compared to what they were supposed to be. There is a flow to nature that really is one-of-a-kind," Ahrayn said, scrunching up her nose.

Ara laughed at this. "Yes. The Druidica always said that you Arcanum folk saw life as a formula and not as nature intended it. We were always impressed with your work, but when it came to dealing with the natural side, well, our professors loved to use you all as teaching moments."

Ahrayn gave her a pointedly annoyed look, then chuckled, tucking beneath the waters after an elegant gulp of air.

The turtles were idly going about their travels, not taking much mind of the headless bodies near the water's surface.

The elves swam down to the bale of turtles, clumsily kicking away at the water. A turtle gestured towards the surface for them to meet, the finer details of his expression being concealed by the lakes gloom.

"Good day, elf-folk. What is it that you are doing in this dale? We don't often see your kind this time of year?" the turtle greeted with a smile. His cadence drawn out to a gentle meander through a glen.

"We have come to say hello," said Ahrayn, grinning and waving.

"Oh. Hello," he said, reciprocating the grin before making to return to the migration.

"Do you have any news from the north?" Ara interrupted, catching him before he submerged.

"It is cold," he said, the smile slowly creeping back across his face.

"Do you have anything to trade?" Ahrayn smiled.

"We have this for you," he replied, handing over an enormous, furry finger with a vicious looking talon on the end.

Ara was shocked; not simply because she did not recognize the species to which it belonged, but also that the finger was the size of her forearm.

Ahrayn's face went blank as she gently accepted the finger from the turtle. "Thank you... This is a precious gift indeed. What is it you would like in exchange?"

"Perhaps a string from your shoe or the smell from your hair?"

"How about a song?" asked Ara, familiar with the peculiar tastes of their reptilian friends.

"Perhaps?" he said with a slow chuckle, pulling a vial from beneath the water.

Ara gave her best rendition of 'St Albert's Flower' that Raethran had sung for them the night before. Ahrayn chuckled at her fumbling attempts and joined in before long. As they sang, a viscous wispy light flowed through the air, into the vial. With the final line of the song, so the vial was filled.

"Thank you for your trade," he smiled, tucking beneath the icy surface.

Ara stared at Ahrayn for a moment, the lake's mist swirling around their meeting. They burst into laughter, shaking their heads. It was the kind of laugh that started from happiness but ended as a release of pent-up emotions from all corners of the heart, a safe channel to release the pressure.

"Well, we have our... finger? I guess we should get back," said Ahrayn, growing tired from treading water.

Ara nodded and they flicked their arms through the ripples. With time dragging on, the first thing to hit was the cold. They were almost at the shore, but their wards were failing sooner than expected. Their pace quickened but it was in vain as when they were able to catch their footing on the shallows, so the flood of water met their skin. Panicked gasps were squeezed from their chests and the rest of the journey was spent, at a frozen jog toward the dormitories, with stiff legs and desperate giggles.

Gift of a Dagger

Alikain dropped the dome silencing their conversation when he saw the frosted forms of Ara and Ahrayn parting the breakfast crowds to get to their table. They were wearing new clothes and, despite being wrapped in blankets from the dorms, were still a few shades on the blue side.

Raethran handed out the hot chocolates he had just ordered sitting in silence, knowing the fate that awaited him if he opened his mouth. Even Alikain stifled his comments, at first.

"When you two are done with your dental drumline, I think we have some preparation to do. Ahrayn, could you organise enough medical supplies to rebuild Raethran three times over?"

Raethran choked on his croissant, shielding the table from the shrapnel of crumbs.

"Ara, if you could organise your own equipment and perhaps ask Nildinar to requisition some arms and armour for these two? Raethran, if you could secure us some gryphons for the trip? I will get the food and other provisions we may need. Could I get everyone's clothing sizes? We may need more than just travel cloaks for our journey across the continent," he said, sliding a piece of parchment across the table.

After a few confused looks, Raethran chimed in, having just caught his breath, "We are heading on a trip around the continent to make friends with the leaders of the other races. Ilvithiir, the land beyond these portals, has an army. We may need one too. The plans will likely take the better part of a week, so we have some time to stretch our legs and double check our sock supply."

The two had likely pieced together the information already, handling the request with ease. They all scribbled their details on the wrinkled parchment, the quill scratching in their acceptance of the terms of the journey. Alikain stood from the table, looming over them with his emotionless visage. He accepted the parchment with a nod, before turning to leave.

To Ara, the chatter around them, in the hall, was rather dull. To the regulars of the University Arcanum, there was a heavy sense of reservation in the demeanour of their fellow diners interspersed with nervous glances.

Alikain paused, looking over his shoulder. "You have a week, perhaps two. There is a lot that I still need to arrange, and I need to trap the chancellors into committing other resources to the peace talks. Daltorus comes," he said, tossing three silver badges, in the shape of the Isfrisairis eagle, to the table with a scatter.

He walked out, leaving the chatter in the dining hall to explode into theories and gossip. Nervous glances became enthralled stares. Shielded faces now walked the tables with their regular smug expressions.

"Daltorus?" Raethran inquired.

"War council," replied Ara, a heavy weight settling on her chest. "They are planning to summon the Thirty Seat Council, to deliberate on military action, with the hope that we may have the assistance of some of the other races. The meeting, last night, was the first of the Daltorus gatherings."

Ahrayn continued, "The last Daltorus was during the Dragon Wars. The humans had already been decimated and were sheltering in Isfrisairis. The dwarves were hiding in their mountains and the elves themselves, grasping at dangerous magic to simply survive."

Raethran placed down the remainder of his food and sent the plate off, rising to his feet. "Ara, if you are all right dealing with Nildinar then I will be able to assist Ahrayn in moving the supplies. Do not let them tell you to take the equipment yourself. Just ask them to deliver it all to room sixty-four and we will deal with it later. If we do not know when we are leaving, then it will be best to have everything in one location until then."

Their breakfasts were abandoned as they rose, following in Alikain's wake to begin carrying out their assigned duties.

***

"Did she make fun of your suturing techniques and get pushed into the lake or is there a different reason the two of you decided to take the plunge?" Raethran asked, breaking the silence of the journey.

The safest route to the infirmary was to cut through the lecture halls, otherwise one might encounter a bored Graxith on his home turf. A more scenic route had one skirting the lecture halls, along the eastern flank of the campus, braving the towers of the arcane faculties as you looped around.

The halls were still warming up from sun and spell, leaving students to walk between their classes wrapped tightly in their robes. The white and grey robes dominating, with the seniors usually sticking to areas of practical application or being locked in the smaller lecture rooms for their classes.

"I had one of those annoying little divination hunches. Ara is someone that will be very important in your future, but I do not know why. I thought... well, I did not think. I just sort of threw words at her. I asked if... I said what I said but then, we were left in an awkward silence. Neither of us knew what to say and she was not answering so I sort of just... Well, I threw her into the lake," she said with a frown, focusing on where they were walking with a flush of embarrassment creeping across her cheeks.

He burst out laughing. "Well, it sounds as if it were the only logical thing to do at the time."

"The turtles were swimming past, so I thought we could chat to them. I cast wards on us but we swam too slowly it would seem."

"The turtles are late this year? Did you get anything interesting?"

"They gave us a finger and Ara gave them your song for her trade."

"Brilliant! Well, not the finger..." smiled Raethran, imagining the laid-back renditions of St Albert's Flower that may soon hit the roadside inns.

She fished around in her messenger bag, slipping out the finger wrapped in waxed linen. "You should preserve it in the lab before we go. It had a sort of glow to it," she said, handing the finger to Raethran.

"Yeah, I think you got ripped off there," he said, inspecting the digit. "And a sort of glow? You divination folk wonder why we cannot take you seriously." He finished, throwing it into the air and counting the spins he could get on it.

She shoved him with her shoulder. "You say that, but who will you be thanking when that finger ends up being some sort of a key to a powerful magical artefact?" she derided, causing him to stumble forward, chasing the finger as he fumbled in his catch.

"Sure. When we need to pick some ogre's nose then I will likely be very grateful for this." He replied, panting, having rescued the airborne digit.

"Oh, shut it," she said, giving up on his cynicism. She huffed a stream of air at her fringe, the rogue strands teetering on the edge of her vision.

The hall opened and they left the bustling activity, crossing along the gravelled paths in the crisp air. The ivory mage towers for each school of magic stood tall, reaching to the sky. The opaline *lenlialarla*, set to their apexes, lying quiescent in these times of relative peace.

Kaylith was amidst a group of first years, scribbling ritual diagrams in the snow, gossiping about the activities of the previous night's market. Such events had a nasty habit of sending a flood through the gossip mill with anything from romances to pranks.

With the infirmary ahead, Ahrayn quickened their pace. A queue had formed outside of the infirmary, the patients holding their heads and shying away from the sun as it crested to the east. Raethran grew hesitant, remembering the great food poisoning epidemic of six years prior, when Grindol and Olethia decided to 'improve' on the meal stone.

A student, in her medical robes, squeezed through the door, pushing away at the desperate attempts of the horde trying to slip past her. "We will not be seeing those afflicted with hangovers. The infirmary is reserved for real injuries, afflictions, curses and diseases."

Resonating groans shimmered from the crowd but no one made a move to leave. "Those caught having nothing else wrong with them aside from a hangover will be used in the experiments and showcases for the council presentations later today," she concluded.

The students dispersed, shuffling slowly back off, towards the dorms. Martial students were complaining about how they had to fight within the hour and could barely stand at this stage. The mages were pointing out the irony in how their impaired mental focus would lead to accidents and then the infirmary would have a serious patient influx on their hands. Ahrayn and Ara simply being content to snigger at their misfortune.

Ahrayn shook her head at Grindol, who had sheepishly formed a member of the departing groups, still holding a blanket over his head and trying to hide the gear imprint in his cheek.

Raethran tapped the elf on the shoulder, wishing him well but only received a yelp in return. The physician saw Ahrayn, and her troubles appeared to melt away before her as she rushed forth.

"*Oronnsela estrala,* Ahrayn, you have come to save the day! We are short staffed as it is, and word on the grounds is that Graxith is preparing to throw the martials at the evokers later." She cried, grabbing Ara by the shoulders in her panic.

"Sorry, Silla, not today. I am on official business, and I just need to talk to Hital," she replied, failing to hide her smile at the junior's flustered demeanour.

Silla's shoulders sank. "Of course, well, right this way," she said, ducking inside and latching the doors behind them.

There were junior students doing rounds with the seniors, whilst others changed bandages and stocked cabinets. The infirmary filled with a bouquet of sterilant and jasmine which Raethran now simply associated with being in a lot of pain, but eagerly awaiting Ahrayn's visits between her other patients.

Master Hital was handing out the daily medication doses to the students presenting their cases and treatment protocols for approval. She had backed herself into the dispensary and was decanting vials with a speed that dazzled the students awaiting their orders.

"...Sprained wrist, no fractures detected. All other values are within normal limits. Treatment involving anti-inflammatories, rest, reperfusion therapy and structured exercises?" posed a junior, likely terrified at being on the frontlines of patient management for the first time. Her hair was wild, and her robes stuffed to the brim with notebooks and reference charts.

"All right, it may be soon for the exercises at this stage, but he is also faking. Remember the five signs of inflammation? Well, if they were present then he would not be able to pour himself a goblet of water like that," she said, pointing at the student. "A quick tip. Ask for their subject schedule for the day. It will help you sift through some of those looking for an excuse to miss training. Turf him out and tell him that if he comes back for anything made up again then Graxith is going to receive a full report. Also, confirm that the contents of that goblet of his is just water and not wine," she finished, ushering the student off with a suspicious glance at her patient.

"Hi, Mum, could we have a chat?" Ahrayn interjected quietly.

Hital beamed at the intrusion, colour rushing to her cheeks. She nodded her head and, with a flick of her hand, arranged a senior to take over her position in the dispensary. They walked to her office where students were running to and fro to deliver assignments and patient discharge requests.

She sighed at the rising stack of paperwork and looked at Ahrayn pleadingly. "Is it wrong to hope that you are here to work on your day off?"

"If I was, then I would hate to steal all these hours of fun you have before you." She smiled, prodding the leaning pile. "No, we are here on... official business, I guess you could say. We need supplies for a trip that we are going on."

Hital raised an eyebrow and a knowing grin pulled at her lips. It was shattered however, as Ahrayn took out the badge that Alikain had given her, the silver catching a glint from the *lenlialarla* chandelier above.

"Ahrayn, he cannot take you with him on this. Inquisitor or not, the audacity of this request—" she began, her face turning maroon.

"Mum," she interrupted. "I want to go with. I am feeling much better now and, besides, I figured that seeing what lies out there in the world… Well, it may do me some good."

Hital fell back into her chair. The gentle gargle of a water fountain, in the corner of the room, saving them from complete silence. She looked up with tearful resignation. "What do you need?"

Ahrayn walked over and gave her a hug. They spoke for a while, compiling a list of supplies to the scratching of Hital's quill. Raethran was kicked out of the infirmary and told to head to the alchemy labs with a list of reagents whilst an army of junior students gathered what they could from the dispensary.

He took a jog, weaving through a group of martials that were making their way to the fields. At the front of the pack was an ambush awaiting Raethran's arrival. He was snatched up by the scruff of his shirt. He spun to meet his attacker and found Thriol staring back at him with an annoyed scowl, a colossal mace resting on his shoulder.

"You do realise that you are meant to be sparring with the group this morning?" he spat. "You better have some armour under that tunic. Graxith wants us running defence formations against the volleys of the rangers and evokers. A run up Gryphon's Peak for every projectile that finds its mark… full plate and packs."

Raethran stepped back from Thriol's grasp, adjusting his tunic. In so doing, he flashed Alikain's badge at Thriol, hoping to convey a message of urgency. "Not today I am afraid. It is someone else that will have to cause those extra laps for you all."

Unexpectedly, Thriol nodded, his expression growing sombre. "That explains all of the drills they are running. There are whispers about campus. I guess, you were always to be one of the first to get snatched off. Look, Graxith is patrolling the western fields. He is on the hunt for test subjects and one look at you, in your casuals, will have him angry enough to snatch you away to fight in some arena of madness that he will concoct. Stick through the halls or to the east and you should be all right. Take this too. I would not want you running out of weapons with the first enemy you fight out there," he finished, handing Raethran his dagger from the sheath at his side.

Raethran nodded his thanks, gingerly accepting the dagger. He turned but caught sight of a small bite shaped bruise on Thriol's neck. Not risking a chuckle, he ran off to the labs, braving the mage towers and skirting around the back of the lecture halls.

Raethran was shaken to his core. He expected a right hook from Thriol sooner than a gift, let alone his dagger. The knife was practical, effective and sharp enough to slice through falling silk. It was a mundane looking piece of steel, on a handle of carved birch. A handy tool or a deadly weapon but given to Raethran in this sense, it was now an oath.

He flushed the thoughts from his mind and ducked into the wall of heat and steam within the labs. Everything was still warming up with Master Oldiir scrubbing the wall of a suspiciously elf-shaped soot stain near one of the exhibits. He saw Raethran enter and strode over to his desk. He pulled a pouch of coins from his top draw and threw them in his direction.

"One of the sentinels took a liking to those arrows of yours. He said that he knew just the person who could put them to use. He brought half of them before they were even officially placed on sale. Kaylith was very excited about the ordeal," he said, folding his arms and puffing out his chest.

Raethran pulled out a few coins from the pouch and tossed the rest back to Oldiir. "She did most of the work anyway, it is only fair. I am here for these, however," he said, sliding over the crumpled list, pinned down with the badge.

Oldiir nodded. "Well… we were warned, I guess. I shudder to think what Alikain has in store for you though. I will need around ten minutes for this. Just wait here and make sure none of the others set fire to the place again," he said, inspecting the list in various mumbling grunts as he rifled through the storerooms.

Raethran turned to the lab and began searching the shelves for gloves, a knife, a board, a slender jar and some formalin. He performed a quick examination of the finger Ahrayn had procured before deciding that its alchemical value was minimal at this stage. Water from the central taps allowed him to dilute the formalin, in the jar, to a ten per cent buffered solution. Then, stifling the coughs and burning eyes, he re-shelved the chemical, having been careful not to spill anywhere. Next, he slipped the finger in the solution and fitted the jar into his bag with a silent prayer that the container would not break or leak.

Oldiir returned with a separate satchel for him, placing it on the table with an exhausted huff.

"There you go. Some of the reagents are too fresh to be used right away but I am certain you can work around that," he finished, eyeing out a student in the far corner that had left his cauldron unattended for too long already. The bubbles of orange tar were now rising dangerously close to the surface with a sparking purple mist gathering around the base.

Raethran saw the events unfolding, nodded his thanks and ran off, out the back door, leaving Oldiir to control the situation. He skirted around the eastern edge of the lecture halls, aiming for the infirmary in a determined sprint.

Fellow students shuffled to their classes with the exchange of jovial pleasantries whilst gryphons flew overhead as horses rode around the grounds. The black tile of the university's roofing was attempting to shine through the evening's snowfall with the alabaster flying buttresses shivering off the last of their icicles.

Ahrayn and Hital were walking south when he ran into them, digging his heels into the gravel to avoid a collision. Master Hital accepted the satchel. "All right Raethran, I have agreed to not stand in Ahrayn's way. She in turn, has promised regular updates, at least twice a week. Between the two of you, see that this is done, or I am sending an army to fetch you. Now, I will have your order at your room, ready to go within a day or so. You have not exactly chosen the best time to drain the infirmary's stocks, but I guess your cause is worthwhile," she finished, giving him an exasperated look.

Ahrayn hugged her mother, and they said a farewell. "I just need to inform my father of the plan and then I will meet you at the summit of Gryphon's Peak?" she said, excitement tangible in her demeanour.

"Sure thing. I will let the two of you have some time to yourselves. I need to chat with my brother to sort out some of the finer details and steal his boots if needed."

Ahrayn shook her head and gave his cheek a kiss before he was allowed to skulk off towards the Arcanum proper. The fights on the field were now in full swing with the striking of steel and the shattering of spells. He could hear Thriol's booming voice from the centre, keeping the group's cohesion in check as wave upon wave of destruction rained upon them. The arrows were meeting steel or magical displacement fields. Thus far, none were getting through with spells being negated or dispersed with their wards.

The twins were on the reserve benches, preparing bandoliers of daggers next to a nervous looking Yalthin. Astril was looking even more self-assured than usual with Lirith in search of an excuse to stab someone. Raethran was not going to be that person, so even with Graxith preoccupied, he avoided the fields altogether, this time skirting along the lakeside.

The Arcanum's main hall was rather barren of activity save for a few of the seniors carrying piles of books and scrolls through the hallways. To find Nildinar was a simple task. He just had to look for the door flanked by sentinels in a hallway flooded with the smell of mint green tea. Raethran swallowed his nerves and requested entry from the steel statues flanking the heavy oak door.

They made him wait for a moment before stepping aside and opening the door to a repurposed war room that Nildinar had created. Chancellor Kilorin and Master Ndolin were on either side of him, staring at their maps. Nildinar rubbed his eyes and pulled Raethran to the corner of the room where he handed a linen satchel over to him.

"Ara has already filled me in. I did not bring much with me but what I have is yours. There are some formal tunics in there – remember; greens, blues, or greys especially in Eastern Anthuria. We do not need you starting wars due to your shabby dress code offending some cardinal. I have requisitioned some basic armour for you and Ahrayn. It is being sent to your room as we speak. As for a weapon, I thought you had one?"

"I have training blades from the armoury, nothing that I will be permitted to take with me," he replied, staring at the floor by Nildinar's feet.

"Fine. Just take my sword. Raethran… I need you to temper Alikain's methods. We are sending a live ember into a nest of twigs here. This is a time for politics to take the lead, not his usual anarchist operations."

"Of course." He bowed, his voice barely managing a whisper. "I will send through reports as I can," he finished, taking the sheathed blade from his brother.

Nildinar gave Raethran an uncharacteristic hug. "You are going right into the eye of the storm, little brother, and your guide has a death wish. Please, keep yourself safe. I cannot defend this plane and look after you. I will not forgive myself if anything bad were to happen."

Raethran reciprocated the hug, not sure how to respond. He elected to give a confirmatory nervous chuckle. Ndolin and Kilorin were beginning to tap anxiously on the table, summoning Nildinar back into the fray. Raethran slipped the coins from Oldiir into the bag and eagerly left the tension of the room behind, relaxing when he was out of sight of the sentinels, back in the open air of the Arcanum.

A Quick Breath

Ara's tasks barely carried her until mid-morning, allowing her to sneak in a tea break at the lake side. She pondered the turn her life had taken whilst the worlds reflection rippled over the glittering waters. Birds fluttered over and fish kissed the surface to give life to the aquatic canvas. The martials had been setting up on the fields behind her and had now begun their clanging of metal, forcing her to relocate.

She took a walk through the lecture halls, wondering if there were classes she could attend, hearing the muffled voices behind the oak doors. Despite the council's interruption, the university's schedule forged on. A group of nervous-looking, white-robed students shuffled past her, all with overstuffed bags and piles of books in their arms. They were gossiping about the abjuration lecture they had just escaped whilst being filtered down, as fragments peeled off to head to their next classes.

A trio of handsome, grey-robed students strode by, nodding to Ara as they did so. Such open actions from the *tarviahaltha* making Ara blush in the presence of their sculpted features. She had tucked the daisy from Ixilth back in her hair, the flower having refused to wilt since that day. She was tired but felt the need to keep her mind occupied for a little longer before being able to justify a nap.

A scattering of pupils had gathered around a notice board in excited chatter. Master Paylorn was pinning up pages amidst the small tussles breaking out between the students as they reached to grab them off. This was all too familiar to Ara, as they had this exact system at the Druidica. She snuck forward to have a look at what the parchments had to say for themselves.

These were the credit writs. Students, lecturers and masters alike would use a system of trading credits to get assistance with their training and their projects whilst seeking to diversify the students' learning opportunities as much as possible. Tasks were given credit values by the university's Writ Master and then posted on boards like these for all to peruse.

Say a student needed sparring training against multiple opponents?

Well, they would post the offer here, likely for around two to four credits for each participant, depending on the exact nature of the exercise. Ara's favourite writs were those given by the alchemists that would involve her venturing into the forest to look for plants and mineral deposits. She would also take any magic writ she could get her hands on, loving to let loose her power wherever possible.

Ara would spend her writs on having ritual pigments mixed for her or getting people to repair Anmas's tack. She did not mind such tasks but there were far more engaging things for her to keep occupied with.

These writs were much the same as the ones at the Druidica. A student named Kaylith was looking for assistance in testing a communication amulet. She needed two students, one to have an amulet and one to try to listen in. One credit each. Master Ruunidil needed students to assist in transcribing and translating a collection of documents for him. Ara knew exactly what that was about. Three credits each.

The scariest was Master Filthin, needing a student to assist him with his 'Cadenced Dynamism Development'... whatever that meant. The writ had some dust on it, so Ara deduced that few were willing to risk finding out. He had other writs on the board though so his tasks were clearly in demand.

Ara grabbed a writ for one credit: pruning bonsai strangler figs. Working with sentient flora was always tricky but she wanted to test a theory. She walked through the carved paths to the greenhouse, noticing an elf from the sinchal game walking in her trail. Ahrayn had said his name was Tuliin, he was the martial that fumbled when nocking arrows with his bow. Raethran had said he had wanted to become a ranger.

The concept of rangers had always interested Ara. These elves that would brave the southern reaches of the continent, being hunted by all whilst trying to assist the many. They left the safety of the elven forests, usually being assigned villages or roads. They would passively protect their designations, taking credit where possible, in an attempt to sway public opinion in the elves' favour. It had never worked but that did not stop Isfrisairis from trying.

Ara had been keen on becoming a warden when she was young. These were the guardians of the northern forest, protectors of the elven lands. Where rangers protected the wilds and sentinels the cities, so they defended the forest. Sinien Tarvia had the mariners but there were no trees out on the ocean for Ara to explore. At least, not above the water.

At the greenhouse, a senior, in their black robes, was leading a lecture of first years on plant adaptations in various biomes. Ara was in the tropical section of the greenhouse and thus, he was explaining the buttress roots of trees supporting themselves in their shallow foundations, the leaves that were designed to repel water, not absorb it and the bounteous colour variations in the flowers, designed to attract pollinators.

Ara watched with her mouth agape as one of the students had settled a touch too close to a snap lily (now known as St Albert's Flower to the humans), causing it to salivate in anticipation. Thankfully, he was just outside its reach, so nothing became of the situation and the group soon moved on, weaving their way through the rows of flora.

Relieved, Ara looked about the house to find the bonsai strangler figs. Tuliin was already taking clippings and setting to work on the northern tables leaving Ara to set about clipping those on the south. Professor Thrindolin, the herbalist and the one who had offered up the writs, smiled as he walked by on his patrol of the greenhouse.

He also got too close to the lily, but it simply leant forward and allowed him to remove a dead leaf from its stem. The elf was definitely of the *forehaltha* but had no intention of opening up conversation with Ara based on this point of common ground. Ara was happy to see one of her kin, nonetheless. His tanned skin, hazel hair and moss green eyes lent a peaceful serenity to his diminutive form.

Wordlessly, she completed her task, first soaking the soil of the bonsais before attempting to clip the stray growths. The plants never hunted in the rain as the water made prey too slippery to bother with expending the energy. That, and the water would weaken the grip of their root systems. The same having now proven to occur in the bonsai versions, thus verifying her theory.

Tuliin, after receiving a few cuts and slices on his fingers for his trouble, looked over to study Ara's technique, silently thanking her and adopting it as his own. Ara chuckled beneath her breath. Tuliin could likely recite the nitrogen sources, protein synthesis pathways and gluconeogenesis cycles in his sleep but the Arcanum never stopped to sit and listen to nature.

Where the students of the Arcanum did impress her, beyond what she thought possible, was with their control over magic. Ara followed that which was taught by the Druidica: be nature's fury. She was passionate with her magic, and it showed. The Arcanum students were precise, expending only the power that they needed to for a given task. They were the delicate chisel to the Druidica's hammer.

She finished up and returned her pruners to Professor Thrindolin who, to her surprise, gave her a credit token for the University Druidica. She smiled at this, running her thumb across the etchings of the writ coin as she exited the greenhouses, choosing the exit by the lake with a biome made to mimic the mangrove swamps of southern Mardacia. She was worried that she had shirked her duties for too long but remained reluctant to abandon the ode to nature that the Arcanum had created.

Ahrayn spotted her return, from across the quad, and jogged up to her. Ara was ecstatic to see her despite the sea of awkwardness washing over her. Thankfully, Ahrayn was in no mood for requests and welcomed her as a friend and travel companion.

"A little birdy told me that you are looking for some riding lessons." She smiled, nudging her in greeting.

Ara laughed and removed the daisy from her hair, placing it in Ahrayn's mousy brown tresses. There was no need for words as Ara felt an easy comfort around her. She sank into thought as they made their way back south, through the grounds and towards Gryphon's Peak. They danced with their steps and hopped across the stones in the forest, straying from the path for a trip more befitting of the *forehaltha*.

An unusual feature of the Arcanum was that they made their buildings from carved stone. It was a different sort of permanence than that which Ara was used to. Having buildings sung from the living trees created a more dynamic presence, where walls could be healed, and rooms could be resized as needed. Here, they had made a commitment to each chisel strike for every block of marble that was placed, creating a testament to their efforts that lasted through the ages. Stories from these rocks becoming as ancient as the words from the tomes within.

What they did well; what the *tarviahaltha* always did well, was utilise light to its full potential. Light was more than just for reading though, it was a source of life to be worshipped and celebrated. Tall windows allowed curtains of sunlight to warm rooms and the rich tapestries that lined the walls. Crystal light sconces were scattered throughout, shedding a celestial glow wherever the elves carried out their business, no matter the hour.

They had lined every other free section of the interior walls with paintings or boo shelves, leaving little to be desired with a world of knowledge placed at their fingertips. Stories unfolded before the eyes, wherever they wandered, with wise old sages and majestic vista's watching over the knowledge that accumulated in the university.

The black robes of the senior students were rather infrequent with the majority of the students being grey-robed. Those who were midway through their studies here and represented the elves that likely knew more than most but not quite enough to escape the Arcanum's grasp. Those new to the halls were clad in pure white robes, unsullied by the volume of work that lay ahead of them. All remained hungry for the knowledge that the university had to provide with the Arcanum being all too eager to provide it, knowing that each student to leave the halls would do so with the desire to further the university's collection.

The University Druidica was more practical in its approach with most classes occurring in the forest, surrounded by nature and the topics at hand. The Arcanum kept their students confined to training fields, libraries or lecture halls. Oceana loved their ships but were a good mixture between the Druidica and the Arcanum in their lecture structures. Then there was the University Astrologica, a creature all of its own. They had entire halls dedicated to the gods of the elven pantheon with towers whose sole purpose was to guide the faculty through its divination rituals. Spires upon mountaintops, caves of solitude hidden behind cascading waterfalls and observatories with their gaze locked on the stars.

The other universities tended to keep away from religious beliefs, allowing for Vexhimarith' to formulate his theory: 'When our prayers fail then it is to science that we sing.'

Ahrayn pointed out the many features of her little part of the forest for Ara to marvel at, only commenting here and there when asking for comparison of certain plants to those found near Foretilatava. The winter chill had set the forest a slumber, the branches hanging lazily, supporting the thawing snow in the afternoon warmth. Bird and wind, the crunching of snow to the tapping of thawed ice raining down. What in summer would be luscious shrubs and bushes, were now skeletons, awaiting the vitality of spring to lift them up as the sun freed them of their snowy burdens.

Paths had been cleared by the early morning students with the walk making for a refreshing hike, that is, until they reached the mountain. From there, Ara found herself heaving like a horse in a gallop, trying to put one foot in front of the other on the steep gradient she faced. The ascent started with her looking at the vistas unfolding around them but soon had her staring at her footfalls, ensuring she did not twist an ankle or step on a loose stone.

Ahrayn shook her concentration free, clearing her throat and pointing out the view to the north, herself struggling to keep her breath. The white marble of the Arcanum shone brightly, a palace of pearls and magical gems amidst the emerald trees. It hugged the lake and was surrounded by the mountains near Gryphon's Peak, making it difficult to spot unless it called you.

The *lenlialarla* caught the light, harking back to a time when the dragons flew over these lands, ravaging the elven nations. It was these very crystals that now protected them. They were the reason for the peace that they all currently enjoyed. Crystals designed in the halls below; halls that now prepared a new generation, one that was expected to live in harmony with their once mortal foes.

The scent of the gryphons' churned with the mountain breeze to conjure a truly unique aroma. Master Filthin was assisting the students with the fledglings; feeding them and cleaning their feathers with a dance of fledglings playing amidst his feet.

The gryphons would snap at their fingers, bite at their hair and rip their tunics all to the musical laughter of the elves. The adult gryphons watched regally over the interactions of their young, ensuring the safety of their little ones whilst making sure that they did not misbehave too much. They lay back from the heart of the activity, content to stay warm in their nests with their forelimbs crossed over, beneath their chins.

Ahrayn arranged a gryphon for each of them, fully tacked and eager fly. Ara was shocked at their size, with their withers standing above the level of her head and their length doubling that of Anmas. They were lean creatures too, something that was difficult to appreciate from far away, with all their feathers.

"This is Foltair," Ahrayn said, placing Ara's hand gently on his neck.

Ara's fingers tucked beneath his icy blue feathers into the thermal layer beneath, touching her skin to his. He shivered at the contact but paid it little mind in the excitement of the impending flight. In awe, she smiled at Ahrayn who simply reciprocated and offered to hoist her up. Not thinking, Ara accepted the boost and launched herself into the saddle, slipping her mind into the rhythm of riding a horse, something she was all too familiar with. She slid her feet into the stirrups, secured the safety straps to her flight jacket and leant forward to the leather neck strap, her reins?

Slipping on her flight goggles, she looked at Ahrayn for guidance. Ahrayn hopped into the saddle of a particularly young and boisterous looking gryphon who danced on the spot, turning in circles like a yearling preparing for a race.

"You have ridden horses before, correct? Well, this follows the same basic principles," she said, giving a sly chuckle before lifting off the ground in a hurricane gust. The manoeuvre sparked an excited frenzy among the fledglings who called out after her, almost tripping Filthin in their stampede.

Foltair did not wait for Ara's command, instead obeying her unspoken wishes whilst she struggled to find the words.

Her body was flung back, wrenching at her arms as she held onto the straps with all her panicked might. She shut her eyes and tried to scream but when she opened her mouth; air simply rushed in with an almighty gulp. She ducked down and buried her face in Foltair's feathers, feeling the heaving of his muscles. With each beat of his wings and each consuming breath. She rose higher and higher, or at least, Ara assumed she did. She refused to confirm her theories for fear of being correct, imagining the ground retreating further and further away from her, taking her safety with it.

After what felt like a lifetime, Foltair levelled off his altitude, shivering in elation at the flight. Ara, still hiding away in his feathers, risked opening her eyes, tempted at the music of the wind sailing beneath his wings. Ahrayn was flanking her, laughing in hysterics at her reaction, unable to compose herself enough to provide comfort.

Ara, rather embarrassed, allowed herself to be infected by the laughter but was unsure if she had tears of joy or of fear at this stage. She looked forward and slowly straightened her back, looking over at the horizons around her.

The forest was now a lake-spotted and snow-dusted ocean of green with the mountains rising in the east and the Onien Mer ocean to the distant north. She fought at the lump in her throat deciding that after all she had been through, heights were the least of her worries.

Ahrayn began casting mental messages into her head, giving her pointers on how to refine her riding technique. Ara accepted the assistance graciously as, at that moment, she was more clamped onto her saddle than she was riding a gryphon.

Most of it was the same as riding on horseback although the principles of a gallop applied more so than that of a trot. She was grateful that her legs were held in place, rather than being free to flap about unsteadily, as she attempted to make herself comfortable. They hunkered themselves closer to their mounts and bent their legs, ready to mould their bodies to retain their balance as the gryphons sailed over the air currents and ducked through pressure pockets in cutting dives.

Icy air flooded Ara's chest in refreshing breaths that filled her sinuses and invigorated her limbs. Rolling clouds formed a landscape worthy for the gods, providing rain for the kingdoms below. Rays of sunlight forming iridescent halo's in the ice crystals above.

They flew in perimeter circles around the University Arcanum, getting acquainted with the saddles and enjoying the panorama. Ara was relaxed in the sense that she knew she was safe, but she was being forced to use muscles that she did not know existed until today. Thankfully, the thrill of the experience overrode most of the burn in those muscles as her heart danced in her chest with her senses drinking in the wonder around her. They did not fly for long, Ahrayn gesturing for them to begin their return after half an hour or so.

With that mischievous smile of hers, she looked at Ara and spoke in her mind again; *Do you remember those helix manoeuvres the gryphon riders were performing?*

Ahrayn, no! she replied, her hands acting on reflex, piercing into the saddle.

It is a manoeuvre used to safely land when archers are firing at you. It was also a method of flying at dragons that would dazzle them just long enough for the sentinels to approach without getting cooked in their armour.

Yes, that is great. But with neither archers or dragon— she attempted, Foltair ignoring her and joining Ahrayn in a spiral dive, the two gryphons spinning around a central axis together. Making short work of their descent with their wings in controlled strain, they weaved the forces of nature in a delicate balance, testing the limits of possibility.

This time, Ara would not be held back by her fears. She summoned her courage, brought forth her resolve and she managed a scream to match the enormity of the terror she felt.

Getting closer to the ground, Ara now thoroughly out of breath, the gryphons levelled out, Ahrayn bent over the side of her saddle in laughter.

"If we were riding stags right now then I would kick your arse!" Ara screamed through a voice hoarse enough to belong to one who had sat sucking on campfire smoke the entire night prior.

Ahrayn continued, uninterrupted by Ara's objections, bringing them in to land at Gryphon's Peak. Not knowing the procedure, Ara had her weight flung about as they touched the ground, earning her an exasperated grunt from Foltair who trotted to the dismount ramp, giving Ara his thoughts on her performance.

"I am sorry, boy. I learned a lot though, thank you! You were so wonderful. Perhaps one day you could show me the secrets of the skies. For now, though, thank you for keeping me alive," she whispered into the warm aura of his feathers.

Raethran was waiting for them just outside the gryphon's landing area, laughing with Ahrayn, having witnessed, and heard, their descent with a gang of first years joining in. He walked over to Ara and offered her some assistance in the dismount.

"You did far better than I did on my first attempt. This one had me swimming out of the lake instead of landing with my gryphon," he said, gesturing towards Ahrayn.

She shrugged her shoulders and hopped out of the saddle herself. Wincing as she hit the ground. Raethran dove over to her, offering a shoulder for support, gingerly lifting her up.

"Are you okay?" Ara asked, a pit in her stomach.

"She is fine. She does this when she is too lazy to walk down the mountain by herself," Raethran replied, a meagre attempt at hiding his own concern.

He lifted her into his arms, gesturing for Ara to follow them down the hill and back to the university. Ara spared a brief glance back towards the gryphons. A white-robed junior and two grey-robed students were removing their tack under the careful watch of Master Filthin, who spared a worried glances for Ahrayn amidst his other duties. They smiled at her acknowledgement and waved her on, seemingly quite happy with the opportunity to help groom two of the adult gryphons, allowing Ara to assist Raethran in the descent.

Raethran regaled them with his abundance of stories relating to his falls and injuries sustained in his own gryphon riding career as he led them down the winding mountain pass, his dextrous hops mimicking Ara's when she was in the forest. Ahrayn was soon able to join with her own and hopped down to walk beside Raethran, locking her arm through his elbow for support.

***

Alikain had been preoccupied in council meetings with Vexhimarith and Nildinar, allowing Ara to take the rest of the day to relax and enjoy herself.

She had followed Ahrayn back to her dorm with Raethran darting off to the dining hall to fetch them all some food. Ahrayn was the perfect host, showing off her collection of scented candles and foreign teas.

Notebooks, baring esoteric designs, lined her shelves with trinkets and ornaments scattered about. Carved animals of beech, hickory and walnut from Raethran's practiced hand with the fruits of their labours in the alchemy and transmutation labs between. Ahrayn had an artistic streak which complemented the sober approach that Raethran took to the decorations. The two had turned her room into a testament to their personalities with all their eccentricities on display, if you knew where to look.

Ara took in the secrets of the room as they ate biscuits and compared notes on the university drama. All Ara needed now was some lost soul from the University Oceana to let their case be heard amidst the chaos of the Druidica and the Arcanum.

The Arcanum had always been the posh academics and the Druidica the free-spirited naturalists. Oceana, on the other hand, were the adventurers. They saw the edges of the map as an invitation and not a warning, daring to push themselves to their limits to reveal the world's secrets. She had not met many of their number but Ahrayn sang tales of these roguish adventurer types showing up at the infirmary, riddled with wounds after fending off a leviathan, risking life and limb to retrieve some or other deep-sea relic.

Much to his relief, Raethran arrived back just in time to enjoy the last of the ginger biscuits. A tray of boiled water and miniature sandwiches were placed in the room's centre for their enjoyment. They all settled back to enjoy the warmth of their selected teas. Ara sat cross legged on the carpet, leaning back against Ahrayn's wardrobe for extra comfort. Raethran tossed her a pillow settling himself on the edge of the bed. Ahrayn propped up the remaining pillows and rested her feet on Raethran's lap, forcing him to awkwardly hold his biscuits and tea aloft.

They gossiped through the hours and as late night became early morning, so an extra bed was arranged in the room for Ara. Her carriage was deemed far too dangerous on account of roaming politicians and a prowling Yalthin who could be heard singing to the moon from the lakeside.

In the comfort of stories spun from excitement, love and wonder, sleep came to Ara. Her mind was swirling with adventure once more and her future became illuminated by her new friends. Dreams brought with them the imagined smell of the rolling dunes of Melsoa with mighty ships sailing upon the sea of sand. Dragons flew across the sky and the wind itself was made from magic. Wings beat beneath her as she rode the motion of her gryphon throughout the continent of Etroah.

With a smile and a contented sigh, she rose out of bed, not caring for the nest her hair had formed. At the foot of her bed was a pile of supplies laid out for her. A warm breakfast with a note, atop the plate lid, containing Ahrayn's schedule should Ara wish to join her.

She tucked into the steaming pile of flapjacks, making short work of the meal. She looked about for her travel pack, eager to get the day started, locating it beneath a set of robes baring another note.

Ara, you are one of us now. You best look the part. It read, Ahrayn's flowing handwriting, artful in itself.

She picked up the black robes, chuckling at the burn marks and character stains it had, before jumping into them and running a comb through her hair as fast as she dared. All dressed, and a member of the Arcanum, she raced off to the alchemy labs.

Ahrayn had a class on *Pharmacology: Analgesia in Draconic Species.* The title being enticing enough to pique Ara's interest. She wondered who had dared give medication to a dragon with a headache to then chart the results.

Snow blanketed the grounds; students laughed and gossiped as they walked through the frosted landscape. Raethran was in the centre of the quad with a mixture of students. They appeared to be playing catch with a ball of lightning and their sinchal gloves. Even Master Ndolin had joined in, the slender elf chuckling as a student dove for a catch, getting a face full of snow and a shock in the process.

"Hey, Ara, could you make us another?" Raethran called, waving a greeting to her with an impish grin.

She smiled and sent a bolt at his glove with her magic. She misjudged it and sent him flying five or so metres back, causing Ndolin to fold over in hysterics. Raethran sat up from the snow, only his top half visible, then, with a ball of lightning in one hand and a thumbs up in the other. "Thanks!" he shouted, spitting out a mouthful of powder.

She chuckled, a touch embarrassed, before ducking off to the alchemy labs. The smoke from the chimneys made her think of the bubbling cauldrons within, hopefully some being the appropriate temperature to warm her hands over. As Ara arrived however, the door swung wide and the class was dismissed. Ahrayn exited and bid Ara a good morning, laughing at the disappointment of her hanging jaw.

"I have 'Advanced Material Transmutations' next. It promises to be a fun one. With the winter market coming here, we will mostly just be using the left-over stocks to make whatever we want. Last year, I made a few sapphire sparrow pendants out of spare corundum and silver filigree. They sold rather quickly. I got a few credits for my efforts there," said Ahrayn, bragging for the first time Ara had known her.

"Well, you cannot go around proclaiming things like that without offering proof!" Ara goaded.

"Raethran still has one. Well, I gave him one. The elf would lose his feet if they did not keep tripping him as a reminder," she said, spotting him in the quad. "Just hold on,'" she added, storming off in his direction.

She grabbed him forcibly by the forearm and dragged him over, his weak protests going unheard by Ahrayn but causing laughter amongst his friends and the Master of Evocation Magic. "He missed his morning 'Transmutation for Biogeographical Adaptations' and threw a coup in his 'Advanced Evocation Tracings' lecture, forcing the class outside to play his little games," she reported, but Raethran was already distracted by a group of gryphon riders overhead.

Ara laughed, not just at his mannerisms but also at the few strands of his hair that were standing on end with the built-up static.

"Where are we off to? I have a bet with some of the first years that I can get Filthin to tap dance for us later and I still need to bribe the folk down in the theatre to 'set the stage' as it were," he asked, now concerned with his time crunch.

"That is one you will have to lose. You have 'Advanced Material Transmutations' now, and plus, you still have that alchemy masterwork level project to turn in!" she said, leading the way to the Transmutation tower.

"Oh, right. I thought Master Ilkiir was just going to let us goof around? Plus, I finished the alchemy project already."

She ignored his plight of justification as they ducked into the tower, ascending to the fifth-floor workshop for their efforts.

The trio worked together for the morning's class. Ara would sketch flowers from her home near Foretilatava whilst Raethran gathered the relevant materials for the colours required. Ahrayn then transmuted the materials into their new forms with Ara's aid; creating crystal versions of her sketches before adding the necessary trace elements, according to Raethran's guidance to match the colours.

At the end of their labours, they had twenty crystal flowers in total, much to Ilkiir's astonishment. Naturally, Raethran leveraged this to get the group one as a keepsake. Ilkiir was all too happy to oblige, himself marvelling at a crystal flame lily in his hands. Ahrayn immediately picked up a crystal daisy to match the one Ara had given her, handing it over and reciprocating the gift in kind.

"Do you still have the bird I gave you last winter?" Ahrayn asked Raethran absently.

He put on a guilty face, before giving up on the ruse, pulling a swallow from his pocket. Its body was made of clear sapphire and its wings and tail from an engraved silver setting showing signs of recent polish.

"A tree swallow…" Ara mused. "How perfect."

She leant over, inspecting it in his hands as he gingerly held it aloft. It was made all the more precious when in contrast to his fraying fingerless gloves with dirty, calloused fingers poking through. She looked at the pair, admiring the honest smile they were sharing. Raethran wrapped the piece in a dirty polishing rag and returned it back to his inner tunic pocket.

"So, you just carry that around with you?" Ara asked, mocking his triumph.

At this, he chuckled and shook his head. "Not just that. I also carry around my lucky rock and a piece of cloth," he proclaimed, revealing the items from his pockets, along with bits of string, brass gears, and scraps of paper.

Ahrayn kissed his cheek with a loving smile. Ara just chuckled, wondering how Raethran could even hope to get along with a character like Alikain.

Dichotomy and Dilemma

Chancellor Kilorin, Vexhimarith and Nildinar were almost never seen instead, being confined to their planning chambers with a string of mages delivering books, scrolls and charged messaging amulets. Ara had escaped the official talks but was not exempt from being shown around the university by any and all *tarviahaltha* looking to make a name for their institution in the eyes of Foretilatava.

She avoided most of them, deciding their offers to be poorly timed attempts at hoisting up their own reputations. Ahrayn and Raethran were nothing like the others, merely floating around the campus doing what made them happy or ticking off their assigned duties to avoid the attention of the masters. Ara found herself gravitating towards them and their more easy-going approach to touring the university grounds.

Raethran was always in someone's sights though. He had secret book deals with Ilkiir, would assist Ndolin in private training sessions and be called upon by Graxith whenever he needed someone to stand up to Thriol or Vexrith.

He was a curious character, spending most of his free time in the library, buried in a fortress of medical and alchemical textbooks, unrelated to his course load. He only took breaks to stretch his legs in the forest or complete various writs, simply passing the time until Ahrayn was free again.

Ahrayn was more grounded. She had a routine that had her taking shifts in the infirmary on an almost daily basis, fitting her class schedule around it. She enjoyed walking through the forest and flying over the lake on the sinchal disks, often inviting Ara to join her on her informal tours.

Gryphon flights were a frequent occurrence although, with a focus on enjoying the surroundings. Each flight slowly stripped away any fear or reservations Ara had about the creatures. Soon, she was as much of the sky as she was of the ground, or close enough at least. She was now flying with eyes open and could even brave the occasional banking manoeuvre to follow the temerarious flight style of Ahrayn.

The days, though few, had already begun to blend into a routine, one that allowed Ara to explore who she was in this new setting.

After a breakfast of hash browns with egg, tomato, spinach and hollandaise sauce; Ara decided that she would assist the infirmary. Vexhimarith had assured her that her presence would not be needed with the current discussions as they mostly involved listening to Alikain recount his stories of Xilmiranth. A story which she was not ready to hear just yet and certainly not one she would want to hear in front of the council members.

She had significant experience in the Druidica's medical faculty due to her assisting Rylia in the *Tamore Narana*. Besides, this morning, Lethrik and Yildrin were nowhere to be seen; with Raethran being tasked by Filthin to assist with planning the winter market.

The infirmary was a serene environment, the piercing smell of sterilant and jasmine indicating a fresh clean had been recently completed. The majority of the martial demonstrations had been concluded so the patient influx had trickled down to only slightly above average, allowing for most of the healers to take a break. Ahrayn walked past, with a tray in her arms: a cup of tea, a bowl of fruit salad and a book of rhymes and riddles on it.

"Good morning," Ara sang, hopping to Ahrayn's side.

"Good morning to you too. Apologies for not joining you in the breakfast hall; they had me up before dawn for my shift," she said, stifling a yawn.

"I do not want to create any obligations for you. Plus, I am rather capable of handling breakfast without a member of the esteemed Arcanum there to guide me."

Ahrayn chuckled. "Well then, I look forward to hearing about your first solo encounter with Yalthin's advances, especially with the romance of the winter market approaching."

Ara laughed at first but when Ahrayn's smirk failed to go away, she nervously changed the subject. "I was hoping to assist you in the infirmary today. I have my basic and apprentice level medical qualifications from the Druidica, with some experience from the *Tamore Narana*, so I thought I might be of some use."

Ahrayn was still regarding the offer, making her way through the infirmary with her tray when a student physician ran up to the pair and held out a suture kit with a pleading look. Initially, Ahrayn looked annoyed at the intrusion but with a curious tilt of her head, she sighed, pursing her lips in thought.

"Ara, could you take these to room fifty-one? About ten or so metres forward, first door on the right. We need to head outside to sedate a gryphon and suture its leg. Come, Silla, I am not going to do it for you, but I will be there if anything goes wrong."

The junior student released the weight of the mountain she had been carrying and scurried off with Ahrayn. She prattled on about the clinical parameters with Ahrayn entertaining her for the most part, merely keeping an ear out for anything wrong with her diagnostic process thus far.

With tray in hand, Ara smiled and walked forth to room fifty-one, clearing her throat and practicing renditions of her patient-greeting voice; "Good morning, how are you feeling today? No... Hi there, how are you feeling? No..." she muttered, under her breath.

She opened the door and attempted her choice greeting, the words freezing halfway out upon seeing Aeradil, curled up on the bed. The blanket was pulled up to his chin with his expression glazed over. The grizzled veteran ranger from Ilvithiir not showing so much as a glimmer of a response in his eyes.

Not knowing what to do, she steadied her racing heart and set aside her confusion, walking over and placing the tray on his bedside table. A chair had been pulled up next to his bed. Ara took a seat and picked up the book, assuming Ahrayn's plan from context. She fondled the dry and tattered corners of the pages, becoming acutely aware of how plain the breakfast was.

Wind flicked at the bleached curtains, adding motion to the otherwise still room. Muffled voices and clanging of drawers echoed in the halls outside the room; the occasional bout of laughter escaping through the window. The book remained closed on her lap as she stared at it; the isolation of the room trapping her in her seat.

"Aeradil, it is me, Ara," she began, unanswered. "How have you been?" She fiddled with the pages of the book with trembling fingers, picking at the loose binding. "How are you feeling?"

She asked her questions to the empty air, not seeming to have reached the ranger who lay before her. Ara was now simply a piece of furniture to add to the shell around him. She sat back in silence, watching the wisps of steam rise from the tea in the light beaming through the window.

Her voice wobbled, barely audible, "I saw my sister again… and Foretilatava. It was home, but… I guess I was not the same person, so it did not quite feel like my home," she began confessing as she stared out the window. "I guess… Well… Thank you. I still cannot think back on the singular day that I spent there, but I know that I would not be here if not for you saving my life."

The elf shifted under the covers and turned over, facing away from Ara.

She looked down at her fingers, not seeing the bloodstains but knowing they were there. Aeradil lay motionless, the subtle rise and fall of his chest being the only indicator of his presence in the husk that lay before her.

She remained a while, sifting through the countless things she could say, finding nothing to latch onto. Her mind's activity faded until the last of the steam from the tea had evanesced. She bid him a silent farewell, looking back at his statue. Once free from the room's guilt, she set a few silent tears free in an attempt to settle her mind.

Ara leant against the wall and slid to sit on her haunches, ignoring the world as she controlled her breathing and silenced the ringing in her head. She pushed out all memories of Ilvithiir before they could form into anything real, biting her lip.

Aeradil's file was on the door leading into his room. She got to her feet, wiping at her cheeks with the sleeve of her robes. Retrieving the file, she flicked through to the patient progress reports and ongoing diagnosis.

He was healthy, physically. Clinical parameters all within normal limits. All his wounds were healing without complications, and he only had mild pain on the charts. Ilvithiir's real damage was the poison of the mind.

He had been on the front line, defending the keep, watching his kin die all around him. He had already come to terms with his own death before Ara had arrived. Aeradil had been there for months and had not only fought off so much, but he was forced to witness the demise of those who didn't, not out of inability but mere chance. A simple roll of the dice or flick of the coin that decided who was killed in an ambush or who took an arrow in the defensive line.

Ara scrunched her brow, carefully replacing the file. She leant back against the wall and absently stared down at her fingers as she picked at the skin by her nails, thinking about Alikain in all this.

Ara had seen no other survivors of the expedition, except for Ruunidil. Out of the three of them, Aeradil appeared to have fared the worst. He had been out in the action and Ruunidil in the inner keep so it made sense that Ruunidil could still function. Alikain on the other hand: not only had he been on the front lines, but he had also been captured, tortured and hunted by the thalenarians with the worst they had to offer.

Her mind reeled at what the inquisitor may be going through and how he was able to cope so well. She thought back on all the horror stories of inquisitors and wondered if this was simply his job? Perhaps he was able to handle this because he had been through worse, or perhaps done worse?

"Speculation can be a blight to the mind," she recited, words Vexhimarith had begun each of her diplomatic history lessons with.

Ahrayn cleared her throat, announcing her approach.

"Apologies are you all right?" she asked Ara who was now fighting her legs to keep standing.

Ara looked up, blinking to clear away the last of her tears. She sniffed indelicately and nodded with a weak reply, "Ah, yes... I just need some air."

Ahrayn smiled sympathetically and led the way outside, heading north and keeping away from the university. They were beneath the trees again, walking side by side with matching strides. Ahrayn stayed close but kept a comfortable distance from Ara. Strength returned to her body as the fresh air entered her lungs and the trees sang her to health again.

"How is the gryphon doing?" she began.

"Well. Thank you. She is sedated and they will soon start suturing her wound. Olethia arrived to take over the supervision. Do not think poorly of me, but I saw potential value in you interacting with Aeradil, alone. He is suffering from post-traumatic stress and has retreated into his own mind. It is getting worse each day. While he can still eat and perform basic functions on his own, he has stopped responding to the normal, everyday occurrences in the world. Smiling, laughing, now even basic conversation. The slightest of reminders takes him back to his time in Ilvithiir so he has been breaking his ties from the world to shield himself from them." She paused for a moment, inspecting every nuance of Ara's features.

Confirming that she was in the clear, she continued, "It is called exposure therapy. The *tarviahaltha* first developed it in the aftermath of the Dragon Wars. You see, Aeradil's body has a full physiological response, equivalent to that which he faced in Ilvithiir, each time he has the slightest reminder of the event. His mind is struggling to process the memories and has formed dangerous links that threaten to take over. He is now shielding himself from the world lest anything stimulate such a response again."

"So, you threw me at him to remind him? See how he reacted?" Ara frowned, sickened at the thought.

"No. To expose you both to each other. I heard that he helped you in Ilvithiir, thus, he represented something close to being called 'good' from that horrid place. From what I understand, you were the reason all of them were able to return. You, thus represent a stimulus that offered solidarity, in having also faced Ilvithiir, whilst being representative of his departure. You two provide safer exposures for each other. I did not want you to feel like you had to hide your reaction from me, so I thought it would be better if you faced him alone."

Raw and exposed, Ara halted. She stared at the trees and breathed deep the damp wood of the forest and loam earth. She listened to the song of the leaves accompanying the chatter of birds. Her exposed skin burned in the cold with her ears calling out for the hood of her coat to be lifted.

She answered, "I suppose it makes sense. The Druidica had tried, but I simply cleared my mind and was able to get by. Any loud noise though, the smell of smoke… You could have warned me. You should have warned me."

Ahrayn sighed, feeling her guilt wash over her. "I should have. It was rash of me, but I took a risk. I think that if I had guided you there, you would have just shielded yourself off. I had a feeling that you going in there would be the right thing to do. Know that I did not exactly plan it that way, I guess the moment just presented itself."

"Is this the same feeling that has you wanting me to look after Raethran?" she asked, not meaning it to sound as severe as it did.

Ahrayn ducked her head. "Yes."

Ara exhaled her pent-up anger, walking over to a nearby elm and stroking the vertical scars of the bark. A shield against the dangers of the world. A shield made of scars and lessons learnt.

"I was only there for a day. I cannot see how I can help him. I want to, I really do but I do not see how I will be able to do so," she said, begging Ahrayn to hold her resignation at bay.

"You just need to be there. Do not be his therapist. Clear your mind of worries for his health. You are there to be a friend who has seen what he has been through. Please, visit when you can. I think you two will be good for each other. Do not ignore the lifeline he has given you and do not keep this lifeline away from him," Ahrayn pleaded.

Ara nodded, accepting Ahrayn's hand, taking solace in the small squeeze she gave, surrounding hers in a delicate warmth. Nothing she had asked of her was for herself but she had asked a great deal of her. Ever the healer, Ahrayn was a wonderful friend for Ara to have but one that came with her fair share of quirks. Everyone at the Arcanum seemed to be afflicted with something or other.

Ahrayn returned to her shift at the infirmary, leaving Ara to her introspection and recovery. She sank into the snow at the base of the elm tree, lifting her hood to let the world move on without her for a bit. A long-tailed scarlet fox had not noticed her presence whilst nuzzling in the snow with little huffs. Its ears twitched, and it cantered off between the trees, out of sight.

She could not decline Ahrayn's request after all, she did feel like stronger for facing such a blatant reminder of Ilvithiir. It had been a shock, yes, but when the flood of memories had come, she managed to stave them off. The wounds were opening but she was getting better at sealing them, with the scars being stronger for it.

It would seem that here, like in Ilvithiir, Aeradil was her saviour. Not Alikain and certainly not herself.

Her sombre mood became a stark contrast to the jovial, jaunty tune of Raethran's voice approaching from her north. The elf appeared from deep in the forest, carrying a saddle on his shoulder, as he sauntered back in the direction of the university.

He was at home in his own little world, almost dancing as he walked, not bothering with his hood, or fashion in general. He had his creased university robes hiding beneath a layer of frost that had enveloped him with his fingerless gloves and loose grey scarf providing the only thing approaching cold weather clothing in his ensemble.

He spotted Ara on the floor and halted his tune. He walked over to her, offering her a hand. She decided that she had felt sorry for herself for long enough already. That, and she had yet to devise a reasonable excuse for refusing to be pulled from her little hiding spot, leading her to accept his offer.

"My lady, a world of adventure awaits. I am unsure which chapter you are facing but know that we go through the bad so that we might appreciate the good. Now, hold this," he said, handing Ara the saddle, freeing up his fingertips to be warmed beneath his arms.

She was not ready to respond so she gave an obligatory chuckle of acknowledgement and carried the saddle for him.

"And just where did you get this?" she asked after they had been walking for a bit, gesturing toward the saddle and its distinct lack of accompanying gryphon.

"I had nothing to do with that one I am afraid to say. This was just some show-off doing his apprentice level work that ate snow and tree limbs when flying too low. He has a fractured collarbone, shattered ego and a concussion, whilst his gryphon has a cut on her leg. I think he is also going to get some creative punishment from Filthin for his efforts. Anyway, I was just retrieving it from the crash site."

"I suppose that sounds fair... I guess. Do you ever do proper work around here?" she queried, confused at his entire existence.

Mock offence struck him back. "I do more work than most!" he began, then with a playful nudge of Ara's shoulder, he returned to his normal self. "The trick is to make everyone think you are useless and never have a plan. That way, when you reveal that you have everything under control, they simply will not believe you, and call it luck. It helps to keep folk from asking for your help unless they really need it."

"Careful, tell me all your secrets and you will have nothing left for our trip around the continent," she warned, his words making a small amount of sense in the context, although seeming a touch too convenient for her liking.

"That is the beauty of it. I told you, but then you will see me in action and forget about it all. Next thing, you are wondering how I remember to walk each morning, yet alone function as an elf," he mused, taking back the saddle with a wink.

"In my defence, you did plan to go wandering off into the forest, in winter, without a cloak," she offered in rebuttal.

Raethran merely chuckled, changing the subject. "Filthin will be on the lookout for more assistance with the winter market. Would you care to ignore that entirely by picking up a writ with me? I was thinking of one that takes us away from the university buildings whilst all the duties get handed out," he asked, leading them toward the lecture buildings, handing the saddle to the first student he saw that had gryphon rider goggles around their neck.

There was a change in the atmosphere of the university with fewer spells and weapons being thrown and more books and satchels being carried about. The duelling arenas in the quad were slowly being replaced with boarded walkways and temporary stalls for merchants to set up at. Master Graxith was grumbling at the upset whilst Filthin was in his element, directing the construction efforts with a flick of his conductor's wand.

They tucked into the main lecture hall and toward the writ board. Astril and Lirith walked past, giving Raethran a hungry glare whilst greeting Ara with a nod that acknowledged her presence whilst dismissing her as a threat. They were formidable sure, but what Ara noticed at that point was how lovely they smelled. Birch? Cedar? Elderberry? Lilies? She could not place the scent, but it was wonderful enough to make her forget their previous hostilities.

The Arcanum's writ board had a few new selections and a couple of the older ones. Master Filthin's private training session remained untouched and partially covered by a writ calling for gryphon riders to partake in aerial combat manoeuvres.

Ara, having already completed a simple writ, looked over the board, deciding to go for one that would take them through the forest whilst being a little more challenging. The writs had various symbols on them that were the same no matter the university. Her hand gravitated to one of her old faithful's; a vial, a plant symbol, a sign of the forest and one for danger. Thirty credits.

"This one!" she said, not bothering to read the details, handing it confidently over to Raethran, using his own mischievous grin and nonchalant attitude against him.

Writ of Passage

Ahrayn had since joined Raethran and Ara in the quad for her break from the infirmary. Amidst the plans for their expedition, the two argued over a local map of the Arcanum's corner of the world, finding the closest sources of the moss required by the writ. The pools of Hamorumma. Ara grumbled at the choice as the pools closest access was nearly a day's march, to the north, and Raethran appeared far too excited about the prospect of going there.

Their stomachs signalled the move to the dining hall in unanimous agreement. It represented a convenient escape from the building sleet that Ara was not dressed for, having abandoned her cloak for a black student tunic from Ahrayn. It was a little tight on the shoulders but otherwise fit her well.

Yildrin and Lethrik were in the hall, enjoying some sensible meal choices with large mugs of mead to accompany them. Neither of them was in their official dress, having been overdue for a break for a few days now.

Lethrik looked as he always did; the groomed naturalist with just enough mystery to get by. Yildrin looked even more intimidating with his armour off. He was still lean, mind, but had enough muscle to swing a dining table around if he so needed. His shorter silver strands of hair were pulled back neatly into a tail, a malachite feather pinning it back.

Ara gestured for Ahrayn and Raethran to follow her, sitting down at her old convoy's table. She pointedly ignored them whilst in her periphery, she watched them break into smiles.

"Ara, how wonderful that you could join us. May I get you some tea? And your friends?" Yildrin began, turning to nod a polite greeting to each in turn. Ara beamed and scooted closer, making space along the bench.

"Yildrin, Lethrik: this is Ahrayn and Raethran," she said by way of introduction, nodding to the offer of tea and ordering a pomegranate salad for herself.

"A pleasure," Lethrik replied, tipping his head to them, before continuing in a sly tone, "and what of your 'Inquisitor' companion?"

Yildrin shot him a look, but the can had been opened and Lethrik was digging into the juicy gossip.

Ara chuckled. "He is likely stuck in some boring council meeting. What are you both up to?"

"He has not invited you on some mission, has he? You have heard what he does to people right?" Lethrik continued, ignoring Ara's prompts.

Ara shot him a warning look, trying to get him to stop whilst discreetly glancing at Raethran in a mild panic. Lethrik seemed to think that she was merely displaying a mixture of confusion and interest at his enticing introduction, as he leant forward and continued with a twinkle in his eye.

"Well, I heard that he would trap mages in their own homes and then set fire to them whilst they were still inside, only rescuing them when they started to scream… As that is when he knew their wards were tapped—" Lethrik began.

"He learnt to tell the difference between the real and the fake screams too…" Yildrin added, his uncharacteristic social theorising shocked Ara as both were now leaning into the centre of the table as if plotting the downfall of a king. He had clearly spent too much time around Lethrik for his own good. That, or his mead was stronger than anticipated.

"Yes, he would then waltz in and pull them out, barely clinging onto life, before even beginning his interrogation."

"Look, this is hardly—" Ara attempted.

Yildrin interrupted, "There was once a rogue sentinel who had trapped a dragon. He was using his magic to call other dragons to the area, trapping them and killing them. This was after the war too… He did that to him after fighting him off and chasing him into an abandoned outpost."

"In his defence, the dragon was the one who started that fire. He just refused to put it out," chuckled Raethran, cutting up a spinach and tomato topped mushroom.

The sentinel looked quizzically over at Raethran's weak attempt at gossip. Ara settled the confusion, much to Lethrik and Yildrin's embarrassment.

"Raethran is Alikain's apprentice. He has been for a while now, I think. He is going to be joining us on our trip," she said, hiding her face in her tea, uncertain of how an inquisitor-to-be would handle this sort of speculation.

A pained silence followed, none daring to breathe.

Raethran finished his mouthful and pointed at Yildrin. "Now, sentinels, they are the real heroes. They do not get caught up in the whole rogue spellcaster business, no! You are on the frontlines of it all. When I first saw a sentinel, my brother was walking me through the valleys at Isfrisairis, mountains all around with the mist of waterfalls casting rainbows in every direction. And then; there you were. These beacons of the *tarviahaltha*! I never knew that fear, awe and excitement could be in the same room at the same time, yet there it was," he said with the waving of his mushroom laden fork, breaking the tension with his characteristic laugh. "Lethrik is it?"

Lethrik nodded awkwardly, staring nervously at the fork pointed at him.

"I have always wanted to be a ranger. Have you had a designation past the borders?" he asked, pulling Lethrik into the conversation as he casually took a sip of his own tea.

"Well… yes. I had Xenia as my allocation. It is a sizable town between Symmian's Rest and Odyssey. In Mardacia," he said, pride fixing his posture.

Ara relaxed. Raethran was a ridiculous individual, but he had a way with defusing tension. He seemed to handle life like it was a sunbeam on a cloudy afternoon. Rejoicing when the warmth came and then smiling in the shade, knowing that another ray was soon to come.

"Now, you must have some spectacular stories! I am sorry. I am being awkward again. I am just a huge fan of the rangers and I really have been envious of you all my life," he said, revealing a rusted arrowhead in the shape of a willow leaf. He had it fashioned onto a necklace, pulling it out from his tunic. "The first time I ever met one of your folk, you saved my life. This shadow that appeared when we needed you most as if the trees called you forth to save us. No offense to you, Yildrin. But, if it makes you feel any better, I knew I could never be good enough to join the sentinels."

Yildrin chuckled with a shrug, finally relaxed enough to risk returning to his food.

"Hey!" exclaimed Lethrik, refusing to have Yildrin out-do him.

"If you are going to deny it," said Raethran, "then I expect you to do so without crumbs on your chin. Also, the rangers take in all types. I am not saying that I would have been assigned an entire town, but I would like to think that at least a small road or hamlet could have been mine. Maybe even something innocuous, like a footpath in the Tirzahn Mountains," he finished, securing the egos of all at the table.

Ara, feeling foolish for causing the situation, began discussing the top food choices and asking what these graduates of the Arcanum had to bring to the table. Her desperation seemed evident to all as they were happy to oblige.

Yildrin had heard of the chocolate volcano but was more a fan of savoury dishes, ordering something he simply called 'The Beast'. A sandwich of monolithic proportions flew to the table; its many layers requiring a skewer to be placed through the top to hold it all together.

There were three types of cheeses, jalapenos, gherkins, onions, corn chips, pulled pork, salsa, basil leaves, lettuce and a chicken patty all set between two roasted buns. He did not stop to explain his creation, letting the crunch of his first bite speak for itself. Raethran had a new hero and Lethrik was up.

The ranger scoffed at Yildrin's creation, and instead ordered a plate that carried a dizzying array of macarons, each a different shade or colour and each with a unique flavour. Accompanying the dish was a cup of mint tea and a small bowl of lemon sorbet. He began explaining each macaron in excruciating detail before devouring it whole, slapping Yildrin's hand away as he tried to sneak one off.

Their lunch took longer than intended and Ahrayn had to hurry off to get back to her shift at the infirmary. Lethrik and Yildrin apologised to Raethran once more. He merely shrugged them off; challenging Lethrik to a game of sinchal and guilted Yildrin into writing down the Beast's ingredients for him.

***

Raethran waded through the forest silently enough, but his movements grated Ara's keenly attuned *forehaltha* senses. She was a part of the forest and as such, moved with it and not through it, as he did.

They travelled north for the day, not needing to rest as the cool weather kept them relaxed whilst their movements kept them warm.

Initially, Ara led the way but soon, she got tired of Raethran wandering off to marvel at a winter orchid or rare herb that they crossed. With him in the lead, Ara could keep track of his wanderings, but their progress slowed with the increased detours that this had afforded him.

He had several pouches on his belt and on a bandolier slung across his chest with pockets that jingled suspiciously. That, and the messenger satchel draped across his shoulder providing him with ample storage for the myriad items he took a liking to. Ara recognised some as alchemical reagents, but others seemed too odd, even for him; an old pinecone, a pebble found in the boughs of a tree and a clump of snow dusted from a conifer.

Ara was in her travel gear but at the insistence of Yildrin and Lethrik, she kept her bracers and breastplate on. She had her bow too, but that was just common sense in the forest, especially when following an elf who could pass for a squirrel.

The long walk provided ample opportunity for her to admire the bow once more, prompting jealous glares from her curious companion. She regretted the loss of her lovely arrows, not having had the time to replace them before leaving Foretilatava. Thankfully, the rangers were all too happy to share their stocks with her and she now had a quiver of quality arrows with mismatched fletching and arrow tip styles. Among their number were some of Lethrik's with silver and green fletching, letting her know that he would be there to protect her the next time she found herself in trouble.

She had a travel pack for her provisions but was less keen on collecting trinkets from the trip. The forest here was a new creature in itself and it brought Ara much joy and a fresh perspective to behold it. However, she did miss the trees of Foretilatava. It felt like an age since she had wandered beneath their towering boughs like this. Simply exploring the hidden depths, without really knowing where she was going to end up.

Looking through the dormant ferns of the undergrowth as Raethran set about scraping moss from a rock, she felt Rylia watching over them. Faint echoes of her voice were now sung in the leaves with whispers of her guidance in the streams. She had not been queen for long, but with each day, her power grew.

"The Druidica, what is it like?" came Raethran's question, signalling that he was now moving on, dusting his hands on his trousers.

"Beautiful. The forest, the glades, the pools. Buildings sung from the trees, and the animals of the forest are as much its citizens as we are," she replied, shaking out her legs, which were straining from the long march.

"I always thought that that would be nice. What did you major in?"

"Well, I initially trained as a druid, switching to politics in my later years. My sister was selected near the end of my studies so instead of becoming a druid to defend our lands, I was to become an envoy who could travel through theirs. In my last year I studied clan politics and histories of the royal Anthurian families, as a primary. All to become her envoy."

"Seems like a lot has changed."

"For the better though. Plenty of forests out there. I do not see why we need to confine ourselves to just the one."

Raethran gave a slight chuckle at this. "So, you are going to save Etroah from the racial feuds? Stave off the greed of the dwarves, end the corruption of the humans, and shatter the pride of the elves?"

"Do not forget about quelling the imperiousness of the dragons," she finished with a wink.

"How far did you progress in your training as a druid?"

"I had finished the theory. Perhaps one day I will complete the practical side. I would have liked to develop an animal form."

"That does seem great. Any idea which form you would have taken?"

"Remains to be seen. Perhaps, if we pass the Druidica than I will be able to convince them to take us through the *fairandamay*[27]. You *tarviahaltha* may even find your forms," she offered.

"That sounds like fun. How would we go about it?"

Ara chuckled, "Well, if we ever get there, I will make sure you find out."

"Huh, well I look forward to it! Now, what have you heard of The Pools of Hamorumma?"

"I know that the divination mages enjoy the water from there. Some say it is one of the subterranean birthplaces of the river Isfrisairis and others speculate that it is where one of the primordials fell. At the end of the day, they are pretty pools. 237uri writ gives us an excuse to go there."

"That is a great way to look at it. I have only been to the surface pools once, and that was a long time ago." Raethran said with a simper, tightening his coat around his neck.

They slipped back into their companionable silence, before Ara's 237uriosity got the best of her.

"What about you? Do you enjoy the Arcanum? You were initially wanting to become a ranger, correct?"

"I have always sought to understand the world a bit more, which is where the University Arcanum came in. It is great! Adventure and the forest

---

[27] Reveal Soul Spirit: The process of finding one's attuned animal spirit

were a close second. I never would have made it in the University Astrologica – now those are the imperious folk you need to worry about."

Ara laughed. All the Isfrisairis and Sinien Tarvia elite would go to the Astrologica. It was the university dedicated to plan the future of the elven race. They were the ones who sought guidance from the gods, discovered new paths in their divination rituals and led the moral direction of leadership. It was small compared to the others, barely having two hundred students at a time, but its undergraduates were considered to be the future.

Raethran continued; "I would have enjoyed being a ranger, I think. Helping instead of hunting."

"Inquisitors do seem a bit… on the predatory side," she answered, softly.

"Hmm… I suppose. I guess I see them as a limp. A limp is painful, but it tells the body to slow down. At the end of the day, which is what your body needs to heal. We need inquisitors and likely always will. I would hate to see a world where politicians, sentinels, mages, or anyone for that matter, can act with impunity. I will be proud to serve such a cause, despite it not being my initial goal. Anyway, no work-talk when on the job. We have a writ to complete, and this right here should do the trick," he said, stopping to point at a pile of moss covered boulders.

Ara had no wish to continue the conversation either. Alikain was a good person, but his inquisitor side was definitely not what she wanted to focus on, especially when knowing that it was the fate awaiting Raethran. She climbed the rocks after him to see what the fuss was about and what could make the writ worth its thirty credits.

The pile was about half her height with a small crack in the top, the sound of rushing water emanating from deep within.

"Wait… Raethran, no," she insisted.

The elf had that annoying grin of his and was already emptying the contents from his pockets. His satisfaction at Ara's reaction only made her more annoyed, thus fuelling his smug little fire.

"There is no way I am crawling down there, swimming in that then trying to escape back through this!" she said gesturing wildly to each obstacle in turn, his grin remaining unchanged. "We do not even have towels!" she shouted, still not receiving a reaction from him. "And nobody knows where we are, to even find our frozen corpses!"

At this, Ara thought she had struck a spark of sense in him, but

Raethran merely crouched over his horde and sorted it into random piles and cast wards on himself and Ara. Ara thought she recognised some of them as the same ones Ahrayn had placed on her to protect her from the lake before, but her mind was focused on more important things.

"It is something of a squeeze, but there is a sizable cavern beneath. Follow close, do not make any unnecessary splashing and do not, under any circumstances, cast any spells. Oh, and here—" he said, taking off his coat and shoes before tossing a pebble to Ara. At contact with her skin, it shed a bright blue light on the landscape around. "Also, you will need to take the pile with the pinecone, maple sap and the cool rock shaped like a squashed egg," he finished, summiting the boulders.

"Just why exactly? And why blue light? This is useless?" Ara gasped, incredulity not even scraping the emotions trying to escape through her tone.

"Well... because it is not yellow," he said, his smile only growing at her increased exasperation.

"And this trash?" She gestured, bordering outrage.

"Hmmm... I will think of something. See you down there. Oh, mind the drop," he concluded, squeezing through the rocks and into the water with a distant splash.

Ara looked around, hoping the forest would have the good sense to back her up at this stage. Alas, the trees stood, stoic and calm as ever. She threw her coat to the ground and removed her shoes. Next, she removed her snow trousers and jersey. When Raethran's wards failed, she would at least have a plan. For good measure, she piled a few dry logs together before climbing the rocks.

The cave was large enough that the light only caught reflections in the water below. The reflections did not help matters, as they should have been a lot closer if they were to make Ara feel any better about the plan.

She checked that she had her trash pile, as per instruction, and squeezed through the gaps in the rock, leaving all traces of elegance and decorum behind.

Down, she plunged. There was a moment in her fall where she was convinced that she should have hit the water already. Next came a moment where she wondered why she had not hit the water already. After that, she decided that it was simply rude that she had not hit the water yet and braved looking down. Her timing could not have been worse as she saw the water right below, releasing a panicked gasp before spearing through its surface.

She spluttered for air and floundered about until she found Raethran, grabbing onto his shoulder in the blue light of their stones. She gave him a stare that she had only ever used once. The victim of which had stolen Anmas for an endurance race and had brought him back exhausted, lame on both forelimbs and with a mighty gash on his flank. Witnesses were probably the only thing that saved that particular soul from her intended fate. Raethran looked at her quizzically for a moment then held his finger to his lips before swimming upstream.

The river wound through the subterranean systems of lakes and rivers with turn after turn, forcing Ara to give up all hope of them ever finding their way home. Lengths of the rivers had them swimming underwater, straining their lungs to make it through to the next pocket of air which may or may not have been there. Stalactite pillars pierced the water from the ceiling, forming a rocky forest where Ara and Raethran were the little shrews scuttling in the foliage.

Raethran found a shoreline and they hopped out of the water, Ara thanking the universe that their wards had not failed yet. The elf was worryingly silent, leading the way on foot. Oxygen was less of a concern, but space was in short supply.

Crawling up now, they squeezed their way through jagged apertures that forced them to pass through one shoulder at a time. Then came a crawl space. Lying prone, they squeezed through with the weight of the earth crushing down on them from above, each breath of air being cut short as their chests expanded to the height of the crawlspace.

Once free of that, their job became a different type of scary. The crawlspace opened up to a cliff upon which, were minimal footholds. Ara could climb a tree better than most vines, but rock had always evaded her. Rock was lifeless making her feel like she was the only one attempting to hold on to the relationship.

Below their awkward shuffle was a crack in the world that extended beyond the blue light of their stones and into the endless void of the unknown. Rocks were scraped off the cliff surface and fell, bouncing off the walls but never finding an end to their descent, travelling out of sight and out of time. Ara pushed her fears from her mind and matched her hands to where Raethran's efforts had smeared the moist rock, marking the handholds for her.

They made a harrowing traverse before tucking into a cave system that wound its way yet further into the belly of the earth. Down they went, each step a controlled fall to a slippery platform of jagged stone below. Finally, Raethran turned to Ara to reveal the nature of the expedition.

"The bacteria grow in subterranean systems like this. The waterway we were in previously is fed predominantly by surface runoff and is too cold. The water in the lake ahead should be warm enough as it has water from the Isfrisairis Mountains as well as a few springs along the way. Just look out for a layer of slime on the floor with small fimbria on the surface," he whispered, handing Ara some tree bark and a configuration of fern leaves tied together to look like a humanoid doll.

She looked at the presentation, confused. "Why are you whispering, and what in the stars' plan are these for?"

"Theatrical flair and dramatic tension... wait... switch those," he finished, wading into the water and tucking beneath the surface.

She slumped her shoulders and followed him into the water. Ara swam weightlessly through the subterranean city of stone, marvelling at the blue light shining off the rock, casting portraits in the shadows. The apparently lifeless beauty of it all.

Raethran made it to the bottom and had found the bacterial film which he was scooping into a pouch. They did not need much for the writ and as such, were out in no time, ready to begin their temerarious journey back.

They began by climbing up the slippery staircase of wet rock, forcing them into a loose scramble to find their footing before starting their awkward traverse back into the crawlspace. The wards had kept them dry and free from mud but would do little to stop a fall into the chasm or keep a falling boulder from crushing their chests.

Ara remembered her ever-growing pile of useless reagents, deciding that an explanation was needed. She was beginning to look like a travelling merchant turtle which hardly seemed fitting when scaling underground cliff faces.

"Are there any other useful reagents in these caves?" she opened, hoping to trick him into providing some answers.

"A few insects and arachnids. Some fish in the pools that lead directly from rivers and the occasional cave moss species. Most of it can be found in the twilight zone though. If you go this deep, then it is usually to find ore deposits or material fed by the springs. A few nastier things if your luck

241

turns rotten."

"And we wanted the warm water for the bacteria?"

"Of course. We wanted to get this done in a day, which eliminated the cave systems to the south or travelling another full day north to the surface pools of Hamorumma which are known for the bacteria in question. This is the closest one I am aware of. And the safest one, believe it or not."

"Fair enough. So, are you going to reveal why we need all these… other components?" Ara finally asked.

"Well, the hope is that we will not need them." Was the only answer he provided.

"Fine, you know what… At least tell me that you know how to get back?"

He looked at her, arching an eyebrow. "If you were on the surface, how would you find your way back?"

Annoyed, she replied, "I would look at the sun. The stars. I would look around for geographical features and smell the ocean in the air."

He laughed. "You are spot on, but I believe that you may find those to be lacking down here."

She simply stared at him in response, hoping her stone's light would highlight the sarcasm in her expression. "Really…"

"Rivers. We went through all that effort swimming upstream. Rivers converge and very rarely diverge. There was no river divergence along our route. We follow the current. A trick for unfamiliar terrains is to listen to the certain fundamental laws of nature and well… hope it works out from there."

Ara saw the logic but was pained at the fact that Raethran may have actually had a plan this entire time. Annoyingly, it made a lot of sense, now that she was focusing on the problem at hand and not the elf in question. Navigating when the sky was not an option was always as simple as finding the nearest river.

The return swim was much faster with the current assisting their travels. Knowing the safety of the air pockets did not help much though, as Ara could not remember where they were, relying on spotting their mirror reflections of light on the surface. Soon, they were in the first chamber through which they had initially plummeted.

All too keen to hear the next part of the plan, she stared at Raethran, who was now treading water and scanning the walls of the chamber around them.

"Need a little help?" she offered, beginning to feel the chill settling in, knowing that this was likely the start of their wards failing.

"No… I just need to remember…" he replied, swimming around the perimeter.

"Raethran, enough. We do not have the time for this. I am growing tired of your games," she replied, bolstering their wards by casting hers over them in a flash of golden light.

"*Aseroena*[28]*!*" he swore. "There. Quick!" he said, pointing towards a corner of the cave with a pile of rocks that would allow for a safe climb. Spurring them into a frenzied retreat, they swam as if a school of piranha were in pursuit, their splashes echoing throughout the cavern.

"What is happening?" Ara asked breathlessly as she scrambled out the water.

"Dragon!" he shouted, throwing her up to the rocks to begin her climb.

The cave shook in a sudden pulse. Then again. And again. Resounding waves of pressure that shook the earths foundation in mighty breaths.

Ripples formed in the water to reveal the presence of the colossal form beneath. An emerald eye opened beneath the ripples, the head of a green dragon rising up with a deafening growl, shaking rocks from the cliffs in an avalanche of chaos.

They were nearing the exit now. Ara's hands kept slipping and her feet were getting torn up by the sharp rocks. The dragon opened its mouth and a vortex of flame appeared in its throat, radiating out from its chest.

Dragon fire erupted from the cracks in the rock, sending boulders and elves flying through the air and landing on the floor around the caverns entrance. Ara's wards shattered as swaths of flame enveloped them. In a mad scramble, they run for it, ducking between trees and finding the nearest root system to hide within.

"Pinecone, sap, now!" Raethran shouted, grabbing the items from Ara's hand as she ripped them from her pockets.

He smeared the sap over the pinecone and set a flame onto it. He yanked some hair from his head and added it to the smouldering wood. He threw the flaming decoy behind them as they made for a great oak that stood near a steep embankment. They dove over and tucked under the buttress

---

[28] Apple worm – A curse Raethran uses to emphasise his poor luck

roots, Raethran grabbing snow and pushing it at Ara, himself eating a handful of it. She copied his action, locking her limbs and praying for the roots to envelope her. They sat there in silence, awaiting their fate, suppressing each breath.

The dragon stalked through the forest to the east of their hiding spot, roaring in pursuit of the smoke trail from the pinecone. For once, Ara could see that Raethran was present, his eyes darting around as he searched for a plan to piece together.

They hid there, freezing in their motionless states, their breath now too cold to form steam and give away their location. Hypothermia was a fast-approaching threat but Ara held off casting a ward, awaiting Raethran's next step.

Light was fading when a soft blue glow flowed from his fingers. It took a while for Ara to realise what had happened. He had used so little magic that she could not see how it could even hope to protect them from the elements. Now that the cold was off them, their body heat could begin repairing the damage done, circulation slowly returning to their hands and feet.

The sound of danger had long since subsided, but they were not going to take any chances. It was past midnight when Raethran finally relaxed, motioning for her to follow him out of their hovel. They still needed to retrieve their belongings and make the hike back. Their coats were a little ruffled by the dragon's emergence but otherwise unscathed. Their packs and Ara's bow still tucked away safely without sign of tampering, much to their relief.

From the look of the tracks, the dragon had returned not long after it had emerged, clearly having decided that they were not worth the effort.

Raethran led the way with Ara following in terse silence. She was fuming, but only most of it was directed at Raethran. Not even the gentle crunch of the freshly powdered snow could break through her mood. She had been pushed around for too long now and this was the point where she vowed to change it. If these little inquisitors wanted to see what Ara could do, then let them look on as she showed them the power of the *forehaltha*.

When the university was in sight, and dawn fast approaching, Ara decided that she could hold it in no longer. "Yellow light? Dragons? Did you not think any of this would be useful for me to know?"

"The yellow light was for the sharks. That river system was not officially part of the pools but an underground system that communicated with the Onien Mer. Mana sharks love cave systems like that and will migrate along them for their breeding cycles to have their offspring ready come springtime. Sharks love yellow light, the more magical the better for mana sharks. I did not want to look any tastier to them than I needed. Your ward was not only yellow but such a massive expenditure of magic that the dragon could not have helped himself. The pinecones were a distraction. The figurine was in case we needed a binding to make an illusionary double to fool anything hunting us… I had a few tricks up my sleeve; I was simply hoping that none of them would be necessary."

"This seems like information I should have had before we went in!"

"Do not get the term partner and leader mixed up. You knew what you needed to know and had your time to do further research as needed. There was a danger marker on the writ, not to mention it being worth thirty credits. Underground systems like that are known to make lovely homes for dragons. This close to the Onien Mer, we were lucky not to be surrounded by mana sharks from the second we touched the water. I know you did not grow up here, but we are going to have to learn to adapt to new environments out there. You need to be able to read situations and make the relevant decisions yourself. I am simply testing you so that you can avoid these mistakes when we are travelling with Alikain."

"What? So, you were just testing me? You are just being a good little puppet and training me for Alikain?"

Raethran stopped and turned towards her, his smile fading away, replaced by the look of an inquisitor. The clouds of a spring storm rolled through his eyes, the dangerous stillness of his expression holding back their ferocity. Ara saw that she had crossed a line, but she had a right not to be toyed around like this. She bit down on her lip and faced him, clenching her fists.

He replied, his tone neither cold nor scathing but one of pity, "Yes. It is time you realise who it is you are going to be travelling with. When you are with him, you are a tool, and you will have your purpose. He will push you to the very limit of your capabilities as that is what he needs from you. If you fail, getting hurt in the process? Well then, that is your prerogative, and we cannot expect any sympathy from him. You, me, Ahrayn, we are there to get results for him, that is all. You need to be better because he will expect you to be better."

Ara could not reply. She hung her head and sighed, exhaustion depressurising her anger.

"You did well in a pinch," Raethran continued, "Your wards were strong, and you followed your instincts in the chaos. Where that was not enough, you used my actions to guide your own. Part of me wishes you had branched out with your own plan, but I guess I was not as forthcoming with my answers to your questions. Old habits."

"I just needed more information. You did not have to keep me in the dark like that," Ara said quietly, as she pushed some snow around with her foot, refusing to make eye contact.

"You have been chosen by him for a reason. It is no small compliment either. Yes, your magic is powerful and from what I have heard, you could take on half of Mardacia with that bow of yours, but there is more."

"I am the sister to a queen," she added, looking up.

Raethran shook his head as he studied her expression. "Elven royalty is not hard to come by for him. We have enough of those, and most of them have been throwing spells around for a lot longer than you or I. He chose you because you have proven yourself in action. In some way, with something you did, you have shown him that you are worth his interest. Do not, however, see yourself as a prize coat for a ball he is to attend but as a piece on his chess board, manoeuvring through the world until you make your intended move. We just need to hope that we are the knight that checks the king and not the pawn that draws out the bishop."

"That hardly seems fair. Why should I follow him if he is just going to treat me like this?"

"Because that is how people treat each other. Alikain is just up front about it. He has a goal that he will need you to achieve, it is up to you from there. I wanted to see how you would react here so that, together, we can ensure that you are prepared for whatever comes our way. We are going to be diving in, head-first to any task required, no matter the danger."

"I guess that is it then. We are destined to be dragged across the continent on the whims of an inquisitor," Ara sighed.

"There is one consolation though: to be on his side means that you will be changing the world for the better. You will be ruled by a code of morals second to none. You know… Lethrik and Yildrin had a point about Alikain. He has done some terrible things in the past, but they have all been necessary. That sentinel they were talking about, the one he killed in the cave? Six dragons and counting. He had become one drawn to violence through hatred and vengeance. He had fallen off the path and killed all those that had tried to pull him back, including his fellow sentinels and two inquisitors before Alikain could get to him. Nobody in this world took that harder than him, but still, he performed his duty. Through his sacrifice, he ended that sentinel's suffering and closed the threat to the peace between *haltha* and *lohikaara*[29]. Ara, he does what needs to be done, and for some reason, what he needs to do now will require you to be at his side. If you want to survive him then you need to be ready. We all do."

Ara frowned, absorbing all of this. The more she thought about it, the worse she felt. Her head was spinning as spots invaded her vision.

She laughed humourlessly, "You do not know what I have been through, nor what I have seen. You have no idea what I have done. My actions, my mistakes! I have already caused death, pain and destruction and now you tell me this? That one of those actions piqued his interest. I cannot do this, Raethran; I cannot do those kinds of things for him, no matter how noble the end result."

"You are strong enough to handle this. I am simply warning you and preparing you for what is to come. He will not lead you but work alongside you. Take his orders as goals but go about them in the manner that you see appropriate. That is what he needs from you. You are not some sentinel that is there to do as you are told. Stop following instructions and start leading yourself. That said, you are not a ranger to let loose on the world with an idea in mind. I guess, what I am saying is that you are Ara. What Alikain needs at his side is an Ara. You need to find your courage in being yourself and stop letting your fear and doubt suppress that," he said, pulling out the rock shaped like a squashed egg, wiping away the mud to reveal a message.

Luestrala marilma ramsoma a'isir.[30]

Ara gave an exhausted chuckle and accepted the rock from his partially gloved hand. "So, this is how it is going to be? Cryptic messages and cruel lessons?"

"I will do better. This is my first time teaching so give me some slack. But you are a good student. If it helps, then remember that I have just given you permission to be yourself. The next time I refuse to answer your questions, to your satisfaction, then you can hit me with another of those lightning bolts. If that is what you would do, then have at it! We clearly need a sprinkle of Ara in our lives and I for one am prepared to see all it is

---

[29] Elves and dragons
[30] The stars light the path from which our heart chooses

that you have in store for this world and, well… and the next."

"Even if my magic has a habit of calling forth dragons?"

"I choose to focus on the positives. Plus, we now have something that nobody at the university could ever hope to have, thanks to you."

Ara rolled her eyes. "And what, pray tell, is that? Friendship? Partnership? A bond forged in dragon's fire?"

"A bag full of goo," he answered, lifting the soggy pouch victoriously into the air, making his way down the hill and toward the Arcanum whilst whistling a jaunty tune.

Small Steps

Raethran and Ara had slept most of the next morning, allowing Ahrayn to get through her work without interruption. They were exhausted from their feats. Ara had also let slip about the dragon which gathered quite the stir in the infirmary, placing Vexhimarith on Raethran's tail.

The Arcanum greeted the first of the merchants for the winter festival. Exotic foodstuffs were a guarantee, with the majority being provided by elven trade caravans from Southern Tour Aine, and the rest sent via the merchant ships of Sinien Tarvia from as far south as Rubahari. The foreign flavours were a favourite amongst the students, and, despite the abilities of the meal stone, there was something unbeatable about the taste of the real thing

Mardacia brought out the weird and wonderful foods with meat carved from the deadly monsters, which ravaged villages, and fruits plucked from trees growing at the feet of the gods themselves. Melsoa excelled at strong spices in the dishes that were unique to the south. They had a large amount of water in their foods thus, stews, curries, and soups were on the menu, which suited the winter climate rather perfectly.

Anthuria had some standard favourites but were mostly famous for having a million and one ways to cook staple foods like wheat and potato. What they lacked in the food itself being interesting, they more than made up for with their sauces which were likely going to be on sale by the jar. All the food aside though, what Ahrayn was really looking forward to, were the trinkets from Sinien Tarvia.

The home of the *merhaltha* was the elves' port to the oceans and beyond. They were adept at finding sunken wrecks and long forgotten ruins in the depths of lands lost to the tides or to the changing terrestrial surface. Recently, Raethran had been preoccupied with various writs and adventures that had him off the grounds. She was thus wanting to spend more time with him and hoped to find a little gift to commemorate the occasion.

Her dorm room was clean and orderly, with an array of potted plants awaiting their routine care. She filled a watering can and set about tending to their needs, removing the odd dead leaf and inspecting the flora for signs of pests or disease. Next, she folded her clean laundry and placed it back into her drawers, setting aside a dress for the night's activities. It was the deep blue of a glacier, with a shoulder cut and a skirt which flowed when she danced, like the rolling of waves. She wanted to look her best should she and Raethran find themselves dancing again. It also served to hide her feet so she would be able to wear her comfortable boots and not have to worry about the cold. Her wards would take care of the rest.

Olethia passed by her doorway and leant in, placing a cup of freshly brewed tea on her nightstand with a kiss to the air. She gave Ahrayn a smile and wordlessly continued with her day. Ahrayn shouted a thanks in her direction, the words travelling down the hall on a musical note.

Next, she perused her assignments whilst drinking the fresh cup of tea, checking that they were up to date and ready for submission according to her standards. One of the pages of her paper: '*Management of Verminosis in Domestic Gryphons* 'had a raspberry stain from when Raethran had snuck her some jam-filled doughnuts into the library. She smiled and shook her head, keeping the imperfection on the page. Looking back fondly at the day, she cringed, remembering Ruunidil's fury upon discovering the crumbs from their lunch.

Raethran had confessed, of course, this simply earning him cleaning duty in the library. The next day, he had shown her various textbooks from the restricted sections, so he had likely planned to leave those crumbs behind. Either that or his dealings with Ilkiir had left him with more than just scribbles, on the Ilvithiir expedition, for his efforts.

Her duties attended to, she got dressed and tied back her hair, choosing a scarf of soft blue wool to accompany her ensemble. Everything was in order and prepared for Raethran to spend the night, his own room having been transformed into a storage area with their luggage. She turned to leave, the prospect of breakfast luring her out with the thought of raspberry jam doughnuts now fresh on her mind.

The snow had not relented the entire day; and fresh powder had blanketed the grounds faster than the students could clear it. The martials were taking a well-deserved break, and thus most of the tours had been held indoors to allow for warm fires and dry boots. Windows were now occupied by students reading, with alcoves becoming home to those huddled around wholesome conversations with flasks of tea in hand.

Snow covered the rooftops and glistened in the mid-morning light. There was a strong wind blowing in from the north carrying with it the faint scent of the Onien Mer. Ahrayn enjoyed the crunch of the snow underfoot allowing her to add a sort of rhythm to the winter ambience in the rise and fall of the breeze with the melody of the student's voices.

The meal hall was thriving with students hurrying in and out, their arms laden with parcels for their day's plans. The warm glow and cheery laughter that emanated from within was enough to brighten anyone's mood. She tucked her head in and placed her order, eagerly awaiting the sweet raspberry jam, but immediately regretted her decision after seeing Ranger Lethrik. He was sitting in the corner, tackling a tower of decadent pancakes with berries and cream being added to each bite. His eyes gleamed as he stuffed his cheeks with the fluffy delight.

The doughnuts arrived in a neatly wrapped pouch of banana leaves allowing her to steal them away for her breakfast on the move. Ahrayn's mother had been struggling to keep up with the paperwork of recent events and she thought she may assist her with some mother–daughter time in the admin office, making the best of a bad situation. Her lectures were up to date and her assignments completed, to her standards, so it suited her well.

The breeze from the north had woken up and turned into a heavy wind, buffeting Ahrayn's cloak, forcing her to tuck her head down and scamper across the quad. She gave a quick wave to those she passed and stopped to give the more familiar of the students a nod. This was not the weather for talking so she forged ever onward, her stomach now beginning to ache, reminding her of her medication.

The infirmary was a welcome reprieve from the elements and was calm enough in itself to allow Ahrayn to sneak through unimpeded, toward Master Hital's office.

Specimen jars were placed on shelves with detailed and colourful diagrams lining the walls. Anatomical models were mounted on tables, abandoned in various states of assembly with textbooks strategically positioned throughout. She had always thought the decor a bit garish, but it assisted her in the job and that was the purpose of it all, at the end of the day. To assist with making it a more habitable location, Ahrayn had slowly been adding a selection of indoor plants over the years, now forming a tour of scents and colours to an otherwise clinical environment. The vanda orchids surrounding the water fountain in the corner were particularly beautiful.

Of her parents, Hital was definitely the messier of the two. Ahrayn spent her first ten minutes simply returning tools to their drawers, reassembling the anatomical models and watering the plants that required it. After the chaos had been quelled, she removed an array of vials from her backpack, taking a sip from some and decanting capsules from others. She made herself a cup of tea and completed her doughnut and medication breakfast in relative peace until Hital arrived.

Her mother entered and let loose a tangible sigh of relief at seeing Ahrayn present, ready to save the day. The two embraced and set about their work, interspersed with pleasantries. Hital guided Ahrayn' to the piles of paperwork that needed the most immediate attention, finishing with the medication order herself.

An exhausted looking Silla was called in to take the order to Oldiir. She was all too happy as this was her final duty before her shift was over. She was running on automated responses at this point, taking the form from Hital with a blank expression. Bumping into a side table on her way out, Silla stopped to apologise to it with a polite bow before scuttling to freedom.

The pair made short work of the admin pile with Ahrayn working uninterrupted whilst Hital handled any emergencies or questions between working on her own pile. Soon, the infirmary was under control. Hital even stopped to share a victorious cup of jasmine green tea with Ahrayn, the two moving to the couches.

"How are you feeling today?" Hital asked, lifting her feet onto her chair to sit cross legged, matching Ahrayn's posture.

"Better thank you. I have been trying to guess at the ingredients of the new pain reliever. Basilisk venom? I do not feel sedated at all, nor do I feel numb, so I was thinking it was a muscle relaxant, and a strong one at that," Ahrayn postulated.

"Good guess. Do the effects last long enough?"

"Almost. I am reminded when my next dose is due, but it works too quickly to extend much past that. Is the venom the reason why Raethran came back looking like he was mauled by a dragon?"

Hital tapped the side of her mug before shamefully admitting, "…Yes. Ilkiir heard word of a male basilisk without a mate near the Ixilth valley. It was beginning to cause a stir and had already begun killing the local wildlife and breaking down a few trees."

Ahrayn sighed and looked down at the roof's reflection in her tea. The chandelier of glowing *lenlialarla* forming a geometric array of starlight from the ceiling. It gently rotated, casting even light over the room in a soft white hue.

"He handled it rather well from what I gathered. He did not go into details though; you know how he is. I think you are the only person who can ever get a straight answer out of him," Hital remarked.

A polite knock came at the door, startling Master Hital and causing Ahrayn to look up from her tea. Hital walked over and opened the door to find Ara, her ears and nose red from the cold with her boots still tracking snow across the infirmary.

"Good morning, my dear! Is everything all right?" Hital inquired, giving her a quick scan for any potential injuries or signs of panic.

"Everything is fine, thank you," she began, noticing Ahrayn in the room, giving her an awkward wave. "I was wondering if I may visit a patient of yours. Aeradil, room fifty-one."

Hital pondered the request for a moment, being rescued by Ahrayn.

"Mother, I was hoping that Ara could assist with Aeradil's exposure therapy. He has already begun reacting to social stimuli and that was after only one visit from her."

"Uh… Very well then. I would just ask that you avoid any verbal reminders regarding Ilvithiir and those involved over there. I see no harm in it otherwise. I wondered what had assisted him so," Hital replied, giving a reassuring smile to Ara.

Ara shifted her weight awkwardly, not knowing if she was allowed to leave.

Ahrayn unfolded her legs and got to her feet, placing her teacup on a coaster on Hital's desk. "Ara, I was wondering if I may join you for this one?"

Ara nodded, panicking slightly, stepping aside to welcome Ahrayn to her task. Hital returned to her desk and set about the remainder of the paperwork she had accumulated thus far, idly sipping at her tea and humming the gentle tune of *'St Albert's Flower'* that had been stuck in her head since the night of the sinchal game.

"How are you doing this morning?" Ahrayn asked Ara, now leading the way to Aeradil's room.

"Well thanks. Vexhimarith insists that I sleep in my carriage for propriety's sake, despite your offer and having been offered a dorm room by the masters." She noticed Ahrayn's confused look and finished her thought. "It is a lovely setup, do not get me wrong. It is the midnight toilet breaks that get annoying. It is an hour-long process getting dressed for not only the weather but for any potential threat of diplomatic encounters that would arise if I were to bump into anyone. All that, only to spend a few seconds actually doing what I set out to do."

Ahrayn chuckled. "That is big talk coming from the druid. Plus, he just turns into an owl every night and flies about the place. I hardly see how that is appropriate from a diplomatic perspective. Not to mention, it has now been twice that he has tried to hunt me!"

This time it was Ara's turn to look confused.

"I can turn into animals too. Well, an animal. A tree swallow to be precise," Ahrayn explained.

"Like your pendants? You certainly have your fair share of surprises. I thought it was rather difficult for the *tarviahaltha*?"

"The *forehaltha* have an easier time of it, there is little doubt there. Where you align yourself with the essence of the creature you wish to turn into, we have to assist the spirit guardian of that creature in such a way that they gift us with the understanding of their form. It is a convenient way of bypassing our need to break everything down into their facts and formulae."

"So, you can actually turn into a tree swallow?"

"Yes," replied Ahrayn with a chuckle. "I try not to do it too often though. Can you turn into any other creature?"

"Nope. I am clumsy enough in my own skin. Before I was to be an emissary, I was studying to become a druid. My course load soon became too severe thus, I decided to delay it for the time being, the practical side at least. Such transformations are frowned upon down south, so I saw little use for it with my new role. How did you assist the guardian of the tree swallows?"

"Not the guardian itself, more just assisting enough of the tree swallows. There was an internal parasite brought into the population by a migratory flock from Melsoa. I figured out a way to assist them. I was even able to get rid of future infections. Turns out it was a magically mutated strain of trypanosoma. I told Alikain about it and he found the culprit responsible for infecting the birds. The problem went away soon after."

"Sounds like you deserved that one. I had heard of something similar to that, but I guess I just figured it would be more along the lines of being able to turn into a lion after removing a thorn from her foot. My apologies for Vexhimarith's behaviour then, I guess."

Ara and Ahrayn laughed together before walking down the hall to room fifty-one.

Ahrayn knocked gently before opening. Aeradil was lying in bed but there were signs of him having moved since Ara had last been there. His expression was still empty, with his slow breathing being the only indicator of life. That, and the occasional blink.

"Aeradil, I have Ara with me today. I was wondering if you may want to sit outside together and get some fresh air? The sun is poking through the clouds and the wind has calmed down. It is beginning to look like a lovely day outside," she offered.

There was no response from the ranger. Ara let loose a small sigh of relief at not being left in the cold. Ahrayn was having none of it though and simply smiled, calling for a student in the hallway to set up some chairs outside.

"Great, well, let us get you up then. Ara, would you?" she asked, walking over to Aeradil and helping him slowly out of bed.

Ara took his one arm and Ahrayn the other; together, they led him outside and onto a chair. Ahrayn went inside and retrieved some blankets for the two elves, setting them to relax in the cold morning air. She even had tea for them and before long, Ara was snug and enjoying herself, unphased by the cold and glad to have Aeradil at her side again, even if he was not entirely there. In her periphery, she did notice him adjusting his blanket and taking a small sip of tea every so often.

Ara decided against talking in general, trusting in the healing powers of time and the natural world around them. Aeradil would find himself again and there was no sense in taking a risk to rush it. He was safe at the Arcanum and perhaps it was better that he stayed here a little longer before returning to his other duties.

Ahrayn had finished ensuring Ara and Aeradil's comfort and decided to now see to her own.

Raethran was likely up by now, getting an early start to the day by bunking his lecture; 'Static Wards and Ritual Shielding'. He was thus, likely in the library if he was at the university at all.

The sun was attempting to warm the grounds in vain, the light reflecting off the snow. Master's Graxith and Selen appeared in the middle of a debate with Alikain at the centre of it, something Ahrayn would rather avoid. She skirted around the eastern end of the university and in the back entrance to the Arcanum itself, aiming for the library.

Ruunidil had a small army of students under his command, copying texts and rescanning documents, bringing him any information he may have missed. He acknowledged Ahrayn's entry with a polite nod and returned to his work. Surrounding him were six quills, all scratching at parchment in response to his magic, only pausing at the breaks in his concentration when he dealt with his students.

Raethran had formed a fort with his books and was scribbling notes on free parchment, not noticing Ahrayn's arrival. His inkpot was running low, and he had already managed to stain his fingertips blue. She glanced over the titles and shook her head. He was forever wasting his time, sifting through the medical textbooks, hoping to find something the infirmary or *Tamore Narana* had missed.

Judging by the state of his hair and the collection of cake wrappers he had stored in his satchel; he had been here since the early hours of the morning. In the surrounding shelves were likely a few students on his payroll, working to gain their writs by assisting him with his pursuits down whichever rabbit hole he had gotten himself stuck in this time.

Ahrayn sat next to him and poked at his shoulder, rousing him from his furious concentration.

He finished his train of thought and completed the last of the line he was writing. The 'Raethran script' may as well have been encrypted as his handwriting was so terrible that only he could read it. The masters gave up on reprimanding him after his third year and eventually just perfected the art of its interpretation.

"Ahrayn, good of you to join me. I was just learning how we apparently have this stuff called blood that flows in our body to keep us alive. Now, this stuff is supposed to stay in our body in order for it to do its job. Do you think we should tell Graxith or let him find out on his own?"

"Yes yes, he would not keep throwing martials at each other if you actually paid attention in his classes," she replied.

Raethran merely gave her a look to let her rethink her words.

"All right fine, but I have another shift this afternoon and I want to spend my free time outside of the library, if at all possible," she pleaded.

Raethran smiled and shut his book, loading his literary hoard onto a trolly and quickly packing them away before following Ahrayn to the dining hall. Their usual lunchtime order of tea, fresh bread and split pea soup flew to the table ahead of them and they sat down to enjoy each other's company.

Ahrayn dispensed her lunchtime medications and tucked into her steaming hot meal. She looked at it, added salt and continued whilst Raethran layered butter on his bread before dunking it in his own soup.

Graxith entered the dining hall with his chest puffed out as if to receive a medal for holding a bridge against an army of Eastern Anthurians, all by himself. A feat which he had actually accomplished but he refused to acknowledge the medal as it wasn't a full army by his standards, only a scouting group.

He began his announcement with giddy anticipation, his resounding voice waking the marble of the hall and shaking the dust from the tables. "We will be having a hunt later tonight. You will be the prey, and the rangers, your hunters. Capture the flag ruling, with the flag being the *lenlialarla* at the centre of the quad. I expect to see an impressive display. All are welcome with prior clearance from myself, but no final year will be exempt from participation. You may form teams of no more than three and may use any non-lethal techniques for the same shall apply to your hunters."

The final years were veterans of Graxith's machinations but so far, it had only been Raethran who had been hunted by the rangers. Nonetheless, they kept their calm, and the political alliances began forming without a moment's hesitation.

Olethia and Tuliin were already sitting next to each other, and with a discreet hand gesture joined forces. Thriol sauntered towards the twins, but they turned him away, not letting their desired conquest get in the way of their victory. Vexrith, surprisingly, approached Grindol, and after a moment of shock, the gangly elf nodded enthusiastically.

Raethran sighed at the news but then looked at Ahrayn with a contented smile. He had the only person he ever needed. He squeezed her hand and returned to his soup, not falling into planning mode like their fellow final years in the cafeteria.

Ara and Alikain entered the hall, idly chatting, seeming more comfortable in each other's presence. They spotted the two at their table and quickly joined, darting through the commotion that had now been stirred.

"So, it seems Selen finally consented for Graxith to have the rangers hunt down all the students, not just me," Raethran said, greeting their arrival.

Ahrayn looked to Alikain for his reaction, but he did not reveal anything, merely waiting hungrily for his vegetable stew, which was now on its way, zooming through the air, narrowly avoiding a collision with a flying chocolate fondue.

"I suppose it was only a matter of time before he wore her down," sighed Ahrayn. "I will admit to being curious about the Vexrith and Grindol pairing," she said with a nod in their direction.

Ara's gaze turned to the unfolding chaos, not sure what to make of all the scheming. She was brought into the conversation as Raethran asked her, "Are you going to be joining?"

Ara frowned, ignoring her tea that had just arrived. "This hunt? I am not sure if I am allowed to…"

Raethran scoffed, "Sure you are. This is a free-for-all. The only reason the juniors will not participate is because they would rather waste their time betting, and the professors are too scared of being beaten by us lowly students, to risk it." He shared a glance with Ahrayn and turned to another spoonful of soup with a smile.

Raethran, not getting the acknowledgement he was looking for, dove back in. "Do not think you are exempt from this either, Alikain. The inquisitor finally getting a chance to sharpen his skills against the rangers? It may even help you during our mission around the continent," he said, risking a close-handed tap on Alikain's shoulder.

Alikain grunted at the impact and turned to face the trio, looking as impassive as always. He and Raethran had another of their silent conversations, glaring at each other. Alikain's lips twitched ever so slightly towards a smile with Raethran beaming in triumph.

"I suppose there is value to be had with me joining. Ahrayn and yourself have had plenty of experience in this sort of thing… So perhaps Ara and I can give it a try, as a team?" He offered, ignoring Raethran's victory grin.

"What exactly is this hunt?" asked Ara, the uncertainty of her future becoming all too real.

"Over the years, Alikain would send me out on writ missions but, to make it more difficult, he would send some rangers after me. Blunt weapons of course but enough to give you the fright of your life if they catch you midway through climbing up the cliff by Gryphon's Peak," he explained, laughing at first but trailing off as he remembered the bruises and fractured wrist. Ahrayn placed a comforting arm around his shoulders at the revelation.

Ara glanced at Alikain, who had turned his grey eyes on her, waiting for her response. She decided that she was going to adopt some of Raethran's quirks. It had kept him safe for all the years that he had been apprenticed to Alikain so why would it not help her out now?

"Great! Sort of a competition then? Us versus you? And the other students too, I guess," she said in Raethran's tone, trying to convince her voice to sound goading and carefree.

Raethran chuckled. "Fantastic! Well, Ahrayn and I have some scheming to get done before the bets have been finalised," he said, hopping from the bench and onto the table top, throwing his arms out and proclaiming to the crowd. "Attention all, we have another team to enter the pool… Inquisitor Alikain and Lady Ara have decided to join the hunt!"

He gestured to the pair, bowing theatrically before stepping down, dodging a flying piece of toast from Alikain. Ahrayn shook her head with a smile, mussing Raethran's hair and claiming his hand. He gave her knuckles a kiss and strolled away, pausing only to throw Ara a wink.

Sounding of the Horns

Hopping down the last of the stairs from the illusions tower, Raethran jogged over into the quad, joining the student congregation. Graxith had set up a *lenlialarla* in the quad and was addressing the students in his vicinity, eager to get the evening's hunt started. Ahrayn welcomed Raethran's huffing and puffing with a casual smile, grabbing his hand and turning her attention back to the briefing.

Alikain sat off to the side with Ara mingling among the students. Everyone was loaded with packs, satchels, weapons and armour, looking to Graxith like pigeons around a park bench. Being new to the ranger hunt, but regulars of these sorts of exercises, they wanted to be prepared for anything heading their way. The main difference here, was that these trackers were the best that Isfrisairis had to offer, a fate normally reserved for Alikain's sadism against Raethran. Sure, they were no wardens of Foretilatava, but they didn't need Thriol to be covered in glistening plate armour in order to spot him in the forest.

"…The rangers will begin within five kilometres of the objective. You will begin between fifteen and ten kilometres away. Get here, touch the *lenlialarla* and you win, if you are first that is. Now, off you run. I will sound the first horn within the hour. The cavalry will be released at the second blast of the horn," he finished, turning from the group and heading to his office with a worrying skip in his stride.

Concerned looks exchanged between the senior students quickly turned to a hum of activity as they formed their teams and set off, according to their plans.

The evening sky was mostly clear, the moon was waning on this, the third day after the full moon allowing for enough light to see despite its low angle in the sky. With no blanket of clouds to trap the day's heat, the moonlight illuminated the mist of the elves' breath. Owls hooted at their intrusion whilst the branches reached out towards them, reeling away from the footpaths.

Now, twelve or so kilometres away, Ahrayn broke the silence of their serene journey. Risking the cold, she dropped her hood, her mousy hair flowing freely to protect her ears from the frigid breeze.

"So, what is the plan? No pretending that you do not have one," she asked.

"Subversion, misdirection and no shortage of luck. We have the advantage with the relatively low light and the area the rangers have to cover, we just need to utilise that advantage," he replied, leading them onto a rocky plateau. Scant tree cover let in a swath of moonlight to illuminate the snowpacks between the stones in the tranquil opening.

"That does not sound like a plan, so I will ask again. What is the plan? More importantly, will it get us out of this cold soon?" Ahrayn asked again, fighting away a shiver.

"I do have a plan, but it is very much a shell. I will tell you that it begins with this," he said, laying a picnic blanket for Ahrayn and setting out a flask of tea pastries, still steaming from their wrappings.

She grinned, appearing placated by the offering. She sat back and watched as he went about igniting a small campfire that allowed her to warm her fingers. Embers darted about the mist, frolicking as they rose to their heights before fading into the sky.

"Hardly the stealthy approach but this works fine, for me," she concluded with a smile, wriggling her fingers over the flame.

***

Alikain followed behind Ara, excited to see the workings of one of the *forehaltha* in the forest. He watched as her feet danced across the leaf litter whilst she spun around, avoiding the rogue branches. Alikain had to guide his footfalls to avoid snapping an ankle when the path became too uneven, yet she danced on. She managed an easy pace through the trees to the north, a heavily forested area and a direction that did not rely on the gryphons to be stolen for the entry into the university grounds.

The air burnt his lungs at around the eight-kilometre mark as he pushed to catch up to Ara. He was trying not to make too much noise lest he attract a passive, aggressive glare. There were multiple entry points into the campus from the north and Alikain was curious to see which she seemed so intent upon. There were the valleys of the northeast that could break line of sight rather nicely but the northwest had the lakes that could separate pursuers, lending benefit to Ara's speed.

They startled a fox with their sudden intrusion into his glade, his tail darting behind a tree like a shadow fearing a torch. Now being the required distance from the campus, they allowed themselves a brief respite until the horn blast signalled the hunt's commencement.

"Thoughts?" Ara asked, her whisper as silent as the breeze that frosted their breath against their face covers.

"The rangers will likely wait for us to duck through their ranks before sweeping back, pushing inward to funnel us into their traps. They will be able to track us that way and it will be difficult to outrun them in these trees. This is also the forest that they were all trained in so I anticipate no shortage of ambushes. I am curious to see what Graxith meant by the second horn for the cavalry…" he replied, watching her closely in his peripherals for the slightest change in posture or sign of action. There was a fierce determination fighting off her fear with the internal battle bubbling to the surface of her features.

"I meant on a possible plan," she clarified.

"Yes… Well, now you know what your plan needs to avoid," he added, raising an eyebrow.

She chased off a look of exasperation with her determination winning out. "All right Inquisitor. If you want to let the *forehaltha* cultivate the plan in a forest, then you best be prepared to keep up. These may not be my trees but all I ever need is soil beneath my feet and leaves above my head."

Alikain smiled at her resilience and in a silent chuckle, leant back and looked to the stars' light, marvelling at the magnitude of the universe above them. The night had certainly begun with its fair share of surprises with many more promised on their horizon.

***

Raethran now had their fire going and was loading various aromatic barks into the flames. When he was content with his efforts, he pulled two coats from his bag and gave one to Ahrayn, adorning the other himself. It was a hideous choice as it had odd stuffing and tassels of fabric in random patterns but would be enough to break a silhouette and provide some camouflage in the darkness. It added another layer of warmth too, for which Ahrayn was grateful.

He sat next to her, and she poured him a cup of steaming tea, welcoming him to the good life that she had acquainted herself with. Nocturnal creatures went about their business around them, grumbling at the smoke but eager to get a start on their activities before the evening got too cold. She let loose a frustrated sigh as Graxith's horn blast carried through like thunder rolling over the land. A flare shot into the air above the Arcanum to mark the occasion, its coruscant blue light adding to the tapestry of the night sky.

Raethran looked up, merely enjoying the sight of the cerulean light falling lazily to the ground like an autumn leaf drifting to the floor. Ahrayn chuckled at his lack of action, indulging in another sip of her mint green tea. Her feet were getting a little too warm at this stage, being tucked right up against the flames to bring feeling back to her toes.

"So, is this where you give me my promise in the moonlight or are you going to reveal your master plan? You survival students always have a list of facts to throw out in times like these," she asked in a mock sigh of exasperation.

Raethran gave a slight chuckle. "I just wanted to enjoy the moment whilst we wait for the rangers to get closer. They will be coming for us, so stay on guard. We have the mountain behind us, so all the cool air is going to sweep down the slope and bathe them in the smoke from our fire. With our scents masked, we just need to stay out of sight as they walk by, hence the coats. If all that goes well then, they will need to find our tracks. This area was host to the alchemists this week as they harvested their ice-truffles. Countless footpaths and a sea of churned earth means that our tracks just need to stay unpredictable to either lose them or waste their time for long enough so that we can get a lead. If there are horses, we need to worry about then we should be able to hear them before they see us. They will not be of much use in the trees, against just the two of us, anyway so we will likely only need to worry about them when we are in sight of the campus. If we tuck around to the lake, then we will not have to worry about them at all, but we will see how things are going when we get near to the grounds."

Ahrayn smiled and leant back, pouring herself a refill of tea, tucking her legs into her chest. "That sounds fair. I am hesitant about the lake part of it all but until then, we should have a grand old time. Is that pecan pie I am smelling?"

He rewarded her keen senses with the pie and sat next to her, resting his head on her shoulder, sipping his tea. He placed his feet near the fire and wriggled his toes to wake them up for the journey to come.

"What are your thoughts on Ara?" Ahrayn asked hesitantly.

"She is lovely. I worry that Alikain has her on board. He is dangerous enough with his inquisitor's badge and now he has *forehaltha* royalty to throw around."

"I meant: what do you think of her as a person?"

"Well… She seems like fun. I have yet to give it much thought, if I am to be honest. She has a good brain between her ears, but she appears too afraid to use it around us yet. I think she has been bossed around in the past and is simply expecting that to continue going forward. Her magic certainly packs a punch, and her capabilities are astonishing to say the least."

Ahrayn smiled into her cup, her eyes fixed on the dancing flame. "Chaotic and passionate. She has a strong soul too. If I were you, I would not misbehave too much around her. Although, I think if anyone can keep you in line then it would be her."

Raethran looked down into the shadows where he sat. He took a moment to order his thoughts then adjusted his tone accordingly. "Well, I guess I will just have to hide behind you. You keep me in line anyway. Well… for the most part at least."

Recognising the sombre look in her eyes, he abandoned the conversation, leaning forward to start packing up their camp. Ahrayn sighed and assisted him with folding the blanket. He stamped out the fire and they made their way into the embrace of the forest's shadow.

***

At the signal Ara set a brisk pace, heading towards the university's north-west approach.

"Do you know about the subterranean tunnel system to the north of here?" she probed.

"I do. The entrances may take me a while to find but I would not suggest those. Plus, it is quite a walk," Alikain said, glancing between the trees. A sudden commotion caused his heart to skip a beat. It was just a white tail deer who raced off, away from their skulking and into the thick underbrush.

"Yes… best if avoided," she finished, blunting her tone before the words slipped out.

She scanned the area ahead, cupping her hands to her ears. The rangers were not making their presence known physically so, she sank her hands into the ground every two hundred metres. Each time her fingers entered the loamy soil, chiselling through the frozen layers at the top. She would whisper to the forest, sending seams of green light into the ground as she shared the worlds magic with the earth.

"Mycelial networks?" Alikain guessed.

"The forest is constantly communicating. These rangers may be stealthy, but they are not expecting the forest to be watching. If we had the wardens of Foretilatava hunting us then, we would not stand a chance," she said, giving a casual smile to the inquisitor, recognising her own expertise in the situation.

Midnight drew close and a second horn blasted, although Alikain paid it no mind. Horses would be of concern in the plains or on a road but here, in the forest, they were merely a slightly elevated viewing position for their riders. Ara appeared of a similar disposition as her trajectory and stride remained unchanged.

The lakes ahead had a thin layer of mist fighting off the cold at the surface, ice crystals gathering on the shoreline. The gentle waves rolling over the stony shores, rhythmically adding to their cadence.

Alikain saw him first. He held his tongue though, curious to see Ara's reaction.

An arrow shot through at her, glancing off her ward, barely altering its intensity. Another two arrows were likely in the air already, but Ara had sprung into action, unleashing a torrent of energy into the ground beneath the ambushing ranger. He dove out of the way as a nest of twisting vines shot out of the floor to envelope him. He did not stick around for further exchanges, merely sinking back into the shadows to stalk them from a safe distance.

She looked wildly at Alikain who offered her a shrug. "You had an excellent plan, but they know they are hunting a member of the *forehaltha* and are likely familiar with the tricks of the wardens. It would have been a shame if they had made it easy for you."

Ara smiled. "A shame indeed. Keep up, Inquisitor," she said, a subtle music to her words.

She took off at a run, excited at the prospect of pitting herself against the rangers' tracking abilities. She danced between the trees as if she were back home, racing through the glades of Foretilatava. She was exhilarated by the hunt, losing herself in the feral chase.

Laughing uncontrollably after a lengthy dash, she dropped her speed, allowing Alikain to catch up to her where she was leaning against an oak, elated at the experience. Alikain could not help but join her in a chortle, gesturing for them to continue but grateful for the more relaxed pace.

"I did not see that one coming. I would be impressed if he could keep up with us after that," she said, casting a spell at their trail, causing the forest to envelope it and hide all traces of their passage.

"Not bad. It has been a long time since I have seen magic like this," he said, marvelling at the renewed ground behind them.

"You are not going to hunt me for that, are you?" she jested.

"Goodness, no. I love magic, especially like this! Destroy an innocent dwarven village or drain the life from an entire lake and we may have a problem. Until then, I encourage as much magic as possible. It is refreshing having people cast spells around me without fear and suspicion."

"Not entirely without," she added with a wink.

***

Ahrayn followed Raethran's footfalls exactly, copying his ridiculous looking fox-walk that suppressed the sound of their passage. They walked over streams, doubled back when they hit footpaths and mixed their approach, taking the most arduous of routes to find a path least likely to be travelled. They were careful not to break spider webs or smack branches against each other whilst also choosing paths that encountered such obstacles as much as possible.

Every so often, they would tuck into a root system or under the dense foliage of a shrub to watch the world go by. Mostly, they were simply staring into the darkness and listening to the insects and birds, conducting their nocturnal symphony. About halfway through their travels, they walked within view of the main pathway, toward Gryphon's Peak.

There, swinging from a rope, upside down and sounding rather disgruntled about the matter, was Yalthin. Ahrayn stopped their progress to point him out, impressed at his determination as he began swinging wildly from the rope. With a flash of his sword, a twist and spin in the air, he landed on the ground with a graceful display of acrobatic prowess. He gave a stage bow to the forest before slipping his bonds and continuing his journey with a haughty skip.

Raethran tipped his hood to the elf's efforts, wondering when the ranger stalking him from twenty metres behind was going to make himself known. Ahrayn shook her head and pushed Raethran back into motion, now having been entirely inconvenienced by the cold.

The rest of the trip was wondrous and uneventful. Only the occasional trap needing to be circumnavigated and the odd lookout point avoided. They did not see any other rangers which was a good thing, as generally, if you can see them then it means that they have been watching you for some time already.

The Arcanum was wide awake, and the light of the crystals shone through the windows with the alluring smell of the dining hall drawing them ever closer. The pair avoided tucking westward, thanks to Yalthin's shenanigans, approaching from the east instead.

Not a horse to be heard, seen, nor smelt, Raethran had them duck into the lecture buildings without much fuss. Shedding their camouflage for borrowed grey student robes. He hid the bag in a lecture room as they pulled up their hoods to blend in with the other students walking around, making idle chatter to avoid any curious glances.

Most eyes in the university were glued to the quad and curiously enough… to the sky.

***

The mycelial network sparked at Ara's fingertips, conveying their reports. The ranger was apparently able to track them, through Ara's tricks, as he was a mere half kilometre behind. She wasted no time in setting off again, keeping close to the waterways supplying the university's lake. Hunter versus the hunted, but what so many failed to understand is that if the prey knew they were being hunted then it was generally them who came out on top. Besides, she was not going to let these *tarviahaltha* show her how to survive in the forest.

They avoided open ground and made quick work of the vegetation, stopping to cover their paths and scout ahead with Ara's magic, whenever they reached a shielded location. Alikain was impressed with her work, especially when she began issuing orders to him. Mostly, it was to keep an eye out, but it soon encompassed adding wards to silence footfalls or refraction walls to hide them when crossing the more open areas.

Tucking between the lakes and taking winding routes through them, any hope the rangers had in catching them lay securely in luck. They were either going to walk into an ambush or run into a ranger who was returning to form a perimeter, closer to the university.

Ara was a shade without impact on the forest. Before long, they had made it all the way to the northern shores of the university's lake. Upon the waters was a reminder that they were not the only ones in the hunt.

Vexrith and Grindol were racing across on sinchal disks, sending a spray of water in their wake, with Vexrith's wards ready to shield them from any and all projectile fire aimed in their direction.

Ara seemed unphased by their lead and set down safely within the brush to watch the show. The two elves sliced through the middle of the lake, carving up the distance. Moonlight broke through as the cloud cover moved on, revealing them at centre stage and allowing for a ranger to summon a tower of water to rise up before them.

Speed was their downfall and they crashed through the water, flying off their discs and into the frigid lake. After a brief moment, they fired off flares to signal their submission. Vexrith was now using all her magic to stay afloat in her armour whilst Grindol summoned their discs back to them.

Rangers from around the lake, tucking back into the shadows, reset their trap. The lake was a natural ambush point with its open views from the concealed shores. What they could not cover was the area beneath the water.

Ara looked nervously at Alikain, "Do you trust me?" she asked, casting wards on Alikain before tossing a small reed pipe to him and slipping into the lake, disappearing beneath the surface.

***

Ahrayn and Raethran snuck through the hallways in plain sight, Raethran deciding to waste more time by sneaking into the alchemy labs. Oldiir had locked up for the night but that had hardly stopped Raethran in the past, and they were in before long.

They flicked their hoods back, moving chairs to the window to get a view of the competition unfolding outside. There were rangers posted on the roof, but they were all preoccupied with the outer defences for the time being. Raethran brought the tea out, reheating it with his magic, for them to then continue their picnic in giddy silence.

There was a flash of lights over the lake and a rush of activity in the area as students ran to get an update on what had happened. General commotion suggested that a team had been eliminated as certain students looked rather disappointed as they exchanged coins amidst themselves.

Master Graxith was nowhere to be seen with Master Paylorn watching over the *lenlialarla* to ensure the integrity of the competition. He appeared as if there were a thousand places that he would have preferred to be and that all of them were warmer than his current location.

Although sunrise was a long way away, Ahrayn grew nervous at the time crunch. They had had a leisurely stroll toward the Arcanum and, thus, others would be close. Raethran, still just sat back, sipping at his tea which was now exiting the flask at a disappointing temperature indeed.

Next to enter the fray was Thriol. He burst through, between the lecture halls and the Arcanum, charging the quad. His shield was riddled with arrows, and he had a severed length of rope attached to his waist, but still, he charged down the gem in a tumultuous stampede. Halfway to the *lenlialarla*, a gryphon descended and lifted him into the air, Graxith in the saddle, swinging a halberd to knock Thriol's sword from his hand with a victorious roar from both gryphon and elf.

Raethran's eyes were larger than the Arcanum's lake as he turned to Ahrayn, his mouth agape. He stifled a laugh and ran his hands through his hair, pondering their next move.

It took him until Ahrayn had finished her tea before he stood up, dusting his jerkin. He looked up at Ahrayn and shook his head, having the sense to place doubt in his own plan.

"Cavalry..." he remarked under his breath, shaking his head in disbelief.

He silently unlocked the door and held his shoulder against the wood, leaning to keep a line of sight on the quad. Ahrayn tucked in behind him and prepared herself to be carried away in the talons of a gryphon.

Next to enter the battle was a team from the lake. A subtle shimmer in the way light struck the water being the only indication of their presence. They shot out from their approach and charged through the rangers that blindly fired into the illusion. Graxith was having none of it and a trio of gryphon riders dived on their position, Graxith sending a beam of red light to shine through the illusion and reveal their quarry.

The spell had little effect, but they dove in nonetheless, causing the team to rely on other means of defence. Arrows, gryphons, rangers and, most of all, Graxith were now atop the two elves in a furious attempt to break through the torrent of magic they were fending them off with. Motes of earth catapulted riders out of their saddles and vines tethered gryphons to the ground. Bolts of lightning shot out at the rangers, stunning them in place, with the clanging of steel ringing throughout the quad.

Seeing this, Raethran causally opened the door, waiting for Ahrayn to walk out before closing it behind them. They took their time to look as nonchalant as possible. Sauntering over to the *lenlialarla*, they grabbed each other's hands, touching the cold stone amidst the crowds that had their gaze transfixed on the battle on the lakes shore. A wave of pink mist erupted out and a flare shot into the sky, signalling the end to the competition.

The pitched battle paused to stare at the source of the pink mist that broke through their hostility, with Ara at its centre, a sea of mixed emotions. Raethran slid behind Ahrayn and gave a nervous chuckle, attempting not to make eye contact. Much to his relief, Ara's focus was broken by Graxith, who walked over to shake her hand in a hearty chuckle.

Cadenced Dynamism Development

Alikain's back ached, waking him up, forcing him to get ready. He had been sleeping on the floor, currently unsure why the only way he could get rest was if he lay on the cold stone and not on his mattress. The dorms brought back memories of when he was in the Arcanum, studying to be a mage for Isfrisairis. Of course, the Dragon Wars were still in full force, so there was more of a focus on evocation and abjuration magic at the time. Still, the smell of jasmine, the stone beneath him and the royal blue curtains brought him back through the memories hidden away in his mind.

He stretched out his muscles, opening the window to greet the cold. The *lenlialarla* atop the Arcanum and the mage towers were catching the first light of the rising sun, refracting the rays over the grounds. They had kept them safe against the dragon attacks, their magic lashing out at any threats that flew too near, providing the elves with a few safe hideouts across the forest. He now wondered how long it would take him to feel safe around them with the thalenarians on his scent.

An owl landed on the window ledge, nearly making Alikain spring from his skin. With a hoot, she stuck her leg out expectantly to reveal a message tied there. The note had a seal of the Isfrisairis rangers containing within it, a registry of merchants for the Winter Market. He liberated the charge from the owl, setting her free into the skies so that he may unfurl the note in his own time.

Nothing unexpected but it did change his plans somewhat. One of the mages in attendance needed to be apprehended; Alikain would need to arrest him.

He got dressed in his inquisitor's uniform, sheathing his sword and reattaching the sheath to his belt before leaving the room. He locked the door and placed a tamper ward on it for good measure.

He had a spring to his step, remembering the maelstrom of magic he was in not nine hours prior. Fending off gryphon riders, with spells of his own blending in with Ara's chaos, making for a stunning display. He moved down the storied halls, the decorated doors of the student dorms baring posters that warned of what lay within.

The fresh magic, despite the acrimonious setting, had helped to clear his mind of Ilvithiir's influence. Just as his morning routine of stretches relieved the tensions in his body, so the magic relieved his mind. Still, he decided that it was safer to adjust to his normal stride before heading out to the quad, not wanting to break his persona.

Raethran and Ahrayn were sitting on a bench by the lake, laughing away in their private corner of the world. He decided to let them be, casting a mental message at Raethran to have them meet up at lunchtime. He needed assistance with some combat drills and Raethran was one of the few folk that would not jump from their boots at the prospect of fighting an inquisitor.

He aimed for the library, trying to ignore the sidelong, and sometimes blatant, glances from the students. Still, he was unable to keep from scanning their every movement for signs of casting spells or reaching for weapons. It was a simple instinct by this point.

The library was filled with the sounds of quills hastily scratching away at parchment like termites gnawing through a log. Ruunidil had just been handed a book by a student and was perusing a passage. Clearly having decided it was not what he was looking for, he sighed and sent the student off with a flick of his hand. It looked like Grindol, Raethran's roommate, but it was hard to tell. He had a few bruises and was avoiding Alikain's gaze at all costs to the point where he knocked into a desk in his retreat.

"That was the one who nearly set fire to the artificery correct?" Alikain asked, falling into a seat across from Ruunidil's desk.

"That is correct," he responded, finishing a mental message to one of the students in the room amidst the thousand other activities he was attempting to run simultaneously.

Alikain had left his detection amulet in his room. It was a handy little trinket that would have allowed him to detect various magics and even listen in on such messages. There was simply too much magic at the Arcanum for him to handle wearing it all the time. He would have been driven insane by now if he had kept it on. However, he would still use it for choice adventures such as last night's hunt where he kept track of the three rangers on their tail and the underwater ambush a group of sentinels had prepared. Thankfully, Ara had led them past, just narrowly avoiding a truly disastrous encounter.

Ruunidil was lost in his thoughts, his brow furrowed in concentration. Alikain fidgeted with a bronze desk puzzle, flicking a ring over another, tucking another one through and – click – the entire puzzle fell apart in his hands with a ring clanging to the floor and rolling beneath the desk.

Ruunidil sighed. "How can I help you this morning?"

"I was just checking in to see if you needed any help. See if any progress has been made? Do you want to get some lunch later on?" he responded, awkwardly pouring the fragmented pile of rings back onto the desk.

"I am far too busy, and I have all the help I trust myself to oversee at this point. If you had a spare set of eyes that did not sting every time, they opened then I would appreciate those."

"That Grindol fellow. Would that trinket he blew up have helped at all?"

"No. We would need to have known the code pattern and various key phrases in order to deduce it. Perhaps, once the code has been cracked, we will be able to streamline our translations, but such a task seems out of our reach for decades or until you bring me a living acolyte. There is then the issue that the text seems to be in constant flux, changing in unpredictable manners. It seems that our only hope is trial and error. You know, in a language we do not understand, on a topic we are unfamiliar with, etcetera."

"Good thing there is no overwhelming time crunch," Alikain jested.

Ruunidil put his quill down to add emphasis to the glare that followed. Alikain stood up and laughed. "You used to be much more fun. Remember when you followed me into the dwarven silver mine in the Tirzahn range? We were after that shaman who was intent on creating a volcano."

"Alikain, I was nearly immolated, crushed and ground to dust on that particular little mission of yours."

"Sure, you mention that, but forget about that red dragon in the ruby cave that fell in love with you. What was her name now, Kilthrixila? Kilthrixilanthila? I am likely missing a few syllables…"

Ruunidil chuckled and returned to his work. "Kilthrixithila," he answered, turning crimson.

"There we go. I mean, when they warn you of the fire of dragons, they certainly made no allusions to that. Anyway, could I requisition these books?" he asked, presenting a rolled-up scroll. "I have realised that I know nothing of the current political landscape of the world despite having signed myself up to be at its centre. Nildinar seems adamant on the idea of diplomacy, and I intend to show him that I at least tried that route first."

Ruunidil accepted the parchment. He paused to look at Alikain, seeming to notice him properly for the first time in this conversation. "It is good to see you are feeling yourself again. Of course. I will likely have it all ready for you by the end of the day. Ara, the *forehaltha* accompanying you? She is the only reason the council is allowing your plan to go ahead; I hope you know that."

"A trained envoy, yes. I am just glad that there are now four people in this world that are able to cast spells around me," he chided, reciprocating Ruunidil's glare.

Alikain left the library, regretting not having his extra coat as he braced against the cold.

Nildinar flew around the corner, nearly colliding with him head on. He had a stack of books in his arms, only just able to hang onto them during the altercation.

"Yes, Alikain. No time to chat. We will have a full brief for you by tomorrow. Come by around midday. We have a plan for the West Anthurians. The *haltha* are on board and the dragons have agreed to a meeting," he said, barely breaking his stride on the way to the library.

Alikain let out a huff, not quite sure what had happened in the previous ten seconds, but content to carry on with his day, nonetheless. Nildinar looked a lot more alive today, having gotten some sleep judging by the faint smell of jasmine – the cleaner that the university favoured for all its linens.

The elf in Nildinar's shadow was one that Alikain didn't know. He did not like that. It was, however, something that could be rectified later. For now, he let his feet led him back to a tree overlooking the lake where a commotion had signalled the start of an impromptu sinchal game.

Thriol and Vexrith were both wearing ice gloves and had taken to freezing walls of water flicked up in front of players to add some heft to their collisions. Kaylith, the elf that had assisted Raethran with his basilisk fang arrows, was the one flicking the water up. She had a sadistic streak that Alikain could not help chuckling at as she cottoned on to what Vexrith and Thriol were doing. They had now created a maze of frozen walls across the field. The trio had even gotten the timing right to freeze one of their opponents inside a wall of ice. The ice pillar with flailing limbs was certainly a sight worthy of a laugh, each time the other players passed by.

Alikain did not dare walk closer, to get a better view lest they stopped play, merely marvelling at all the spells flying around in high spirits. They were good, but nobody could handle a lightning glove better than Raethran. Ara would make for a fantastic water mage although she did have that *forehaltha* dexterity so perhaps even a fire glove? You needed an edge of chaos for such and after seeing her in action, Alikain saw her as fitting the bill rather perfectly.

Ruunidil on the other hand, was a touch on the boring side. Perhaps a water mage? Else he could handle an ice glove and focus on defence, shielding players as they flew across the field. He was dextrous when he wanted to be but his annoyance with water, and with being outside in general, may hold him back. Alikain would have to continue searching the corners of the continent to find the other players to fill his roster.

The game ended with the other team now using the ice pillar maze to sneak through their defensive lines, unimpeded. It was a good tactic but there is a reason why moderation is key. There was also a reason why the opposing fire mages were not simply blasting them down, as they were created.

Lunchtime fell upon the campus as a general migration began, toward the dining hall. Alikain waited, not wanting to join the crowd, choosing to stand by his tree and plan his meal.

Ara walked by the lake with Aeradil, not talking, simply skirting along the water's edge. They split up, with Ara heading toward the dining hall and Aeradil to the infirmary. He seemed to dart back, retreating whilst staring at the ground in front of him. Ara did not see Alikain. She strode off into the dining hall and out of sight.

He followed the last of the students, walking over to the table with Raethran, Ahrayn and Ara. They were chuckling at Ara who had just spotted Yalthin across the room, seductively picking at a bowl of olives. His captivating show of eating them one at a time, allowing him to keep her in his peripherals.

Alikain joined the table, shaking his head and joining their laughter. Raethran welcomed him to the group with a cup of black tea and an appetiser of what he called 'Mini-beasts'. They were miniature sandwiches that were towering in their own right, giving a satisfying crunch to accompany their confusing explosion of flavour. It was a meal adapted from one of the sentinels' creations, but Raethran appeared disappointed with his adaptation.

"That was quite the show you gave the crowd yesterday," said Ahrayn, addressing Ara with a nod.

"It was fun. I think I needed to let loose. Who knew that madly running through the forest, whilst being tracked by rangers and attacked by maniacs on gryphons, would allow me to do that, let alone be so cathartic?" she responded.

"Did you have any run-ins with the rangers? I heard it was Grindol and Vexrith who were caught out on the lake. I have not seen her this morning, but he is more bruise, than he is elf, at this stage," Raethran added.

"One of them struck my wards with an arrow. He was following us for a while, after that, but we had speed on our side. I knew they were good, but I never expected them to be that good. I will admit to having some favouritism towards the *forehaltha* and our wardens in that regard, but I learnt my lesson. How was your trip?" Ara asked before securing herself a mini-beast and devouring it with decisive crunch.

Ahrayn replied, "Not too bad. Cold. Uneventful. Dirty. We did see Yalthin hanging from his feet, having been caught in a trap, on the path from Gryphon's Peak. He handled it pretty well but the ranger, whose trap it was, seemed to just be having some fun with him. He just watched him slink off afterward, likely waiting to give him the largest possible fright with a well-placed arrow at some point down the line."

"I think I owe that ranger some coin. Which reminds me – Raethran, what are you going to do with your share of the credits after having had us do all the work, so that you could win?" she asked, failing to hold her composure, smiling through the remark.

"It is not my fault that you two were better suited to carrying out the distraction. You should thank me for helping the two of you realise your potential. I was expecting some magic, but you really did surprise me with that display," he responded, Ara blushing at the compliment. "And you, Mr Scary Inquisitor. You may as well have been dancing with joy after all that. If you smile any more, then people may mistake you for having a heart," Raethran chided, stabbing with a fork in Alikain's direction.

Alikain did not deign to respond to the accusation. Seeing the look on Raethran's face, the one that meant he had a plan, was never a good sign.

After a moment, Ara asked, "So… forgive me a branch of gossip, but there was a writ on the board that has been stuck in my mind since I first saw it. It was from Filthin, requesting 'Cadenced Dynamism Development'. What is that about?"

Raethran responded whimsically, "Dance lessons. Word in the dorms is that Filthin is on the prowl for a paramour and wishes to announce his eligibility through interpretive movement."

Ara nearly spat tea out of her nose. She took a moment to hang onto life, pulling at the air for a few breaths to stabilise her choking.

Raethran chuckled at her struggles, continuing as she calmed down, "The problem is… He is a very good dancer, but it can get rather…"

"Intense," Ahrayn finished.

"Exactly. Ahrayn believes that with him being so tuned to illusion magic, and the master for the field at the university, that he is displaying a vulnerability with it. He is able to project perceptions but here, he cannot hide behind his magic and it is the dance that is on display. Thus, he will settle for nothing other than perfection to match his magical abilities."

Ara nodded at this. It made sense, almost poetically so. Even Alikain gave a nod, taking another sip of his tea.

"Now I, on the other hand," Raethran continued, much to 'everyone's fear, "see it as him having achieved high status in academia. Now, he wishes to seek an identity outside of his contributions to the Arcanum: both physically and creatively, through his many side projects. He is the Master of Illusion at the University Arcanum where perhaps, he wants to be Filthin, gryphon carer, dancer, music lover and avid fitness seeker who works at the University Arcanum as the Master of Illusion," he paused, awaiting his approving nods before finishing, "You all expected me to say something daft, well there! Also, he is just crazy and wants to shake those alabaster stilts he calls legs. Now you get both statements."

Lunchtime concluded with a valiant attempt to conquer the chocolate volcano that Alikain had ordered for the table. Raethran only tasted the composing elements but revelled in the glares they received from the onlookers. Ara and Ahrayn stayed behind to finish the dish, allowing Raethran and Alikain to head into the forest for their training.

***

The snow was packed ankle deep in the secluded grove they chose, pulling at their feet with each step and setting their balance into question whenever they landed on a rock or root. Alikain threw a large pack to the floor, the suspicious clanging of metal erupting from within. Raethran merely tucked his arms in and blew hot air into his hands, jumping on the spot to warm his legs.

"Just some combat drills today, one versus one, no magic and that includes your wards," Alikain explained.

Raethran nodded, fishing through the bag's contents for a longsword. The one he found was a training blade from Graxith's collection. It was not the best, but it had fewer chips on its edge and a stronger core that had kept it straight.

He gave a few practice swings, nearly tearing his muscles right then and there. Seeing the need for stretching, he cleared an area of snow and set about the series of exaggerated movements. His body cooperated rather well, despite the cold, although his hamstrings required some convincing before he could get his forehead to his knees.

"My reactions have been slow, and my footwork needs refining. Do you have any areas you want to work on?" Alikain asked.

"I am rubbish with axes, but I am not going to duel an unwarded opponent with those, even if I am unlikely to land a hit. Could we do some magical duels after? Paylorn lacks creativity with his wards and Ndolin is far too explosive to duel in any environment that is not the magic bunker," he responded, excitement beginning to pick his tone up.

"Set up simulacrums on the side-lines. Instead of floating metal ring mazes around our heads, we will spar with those whilst we duel. Nothing with an area of effect that could reach us though. Your robes look like they are going to blow away without the addition of fire volleys," Alikain compromised, unsheathing his longsword, not bothering to dull the edges but casting a ward on the blade to keep it from chipping.

"Yes, well, armour is expensive. I have to save up for that. I fail to see how buying the cheap steel will help me in the long run so I am just going to wait until I can afford the moonsteel. I have enough for the peripherals, it is just the breastplate that is setting me back," Raethran replied, setting dead branches up in the snow in a small A-frame to represent each of them.

"And a sword…" Alikain said, throwing a test lunge at Raethran's casual guard.

Raethran was not ready for the duel, so he lazily flicked the blade away as he fished for some training armour in the bag. "Have you seen the prices of swords? Smiths these days are only taking on jobs that test their abilities as an artisan of the trade, with nobody left to cater to those not requiring a legendary work of art to hang at their side. Speaking of savings, I do not suppose you would like to purchase two bottles of mint flavoured mead? They are very reasonably priced and only partially watered down by Grindol." he offered, rhetorically.

He adorned a pair of vambraces to cover his wrists and forearms, some greaves for his shins and a helmet. It was a frog-mouth helm, which allowed for only a fine sliver of vision but provided maximum protection. The problem is that sacrificing vision is only a good trade if the rest of you is also covered with steel.

Alikain let loose an involuntary chuckle, seeing the awkwardly armoured Raethran turn and face him. Raethran shrugged his shoulders and shot a bolt of lightning from his own A-frame at Alikain's. The energy was deflected into the snow, kicking up a wave of white powder to hide Alikain's opening lunge at Raethran's gut.

They had duelled so often that he half expected it. He flicked the blade and pushed back to send a high kick at Alikain, his efforts being easily dodged by a hurried step back. Alikain lifted a spear of ice and flung it at Raethran's marker, forcing him to focus on redirecting the trajectory, whilst Alikain swung in to test his high guard.

They spun around and gained ground only to lose it three strikes later. Spells were shattering against wards and ice shards rained down on them after the impacts. The snow, which held their A-frames up, remained as untouched as the structures themselves. The ground around them however was scarred and beaten, both elves managing to avoid the living trees out of respect.

Raethran was holding his own, but he was falling into a trap and he knew it. Alikain had him in a rhythm and was merely guiding him to an opening that would have his sword at Raethran's throat. It was only a question of when.

Raethran attempted a breakout that earned him Alikain's heel to the temple of his helm, sending him sprawling through the snow. At the impact, he heard the splintering of his A-frame, signalling his loss on all fronts.

"No use blaming your reduced vision on that one. That was just sloppy. On the magic side, your attacks were all right, but your wards were focused on redirecting the power of the strikes and not harnessing it to bolster them.

It was wasted power. There is a time for redirection and a time to harness, and a time to use both. This situation was option three," he commented, walking back and resetting his stance.

Raethran set up his A-frame again before dusting the snow off his coat. He picked his sword up and reset his own position. He sprung forward, redirecting each strike to keep Alikain off balance. His strikes were easy to read but he threw enough weight behind them to force Alikain to block them. It was barbaric but it had him where he wanted. Alikain attempted his breakaway jab after Raethran flew a high swing that he could duck. This brought his weight forward.

Alikain was barged to the ground, forcing him to roll out into a crouch, then spin in time for Raethran's follow-up. It was a high strike, which he could block, but Raethran would have him on his back with a sword at his gut in six more strikes. He pulled a dagger with his off hand, slicing at Raethran's thigh.

The skin split and Raethran backed off, cursing under his breath, "*Aseroena!*" The magic duel had also been lost, as Alikain, having caught Raethran's lightning strike, timed its return with his own fire blast, sending the dead limbs flying across the grove.

"You are too predictable with that lightning of yours. They are powerful strikes, but it is me that you are fighting. I have seen it before. As for the duel, you had me there. I had to get creative," he said, standing up and fixing the A-frame for Raethran.

"Yeah, I thought that would happen. I was just hoping I would catch you out on the martial side before you got clever with the lightning. Your footwork is fine by the way, you are just too stubborn. Know when to retreat and you are good. How did you time the lightning dump with that fire blast over there? The one element I could handle but both at the same time was a bit much."

They compared notes on their duels and went nine more rounds before Raethran called time out. He had multiple slashes and did not fancy any more holes in his coat. He was out of breath and fatigued from the magic use. The duelling arena they had for themselves was now a scarred break in the trees with soaking ground from the melted snow.

Raethran sat back on a tree trunk and steadied his breathing. A colony of floating wisps joined them in the grove, having been attracted to the amount of magic that had been expended. They clung to Raethran like fish to bait, dancing around his head and between his legs.

"Some say that wisps are the soul remnants of a primordial race," Raethran said, marvelling at the wisp that had settled on his outstretched hand, floating in its incorporeal light.

"I believe the prevailing theory is that; it is magical energy caught in pockets of air causing electrons to hop their orbitals and emit light. I much prefer the story about them being tricksters that lure folk into the forest though," Alikain added.

"They just want people to play with." Raethran averted his gaze, picking at the loose thread on his gloves. "Alikain, are you all right? I have never seen you like this. I am not expecting you to answer, but I do need you to know that I am here if you need to speak."

A muscle jumped in Alikain's jaw, the only display of emotion in his otherwise stony appearance. "Thank you. I will be fine. Time is providing a reprieve. I need to hold onto this pain though, it will remind me of why we are trying to stop all this."

"All right. In that case, you seem business-like today. Any news on the trip around the continent?"

"Your brother is sure to have every possibility accounted for. He has promised me an update tomorrow and Ruunidil should have all the books we need by this evening. Do you have a proper sword and some armour? I have arranged the travel clothes for you all."

"I do. Nildinar's one. It is not the best, but it has an end to grab and another to stab. I think I was the first person to remove it from its sheath since it was crafted though."

"Excellent. I may also need your assistance tonight. I received word this morning that a rogue mage will be at the market," Alikain began.

Raethran's ears pricked up as he lent forward, giving a quick readjustment to his leg binding.

"He has been peddling *lenlialarla* for the dwarves but not through the legal of channels. He has been getting the gems from their mines, having people at the Arcanum and other such locations do the engravings, where he then enchants them himself. All with disastrous results, from the reports I have received. He is a thug, but magically proficient and crazy enough to not understand his boundaries. He will be at the market tonight, so we may as well deal with him now," he finished, looking to Raethran for his suggestion of a plan.

"Spell gem peddler. Tricky one that. He is likely going to have a few tricks stored up his sleeve. I guess we just get close and lock him down as soon as possible? Search him thereafter and give him a quick scan. Is this merchant the type to have any *lenlialarla* implants?" Raethran asked.

"Difficult to say. I guess we have the infirmary on standby in case. I do not fancy a dissection in the middle of the market," Alikain added.

"Let us keep away from the market in general. We can get close from the front, ask a question that sends him to his stocks where you can take it from there, myself in close support," offered Raethran.

"Good start but switch those. You have been messing around with writs too often to pretend that this is not within your capabilities. Just drop him, get some draining cuffs on and give us a shout when you are ready for us to help with the clean-up," he revised.

The sun was setting, an indication that it was now late afternoon for the northern winter landscape. Master and apprentice discussed a few eclectic points of magical theory before turning in for the day, Raethran carrying the bag back to the university whilst Alikain provided further tips and instruction on their duel.

New Robes, Old Wounds

Ara had to admit that, when it came to winter, the Arcanum knew how to do it right. The forest was stunning, but the snowfall gathering on the mountain tops and crunching underfoot was an experience all on its own. The trees were still clinging onto some of their bronze and golden leaves, mingling with the evergreens that braced against the weather instead of sleeping it out.

The university was alive with festivities once more, the band having been set up in the late afternoon. Crystal light sconces lined pathways across the grounds to guide the steady stream of merchants and patrons that had arrived for the market. They would likely leave the next morning, only spending one night camped near the lake before moving east to Isfrisairis where they would wait out the winter. It seemed such a shame to Ara that they would only be here for such a short time, nonetheless it was a festive outing for all.

Ara fished through her clothing, needing the perfect outfit to match her mood for the evening. She was something of a celebrity around the campus after having picked a fight with Graxith, hung out with an inquisitor and outrun a ranger.

She chose an emerald cloak with silver inlay, and an inner lining of treated alabaster cashmere. She beat the dirt off her brown leather boots that reached halfway up her calf, then pulled them over her fluffiest socks, still fresh from the laundry. She had never been one for much jewellery, but she fished out an emerald pendant of white gold, thinking of the silly little defensive charms she had placed into the gem when she was still in the Druidica.

She ran a brush through the wavy lengths of her chestnut hair, ignoring the collection of hairs clinging to the bristles. She gathered a piece of shorter hair from the front and carefully pinned it back using the crystal daisy Ahrayn had made for her. Finally, she flicked her hood over her ears and stepped from her little carriage, appreciating the opportunity to stretch her back in the open air.

Ahrayn was laughing musically at the campfire with Lethrik and Yildrin, who were fully dressed in their armour. Ahrayn was wearing a stunning blue dress with a long skirt that gently trailed on the ground behind her. Clearly, she had her wards up otherwise she would have frozen the minute she had stepped outside with the thin fabric cutting short at her shoulders.

Ara smiled, noticing a small silver pin on Ahrayn's dress, in the shape of a tree swallow. No gems adorned the decoration, it was perfect as it was, in its simplicity.

Ara looked down awkwardly at her ensemble but was quickly pulled from her inspection by Ahrayn's greeting. She walked over to the jovial crew. After handing over an order form to a fellow ranger, Lethrik waved to Ara and then scampered off into the forest. The other ranger grumbled at the extensive list he had been provided, so that Lethrik could still get his due supply of items from the vendors. He was due for perimeter watch and was thus prohibited from perusing the wares at the beginning of the market when the merchant stocks were fresh and full.

"Ara, you look resplendent as always," Yildrin greeted with a formal bow.

Ara smiled. "Good evening. You are looking rather dapper yourself. You sentinels will never cease to amaze me, although I hardly see how all that moonsteel could be comfortable."

"We do our best and you would be surprised how cosy it is in here. May the two of you have a wonderful evening and be sure to check out whatever is creating that toffee aroma I am smelling. The rangers and sentinels have been banished to the outskirts for this one; I am afraid. Patrol duty near Gryphon's Peak for me. It could be worse though. That scoundrel of yours, Lethrik, has been tasked to the lakes," he reported, looking dreamily toward the market.

"Would you like us to get you anything? I am certain we could sneak a toffee apple to your post. What about a fancy hat?" Ara offered.

"I am more of a 'One-hat is enough' sort of elf but thank you. I am just out for the first half after which, I can have my fill of shopping," he replied, placing his helmet on his head, shining in the flickering light of the campfire as he departed. Everything about him screaming his authority, from the plate armour to the flowing grey cloak that folded and creased only where allowed. His greatsword appeared too large for Ara to carry with his spear being long enough to reach the heart of a dragon.

"So, are you ready for a night of frivolous spending and glutinous treating?" Ahrayn asked, offering her arm.

Ara happily accepted it and the two walked to the market together, following the sounds of the orchestra in the light of the sconces.

"How was your afternoon? Is Raethran going to be joining us?" Ara asked, passing the time.

"It was calm, thank you. I managed to get an advance on the sale of the crystal flowers, which we made the other day. No small compliment I might add. Master Ilkiir likes to play the miser with such, but he was certain that they would fetch a good price; if not here then in Sinien Tarvia," she said, handing Ara her share of the writs. "Raethran has not shown up yet. There have been rumours that he and Alikain were attacking each other in the forest to the east. He should be fine, as the infirmary would have informed me otherwise."

"His training seems harsh. We had duels and such at the Druidica but nothing like what he has faced here at the Arcanum. On top of that, he then has to deal with Alikain's tendencies. I guess that I see why it is needed but still. Wait, this is a lot!" Ara finished, taking a peek at the writs.

Ahrayn shrugged. "He can take it. Dare I say that; he deserves it every so often? As for the writs, I cannot stress how impressed Ilkiir was with them. I half expect him to be wearing one this evening. I wonder if any might find their way to the court in Foretilatava?"

Smiling, Ara pictured the walkways in Foretilatava with her fellow *forehaltha* adorned in the collaborative efforts of the *forehaltha* and *tarviahaltha*. From the Arcanum of all places.

She carefully lifted her hood back and gestured proudly to her crystal daisy. "Well, they certainly shall when I next visit."

Ahrayn let loose an ebullient smile, and turned her head to the side, showing Ara that the daisy she had been given by Peppa was tucked safely into her half-braid.

"What did you get up to after lunch? Have you seen the greenhouse yet?" Ahrayn asked.

"I have. I took a writ to trim some strangler figs over there. Beautiful indeed! Albeit, exotic in places. After lunch, I went to visit Aeradil again. We walked up to Gryphon's Pass. The light was fading so we did not climb the mountain, but he is getting there. He even started smiling," she reported, victoriously. "I decided to avoid inviting him to the festival lest there be any sudden displays like there have been over the last few days. You are a theatrical bunch, I will give you that," she added, now in range of the market to eye out some of the stores.

"Perhaps you should get him a present? I am on the lookout for a gift for Raethran. He has been working himself into the dirt lately and I am unsure if even he realises it. It is possibly the thing that I am looking forward to most about our trip. All the travel time between exciting adventures where we can just be ourselves." Ahrayn said, scanning the shelves of the first stand they arrived at.

It had a dizzying array of painted porcelain and ceramic crockery. Plates and teacups were the display items on the shelves that advertised the full sets stashed in the merchant's stocks. There were vases too, as tall as her knee and portraying epic tales of heroism from across the shores in Mardacia. The crested helms and stylised creatures, making for an easy guess.

Raethran was not the type to appreciate fine crockery, so they moved on. Ara got caught by a stand selling roasted hazelnuts with a honey-spice coating. An obvious choice for her, even amongst the countless other treats tempting her from the sides. She ordered a small bag for them to share so that they could peruse the stands further, whilst entertaining their sense of taste along the way.

They could not believe their luck as they walked by the centre of the quad, where the orchestra was performing. Filthin was spinning through the other dancers on the stage with a partner that neither of them recognised. Every movement of his was perfect but what made the scene was the smile glued to his face, spanning almost ear to ear.

It took them some time, and the addition of Alikain to their group, to break the trance that the Master of Illusion and his golden-haired partner had trapped them in. They cheerfully greeted the inquisitor, allowed him his due time to marvel at Master Filthin, then led off down a line of stalls where it was quiet enough to speak.

"All right, Alikain, what did you do with him?" Ahrayn probed.

"He is on his way. He is just helping me out with a task first. It does however remind me, there is a stall I was on my way to visit before I bumped into you lovely ladies—" he began, Ara interrupted by offering him some of the hazelnuts, distracting him from his train of thought.

"Then you would not mind a slight detour. I could use your help. I have been looking to buy a gift for Raethran. Ara may also like to purchase a memento from the market for Aeradil. Thoughts?" she asked.

Alikain nodded his consent, knowing that it was pointless to argue with Ahrayn. Of all the people in the world, he had the least power over her. Just one of the many reasons why he really enjoyed her company. She was one of those rare people whose very presence was like a soothing balm. Something about her could render him speechless in three words but lift him up to new heights after two more.

"Thoughts? Let us see. Well, Raethran… If you are certain he is deserving of a gift, perhaps then… some moonsteel? He needs a sword and a breastplate. I would think that a sword from you, with a heartfelt inscription, would mean the absolute world to him. A symbol of his trade and a weapon of defence."

"That is not such a bad idea. I was thinking of something similar. Raethran was the one that purchased my very first stethoscope for me. The one I use to this day. There are a few smiths in Isfrisairis I could approach to shape the steel. I would need to get his details sent over. I believe you martials can be rather particular about your blades," Ahrayn postulated.

"As for Aeradil, I do not believe he would care much for a trinket so much as he would, a story. Perhaps a fair game to win him a trinket? Regale him with an array of epic chronicles and allow him to have a token, of your appreciation and care, to keep with him," he added, staring in awe at a cascade of falling embers that fell over the crowd, a snowfall of illusion magic to mark Filthin's grand finale on the stage.

"That sounds like fun. I think he would love that!" Ara answered, accepting the suggestion.

They scanned the stands, finding an appropriate game, getting distracted at a stall with ornately carved music boxes. Some of silver and gold, others of brass, copper and wood. The larger boxes played the resonant anthems of Isfrisairis whilst the polished wooden boxes had the flowing sounds of Foretilatava. A song from Sinien Tarvia came from a box shaped into a three masted ocean rider galleon, an inspiring tune building within.

There were a few wind chimes and handheld instruments adding to the selection but the market was in full swing and there was still so much for them to see. Plus, Alikain needed to stop and refill Ara's packet of honey-spiced hazelnuts after finishing them too quickly. The group added nougat and chocolate treats for some sugary variety before continuing their hunt for a game with a fitting prize that Ara could win.

There were archery ranges set up, halls of illusion and the odd bean-bag toss. All had a simple yes-or-no outcome with minimal opportunity for a story to be made. Slight interest was sparked at a game of pendulums they had going at the archery range, a queue of eager students already forming with Tuliin amongst their ranks. It was Raethran who arrived to save the day, presenting Ahrayn with a poster for the activity.

"Watermelon eating contest. Who is challenging me and how much of their head is the loser getting shaved?" he said, greeting the group with his excitement.

Ahrayn and Raethran shared a hug whilst the group took turns, scanning the details of the poster.

"You know what, this is not half bad. All right, Raethran, you have a deal. Not the head-shaving thing. You would look ridiculous, and you are not the one that has to look at you," Ara replied, her response being greeted with a respectful nod of acknowledgement from Raethran.

"The *forehaltha* have claws. Have the rest of you found anything interesting?" he asked, scanning their shopping orders and stealing a piece of nougat from Ara's pile, earning him a shove in the process.

"Not much, yet. Is there anything in particular that you are looking for?" Ara asked.

"A new coat, I guess. This one is beginning to test my sewing ability," he said, idly flapping his coat tails.

"Yes! You are going to be travelling the continent as an inquisitor's apprentice after all. Best you look the part. I am sure we can find you something," offered Ara, not giving Raethran a choice but seeing Ahrayn's relief in her statement. She grabbed her hand, and they whisked the group off toward the cluster of stalls selling clothes.

Raethran hung back and handed a piece of scrap parchment to Alikain. "Ustair, the merchant we are after; he has enough gems in his cart to summon the interest of a dragon. Seems like he is just getting informal writs from the juniors, having them use the tools at the Arcanum to perform the basic engravings for him. I did not dare get close to him, so I am unsure what he is carrying on his person. His stall has a few odds and ends, mainly quality of life trinkets. The self-tying shoes seemed rather extra, but I guess

I can see the advantage of such."

"Not bad. All right. After you have stuffed your face with watermelon, you can make an excuse to sneak off around the back. We will go forward and get him to fetch a different size of those boots, or something that will have him head back. He will be spooked at seeing me and will likely be distracted enough for you to jump him. Be careful and do not get yourself immolated. He has injured rangers, who have attempted to question or apprehend him, in the past."

"I found some of the trigger words for his gems. If he gets out of hand, then he is going to turn into a walking pyrotechnic display. It is weird that he came here though. I mean, surely, he would have tucked tail when he saw the small army of rangers and sentinels we have camping over here? Plus, an inquisitor of the arcane disciplines," asked Raethran, concerned at their prey's brazen attitude.

"He is part of a convoy. He goes where they go, according to the ruling of the caravan leader. It would have been suspicious for him to leave and his place in the caravan could have been taken by another gem salesman. Nildinar has also taken great care to keep anyone from spilling the beans of the groups here, lest it pose a security risk to the chancellors," he offered.

"All right. Seems like he may have a plan though. Are you going to question him, after?"

"No need. The ranger working the markets in Myngora Haezelahol has been investigating him for a while now. She has all the evidence needed for his arrest. We will detain him, and the sentinels can take it from there. No need to get caught up in the bureaucracy unless we really have to. Plus, I am mainly just doing her a favour. It will save her having to arrest him, question him and then lug him all the way up to Tour Aine thereafter."

They arrived to join the ladies at the second clothing store, the first having items that looked too practical, something Raethran did not see as a bad thing.

"A uniform portrays its purpose in its silence, in its elegance. Your clothes are going to say something about you. Sure, you want them to be practical, but you want them to look as if they are not, so that you are ready even when it appears that you are not," Ahrayn said, fishing through the racks of hanging cloaks. "Take Alikain's coat, high collar without folds, double breasted with squared shoulders and split tails. He can move all the parts he needs to, be wearing a chainmail shirt beneath and none would be the wiser. It also has pockets and likely, quick access to a pouch of emergency reagents or spell components. We need to find that, but for you."

The merchant at the stall gave Raethran a sympathetic look but heard Ahrayn's plight, tucking behind a divider. He emerged moments later clutching in his arms, no less than six options that fitted the description. Ahrayn and Ara deliberated over those presented, holding a few up against Raethran's chest for sizing until eventually, deciding on the perfect one.

It was ink black, with a high collar, stiff shoulders and coat tails to his knees, much like Alikain's. Where Alikain's had a double-breasted option with silver buttons, Raethran's was single-breasted with tarnished silver buttons. It was a smooth material, unlikely to pill. The high-quality stitch may even be up to the task of surviving Raethran, for a few years at least. A fine mesh of chainmail had been sewn into its inner lining and the fibres were ordered such that magical reparations, of any tears, would be possible.

The two did not stop there though. They purchased an entire outfit for him with new boots and all. Raethran had surprised himself with being drawn into feeling excited about the ordeal. A new adventure with new clothes. It seemed rather fitting, although he would miss his current, well-aged coat. He had worn it so much that it knew what he wanted to do before he did it, having zero tensile strength to restrict his motion even if it wanted to.

He handed over some coins from the pouch Ahrayn had given him earlier, thanking the merchant for his patience and rapid work with adjusting the odd hem and supplying them with the countless choices from which they found his current setup.

A feature of the cloak that he had pointed out, which seemed particularly interesting, was the detachable hood. There were fastening points on the inside of the collar allowing for a hood to be attached. The hood had flaps to tuck both inside and on the outside of the collar to prevent any possible leaks of warmth or rainfall.

During the fitting Alikain, who had been scribbling various notes on scrap parchment, had approached Ahrayn for a brief discussion. The details of which, Raethran was unable to make out. She thanked him with a hug and tucked the parchment in with her other shopping items.

"To the watermelons?" Ara asked, their first task having been met with resounding success.

The group cheered and made their way to the raised table that had been set up for the more prestigious of competitions.

Students made up the majority of the participants but there were some new faces as well. Some *forehaltha* and even a few *merhaltha* had mingled in to form the heterogeneous crowd. Ara found her seat, between Raethran and an empty chair. She tucked herself in and warded her clothes to prevent any shrapnel of watermelon from landing on them. Raethran, on the other hand, looked about ready to dive into a summertime bog with the sleeves of his old coat rolled up.

Other contestants included Silla and Tuliin. Olethia was in the front line, staring Tuliin down, herself looking mischievous and involved with his position at centre stage. Next to Ara, in the free seat, sat a petite little creature: to her surprise she recognised her as the young elf, Peppa, from the Ixilth bakery. She was wearing a white dress with a daffodil pattern on it, having placed her white coat on the back of the seat.

"Hi, friend! Are you ready to be amazed?" she squealed, recognising Ara.

"Of course! I look forward to the competition. I must warn you though, I have eaten many watermelons in my time." Ara laughed, handing her a serviette so that she might protect her dress.

In the front line of the crowd, with Olethia, were presumably; Peppa's parents, getting ready to cheer her on. Yalthin stood next to them, preoccupied with a music box, running his hands over the detailing. Alikain and Ahrayn were there too, gossiping about the contestants. Masters Hital and Oldiir were standing behind Ahrayn, occasionally incorporated into the gossip mill with stolen moments of bliss shared between them.

Announcing the competition was a member of the *merhaltha*. The sea elf's sun-kissed hair and bronzed skin sung the tales of his adventures across the seas. They were the merchants to look to if you wanted to trade in goods from outside elven territories. Their ports had connections to Anthuria, Melsoa, Mardacia and beyond with adventurous spirits that connected them all together.

He controlled the crowds with his confident baritone, commanding their attention and guiding them into a cheer for the contestants. Wasting no time, the competition was in full swing. The more civil of the elves, like Tuliin, brought knives out to slice the watermelon. Ara copied him with Raethran saving time by cracking his open with an elbow and gnawing at the fleshy fruit.

Peppa was the victor from the word go. She lifted the watermelon up and, with a mighty roar, she threw it at the table, shattering the fruit before attacking the pieces like a possum. She was a creature of unbridled savagery and soon, the other contestants were merely looking on at her progress, in awe. Her watermelon shattered and devoured; she rose her arms to the stars in victory, allowing the *merhaltha* to declare her the winner.

Ara did manage to terrify Yalthin in the process of her efforts, making quick work of the skin with her knife and showing enough ferocity in her bites to make anyone think twice. He apparently had different thoughts though as he snatched Ara's hand when she left the podium, swinging her around to steal her away. Raethran looked back and chuckled, wishing her luck with a grin and a double thumbs-up.

"Wait, but—" Ara began.

"Have no fear, I come in peace. Here, you have watermelon… just… everywhere," he said, handing her a serviette to brush the fruity debris off the membrane of magic that her wards had created.

She thanked him and cleaned her face, glad that it was Yalthin and not Vexhimarith or Nildinar that she had run into.

"I was hoping to get your assistance on something. I need a touch of the *forehaltha* in this and Master Thrindolin lacks the romantic flare required," he explained.

"Wait… What exactly are you asking for?" she inquired, dubious at his request.

"I plan to profess my feelings for Vexrith this evening," he began, much to Ara's surprise. "I have spent the last three years madly in love with her but, too terrified to actually do anything sincere about it. I have written poems, songs, plays and ballads but none have been able to truly capture her essence. Eventually, I decided to not hide behind theatrics and to just tell her. The problem is, I know that I am not enough for one so radiant and consummate as herself. So, I was hoping a gift would assist in bridging the gap to give me slightly more of a chance?" he asked, laying his soul bare for Ara to inspect.

She smiled honestly, but shook her head, disappointed in the world for trusting her with so many important tasks.

"All right, I will help. Only because Ahrayn thinks that you two are going to be great together."

He beamed, looking about ready to hug her. Ara raised a cautionary hand. "I still do not trust you, and I think that you should have a bell around your neck, or something. Wait here, I am going to go to the greenhouse, and I will be back in ten or so minutes. Meet me right here," she said, darting off south toward the greenhouses without further delay.

***

Raethran reached Alikain and Ahrayn after his failed attempt at eating watermelons. They tapped him on the back, consoling him in his hour of defeat. Ahrayn was too excited to commit fully to restoring his bruised ego so she instead, sent him off to get changed into his inquisitor attire.

He returned looking like a new elf. He had even strapped Nildinar's sword' to his side, having spent the previous day or so sharpening and polishing it in his spare time. He looked equal parts dashing and terrifying, the perfect inquisitor. He walked out, attracting a looks from his fellow students as he was now the opposite of the Raethran they knew and loved. They were all reminded, in that moment, that their fellow classmates were destined for the world outside the Arcanum where relaxed folk, like Raethran, could become uncompromising agents of justice.

"Perfect!" Ahrayn proclaimed, admiring her handiwork. "Just one more detail," she finished, removing her tree swallow pin from her dress and pinning it to his coat over his right breast.

"Now it is perfect," he agreed, admiring the pin.

"All right, you two. Raethran, now that you look the part, I think it is time," Alikain ordered.

Raethran nodded, kissed Ahrayn, slipping off toward the lecture halls with a carefree hop.

"Nope. I do not want to know," Ahrayn said, raising a hand to halt Alikain's explanation.

"All right, well, you have the details of Raethran's sword now. You just need to decide on an inscription," he offered.

"The inscription I have written. It is the design I am still pondering. Are there any vendors for the moonsteel you have seen?" Ahrayn asked, scanning the stalls again.

The two wandered through the less decorated of the tables, into the section that would have had Ilkiir and Oldiir dancing for joy. There were raw ingredients everywhere, from uncut gemstones to metal ingots.

Powdered minerals and vials of labelled liquids in a diverse spectrum of colours and viscosities, some even moving around at their own volition, within the confines of their stoppered vials.

The moonsteel was not cheap but Ahrayn had been saving up for a long time, for just such an occasion. She had earned a fair amount of coin through her work as a healer, taking care of wounds or ailments that students were too embarrassed to get treated through the infirmary or take a writ out for.

With that taken care of, they made their way towards the gem merchants stall, Ahrayn looking nervous whilst Alikain lost himself in the floating embers around them. She noticed that his breathing had quickened, which was never a good thing for one of Alikain's reputation.

***

Ara searched the greenhouse in the high-altitude section where they had dropped the pressure, kept the cold and dried the air for the plants. She reached for a stem and pinched it between her thumb and forefinger, summoning waves of magic to cause a bud to form, from which, a small star-shaped flower bloomed. She thanked the plant and picked the flower.

Yalthin was nervously pacing in a tight circle, glancing over his shoulder and scanning the crowd. He sprang into action, seeing Ara return, jogging over to her.

"This," she said, handing over the small pearlescent flower.

His smile turned to confusion, handling the flower, checking it for hidden features. "Lion's foot?" he inquired.

"Indeed. The dwarves call it edelweiss. Well, they call it Lion's foot but there is a poem crediting the name edelweiss, for it," she answered, proud of her own recollection.

"So... I am to just give this to her?" he asked, doubtfully.

"That is generally how gifts function, yes. Look, this flower has been credited with ending the clan wars between Myngora Haezelahol and Myngora Rotarmarmur. During peace talks, the clans flew into a rage and began jumping at each other's throats. The late King Bromik Ironheart went for a walk in the mountains, resigning himself to the fate of their nations. There, he bumped into a maiden so beautiful that she stole his heart in the first breath they shared in each other's presence. He panicked, having packed away his gold and jewels so as not to be noticed as king, now having nothing to present her with. He found this, the lion's foot flower. With it he proclaimed, 'It is the first flower and likely the only I shall ever pick. You are so stunning as to make a dwarf change his ways.' Not knowing her to be the daughter of the late King Jorgun Stonefist," she finished, recanting the love story she had found in the dusty old history tomes of the dwarven clan politics.

"That is beautiful. I have picked many flowers I am afraid and, thus, I fear this gift may be wasted coming from myself. I guess I should have waited for the flower that my heart felt was worthy of picking," he said, his shoulders sinking into the sea of raw emotion.

"It is more than that. If you are serious about this, then the symbolism can carry it through. Think of it as a staff or *lenlialarla* – it is a conduit through which you can channel your own feelings to give weight to your words when you present her with this gift. It is also a flower known to grow in the heights of the Isfrisairis mountains and from what I have heard, it can blanket some of the peaks around the sentinel's' lodge over there, making for an inspiring view," she offered.

"Ara, thank you," he said, a hopeful smile picking at the corners of his mouth.

Ara saw him off before returning to the market to find Ahrayn and the crew. They were heading to a store selling an array of odd trinkets and *lenlialarla*. Ara had seen it earlier, thinking such gadgets to be items that would be used once then shoved in a closet to take up space from that point on.

***

The group welcomed her with Ahrayn looking nervous, Alikain simply lost in the lights of the market, and Raethran missing once more. They had a fresh selection of treats, this time with a berry sorbet for Ahrayn and Ara and a bowl of diced fruit for Alikain.

"So, what are we doing now?" she asked, secretly hoping the answer included hot chocolate.

"Alikain is wanting to buy something from this store over here. We are keeping him company lest people think him asocial," Ahrayn answered, giving the inquisitor a facetious smile.

Ara chuckled and fell into the group, standing on the other side of

Alikain. The merchant had the usual look to him that people developed when around an inquisitor, although slightly more severe. Then again, he had a mage hunter inquisitor inspecting his magical wares. It was a miracle that he did not simply dive beneath the table at their approach.

Alikain scanned the items before inquiring about a pair of glasses. "What are these?" he finally decided to ask, rather glumly.

"Uh, yes, well those are glasses that lengthen wavelengths allowing for ultraviolet light to be seen on the visible spectrum. A delight when bird watching and such."

"How clever. Do you have anything that can shorten wavelengths? Visualise the infrared spectrum?" he inquired.

Ara nearly scoffed at the thought of a mage hunter with heat vision. "You are going to need two though. Your apprentice looks like you now. You will have to get him a pair as well otherwise you may break the motif. Where is Raethran by the way?" she asked, looking around.

The merchant began looking curiously at the group then tightened up. "I will have to look in the back for those glasses, one moment please."

Alikain did not break his gaze with the elf, looking like a cat ready to pounce. Ara now saw that she was in the middle of something dangerous and judging by the concern on Ahrayn's face, she was not the only one who thought so.

Alikain made a twitch towards his sword. The merchant threw out a spell, surrounding them in darkness. The market was shocked at the development, but rogue spells were not uncommon, and they soon returned to their business, merely avoiding the area, thinking the magic to be a part of a sales pitch.

Alikain dove over the counter, rolling to break the impact. He ran out of the darkness and searched for signs of the merchant. He was in the forest already, branches still swinging at his rushed penetration into the boughs. He sprinted after him, drawing his sword and throwing wards up, around himself.

Ustair panted heavily as he rushed through the forest, fighting off the foliage that tore at his clothes. Alikain decided to copy Ara and he threw a spell at his feet, bursting vines and roots from the ground to tangle his legs and trip him up. The spell shot out but caught a ward. Ustair, however, was used to running from elves. The magic would need to be a lot stronger to get through his defences.

The distance closing between them, Ustair panicked and inverted a pouch on his belt, toppling the contained *lenlialarla* onto the ground, sending spells in every direction. Alikain cast a ward over them, but Ustair was far stronger than he had anticipated and had set multiple triggers to the gems, Alikain only blocking some of them.

A third of the *lenlialarla* sprang up into the air and exploded at head height after hovering for a brief, timeless moment. The world took a deep breath before the explosions shattered reality, blinding him and sending him flying backward, his wards shielding him from any real damage but at a cost.

He heaved on all fours, his chest collapsing in on itself. Flashes of the Ilvithiir skyline. Goronil's face in the moments before he died. The golden masks of the thalenarian acolytes glinting in flickering candlelight as they wrenched open his mind in their torture. Eruptions of dirt during the reaver ambushes and the sickening grin of the salivating smilers.

He got to his feet, but his world was spinning. He could not hold on. He fell to his knees as his body gave up on him, his mind weighing him down. He looked up and through his tears, Ustair had doubled back and was now standing over him, a dagger to his throat.

He was speaking. There was definitely a rumble in the air to confirm that fact, but Alikain could no longer communicate with his senses. The merchant's voice came to him like the grating of rocks beneath the sea. Alikain was a world away from his body and had resigned it to whatever fate that awaited it, desperate for the release.

A figure, clad in black, burst through and fired spells at Ustair's wards, sending him into a full retreat. Escape was not his destiny though, as a rope of lightning tethered the merchant and pulled him forward as Alikain blacked out.

The Songbird's Cry

The infirmary is a cold and lonely place. Alikain remembered far too many nights lying in the bleached sheets of the patient beds, begging his body to heal faster so that he might escape the clinic and return to his life. This time, he had a private room to himself. He said a silent *thank you* to Ahrayn under his breath for that, fearful at the thought of welcoming prying eyes into his weakened state.

Alikain was wearing patient robes, distracting himself by thinking how he had gotten into them. A few of his more stubborn scars had been knitted together properly and he felt better than he had done in months, physically at least.

His normal clothes lay on the side table with his sword leaning against the wall. He reached over to grab his belongings, but they flickered from existence at his touch. A programmed illusion that set off the ringing of a silver bell at his door. He was getting rusty.

Ahrayn entered, carrying a meal tray with fruit salad, yoghurt and a steaming pot of tea.

"I brought you breakfast. I hope you do not mind but I brought an extra cup." She began by pouring tea for each of them, placing one on the tray for Alikain, settling hers down on the table beside his bed to cool. She gave her best bedside smile and adopted the tone of voice that she had perfected over the years. "So, how can I help you this morning?"

Alikain regarded her carefully for a moment, as if he couldn't quite remember what he had wanted to say. Ahrayn simply held his gaze softly, her gentle demeanour finally breaking through the ice of his recalcitrance. His shoulders slumped ever so slightly, and his lips twitched, letting slip the ghost of a defeated chuckle.

"Help me? I am not so sure that you can. It feels different this time," he began, admitting the weight of the burden he was carrying. "I thought I was fine. I thought this was just like the rest of my missions, but it broke me."

"Which mission? Ustair? Or Ilvithiir?" she asked.

"Ilvithiir. It is more than anyone can imagine, there is so much more. I cannot think of the past, nor can I plan for the future as it is so far beyond my abilities, yet here I am," he said, his hands trembling uncontrollably. "It is so hard to do what I intended. I am drowning and there is not so much as a glimmer of light to show where the surface may lie."

"If you look to the future before healing from the past then you will never be able to face what is to come. You are a mess, Alikain, those scars, your emotions. I know you. You have been all over the place since you returned, and if you do not give yourself time to heal then you are going to find yourself six feet under with nobody knowing that you are gone," she said, her tone sharp and methodical.

"I have been through worse, but there is something different about this one. It is personal."

"It is personal, you are right. That is not the reason why it is affecting you. This fight does not just involve you but you all Etroah. You are watching your friends stand up against Ilvithiir when you know what they are capable of and thus, you know what awaits them if they fight. You have seen death, experienced their torture and faced their armies. Realise that you cannot do this alone. You need your friends to help you which means that you need them to risk fighting. To risk dying."

"Then how do I get better? There is a way to do this, I just need time. I need my mind back; I need my body. I can't do this as a fractured person."

"Admit to yourself that you need to heal. You are denying yourself this simple luxury and it is tearing you apart. This would have been your end if not for Raethran and you know what? I think a part of you would have been relieved if he did not arrive in time."

"What am I supposed to do? Tell me how to fix this."

"Give yourself time. Allow yourself to process what it is you have been through. Go about your life but allow your mind to go over this in its due time or it will consume you. If you do not then you are going to be flooded like this every time you face a reminder of your experience over there."

"I have tried. It is locked behind walls that I am unable to break down. There are just… these leaks that form, the slightest of stimuli causing them to spill forth. Just the pain though. I seem unable to remember what caused it, merely flashes," he said, not able to make eye contact.

"Your mind is protecting you. You have been through much but nothing as severe as what you face now. Still, you know how to get through it. You have done it before, perhaps not to this extent but you have the ability. Little by little. Give yourself time and allow yourself to talk through it. You are not alone, despite what you might wish. Raethran will split the earth itself for those he cares for and over the years, he has become a fine ally to have. You have me, whom you have trained to always pick up your pieces no matter how broken you are, and you have a new friend in Ara. Raethran has been through more than he cares to admit and as such, he can provide a fresh perspective. Go through your experiences with Ara. She was not in Ilvithiir for long but her empáthy is at the forefront of everything she does, meaning that she suffered more than most despite her short time there. Let her be the ear that understands, the voice of wisdom and the shoulder of support."

Alikain made a motion to object with Ahrayn stopping him in his tracks.

"If you do not, then it would be a grand disservice to us all. Ara needs your help as much as you need hers. Raethran needs you to show him the ropes to keep him safe, and I need you because I love you. As infuriating as you are, I think we all do. Ilvithiir is inevitable. We are going to face it. You best be ready when that time comes."

"I just… Is there anything you can give me to stave off any ill effects in the interim? If the memories do come rushing back…" he pleaded.

"No. You need to face this, just as you have faced so much before. If we stave off the effects, then you will simply dam the swelling tide and become overwhelmed when the walls break. Plus, you have Raethran to keep you out of trouble," she said with a wink.

"And if something happens to him because of this threat… that has been brought through? He has become the closest thing I have ever had to a friend, and here I am, about to throw him into the crucible."

"We all have our crucible moments. That is part of life. He can handle it. I know that he will handle it."

At this, he locked his gaze with hers. He saw his pathetic reflection in the deep blue pools of Ahrayn's eyes through his gathering tears. "He has not stopped looking, you know. He hunted a rogue basilisk for the venom to assist in your medication. He has half the lecturers under his thumb, doing research on his behalf, even Ruunidil. He has done so much for them and now they are returning the favour, not that they know who they are doing it for. The Arcanum is behind you. Those writs he earns quickly find their way to healers and researchers across the universities with healers as far as Melsoa being consulted."

A tear ran down her cheek. "Alikain, you underestimate my abilities," she said, a voice of crystal through a pained smile as pure and untarnished as the trickle of a mountain stream.

"You know?" Alikain asked, looking into her eyes, desperate for her to do something, anything, to pull him off course.

"I know enough. You may think you have your secrets but there are forces at play that not even you can foresee," she said, clasping his hand in hers. Love, understanding, forgiveness; all passing through her hands as he blinked away the tears flooding his vision. "Now, it is a miracle that we have kept you here for this long, but I see no reason for us to keep you in, medically speaking. Remember, you are still my patient, no matter where you find yourself."

"I was not supposed to be. You just have a knack for revealing my weaknesses, for allowing me to... feel that weakness. Now, before I reveal my deepest and darkest secrets, I need to ask you to find Raethran. I am meeting Nildinar later; he is giving me the final brief. We will likely head off after that, the sooner the better in fact. If we grab the gryphons and get in the air this afternoon, then we should be able to reach Ixilth before dusk tomorrow to catch enough sleep to get a good start on the journey the next day."

She stood up and embraced him. He wrapped his arms around her slight form, returning the gesture. She squeezed him tightly for a moment before holding his shoulders out at arm's length. "Nobody knows that you are here, and if you turn right out the door, then nobody ever will. I will go and find Raethran. I have some final goodbyes to say before I go through to Gryphon's Landing. *Ommerim sinrenon siella[31]*," she said, the love of a friend and family member in her eyes and the softness of her touch.

"*Ommerim sinnanoir siella,[32]*" he responded.

Ahrayn left the room, flicking a spell at the cupboard beside the doorway, revealing his actual belongings. He smiled and took a deep breath before hopping to his feet and adorning his inquisitor's scowl. He got dressed slowly, savouring the last few moments of peace before returning to face what the world had in store for him. He paused for a moment at the

---

[31] I will meet you there
[32] I will see you there

threshold of the room, looking back at his bed. She had left tulips in a vase by the window and had kept the window open to allow light and fresh air through. She knew him better than he knew himself at times.

***

"…The merchant was selling black market *lenlialarla* to the dwarves in Myngora Haezelahol. Check his stocks. The ones he attempted to atomise Alikain with were not the only ones, that much is certain. Look, we were not the ones who called for the arrest so if you could hang onto him until Ranger Merewin arrives then you will have all the proof you need," Raethran explained, thinking the handcuffs were rather unnecessary.

He did not mind too much, however, as he had already figured out the lock and was idly locking and unlocking it with some scrap wire and a simple bit of magic, keeping his fingers busy.

Yildrin, the head sentinel, leant forward to halt Master Selen's response. "After Raethran's initial statement, we were able to make inquiries. We contacted Merewin and she seemed to corroborate this story. Raethran was working under the orders of the inquisitor and from what we found on Ustair; I believe we have enough evidence to warrant a search of his stocks as well as his temporary detainment."

Master Selen sighed at her loose grip on the situation. "The caravan left for Ixilth at first light. They will head off to Isfrisairis thereafter. See if you can send a team to catch them before that, as I feel that the entire caravan will need to be searched. Have rangers comb the grounds and the forest alongside the paths for signs of any hidden stashes. The last thing I need is for a student of mine to get a hold of contraband magical items."

Yildrin nodded, standing to attention, leading Raethran from Master Selen's office.

"You need to get ready. Your brother has arranged a meeting with Alikain, this afternoon, and the last of your provisions will be sent through shortly. He needs you in Ixilth before you can cause any more mischief over here. Master Selen may even begin to relax," the sentinel said, leading Raethran through the halls to the south entrance of the Arcanum. "Well, I suppose, not entirely," he mused, surprising Raethran. He caught his quizzical expression in his peripherals and elaborated, "Here, she can keep an eye on you. Out there, anything can happen. Although, I would not test

302

the reach of her power though. Are you ready to go?"

"About so. Does Nildinar need his sword? I feel bad for taking it. Plus, it is rather shoddy," he said, eyeing out the blade of what could barely be classified as steel.

"Take it, please. It is embarrassing having him walk around with that thing. He needs to update his image anyway. He is beginning to get whispers that he is not flashy enough for Isfrisairis court."

"They should have seen him before his courtly duties. Barefoot, knife between his teeth and living off the land like the best of us. He was a pretty rubbish survivalist though."

"Hah! You will need to share those stories with me over a drink one day. For now, keep yourself alive. You mean the world to him, even if he is unable to look up from his books for long enough to articulate it. Oh, and keep Ara safe too. Ahrayn as well. You know what, ask Alikain if you need a sentinel to come along," he said, jokingly.

Raethran chuckled and handed the wide-eyed sentinel his handcuffs, bidding him farewell with a respectful bow. Not wanting to give Yildrin any excuse to detain him again, he ran off into the quad, making for the dorms.

He had spent the last few nights in Ahrayn's room, giving Grindol a break from his presence. The only downside to the arrangement was that Grindol had full access to their supplies and was likely halfway through constructing some or other obscure autonomous shoe cleaner or horse brushing device from what he had found.

The university was going about its usual business with the small exception of those tasked to clean up after the winter market. Ahrayn left the infirmary and joined Raethran, slipping seamlessly into conversation.

"How did the hearing go?" she asked, wiping tears from her face.

He wrapped an arm around her shoulders and brought her in close. "We will be sure to check in as often as we can. We can also fly back whenever we want. The hearing was a waste of time. They already knew what we did was necessary, they simply wanted to make sure that they followed procedure. The next time Alikain takes on a task that he did not prepare for himself, I will be sure to knock him about before his target gets a chance to do so themselves. How is he doing?"

"He is fine. He is just overwhelmed. I know the two of you love giving each other a hard time but I think you should relax for a bit. He has been through a lot with his Ilvithiir experience and is not yet himself," she replied, resting her head on his shoulder.

"Makes sense. They have opened up the dissection halls for some of the specimens they got from the portal site at Tour Mardesi. I thought the bestiary was a dalliance in the realm of overkill until I saw those things," he said with a shiver.

"I am glad you are doing your research beforehand. I need to go and say my goodbyes to my father. Are you all right to handle the luggage from your room?" she asked, continuing after his brief nod, "Then I will meet you by Gryphon's Landing, where we can get a head start on our journeys," she finished, giving him a tight embrace and a kiss, lingering upon his lips as she squeezed his hands. She offered him a smile before trotting off toward the alchemy labs.

Raethran arrived at his dorm room, giving a knock on the door before entering. Grindol was nowhere to be seen. Evidence of his interactions with their supplies was well concealed, clearly nothing having sparked his interest as no new half-assembled device lay on the floor.

Raethran stopped for a moment, sniffing the air. His face turned ghostly pale. "Twins!" he whispered, shutting the door behind himself and latching it as fast as his hands could manage.

"Nice try, Raethran," the duet came from behind him.

He hung his head and turned to face his final judgement.

"You are right to be afraid, but we come bearing gifts this time," Lirith said, her voice as lethal as always.

They had been hiding behind a refraction wall and were impossible to see, Grindol likely having let them in out of fear for his own behind. They had poured themselves each a drink with the glasses that were clearly visible on Grindol's desk, something Raethran chastised himself for not noticing.

The twins strode forward, with each placing a hand on the wall on either side of Raethran's head, leaning in to deliver the killing strike. Astril pulled a dagger from a sheath but, instead of sliding it between his ribs, she handed it over to him, presenting the handle.

"There seems to be a lot going on in the world. We want in. Call us when you realise that you are out of your depth," Astril said, both elves kissing Raethran on the cheek before unlocking the door and leaving the room.

Raethran took his first breath since they had revealed themselves. It would be a terrifying day indeed if he were to come across a task that required the particular talents of the twins. Thriol's assistance was immense, but Lirith and Astril could topple kings if they so chose. Perhaps an emperor too.

***

Ara rummaged through the snow, collecting pea-sized pebbles. Her fingers froze through her gloves, but it would all be worth it. Once they had filled her palm, she began flicking them at a window of the infirmary, one at a time like a bird pecking at the glass.

She was starting to get worried, seeing her supplies dwindle when the window finally swung open. Aeradil scanned the snowbank, spotting her green cloak with confusion. She gestured for him to join her outside. He blinked. Ara put her hands on her hips with a mock pout. He stared at her in deliberation for a few more seconds before giving her a small nod. He put a jacket and boots on and made his way to meet Ara.

She silently took him by the shoulder and skipped through the snow toward the sentinel camp where her surprise awaited.

"It was a beautiful market last night; the food was delicious and the music was wonderful! We saw Master Filthin dance, and Yalthin, the crazy final year I told you about? He finally confessed his love for Vexrith. The two were sitting on the bank of the lake, early this morning, so I think it went well. It all got a bit strange near the end of the evening but there is no need to go into that. Here, I saved you some hazelnuts," she said, handing a half-finished bag to Aeradil.

He accepted the charge with a dutiful nod, placing it in his coat pocket for safe keeping, pausing to fasten a button to secure the pocket closed. Gryphons screeched up ahead which caused him to shut his eyes until they flew off. He had come a long way and Ara could not have been more proud of his progress but he was far from being himself.

Ara waited patiently until he opened his eyes again. She gave him a reassuring smile to which he responded with another nod. He marched through the snow at Ara's side until they reached the communal tent at the centre of the campsite. It was warm enough and, if you did not mind broody rangers everywhere, rather pleasant with rich upholstered furniture from the university along with spare paintings to add some colour.

Three of the junior students from the Arcanum were playing tunes on their string instruments in exchange for some of the rangers' help in plant identification. They played away whilst rangers argued over pine tree bark and the numbers of needles per cluster to indicate their species of origin.

Other rangers carefully went about waxing bow strings, sharpening knives, oiling leather straps or mending coats. Lethrik was at the centre of the table, close to the hearth, showing off a bushel of finely crafted arrows with green fletching and an enamel type finish to their tips. He was prone to exaggeration, and nobody was paying attention to the advertisement of these one-shot arrows that Yildrin had gifted him.

Ara led Aeradil over to a table where they could be separated from the commotion but able to watch it peacefully, feeling as if they were involved. The tent had no meal stone but an oak table at the centre of the tent supported an urn of boiled water, a basket of fresh muffins and a truly inspiring selection of teas.

Ara took three cups, one with a honey ginger for herself, another with a strong breakfast blend and the final one being a cranberry fruit tea. She pocketed a few muffins for good measure and returned to the table, Aeradil staring blankly across the room into the fires of the hearth.

She placed the breakfast tea in front of him, sparking his curiosity with the third cup. Ara was mainly focusing on her talent, in not covering herself in boiling water, with the journey. Aeradil remained silent and returned to watching the fire, cupping his tea to help warm his hands.

Peppa and her parents walked into the tent, hanging their coats on the hooks at the entrance, allowing Peppa to barrel over towards the table where Ara and Aeradil sat. The young elf had changed her hair to the same hue as Ara's soft, chestnut waves, whilst keeping her own sparkling blue eyes. Ara welcomed her but Aeradil remained a mixture of on guard and concerned at the development. Peppa dove at Ara, giving her a massive hug before hopping onto her chair, sitting on her knees.

Ara decided to introduce their guest, lest Aeradil's mind seize up. "It is my most esteemed honour to present; Peppa. A group of us entered a watermelon eating competition and it was she who took the crown. An entire watermelon before the rest of us had even made it through half. She is also the best baker in all Ixilth—"

Peppa interrupted, speaking with a mouth full of raspberry muffin and butter, nodding furiously, "The world actually."

"—Uh, yes, the world! Peppa, he has a present for you," Ara said, gesturing toward the saucer upon which Aeradil's tea sat.

The crystal daisy lay on the porcelain, to Aeradil's shock. He looked up and saw Peppa's mouth agape with raw excitement and joy. He panicked and handed the trinket over to her, her tiny hands accepting the gift with ebullient grace.

"Thank you! I do not even know your name! Are you a ranger? Have you been on many adventures? Have you been to Mardacia? Have you seen a hydra?" she began, firing questions faster than arrows from Ara's bow.

Aeradil was in shock and had no idea how to handle the onslaught, so he simply began with; "Aeradil. My name is Aeradil."

Because, I Love You

Ahrayn breathed in the scents of the mid-morning breeze, blowing in from the forest. It had been ages since she had left the confines of the University Arcanum and Isfrisairis. This time, it was different too. This was not some journey to see a healer or to have the next round of invasive testing done but instead, a journey to see, and to save, the world. A journey for her.

Water, from the frost's thaw, dripped to the sleeping ground as the limbs of the forest danced in the breeze above. The squirrels appeared to be hiding from the cold, but Ahrayn wrapped her coat closer to her body and forged ahead, to the mountain's base.

A class of juniors had gathered and were making their way to the pass with a scattering of rangers in their ranks, keen to get some flight time with the gryphons, themselves. Ahrayn played with the daisy in her hair, smelling the lingering scent of Raethran on her coat, nervous at the prospect of their journey ahead, quickening her pace to just below that of a skip.

Copper and golden leaves rained down, catching in her hair and on her coat. A flock of birds took flight to her flank, Ahrayn chuckling in embarrassment at the fright it had given her. She was now catching up to the group ahead with them collecting themselves before attempting the ascent. She smiled at the group, spotting the gryphon fledglings amongst their number, roaring away at the games they played with them, others simply tearing at unattended bags in search of treats.

***

Ara had enjoyed watching Aeradil fend off the barrage of questions that Peppa had for him. He had some colour to his cheeks and had even stood up from the table to refill their teas. Peppa had shown Ara that there was an innocence in the world worth fighting for, worth protecting, and now she could see the same medicine working through Aeradil, right before her eyes.

Ara had thanked Peppa's parents for indulging her request. They were all too happy to comply and had enjoyed their time in the tent, chatting with the other rangers and the sentinels there.

Aeradil was beaming the whole walk back to the infirmary. He gave Ara a tight embrace before heading into his room, not climbing into bed but sitting in a chair by the window instead. He had a pile of books from which to choose and he thanked Ara again before settling in for the rest of the morning.

Alikain had warned Ahrayn that today was the day that their journey was likely to begin. Ara was thus advised, by her, to begin making final preparations.

She had been able to arrange pieces of training armour for Raethran and Ahrayn as well as a bow and some arrows for each of them. She was disappointed with this achievement and had a plan to send a message to Rylia in order to request something more substantial to await them when they passed through Tour Aine.

For now, though, she had to wait out the time until Alikain called them together to go over their final plans before setting off on their journey. She stood at the lake edge thinking back on the past few days.

She certainly had her fair share of stories to take home to Rylia, once all this portal business was over with. She knew what they had to overcome was no small task but with Ahrayn, Raethran and Alikain at her side, all of it seemed possible.

Ara turned back to look at the Arcanum. She was going to miss her new home. The marbled architecture, the creativity of the meal stone, the awe-inspiring beauty of Flithin's movements as he spun around the dancefloor. The university was unique in so many ways with each movement being grander than the next.

A group of martials exited the halls, setting up on the training fields and so, she made herself scarce, feeling the need for a more aerial view anyway. The university was returning to its routine with the official business of the chancellors beginning to settle.

She summited the stairs of the abjuration tower and looked out, over the grounds, before her. The lake was shining with the sun's light, with a forest of frozen green leading to Gryphon's Peak to the south. An icy gust blew through in a deep breath, rustling the cloaks of the students below.

**

Alikain left Nildinar's war room, gliding through the halls and out towards the greenhouses. The weight of his task was now firmly set upon his shoulders, and he was all too glad to get to the fresh air of the forest. He closed his eyes and breathed deeply, easing the trembling of his hands.

Satisfied with his reformed composure, he began his now leisurely stroll. There were some reagents that had varying properties according to the manner in which they were harvested. The alchemists at the Arcanum being far too orderly about their procedures to have adhered to such criteria themselves. A personal trip to the greenhouse ensured that Alikain could do this himself.

He had enjoyed being at the University Arcanum again. It had been many years since his studies, but he remembered them fondly. The greenhouse was one of his favourite places to spend his study breaks and any excuse to visit, even now, was a welcome one.

He loved the smell of all the flowers, the textures of the leaves and the dazzling displays of colour that nature could accomplish with such ease. He was brought back into reality by a deer that sprang over the path ahead of him, sprinting through the trees and out of sight.

***

Raethran exited the dormitories and began his short jog towards the landing at Gryphon's Peak. He had packed the items in a dizzying assortment the saddlebags, backpacks and satchels that would be easy enough for them to load onto the gryphons once they had brought them down from the mountain roost.

He made a mental note to say goodbye to Grindol before he left, and to kick him in the shin for the part he had played in his ambush, but that would have to wait until after. He still had to fetch the gryphons and get the final brief from Alikain before saying his goodbyes.

He was wearing his old cloak, saving his inquisitor robes for a day that he didn't plan to spend hugging a musty gryphon. He had stuffed two sets of gryphon rider's goggles and flight cloaks into his satchel and was now well on his way.

He cut through the trees, dodging the roots and jumping over the fallen branches. He lost his footing as the ground gave way beneath his stride, pitching him forward onto his stomach. He caught his breath and chuckled at himself. He sat up in the small clearing, taking time to gather his composure.

The flowers were wilting around him with the leaves decaying a shade faster than they should have been. He glanced around, disconcerted at the aberration. A yew tree to his right had a chasm in it, opening up amidst its roots, likely the cause for its recent demise as evidenced by the few remaining leaves, now desiccated beyond all traces of vitality.

Sounds of screams and a full pitched battle erupted to the north, at the fields. A training exercise at first but then more. Much more.

Alarm bells began to ring as if from all around him, the ground opening up as he scurried back from the earth's maw. He took to his feet and started making his way around the sinkhole, now sprinting towards Ahrayn. His path, however, was blocked by a creature roughly twice his size with hideously long claws and a mouth spanning ear to ear in a savage rictus grin. Its five eyes blinked independently and its mouth salivated at the sight of Raethran. Hundreds of teeth appeared to grow from its gums in row upon row of sickly yellow serrations.

Raethran threw a hand to Nildinar's sword as the creature sprung at him, colliding in a tumble. Raethran dropped his legs, dodging the primary centre of mass, but was thrown off his feet, its claws raking at his shoulder.

He dove instinctively to the side, anticipating another pounce from the creature. There was a manic, fluid choked laugh coming from that direction. He drew the sword and dove a third time. Each manoeuvre was met with more cackling and the sound of the ground being shredded in his wake. Raethran decided to flee, weaving between trees and matching its agility against his own, breaking any chance it had at a successful pounce.

He steadied himself enough to turn around and face the creature, drawing Thriol's knife as he did so. There was nothing. Silence had fallen on the immediate area. He made a choice and sprinted in Ahrayn's direction, being immediately tackled from above. Swords are useless in a grapple so as the creature sunk its teeth into his lacerated shoulder, he began plunging the dagger into its flesh. Stab, twist, pull. Stab, twist, pull.

The creature let go after the second, retreating along the ground, Raethran now in pursuit. He dove at it, pinning its leg to the ground with his sword then rolling away from its retaliatory strikes. He picked up a rock and stunned it with one swift impact to the head, then finished the job with the knife.

***

The tower trembled and the students on the field froze. A shockwave knocked them off their feet as multiple portals appeared at once, all around the grounds to the north.

Time slowed as Ara watched the scene unfold before her. The portals tore at the fabric of their reality. Ara had seen what could come next. She shouted out warnings to the elves below, bracing for the horrors to come.

"We are under attack. It is the portals!" she screamed, fear threatening to paralyse her.

She threw herself down the stairs, colliding into the walls and bouncing off in her intended direction. She looked around the halls for a weapon, a shield, anything! There was no time to scan the rooms, so she burst out of the doors and into the chaos of the training fields. Swarms of reavers were attacking the students in full force. Mages were casting barriers, and sentinels were diving into the fray, but there were just too many of them.

Thriol had formed a square with the martials as the others scrambled to them for safety. Graxith had a battleaxe out, but he too was slowly being overwhelmed, and was hastily retreating to the ranks of Thriol's contingent. The sentinels ushered those they could to safety but as their backs turned, so they were flanked. As they killed one, three more charged in.

Through tears, Ara looked down at her hands, summoning an eruption of flames. She screamed as she bathed the Ilvithiirian forces before her with a phoenix of fire that swept through their ranks in gargantuan wing strokes. A moment's reprieve was all she could manage for the *haltha* before she collapsed to her knees, drained from the magic.

Yalthin, appearing as if from nowhere, pulled her to her feet and dragged her to the centre of the field where the sentinels and martials enveloped them, the screams of the students turning into cries from the reavers.

Ara steadied herself in time to see a sentinel break from the ranks. A blight-shambler had come through, its black aura rotting all it touched, the reavers screamed and were vaporised as they strayed too close. The blight-shambler let loose a cry like that of a war horn and began a lumbering charge towards the ranks. Without hesitation, the sentinel charged the creature down and with a spectacular leap, launched himself forth and speared the blight-shambler through the chest. It let out a colossal scream that rattled the foundations of the towers around. Its howl reverberated, threatening to rupture Ara's hearing then, it stumbled back, crashing over a sea of reavers.

Two sentinels ran forward to retrieve their comrade whose armour was now smoking. They successfully returned with him but, what they brought back was an elf screaming in agony as his armour fused to his skin, melting the flesh beneath.

"Quick, get his armour off!" Ara shouted at the junior students, who recoiled back, staring in horror.

She knelt beside the elf and, with shaky hands, focused her magic on blocking his mind, shielding him from his pain. The sudden flood of agony was too great for her to anticipate as his pain overwhelmed her barriers. What was left was still too much for him, so she split it between herself and the sentinel, crippling her in an instant. She crumpled to the ground next to him. The arcane tether had her begging for death with each passing second, as she lay writhing in the dirt with her own screams ripping at her mind.

***

Alikain felt the shockwaves. His heart sank. He drew his blade and sprinted towards the mage towers. A reaver swarm flooded the grounds, shredding all that were caught in their path. He looked to the fields where the students were fighting for their lives, throwing spells and training weapons in vain. The rangers were still positioned around the field, unleashing volleys of lethal arrows on the charge, but this was a full nest. No number of arrows would be enough.

The route to the west; he could slice through the creatures and help the fields, but the east was… He set off at a full sprint, barely a blink going by for the decision. The screams were hideous, combined with the useless clashing of shields, as they tried to break the tide of reavers. He had seen this before and he knew what the outcome would be. A few stray students emerged from the eastern exits of the lecture halls.

"Inside! West windows from the third floor. Assist your kin!" he yelled, forcing them back inside.

The war horn came next. Blight-shamblers. He felt the energy leach from his body, and the thoughts from his mind, at the sound of what awaited the elves. He ran forth, intent on his singular goal. Reavers were flooding around the hall now, right into Alikain's cleaving arcs. Wide sweeps from high. He sliced through their limbs, ignoring the killing blows, striking at their arms that would be causing the damage. Slow blood loss would do the rest. He did his best to bait a small group into following him and then, focused on his charge.

The mage towers were in sight. He scanned them, thinking back. Second to the east was the Evokers', so there he went. To his west, a sentinel charged the blight-shambler. That brave fool. Alikain threw a ward over him, sparing what magic he could afford. It would get him to the blight-shambler, but few abjurers would be able to spare enough magic to get him there and back again. He spurred his resolve and took the stairs three at a time. Long-long-short-landing, long-long-short-landing, the rhythm went. He heard the furious skittering of a reaver on his heels but paid it no heed.

He reached the apex of the tower and with all that remained of his magic, he channelled his anger, rage and fear, all in one; into the *lenlialarla* that was mounted there. Beams shot out from the gem to those in the other towers then, all at once, they reached out to the *lenlialarla* atop the Arcanum. Alikain turned to the reavers in his pursuit, they were now upon him and with nowhere left to run, he readied his sword.

The first, he dismembered and tossed into the *lenlialarla*. A pulse of energy erupted from it as the stone devoured its physical form. The creature was consumed as the reavers around the campus cried out in agony. The second; he stepped back to dodge its swipe, then stepped in with a clean strike to its head, through its gnashing mandibles. That one went in next to summon a second pulse from the crystals, this one stronger.

Pulse after pulse, the creatures of Ilvithiir cried out across the university grounds. Alikain fed more bodies into the spell, assisting the *lenlialarla* in finding their targets. The reavers were affected the worst, then the matriarchs and finally the yurinduur and blight-shamblers.

After that, the three blight-shamblers who had stepped out were slowly being dragged down by the magic. One of the creatures had strayed too far from the group but the masters were out now. Ndolin incinerated one on sight. Paylorn had collapsed their auras and Ilkiir was slowly tearing one apart, limb by limb.

Alikain had given them a chance, but this invasion had a purpose. The thalenarians thrived off of fear but were far too efficient for such displays to hold a singular purpose. He flew down the stairs, cursing the tight spiral, nearly tripping multiple times in his haste.

His eyes scanned the grounds. The portals had appeared to the north, all at once. So, he ran to the south. Now thinking of the codex that Ruunidil was translating in the library there. The tide of the battle had not yet shifted but the *lenlialarla* had been activated and the ranks of defenders formed. Now, it was up to the training of the soldiers and the strength of their leadership.

Upon arriving at the entrance to the main hall, he found that a portal had formed with no reavers appearing to have emerged from its shimmering disturbance. Tracks led into the Arcanum but Alikain found that he could not follow. His chest tightened and his legs froze. His stomach churned as a familiar pain began leaking from behind the walls in his memories.

Flashes of blinding light stabbed at his mind as he fell to his knees, vomiting on the ground, unable to open his eyes. He clenched the soil in his fists and gritted his teeth, but the pain simply swelled within him, overwhelming his mind and tearing at his skull.

It will consume you... Ilvithiir is inevitable. He heard Ahrayn's words repeating in his head, pulling him down into the earth. They were her words, but her soothing tone had been twisted in his mind, tainting the healing she represented.

An eternity of agony drew him down, as he begged himself to hang onto his consciousness. He heaved at the ground, sobbing uncontrollably.

I know you... You need to heal. Her words rang through his mind, questioning his weakness this time. That questioning, that doubt. It was hope, she could pull him from this. The music of her voice was taking over.

A warmth enveloped his shoulders, spreading to form a circlet around his chest, where Ahrayn had embraced him. The comfort radiated throughout his body, spreading from his chest.

Raethran needs you... Ara needs your help... I need you because I love you... We all do...

The warmth of her unconditional love, her friendship, the strength shared through their bond. He gathered his wits and tightened his grip on his sword. His teeth gritted and he tore himself through the pain's surface, escaping its depths with a gasp.

He stumbled into the Arcanum, his legs shaking, and his vision blurred.

The library was not far off with the sounds from within letting Alikain know that he was already too late. He summoned the remainder of his strength and sprinted in. Two thalenarian mages were currently in a battle with the sentinel guards, Ruunidil and Nildinar. A third was standing over the corpse of Chancellor Kilorin, his throat slashed with a blight seeping, up his neck and down his chest, in lashing tendrils that leapt from the open wound and crawled over his skin.

Alikain threw a ward to block the door and flanked the thalenarians that had engaged the sentinels. They read the situation and baited the thalenar forward, committing him to a strike. Alikain made short work of him with a blade through his heart, his wards shattering at the augmented strike. His sword pulsed with magic, fighting back at it, the blade drinking in the energy and turning it against his foe.

The second, was then swarmed by the sentinels and stood little chance but it was the third who needed to be dealt with. He began casting a spell with rapid twisting fingers and mumbling lips in the thalenarian tongue. Alikain threw a hand into his pocket, grabbing the powder within and flinging it at the thalenar's face. The mixture of enchanted iron, salt, and powdered valerian sparked with the wild energies of the foreign magic. The distorted magic twisted itself as it was summoned into the spell. The thalenar's teleportation failed, shearing off part of his arm and removing the bones from his left leg.

Alikain made short work of him, thereafter, struggling to get through his wards at first, but succeeding before what was left of the acolyte could cast another spell. Their bodies withered away as their flesh rotted, their own magic dissolving their remains.

Ruunidil had been struck by a blight spell as a spider web of necrosis slowly crept up his arm, towards his shoulder. He gasped in an attempt to grab Alikain's attention then turned away, biting his opposing shoulder in anticipation of the pain to come. Alikain grabbed an axe from a sentinel's belt and swung at the arm, cleaving it off in one decisive, crushing strike.

Ruunidil was screaming, but this was nothing compared to the fate from which he had been spared. Alikain jumped forward to cauterize the major vessels, wincing upon seeing the splintered bone. A sentinel took over with a medical kit, putting pressure on the wound and pulling out potions to dull Ruunidil's pain.

Alikain stumbled back in shock, raising his hands to his head, recoiling at the slick blood on his fingers. He took a deep breath and composed himself, retrieving his sword from the floor.

***

Master Hital brought Ara back to consciousness by stabilising the sentinel. She was muttering incantations at a furious speed, causing his skin to seal up and his pain to subside, black mist being pulled from the tissue and captured in bottles. Ara sat up, relieving the duties of the student watching over her. Martials, sentinels and rangers alike, held the perimeter around them, fending off the tide of horrors.

Ara looked around, her breaths coming in short, dizzying bursts as she beheld the familiar view. Like in Ilvithiir, they were surrounded, and the sounds of battle raged, punctuated again and again by the screams of the dying. But they were not in Ilvithiir, and she slowed her breaths, calming herself enough to see clearly. The tides had turned. The blades of grass reached through her fingers with the life of the earth holding her aloft.

Reavers were being dragged down by bursts of magic from the *lenlialarla* around the university, most not even making it to the defenders. It was the yurinduur that were the real threat now. Stampedes of the hulking monsters crashing into the shields, the effects of the gems serving to weaken them but not kill them. Yurinduur that jumped over the shields were met with arcane volleys as the mages made short work of them. The savage training, that the students had endured, had changed them into the fighting army of the Arcanum.

Ara ran to the line of mages, seeing a smiler crawling on the wall of the lecture building, preparing to grab a student from out of the window. She shot forth a bolt of flame, shattering the creature and forming a crack in the marble around it. The remaining pieces fell to the floor, bringing her attention to a lone sentinel with a ranger on his shoulder.

Yildrin had just decapitated a yurinduur and stomped on a reaver's chest, his foot burying inside it. He was facing threats before him but did not see the reaver matriarch, which had rounded the corner, now charging the lone defender.

Ara pushed through the frontline, their ranks only moving when they saw her intention. Yildrin had been alerted to the threat and braced against the charge. Rangers were firing arrows that harmlessly bounced off the

317

thick chitin. Ara did not have the time to explain what needed to be done, only trusting that they would keep her safe until she was close enough. Yurinduur fell at her feet as the rangers desperately kept her alive with lines of magic skirting around her.

Ara ran and dove at its flanks, narrowly avoiding its legs that stabbed into the ground as it ran over her. Reaching up, she touched the matriarch's ventral plates and screamed as she unleashed her spell. Pieces of the creature scattered in all directions as she threw the full force of her emotions behind her magic. Yildrin threw her on to his other shoulder, having lost his sword to a yurinduur's chest.

With a roar, he charged back into the ranks where he thanked Ara, dropping Lethrik at his feet. He had lost a lot of blood but would be fine. Hital spared him a glance, threw a some herbs into a potion before tossing it to Ara. She fumbled, trying to catch it, before securing it to his lips and pouring the contents into his mouth, lifting his head so as not to choke him.

Lethrik was still conscious but having received medical care, he was beginning to look more stable. He handed Ara his bow and pointed out a wrap of arrows, only managing the words, "Blight-shamblers—" in a pained whisper.

She grabbed the bow and prepared the arrows, turning to face the continued influx from the portals. Six more blight-shamblers were now charging at the defenders, their thunderous cries resonating in the air with a stentorian roar.

The arrowheads had wax coverings that she removed with the tabs, revealing the enamel arrow tips beneath, glistening with a glossy sheen. She fired them off, one for each, hoping Lethrik had a plan. The green fletching spun forth and guided them to their marks. They were heavy arrows and made solid impacts, barely surviving the blight-shamblers' aura's but pushing through far enough.

They punched into the flesh of the blight-shamblers before being vaporised. A pit formed in Ara's stomach as she placed the bow by Lethrik, summoning forth the last of her flames to her fingertips. Ndolin stood next to her and did the same after an exhausted nod in her direction. Ilkiir joined too, a worried smile at the others and blood trickling from his eyes.

They unleashed their magic but, at that, the blight-shamblers fell to the floor, crashing into the dirt, paralysed by the venom in Lethrik's arrows. Ara looked to Ndolin for confirmation, but he was not slowing down. He pointed to the *lenlialarla* at the tower, of the Arcanum, and unleashed a beam of energy towards it. Ara and Ilkiir followed suit, calling the rest of the mages to do the same.

The creatures began burning where they stood, the *lenlialarla* too much for them now. Even the paralysed blight-shamblers being incinerated at their power. The portals shuddered and were torn from existence in a cataclysmic explosion. Creatures, that remained, could be heard retreating into the forest, fleeing the university. The Arcanum was safe.

It Takes Two to Stand

Raethran wrenched his sword from the creature's leg and ran towards Gryphon's Peak. There were shadows in his peripherals, darting by at incredible speed. He urged his legs to be faster but, with each heartbeat, he felt his strength being drained. His shoulder was throbbing and... dripping.

He had been poisoned, but he was not finished yet. He charged forth until he had the landing in sight. Junior students and gryphon fledglings, were being defended by six rangers that had flanked Ahrayn as masses of hulking yurinduur charged out at them.

Arrow after arrow, the yurinduur collided with the earth, spraying dirt into the air in mighty waves. Ahrayn threw bolts of lightning out at the creatures, hitting one before it snaked out to those around it. The strikes would kill the first, stun the next few and stumble the others in powerful webs of destruction.

Master Filthin emerged from within the group, casting wards around them between volleys of flame that he sent into the ranks of the charging creatures. He carved out swathes of yurinduur at a time but they could not fire fast enough as the creatures were soon crashing into their barriers.

They beat at the displacement barrier with mighty battle axes and broad blades, the energy of each strike strengthening it as Ahrayn channelled magic that allowed her to shift the forces. She was concentrating on too many spells at once, and near collapsing. Raethran, through his poison induced mental haze, knew that he needed to get there. He added his own magic to ease her burden, stretching his mind to connect with her magic. A net of lightning flew from his hand, surrounding them, striking down rank after rank.

Ahrayn locked eyes with Raethran and fear set in. A war horn sounded from behind as a creature the size of the mage towers stepped forth. A blight-shambler. It was surrounded by a black mist that shrouded its lumbering form. Its humanoid body had elongated limbs with skin barely attached to the skeleton beneath. The wishbone horns on its featureless face spawned a vortex of shadow that shot forth into Ahrayn's barrier. She collapsed as the rangers prepared for the melee.

Filthin pushed the juniors back, having them cast what barriers they could, over the group. He turned his attention to the blight-shambler, his spells colliding with it but not having enough power remaining to finish it off.

The creatures were on them in a blink, but Ahrayn was not out of the fight. Periodic bursts of lightning grew forth from the mass of fighters, felling dozens at a time.

Raethran, barely able to stand, was now fighting these behemoths for his own life, but he kept moving forward to get to Ahrayn. They would be safe, they just needed to be together. He slashed, stabbed, rolled and swiped, seemingly at random to his own distorted mind. He let his training take over as he focused on recasting the barrier around Ahrayn's group.

Another shadow spiralled forth as Raethran felt his soul being wrenched from his body, his own barrier spell collapsing, leaving the group exposed. Three more blight-shamblers exited the portal.

The yurinduur in front of him took advantage of the break in his concentration and sent him flying with the strike of a hammer. His ribs caved in, and all his breath left him. The rangers had gained the upper hand on the melee and thanked Raethran by felling his attacker with a quick arrow to its temple.

The yurinduur had fallen, but still, the blight-shamblers advanced. Spells and arrows vaporising in the black mist around them. A third bolt of shadow shot out from between its horns, this time, Filthin deflecting it at great cost to his remaining magical reserve.

The portal behind it, shimmered again, repeating its shockwave, throwing the elves to their backs.

Two more blight-shamblers emerged from the portal with a humanoid figure at their feet, bathing in the swirling mists and cackling at their failing defences. The, now six, blight-shamblers were marching steadily to their prey.

Raethran's feet struggled to find traction in the leaf litter, kicking about as his mind reached out to hold onto the world. The new threat needed to be dealt with. Ahrayn, he needed to get to Ahrayn.

He shook his head, finding a foothold on a root, he climbed to his feet. Stumbled at first, he gained the momentum to run towards Ahrayn. He looked up to her, desperation clinging to every iota of his existence.

Tears were streaming down her face as she smiled. A smile with the purity to cure the world of all its fears. Raethran gasped, trying to cry out to her, trying to steal her from the world. She ran to the creatures and into the aura of darkness, deflecting spells from the thalenar in explosions of magical entropy.

No cry of pain. No shout of anger. She ran in, her body melting away in the mists. In a flash of purest starlight, they were destroyed.

Raethran fell to his knees; this final image burned into his mind as his world faded away.

A New World

A heavy fog had pulled in with dusk's fall. Solemn torches fought back the darkness, illuminating the wraiths that tended the grounds of the University Arcanum. Rangers perched as crows upon the rooftops, twitching their heads to movement whilst their bodies remained motionless, gathering frost and shadows.

The dead had been laid out across the training fields, grey blankets from the dorms forming their shrouds. Ara could not bring herself to count them and simply sought to keep herself busy by assisting the infirmary team with the wounded; Olethia and Silla leading their efforts.

Aeradil was dressed in the armour of a ranger with a sword at his side and bow at the ready. Peppa and her parents were huddled in a corner where he brought them hot tea and blankets to keep them warm. In his silence, he acknowledged Ara as they both returned to their duties, the world not waiting for them to heal.

Alikain glided forth, his hood up and hands tucked into his sides. He slipped through the perimeter of the *lenlialarla* defence sconces that had been set up by the mages, ignoring the glares given by the helmets of the sentinels.

Not even the insects stirred in the forest with the tree branches slouching ever closer to the ground. The fog obscured whatever solace the sky was attempting to provide, leaving those below to fade into themselves. Each of Alikain's footfalls made the fauna wince as his very presence poked at the fresh wounds of the world. He ducked through to the south, taking a wide berth around Gryphon's Landing by taking the eastern approach into the mountains.

The midnight cloak clung to the armoured inquisitor's form as the saturation of the mist overwhelmed it. Alikain dared not shiver lest it open the gates to all else he needed to feel. He ascended the mountainside in utter silence, ashamed at his existence. Nearly at the summit, the fog began to thin. Rising out from the clouds, he reminded himself to look up, to scan the surroundings.

Raethran's silhouette cut through with the lightless stars behind him. He was staring right at him, the faint glint of his eyes piercing his soul. Alikain advanced, not knowing what he was going to say, not having a plan. He knew that they needed to talk but beyond that, his mind would not dare speculate.

"How are you feeling?" Alikain inquired, the words slipping out in a dark whisper.

Raethran turned away, walking to the west. Alikain followed, keeping a respectful distance between them, pulling the hood of his cloak back to his shoulders.

Raethran hunched over a hole; he had dug a small runic circle at its base with etchings in the surrounding stones.

"Six months. I had six months left with her," said Raethran.

His voice hoarse and his tone was empty. Alikain shifted. A thousand thoughts ran through his head, his mouth making a motion to begin his reply with each. He could do nothing but stand there.

He continued, "She had so little time. Everyone could not help themselves but remind her of that. We were finally going to do something that she was excited for."

"I think she would have loved the ocean the most. The nights of two skies when the sea is so calm that it forms a mirror. Beneath the ocean too…" Alikain added, tears forming as he stared at his feet, kneeling to fidget with the soil.

Raethran shifted his stance. "She was born into a life of agony, spending each waking moment in the shadow of her own grave. Amidst all that, the world simply played with her, expecting her to heal others. There was no one better at it than her. I wonder what it was like seeing all those cured patients leave the infirmary, knowing that she could not. Then, in her final moments, she sacrificed herself to save us, to those whom she had already given so much of herself."

Alikain looked up. "She left on her own terms, Raethran. In a world that guided her every move, she took control at the very end. She lived for a cause, and she chose to die for it too. We need to honour that."

Raethran whispered an incantation and planted an oak seed into the ground. The runes, around the planted seed, pulsing with each load of soil placed over. At the end, remained a small seedling that had already sprouted to the magic. Alikain now recognised the runes as being protective. An oak tree would be unlikely to survive this altitude, yet with these runes, it would survive a century at least.

"The worst part? I… am so damned proud of her. With all the world of terror summoned before her, she stood resolute," he began, grief tearing him down again. "She is my hero, Alikain. I have seen so many great rangers and mages, powerful sentinels and inquisitors walk through those halls down there but none of them compared to her. Her legacy may not be known to all, but it is known to us, and we will be damned if we do not save this world from Ilvithiir. We will control the portals, break their armies and shatter their god." He turned his face to the sky, bathing in the moonlight. "And at the end of it all? It will have been Ahrayn that made it possible. Let that be my promise."

Glossary

1. *Arensela lu alunala*.................... For the light we fight
2. *Oronnsela estrala* .... By the stars
3. *Arensela luestrala selunua foretdinela* .... For the light of the stars and the life of the forest
4. *Forehaltha*...............................Wood Elves
5. *Tamore Narana* .... Council of Healers
6. *Tarviahaltha*.............................. Sky Elves
7. *Merhaltha*...................................Sea Elves
8. *Foretarla*................................. Heart of the Forest – The great oak tree at the centre of Foretilatava
9. *Eleia iaraiña Rylia, foretarla unua arlarla'a orela* ... All hail our Queen Rylia, heart of the forest and heart of our hearts
10. *Yralui* .... Good rain
11. *Haltha*....................................... Elves
12. *Forsonrander* ....Greetings
13. *Lenlialarla* .... Spell gems – Able to store magic or spells. Often inscribed with runes which must be read to activate the spell contained within
14. *Im sinarle*..................................... I love you
15. *Im sinarle ilor*................................ I love you too
16. *Sa sela estrala sinmarilma unua lual sinuruasa* ... May the stars light your path and bless your travels
17. *Sa sela estrala sinmarilma* .... May the stars light your path
18. *Yra irasestrala* .... Bright stars to you
19. *Raéna ilpa* .... Baby fox or little fox
20. *Raéna ilpa, arensela luestrala selunua foretdinela alunala* .... Baby/Little fox, for the light of the stars and the life of the forest, we fight
21. *Marilma. Opas. Yvlynne. Faire* .... Path. Guide. Yvlynne. Reveal

22. *Oronnsela lu* .... By the light

23. *Inunelunail*............................... My moonwing (swallow)

24. *Erilsrahas alemen a huliasomene*..... Unwarranted haste leads to unwanted mistakes

25. *Oronnsela lu* .... By the light

26. *Luestrala inunore* .... Light of my stars

27. *Fairandamay* .... Reveal Soul Spirit: The process of finding one's attuned animal spirit

28. *Aseroena* .... Apple worm – A curse Raethran uses to emphasise his poor luck

29. *Haltha* and *lohikaara*..................... Elves and dragons

30. *Leustrala marilma ramsoma a'isir* .... The stars light the path from which our heart chooses

31. *Ommerim sinrenon siella* .... I will meet you there

32. *Ommerim sinnanoir siella* .... I will see you there